NIRVANA

By Sophie Branchaud

For McKenzie,
who wanted to be able to say,
"My mom's an author."
Here you go.

PROLOGUE

"This way," the man whispered, shining a dim light at the forest wall. It revealed a small, almost invisible gap in the tall grass that filled the treeline.

The small group had been walking close to the forest's edge, careful to keep out of sight. Though it had been hours since the sun had tucked itself away, the night sky glowed brightly with deep pink and blue tones. The stars lit the sky with such brilliance that the figures would have been visible if they had not kept tightly to the shadows of the trees.

Tonight, two moons hung overhead. On some nights, all three of Nirvana's moons were visible at once, and on those nights, the sky was far brighter.

The leader disappeared through the gap in the treeline and into the dense forest. Several shadowy figures followed closely behind, wearing matching red hooded cloaks that concealed their identities.

The path ahead was surrounded by the grass which grew thick across the forest floor. Enormous trees rose from the ground, their trunks thick with coarse bark that glowed soft purple in the filtered moonlight. Each trunk soared straight up a hundred feet, ending in a gnarled canopy which formed a living ceiling. Millions of tiny leaves shielded the group from the watchful stars above.

"Stay close," the leader murmured. His tone carried both urgency and a practiced calm, as though he'd led such clandestine missions many times before.

The darkness deepened as they pressed on. Lagorici buzzed in and out of the grass, their large flickering bodies casting patches of warm amber light, barely illuminating the path ahead. Deep in the shadows of the undergrowth, the rustling of wildlife blended with the hum of the lagorici, filling the night air with a gentle drone.

"We're here," the man finally announced as the group approached a small clearing in the woods. Though their eyes had adjusted to the darkness, it was still difficult to see their destination. The lagorici cast a patchy glow on an unusual space, free of grass, where the forest floor was bare. The exposed ground formed a perfect circle, roughly twenty feet in diameter, surrounded by six large trees.

The man pulled a small silver device from his pocket and let the moonlight glint across its smooth surface. It was oval and flat, about half the size of his palm, with a shallow indent on one side. He pressed it against the nearest tree trunk. The bark around the device softened, as though welcoming the device home, allowing him to push the metal oval into place. It glowed softly, lighting the bark around it.

The man pressed his index finger into the shallow groove, causing the device to emit a soft blue light. As he stepped back, the light pulsed, traveling down the tree trunk. It flowed like liquid through the thick cracks in the bark until it reached the forest floor. The light pooled slightly, then began to move clockwise, tracing the circular clearing. At each tree, it paused before continuing to the next, leaving tiny pools of light at their bases. When the light completed the circle, it pulsed once more, then climbed upward through the cracks in all six trees.

"Step back," the leader instructed. The cloaked figures moved several feet away from the glowing trees. Just then, a wall of light rose from the ground, enclosing the trees in a blue hue. The group craned their necks as the light stretched high into the canopy, nearly a hundred feet overhead.

The blue light softened and dimmed, revealing the outline of a skyscraper made entirely of dark, mirrored glass. The six giant trees stood like pillars, half inside, half outside of the structure. The lagorici continued to fly around, hovering above the grass, their glowing bodies shimmering like stars against the tower's dark, reflective surface.

"Octavian tech," someone murmured. Indeed, the building was a masterpiece of ònakai design, incorporating the existing trunks as part of its support. It would have been admired for miles, if not for the dense forest.

"Yes," the leader said with a wry edge. "Ironic, isn't it?" Then, he stepped up to the glass wall and waved his hand. A portion of it dissolved into an archway. "Come."

He led the group inside. As the last person stepped through, the opening vanished, and the entire structure flickered, then dissolved, becoming completely invisible from the outside.

Inside, the beauty was even more evident. Two grand staircases spiraled up the dark walls ascending ten floors. The center of each floor was made of glass, so moonlight filtered all the way down, illuminating a dais in the center of the room on the first floor. A low-burning blue-purple flame licked at the air from a central fire pit.

They took seats on ten white chairs arranged around the fire; each glowed faintly in the shifting light. The group removed their hoods, revealing an assortment of men and women—some older, some younger. Yet, in the faint firelight, no single face was fully distinct. They seemed to prefer it that way.

"Did it work?" one of the women asked, scanning the room for any sign that the cloaking feature had been activated.

"Yes," the leader confirmed, seating himself last and removing his hood. He had a sharp profile, with eyes that glinted in the bluish firelight. "No one can see or hear us. Octavian T'Dava technology is practically undetectable. We're safe."

He looked around at them, an air of practiced confidence in his posture. "I won't waste your time. We have much to discuss. It's time to put an end to the Doyen and our treaty with the ònakai.

"We've waited a very long time for this—too long. For generations, our ancestors worked quietly in the shadows, waiting for the right moment to act.

"Rumors of 'The Link' are spreading." He paused. "Link or no link, we can't stand idle. We've placed people in positions to influence the council. As soon as we finalize our device, everything else will fall into place. Each of you has your assignments. But before we begin, we must address something critical."

He paused once more, scanning each person in the circle. "We have a spy in our midst," he declared.

Gasps arose as two men stood and approached a figure near the door. They lifted her from her seat and removed her hood. Her red hair glowed brightly in the firelight. Large green eyes widened in fear as she stared at the leader across the flames.

"We have plans for you," he announced, his gaze locked on her. One of the men tied a piece of fabric over her mouth, muffling her shrieks as they dragged her from the building and into the darkness of the forest.

CHAPTER 1

CAHYA

"...It was the Octavian year 8579 P.E., and that's
when humans first arrived in the Gardia system."

"Pause," Cahya instructed. The video on the visor froze.

'P.E.,' Cahya thought. *'P.E.'* She knew what it stood for but was drawing a blank. The rule in class was that if you weren't sure about something, you had to pause and ask for clarification. She tried to remember on her own first, though. She had heard the stories of how her ancestors found themselves in the ònakai's solar system—the elders talked about it all the time—but the dates and facts sometimes got fuzzy.

"Myat, remind me what P.E. stands for," Cahya prompted.

The voice in the visor obliged, "P.E. stands for 'Post Exploration,' meaning the time after which the ònakai ended their deep-space travel programs choosing to settle into a peaceful existence on Octavia. This era falls just before the Human Colonization Era, H.C., and immediately after the Peace Accord Era, P.A."

'Oh yeah,' Cahya thought. *'I knew that.'*

"Continue," she instructed.

A prompt flashed open on Cahya's visor screen that read:

5

'WHAT DO YOU WANT TO LEARN NEXT?'

Cahya's eyes scanned the three options as they were read aloud in her ear by the voice in the visor:

1. "What did the Carta solar system look like when the humans arrived?"

2. "How was the human ship after such a long journey?"

3. "What happened next?"

Cahya flicked her fingers to select the prompt, *What happened next?* Immediately, the screen went dark and a vast sky full of stars appeared before her. In the distance, a small blue and green planet hovered quietly.

The voice continued:

> *"As our ancestors traveled deeper into the solar system, they found a planet that, from scans, looked like a promising place to set up our new home. However, before they could reach the planet, their ship was intercepted by an ònakai vessel. That's how humanity first learned about the ònakai people and their home planet, Octavia."*

A tall ònakai woman appeared on the screen. Her skin shimmered pearly white with the softest hints of pink. Her large, sparkling gray eyes were alive with ancient wisdom—or at least, that was how Cahya perceived her. The woman's wavy white hair was tucked behind her pointed ears, giving her a regal air.

> *"We learned that the ònakai were the only inhabitants of the Gardia system and that they hadn't encountered another space-faring species in thousands of years. We also learned that the ònakai used Nirvana as a farming planet, and we would have to get their permission to settle here."*

Once again, a prompt popped up on Cahya's screen:

'WHAT DO YOU WANT TO LEARN NEXT?'

Before the options appeared, Cahya removed the visor and glanced around the room. Nine other students sat in a circle on the

6

floor. Some had their legs crossed; others lay back with pillows under their heads. One student, Linchel, was standing close to the window, swaying side-to-side as he listened to the voice in his visor. Cahya watched him for a moment, curious about what part of the story he was watching. Cahya knew Linchel loved ships and technology so he was probably learning about that.

Next to her, Nethos sat with elbows on his knees, chin in his hands, utterly absorbed in the lesson. Cahya exhaled quietly, pondering how someone could be so intensely focused. He's always like that, she thought. He was just a year older than Cahya, but he was much more serious.

"Cahya," came Mr. Hickleman's soft voice. "It's not quite time for group discussion yet. Please continue your lesson."

Mr. Hickleman was a nice teacher. Cahya liked him; he was kind but firm. Though she was feeling oddly restless today, she preferred not to be singled out, so she simply nodded and pulled the visor back over her eyes.

The voice continued with three prompts:

1. "Tell me more about the ònakai."
2. "What sort of ship did the ònakai have?"
3. "What happened next?"

Cahya was fascinated by the ònakai. They were advanced and beautiful—something about their shimmering skin and pointed ears seemed almost magical. She thought they were the most beautiful creatures in the universe. Still, she already knew plenty about them and didn't really care to know about their ship, she decided.

"Continue with the story," she said aloud.

The final prompt, *What happened next?* glowed, and the screen went black once again. Slowly, a beautiful planet came into view. It was clean and pristine, full of lush greenery and turquoise blue bodies of water. Cahya recognized the planet, of course—Nirvana.

"The ònakai agreed to allow the humans to inhabit a portion of their sister planet, Nirvana, as

*long as they agreed to certain terms. These terms came
to be known as 'The Gardia Treaty.'"*

"Okay, class," came Mr. Hickleman's voice, "discussion time."

Cahya was the first to remove her visor. She looked around as the other nine students finished their lessons. One by one, they removed their visors and turned their attention to the front of the class where Mr. Hickleman sat cross-legged on a large cushion.

"So," he began, "what did you find most interesting about today's lesson?"

Nethos was first to raise his hand.

"Go ahead," Mr. Hickleman encouraged.

Nethos looked exasperated—like he'd been stewing over something the entire session. "I don't see why the ònakai stopped exploring," he burst out. "I mean, sure, they found a lot of violence out there, but there had to be some good, right?"

"Good question," Mr. Hickleman nodded. "Anyone have a perspective for Nethos?"

Alteeya raised her hand. Though only thirteen—two years younger than Cahya—she was the brightest and most inquisitive in the class, at least in Cahya's eyes.

"Yes, Alteeya, go ahead."

She turned to Nethos. "The ònakai realized they didn't need anything from the galaxy at large. They had all they required right here in the Gardia system. I think it was smart that they stayed hidden in these outskirts, out of everyone's way."

Mr. Hickleman nodded and looked around the room. "Anyone else?" he asked.

Nethos blurted, "But *we* found them, didn't we? They couldn't have been that hidden if humans randomly appeared in their system."

Another boy chimed in. "That was one-in-a-billion odds, basically luck." It was Hoshia, he was a year older than Cahya and he sported a short haircut that suited his sharp jawline.

Mr. Hickleman offered a smile. "We might see if we can invite an ònakai rep to the class so that we can discuss it further. Could be enlightening." Some students nodded eagerly.

Another hand shot up: Nandini. She was a close friend of Cahya's. "Is it true that the ònakai can speak with plants?" Nandini asked, eyes wide with fascination.

Cahya raised an eyebrow, skeptical yet curious about which prompts Nandini had chosen to lead her down that storyline. Although they were similar in many ways, their lessons diverged since they rarely selected the same prompts—besides, Nandini asked a lot of her own questions. That was the point, after all: students chose pathways that resonated with them most. It was how they discovered and refined their unique skills—and eventually how they would be sorted into society, filling roles where they could best serve the community.

Mr. Hickleman laughed. "I've never heard that one. But we can add it to our list of questions for the ònakai visitor."

Before Nandini could protest, the classroom door slid open. Ms. Halthia entered, her expression grim.

"Ms. Halthia?" Mr. Hickleman said, standing from his pillow.

"I'm sorry to interrupt," she said softly, "I need to speak with Ms. Lighthold."

Ten pairs of eyes swung toward Cahya, whose stomach seemed to drop into the floor. She froze, uneasy dread tingling through her body. What's going on?

"Cahya," Mr. Hickleman said gently, "please go with Ms. Halthia."

Cahya pushed herself up from the floor and forced her legs to move. The room blurred around her as she followed Ms. Halthia, who placed a hand on Cahya's shoulder, tears filling her eyes.

"Come with me, dear," the older woman whispered.

Something was very wrong, Ms. Halthia never cried. In that moment, Cahya felt her heart pound—somehow knowing that something terrible had happened and her life was about to change dramatically.

CHAPTER 2
SANDY

'Dammit!' Cahya was late... again. She'd been tucked away in her secret room at the Transfer Station and had completely lost track of time. It happened often; when she was in this space, hours seemed to slip by in a matter of minutes.

This was her refuge. The one place where she could let her mind breathe. Even her home didn't offer that kind of solace anymore. Neighbors and acquaintances felt free to drop by at any hour, always unannounced. She knew they meant well. After all, she was the Dohan—expected to be approachable, available—but it weighed on her. Their constant presence reminded her of how isolated she truly was

The station, on the other hand, was almost always deserted these days. Still, it was impeccably maintained, as one would expect on Nirvana. The only time anyone visited the Transfer Station was when ònakai dignitaries or exchange students arrived from Octavia, which was a rare occurrence lately. The ònakai hardly visited the human planet of Nirvana anymore, and when they did, their stays were short and confined to the city of Deshka. Many children—sometimes even teenagers—on Nirvana had never met an ònakai in person. The ònakai did come from time to time, but Nirvana was large, and their visits were short and limited in scope.

This meant that, most of the time, the Transfer Station sat silent and empty, allowing Cahya to come and go as she pleased without anyone noticing. It was here she'd spent so many hours with her parents as a child. When visitors from Octavia were due to arrive, Cahya and her family would often spend the whole week in Deshka to make preparations; and while her parents worked, Cahya explored. She had so many happy memories from this place.

Her parents had been gone twenty-three years now, ever since Ms. Halthia had collected fifteen-year-old Cahya from her classroom to break the terrible news. Twenty-three years. That was more than enough time for most people to have moved on—long enough that nobody talked about it anymore. Long enough that if Cahya so much as hinted at suspicions surrounding the nature of their deaths, she'd probably be sent to the health center for another round of counseling.

It was widely accepted that Laurel and Trebolt Lighthold had died in a terrible accident at the Transfer Station caused by an unexpected energy surge. The matter had been thoroughly investigated, and new safeguards had been put in place to ensure that no such accident could ever happen again.

But fifteen-year-old Cahya hadn't joined her parents on that trip, she hadn't been there—and maybe that's why she hadn't been convinced. She needed a better explanation. On Nirvana, fifteen-year-olds didn't lose their parents. Accidents like that didn't happen.

At first, people indulged her questions, walking her through the official files, scrutinizing every piece of evidence. She'd lost her parents after all, they felt tremendous pity for her. Ultimately, it all ended the same. Case closed. Over time, people's patience wore thin, and her persistent claims that "there must be more" began to grate on them.

In her early twenties, she attended counseling; the adults in her life wanted her to come to terms with her parents' passing and build a life for herself. And in many ways, she did—at least on the surface. She stopped mentioning her parents or the accident, threw herself into her studies, and became a model student and exceptional citizen. Yet, in secret, she still clung to her tiny hideaway at the Transfer Station. The room she had discovered as a child was an out-of-service maintenance space, accessible only by removing a wall panel. Here, in this hidden refuge, she could exist, free from the expectations of others.

She loved it here. The walls were plastered with photos of her parents—so she'd never forget their faces. She also had the station's floor plans, diagrams of its energy core, and a few technical references she thought might prove useful. Alongside these, she had the official accident reports and announcements posted in chronological order. She spent hours staring at the walls, a puzzle with a missing piece she couldn't quite see yet. She hoped that something would leap out at her, vindicating her gut feeling that something else was at play. But nothing ever did, she didn't have any evidence that hadn't already been poured over during the investigation. Even if she did find something, she doubted that anyone would take her theories seriously after so long.

Somehow, today felt different. Something in the air had shifted. She could feel that something was changing; she just didn't know what. She sat in her secret room, staring at the walls, scanning for a detail that might justify the feeling in her gut.

That's what she was doing when she noticed the time and realized she was late yet again. She grabbed her tunic and climbed out of the room. As she squeezed through the narrow opening, her sleeve caught on a grooved channel in the wall. She yanked and it came free with a sharp snap.

"Ugh," she groaned, quickly replacing the access panel before she sprinted out of the Transfer Station.

Her feet pounded along tree-lined pathways that twisted in quiet arcs behind the Transfer Station. Once the main hub of Deshka came into view, she forced herself to slow, her chest heaving, her breathing ragged.

"Dohan," came a gentle greeting from her left. A woman bowed her head respectfully as Cahya passed. Cahya bowed in return, managing a polite smile though her heart pumped in her chest.

Don't run, she told herself. The Dohan did not run. Officially, the Dohan could only walk with purpose when they were on their way to something important, but they could never run. Running implied poor planning—or worse, an emergency—and there was no sense in causing a needless panic. No, the Dohan moved with grace and poise—always.

Yet even eight years into the role, Cahya found it hard to remember to maintain that composed front when she was truly flustered. And flustered she was. She was late for her training, and she knew everyone would be waiting for her.

A new voice called from a bench by the path: "Good morning, Dohan." This time it was an elderly man, Mr. Gashwald, sitting with a younger woman. Probably his granddaughter, Cahya thought. She bowed gracefully and offered, "Good morning, Mr. Gashwald," but didn't pause—couldn't pause. That was obviously too abrupt; she saw him open his mouth to speak, only to realize she was still moving, that she wouldn't be staying for a chat. Oh no, that was rude, she thought, but she had to keep moving.

As she continued toward the central hub, she was sure that everyone was watching her, certain they could all see that she wasn't really cut out for this job.

"Focus," she told herself as she came to the tall glass walls of the central hub. A broad door slid upward, and she glided inside, forced to slow her steps. The massive building was at least a kilometer wide, with a high, vaulted glass dome overhead that let sunshine stream down. Beneath the glass, there were gardens, pathways, small pavilions—if one didn't know better, they'd think they hadn't actually entered a building at all.

The hub was lively. Grown-ups walked to their various offices, while kids hurried off to educational centers around the perimeter. Plenty of them stopped to bow greetings to Cahya. She returned every gesture with a delicate nod—feeling self-conscious about how breathless she still was.

Finally, she spotted Nandini near the entrance to the central spire. Nandini's arms were folded, her expression carefully neutral, though her eyes betrayed frustration. The corners of Cahya's mouth twitched in amusement. Nandini looked comically stern.

"Where have you been?" Nandini whispered, her tone polite but tense. She glanced around to ensure no one else was listening. "I'm going to start picking you up in the mornings. I can't keep stressing out about whether you'll show up on time."

"No, Nandini, I'm just running a little late this morning. I'm sorry, ok?" Cahya's apology hadn't come across as particularly sincere, but she couldn't help it. She did not want to be escorted from her house every day. It was hard enough having her companions with her most of the time. She needed at least a little bit of space to breathe and feel normal.

Nandini frowned, and Cahya felt guilty. She knew that Nandini wasn't trying to impede her freedom. After all, it was her job to keep Cahya safe, and aside from being a sort of personal bodyguard, Nandini was also Cahya's friend.

"I'm sorry." Cahya said, in earnest this time, "I didn't sleep well last night, and Myat didn't wake me."

Nandini raised an eyebrow.

"Okay, okay," Cahya admitted. "He tried to wake me, and I muted him."

Nandini rolled her eyes and quickly scanned the area to ensure no one had noticed. She gestured for Cahya to follow her toward the spire. "Let's get you to your training."

15

Cahya's stomach churned as she looked up at the large tower before them. Today's cycle was short—only a few hours—but she was still nervous. She wasn't making as much progress as she was supposed to. No one had said anything to her about it, but she could feel it.

Maybe it was because she wasn't meant to be the Dohan. A good Dohan was kind, charismatic, and effortlessly connected with others. Cahya didn't know how to do that. No matter how many cycles she ran, she always returned to the same place—the place where her parents were dead, where she was alone, and where she couldn't seem to trust anyone. Not really.

Maybe it would be better if she weren't the Dohan; then she could focus more time on solving her parents' deaths. Her Dohan obligations kept her far too busy. She hadn't dedicated the sort of time her parents deserved, and the guilt ate away at her.

Nandini and Cahya made their way to the central tower, and a large opening appeared as they approached. Inside, the walls were white, and there were several rooms with glass walls surrounding the perimeter of the first floor. At the center was an elevator encased in a glass tube. They made their way toward it en route to the ELC Lab.

When they arrived, as predicted, everyone was waiting for them. Nethos stood in the center of the room, speaking with the three instructors. They fell silent and looked toward the entrance as Cahya and Nandini entered.

Cahya made eye contact with Kole first, who, though his face remained calm, was clearly distraught at her tardiness. Cahya bowed her head apologetically at her instructor as she made her way into the room to join the others.

Kole didn't waste any time. "As many of you may know, we'll be hosting our first Onakai-Human ELC Exchange Program next week, and I'll be assisting with the first few cycles to make sure everything goes well. As such, our Dohan Training Cycles will be paused, but your training is not paused. You'll be working with Kacha and

Hathina in class on several theoretical cycles, and I'll expect a full report for the following week."

Cahya was grateful that he didn't spend any time lecturing her on her lack of punctuality. Scolding people wasn't really his style; he was always very composed. Still, Cahya felt that she deserved some sort of reprimand today. Maybe it would come later. Maybe she'd be fired as Dohan; maybe they'd replace her and send her off to another city to work as a teacher. She wouldn't mind changing vocations, but the thought of being away from Deshka was torture. It would mean leaving the Transfer Station behind, leaving her secret room and everything it contained.

She'd spent a lot of time in Deshka when she was a child. It was where her parents had died. She couldn't really imagine living anywhere else; not even her childhood home of Catithia.

It was happening again. That tightness pulled at her chest and shoulders. That feeling of being confined and restrained. She took a deep breath and tried to push it away. Years of counseling had provided her with tools for keeping these sorts of feelings in check.

Those years of introspection had also afforded her a lot of personal insight. She knew that the reason she accelerated her education was because she used her studies as a distraction after her parents' accident. She was smart, as it turned out, and intuitive—it's why she'd been chosen by the Doyen to become Dohan. He saw something in her—something that he said made her 'special'. Cahya cringed at the word. *Special*. It took everything inside of her not to roll her eyes at the thought.

Nandini seemed to have relaxed now, her anger depleted into concern. "Cahya, you okay? You seem like you're off on another planet today." Nandini put her arm around Cahya's shoulders and gave her a gentle squeeze. Cahya tensed at her touch. Nandini was kind, but Cahya wasn't a very touchy-feely sort of person. She liked her personal space. Nandini must have sensed her discomfort because she dropped her arm almost instantly.

Cahya caught sight of herself in the reflection of the glass dome. Her long purple hair was tied back in a neat braid, and her violet eyes stared back at her. The glimmer of her black tunic caught the light, but her attention shifted to the tension in her body—her stomach was in knots, and her head ached, feeling unusually heavy. She knew she was acting strangely. Something was off, though she couldn't quite pinpoint what. Most people wouldn't notice such a subtle change, but Nandini could read her like a book. She was still watching, waiting for a response.

"Oh, sorry, yeah, I'm fine, thanks. I guess I'm just daydreaming a lot these days."

Cahya studied her friend, who didn't seem convinced by her response. It wasn't that she didn't trust Nandini; she trusted her more than anyone else she knew. But even Nandini, kind and understanding as she was, wouldn't understand why she was still obsessing over her parents' deaths. It would just cause her to worry; there was no sense in telling her.

Her training. Her life as Dohan—this is what she'd signed up for when she agreed to the role. She knew it would be hard. She knew it was a huge commitment—a lifelong commitment—and she had agreed, hadn't she? Maybe she'd secretly hoped that she'd be too busy to think about her parents. After all, her entire life was laid out ahead of her. She had another forty or so years of training, and then she'd shadow the Doyen for twenty years. Ultimately, she'd take over his role and become Doyen herself one day. She'd be nearly 100 years old by then, and that's when her vocation would really begin.

Doyen. It was a very important role—some might say the most important role. She would never say that, of course, since placing too much value on a person's vocation was frowned upon. Still, being Doyen would require her to make some major decisions that impacted the course of the entire planet, so, you know, that felt significant, even if she shouldn't say so out loud.

Sometimes, she felt a deep sense that she was not where she was meant to be. She felt like a small child stomping around in her dad's oversized shoes; no one seemed to see it, but she could feel it.

Some days, it all felt like too much. On those days, she wished she'd wake up from all of this and realize that it had just been a dream, or maybe another cycle. Sometimes, she wished she could disappear—become invisible to all of the kind eyes that greeted her everywhere she went.

Everyone was lovely; of course, they were very civilized. No, that wasn't the right word. They were more than civilized; they were evolved. Their kindness was genuine, and their understanding of Cahya's sacrifice was genuine as well. They didn't mean to overwhelm her with their attention and support, but they did. All she wanted was to blend in. She wished she could take off her role sometimes, like slipping out of a tight garment at the end of a long day.

Maybe she could even try on some other roles; perhaps she'd find a path that fit her better. This was all nonsense, of course. She was exactly where she was meant to be. Everyone told her so—often.

So here she was, getting ready to enter a cycle as though everything was fine.

"Nethos, you want to help me out here?" Nandini turned to the man standing on the other side of Cahya.

Cahya snapped out of her thoughts. Nethos, who had been staring out the window, looked at Cahya and then shot a glance at Nandini. "What? She said she's fine."

Nandini rolled her eyes. "Hey, if there's something you want to talk about, we're here for you." She shot a look at Nethos, who had resumed staring at something outside. "Well, *I'm* here for you at least. You know that, right?"

"I know, Nandini. Thank you," Cahya replied, giving her an earnest, if unenthusiastic, smile.

Cahya shifted her gaze to the window, trying to see if she could spot what was holding Nethos' attention. She didn't see anything particularly interesting, but Nethos was captivated by odd things. Since he was one of her two companions, she knew Nethos well, and yet she didn't rely on him in the way she did Nandini. He'd always been there, and she knew that he always would—not that he had a choice in the matter.

"Cahya, Nandini, and Nethos." Kole called out, pointing at each of the three pods sitting in front of him.

Cahya removed her tunic and moved toward her pod. As she was about to hang it up, Nandini grabbed the sleeve and inspected it.

"What happened to your cufflink?" she asked, running a finger over the hole where a small black cufflink was supposed to be.

Cahya scrunched up her face, equally confused. Then she remembered that she'd caught her sleeve at the Transfer Station. It must have come off there. She'd have to look for it the next time she went.

"Strange," Cahya shrugged, not wanting to let on that she knew where it was. "Must have fallen off."

"We'll have to get this to Carsen so that he can fix it," Nandini decided. "Cufflinks shouldn't just fall off. We can't have the Dohan walking around with her uniform falling apart."

Nethos was already lying back in his pod at this point, and Cahya and Nandini quickly took their respective spots. The pods were long beds covered with blue glass domes. The domes were raised, floating a few feet above the beds so that the students could get in.

Nandini gave Cahya one last concerned look, and Cahya flashed the most reassuring smile she could manage. "Shall we catch the game tonight?" she asked, trying to shift the mood before their cycle.

"Sure," Nandini agreed, the concern in her eyes softening a bit.

"Settle in, kids; I'll see you all in a few hours," Kole said as he pushed a glowing blue button on the glass screen, which hovered in the air in front of him. The glowing domes lowered, enclosing the three students in their pods.

Nethos closed his eyes, and Nandini turned her head and stretched her lips to give Cahya one last smile before the dream-like state overtook her.

As Cahya drifted off, she pondered the cycle. They had gone over the details in class yesterday, but she had been too distracted to absorb much of it. Who was she going to be? She strained to remember... 'Sandy!' Yes, she was going to be Sandy. She tried to recall her companions' identities in the upcoming cycle, but she couldn't. It didn't matter now. The weight of her thoughts lifted, drifting into the void as the world around her faded to black.

✳ ✳ ✳

Sandy pulled up close to the drive-through window, realizing too late that her mirror was way too close to the building. As she reached the window, her mirror hit the wall of the building and immediately clipped inward, tucking itself awkwardly against the car door.

She jumped at the noise and quickly looked in through the window to make sure the young man on the other side of the glass hadn't caught the commotion. He was tapping furiously on his computer screen while speaking into his headset.

"And a hashbrown with that? No, no, a hashbrown. Well, it's like a small, deep-fried potato patty. No, ma'am, it's not the same thing as a french fry."

Sandy exhaled slowly, relieved that her mishap had gone unnoticed. She reached for her black faux-leather wallet and pulled back the gold zipper to reveal a few receipts and pockets filled with bank cards. She slid a black credit card from its place and tossed the wallet back onto the seat.

"Ma'am?" said a voice from the window. She turned to see the young man hanging out the window, holding the debit machine toward her. "That'll be $8.76, ma'am."

"Sorry, I'm a bit slow today," she confessed and held the card up to the reader. The machine beeped its confirmation, and the attendant pulled the machine back through the window with one hand and simultaneously thrust a hot coffee toward her with the other.

Man, this guy's a ninja, she thought to herself.

This made Sandy feel even more flustered, so she tossed her bank card on the seat next to her wallet and moved an old, used cup out of the cup holder to make room.

She took the cup from the young man who was now holding a paper bag containing her breakfast and pushed that toward her as well. She took it with the same hand that already held a coffee, struggling to strike a balance between moving quickly—mindful as she was of the long line of cars behind her—and trying her best not to drop anything.

"Have a nice day," the attendant said and smiled.

"Thanks, you too," she smiled back, taking the polite cue to *'get the hell out of the way'* from the gentleman. Sandy simultaneously placed the coffee in the cup holder with her right hand, rolled up the window with her left, and steered out of the parking lot skillfully, guiding the steering wheel with her knee. She was used to juggling multiple things at once with great success, but she normally handled it with more grace.

Sandy was a nurse. Head nurse, to be precise—at the Ajax Pickering Hospital in Ajax, Ontario. Her role required her to be quick on her feet and to juggle massive pressure from all angles at all times. She handled it well, but this morning she was off and flustered. Her husband, who normally handled the morning routine with their kids, had an early meeting, so it fell to Sandy to get everyone ready. She'd woken up late, had to drive the children to school after they missed the bus, and was so behind schedule she ended up putting on her makeup in the car while waiting in line at the drive-thru. Then, clipping the wall with her side mirror was an exclamation point on the morning—and it wasn't even 9 a.m.

As Sandy pulled into traffic, she picked up her coffee and took a sip. *Shit! Too hot!*

She checked her mirror only to realize that it was still tucked into her car. Holding the steering wheel and coffee with her right hand, she rolled down the window with her left and reached out to push the mirror back into place. As she did this, she heard a loud, exaggerated *"honk,"* and a car zipped by closely on her left. She jerked the wheel to the right to make some room, and a splash of coffee jumped from her cup and landed hot in her lap.

"Dammit!" she yelled at her coffee. Maybe she was yelling at the car... maybe at herself. What the hell was going on today?

Sandy managed to get the rest of the way to work without another mishap, but she was feeling rattled and anxious as she made her way through the sliding doors, carrying her bag so that it hid the coffee splotch that muddied the front of her pants.

"Girl, you look like somebody murdered your puppy today," Adam grinned as he made his way toward her. When he reached her, he turned 180 degrees on his heel and began walking in step beside her. She gave him a weak smile but didn't say a word.

"Wait," he said, adopting a mock-horrified tone. "*Did* someone murder your puppy?!"

Sandy cracked a faint grin. "You know I don't have a dog," she replied. "It's just... everything's off today."

He gave an exaggerated sigh. "Well, aren't you lucky you get to spend the day with *me*? We'll keep it interesting," he said with playful drama as he draped an arm over her shoulder.

"You know what, I'm actually hoping for an exceedingly *boring* day. I'd prefer it if nothing even *remotely* interesting happened," she told him.

"Oh! Speaking of *interesting*," he said, ignoring her comment, "did you hear about that new corduroy pillow?"

Sandy gave him a puzzled look. "Huh?"

"No? That's strange... it's really been making *headlines*."

Rolling her eyes, she peeled away from him. "Since when did you start making dad jokes?"

Adam gave a slight curtsy. "Just keeping things fresh, mama."

He's a loveable weirdo, she thought, noticing for the thousandth time how broad his shoulders were in his scrubs—the reward he'd earned from all the hours spent at the gym when he wasn't working. Despite his mostly-failed-attempts at comedy, Adam was a great guy—and he was very handsome. He had piercing blue eyes and a kind face, thanks largely to his adorable cheeks. He hated his cheeks because they were a little pudgy, no matter how trim he got. But when he smiled, he had the biggest, deepest dimples anyone had ever seen. Personally, Sandy thought Adam's cheeks were beautiful.

Besides being easy on the eyes, Adam was a true friend. He was always there when she needed to talk through issues or ideas, and he was a huge supporter among the other nurses. Like that time in the break room when Amanda Cooper made a comment about how the shift changes had been a nightmare and blamed it on Sandy—Adam jumped in like a mama bear protecting her cub. He pointed out that Sandy had fought hard to keep the old rotation and that things would have been much worse if she had let the administration proceed with their original plan. Sandy always fought hard for her people—always.

Sandy was about to thank him for the comedic relief when he turned abruptly serious. "Okay, so I have an idea," Adam exclaimed, suddenly becoming very focused. "We should have a double date—you and Steve with me and Stephen."

Sandy stopped walking and turned to face Adam. "Who's Stephen?" she asked. "Are you seeing somebody?!" Sandy felt a little pinch of excitement rise until she caught a glance at Adam's silly face.

"Oh, no, no, honey. That's what I'll be calling your husband when he's playing the role of my gay lover." He flicked his hand by his ear and shook his head, pretending to toss his long, invisible hair back over his thick shoulder.

Sandy rolled her eyes and began to walk away.

Adam called after her, "You'd be a bit of a third wheel if I'm being honest, but I feel like we could make it work." Catching up to her, he continued, "I don't think your daughters would mind sharing their daddy with me, right?"

She shook her head. "Dear Lord," she said, laughing out loud this time.

"It's going to be a *wonderful* day, darling," Adam assured her, wrapping his strong arms around her shoulders and giving her a little squeeze. They walked into the break room together, where the TV played a breaking news report. The announcer spoke in a dire tone:

"More news from the Nuclear Generating Station, which has reported a serious reactor breach leading to radioactive material released into multiple parts of the facility. No word yet on casualties or containment efforts, but we'll keep you updated as more info arrives."

All conversation in the break room stopped. Worried eyes turned on Sandy, the head nurse. She took a moment to gather herself, scanning the fear around her. Then she gave a quick nod. "All right, everyone, let's get ready," she announced. She locked eyes with Adam, "Looks like our day's about to get interesting."

Sirens wailed, making their way closer and louder with every passing second. Distress calls from the power plant had triggered city-wide medical mobilization. Protective gear was doled out. Sandy and her team had done countless drills for nuclear or radiation disasters, though they'd prayed never to use them for real. Today, those prayers went unanswered.

Everyone stood waiting at their respective posts, like soldiers on the front lines of battle sitting in relative silence, waiting for the chaos to begin. Sandy took up her spot at the emergency entrance, wearing white hazmat gear that hid her coffee-stained pants. Beneath her mask and face shield, she kept a cool expression. But inside, her heart pounded in sync with the wailing sirens that drew closer.

25

She watched, her eyes fixed as far down the street as she could see, waiting for flashing lights. Time seemed to stand still. She knew she should try to treasure this momentary peace since her day was about to become a relentless, emotional blur.

She was ready.

Though the wailing grew louder as the slightest flicker of red and white lights flashed into view, everything in Sandy's mind went dead silent. She watched and waited for the ambulance to pull up to the door, her brown eyes peeking out over large protective goggles. Her gloved hands sat waiting at her sides, resting while they could.

A deep silence filled her as she watched the white trucks pull into the parking lot. They stopped, parking side by side with their back doors facing the emergency entrance. Paramedics in full hazmat gear pushed open the ambulance doors and began unloading stretchers from the trucks. Sound suddenly rushed back in, and all at once Sandy could hear sirens and shouting as paramedics began calling out the age, gender, and injuries of their patients. Sandy ran to the closest stretcher.

"What have we got?" she asked.

"Thirteen-year-old female. Radiation burns on her arms. Trouble breathing," the paramedic rattled off as he pushed the stretcher toward the door.

Sandy looked down, startled. "Thirteen?"

"Yes, ma'am. The plant had a 'Take Your Kids to Work Day' event today. They had forty kids in that facility when it blew."

"Take her to Isolation Room One," Sandy managed to sputter, hardly able to conceal her dread. Her oldest daughter was thirteen. Some of her friends might have been in that building. There was no time to think about that now; she had to double down on her focus today.

Ambulance after ambulance rolled up with a total of twenty-five injured children and twelve injured adults. Three people were pronounced dead on arrival: a man in his late fifties and two women, both in their thirties—younger than Sandy. All three had been closest to the blast when the reactor blew.

Thirty-seven patients suffering from radiation injuries had suddenly descended on the hospital, and they didn't have the capacity for this sort of onslaught. Some of the injuries were minor, so Sandy sent those patients to the ER waiting room, where nurses could treat their injuries while they sat in chairs. Other patients had to be sent to isolation rooms as their radiation exposure was dangerous to those around them. Ten teenagers were included among some of the most critical cases that day. Sandy managed to keep all these numbers straight because she had to know where absolutely every person was at all times.

Every machine in the ER was beeping and squealing as each doctor and nurse treated three or four patients simultaneously. Everyone who was on call had been brought in to help. Still, Sandy found herself flooded with questions and requests from every direction. After one question was answered, she'd take half a step and find herself stopped in her tracks to answer another. This went on for three hours. The doctors and nurses treated patients while Sandy orchestrated. They'd lost four more patients in that time—two of them were kids. Sandy was devastated, but she couldn't stop now; she'd grieve later.

Suddenly, the dreaded long, unwavering *beeeeeeeep* of an EKG machine announced that someone's heart had stopped. Sandy looked up and scanned the room, searching for the source of the noise. Her eyes met Adam's, who knew exactly what she was looking for.

"Thirteen-year-old female in Isolation One," his voice was muffled through his N95 mask and face guard.

Sandy's heart sank. She couldn't lose another kid today. She looked into Adam's eyes and nodded. "Got it. Cover the door for me," she instructed.

"San! You can't—" Adam shouted after her. But he knew it was useless to try to stop her.

Sandy pushed her way through a zippered doorway and into a room where a young girl lay lifeless, with two nurses standing next to her, one administering chest compressions.

"She needs oxygen," Sandy shouted.

The nurse administering the compressions looked up with wide eyes. "All of the air pumps are in use, Sandy," a look of helplessness on her face.

The only way to administer oxygen right now would be mouth-to-mouth, and that could be lethal. Sandy couldn't ask one of her nurses to risk it. She made her way over to the young teen and motioned for the nurse to move out of the way. Sandy removed her face guard and mask, leaned over the girl, tilted her head upward, and blew air into her lungs in two puffs. She then resumed chest compressions before giving more air. She continued like this—compressions, air, compressions, air—for what seemed like an eternity.

She watched the monitor with a desperate determination.

"Sandy," one of the nurses said, "she's gone." The monitor continued with its unchanging, unrelenting *beeeeeeep*.

Sandy ignored the comment and continued to work, alternating between mouth-to-mouth and chest compressions. *Pump pump pump. Breath.*

"Breathe!," Sandy whispered, "Please breathe."

Pump pump pump. Breath. Pump pump pump. The EKG line began to waver. Beep... beep... beep. The teen took a shaky breath. She opened her eyes—just a sliver—and locked gazes with Sandy, who gave a trembling smile of relief.

Sandy watched the girl's chest rise and fall, each shallow breath like a fragile thread of hope. Relief flooded her as she smiled gently at the girl, who managed a painful smile in return.

She was alive!

Sandy's relief faded quickly as a sudden, searing pain shot through her chest. Her vision blurred as the room tilted violently.

She clutched at her suit, gasping for air that wouldn't come, and then the floor caught her in a cold embrace.

She dimly heard voices. Nurses barked orders, Adam yelling her name. She hovered above the scene, watching as if from a distance. Adam cradled her in his lap, tears making tracks down his cheeks beneath his own protective mask.

Oh, Adam, she thought, *I'm so sorry,* as the blackness swallowed her.

Everything went dark in an instant. Then, a moment later, a bright, light-filled tunnel appeared before her. Sandy felt herself being pulled through it, slowly at first and then very quickly. Her entire life played back in front of her as though small movie screens lined the walls of the tunnel. Her daughters hugged, consoling one another after their cat died. Her husband kissed her on their wedding day. Her father pushed her around on a bicycle when she was five. Adam held her in the hospital lobby after she learned that her mom had died.

As she moved closer and closer to the brilliant ball of light at the end of this long channel, the pictures flew by at an ever-increasing speed.

At the end, she felt a deep sense of love—for her two daughters, her husband, her parents, her friends, and her family. The entire world, in fact. She felt no fear, no anger, and no negativity at all. She was floating through the speeding tunnel, feeling elated and free. All at once, everything exploded into brightness.

CHAPTER 3
JOHNNY

Cahya woke with tears streaming down her face. Nandini and Nethos remained asleep in the pods next to her. She wiped her eyes, and Kole was by her side a moment later.

"Tough one, huh?" Kole asked sympathetically.

Cahya nodded.

"You're clear; you know the drill," Kole continued gently. "Deep breaths." He waved his hand over the blue dome above Cahya's head, which rose to make space for her to exit the pod.

Cahya took a deep breath and sat up, swinging her feet over the side of the pod and planting them on the floor. She sat quietly for a few moments, letting the tension ease from her body.

"How long have they got?" Cahya asked, nodding toward Nandini and Nethos.

"Well, Adam and Steve will mourn your loss together, fall in love, and have a few decades before they pass. So, they've got a couple of hours."

"Poor Adam." Cahya smirked, glancing at Nandini.

So Nandini was Adam, and Nethos was Steve, her husband. She hadn't remembered before the cycle started, but it was all coming back to her now. Made sense.

Kole handed Cahya a glass of water. "Here you go," he said. "Need anything else?"

"No, I'm good, thanks, Kole. I think I'll head home and take a nap. Could you let Nandini know that I'll meet her at the arena?"

"Sure, I'll set a reminder for Myat to notify her."

"Thanks."

Cahya was looking forward to her nap; she was always tired after a cycle. One might think she'd be used to this by now, but she wasn't.

The walk from the hub to her house was only about 15 minutes, but Cahya wished she could jump into a shuttle capsule and get a ride home. The idea of walking, even for 15 minutes, was exhausting. Plus, she knew she'd have to talk to people along the way.

Capsules were for the elderly or parents with young children. They certainly weren't meant for young Dohans who were simply tired from their latest cycle. It would look completely unprofessional for Cahya to be riding instead of walking. Nirvanians were encouraged to use their bodies as much as possible. This was one way they managed to stay fit, both mentally and physically.

"Cahya!" a high-pitched voice called from somewhere behind her. Cahya spun around to see Ash running toward her. Ash was seven, but she was incredibly smart for her age. She'd bonded with Cahya shortly after her mother passed away. Young deaths were highly unusual on Nirvana, so few people could relate to Cahya and Ash in that way.

Ash's olive skin and bouncy brown curls caught the sunlight and glowed almost as brightly as her smile.

"Did you just do a cycle?" Ash asked, catching up to her friend.

"Yes," Cahya replied, smiling softly.

"Ooooh! Who were you this time? A knight of the round table? A princess? The president of a big, important country?"

"Nope. I was a nurse, a mom, and a wife. I lived in a small house in a small town. I didn't even get to *see* a castle," Cahya exclaimed, a look of mock-exasperation on her face.

Ash shook her head disapprovingly. "Well, that's boring."

"I wouldn't say that. You learn a lot about yourself in every cycle—not just the ones where you're some big, fancy leader or famous person."

"Oh really?" Ash asked skeptically. "So, what did you learn about yourself this time?"

Cahya thought for a moment, then declared, "I learned that I'm very lucky to live in a place with automated vehicles."

Ash raised an eyebrow. "Boring," she reaffirmed.

Meditating on the cycles was an important part of the training. Cahya would have to spend time reflecting on how Sandy's life had changed her and what she'd learned—but right now, she just wanted to rest.

Later that evening, Cahya sat outside the panigêm arena, waiting for Nandini. She was well-rested from her nap but hungry, having skipped dinner. She'd have to remember to grab something from the concession stand before heading to her seat.

"Well, that was exhausting!" Nandini exclaimed as she approached the bench where Cahya waited.

"The cycle?" Cahya asked, wanting to confirm that Nandini wasn't talking about something else.

"Obviously. I just got out about 20 minutes ago. I haven't even showered."

"Gross," Cahya joked.

Nandini rolled her eyes.

"I showered *and* took a nap," Cahya added.

"Must be nice," Nandini chided.

"We don't have to go to the game if you're tired."

"No, it's okay; I want to. Maybe we could just sit out here for a minute, though? I don't think I can jump straight into a crowd just yet."

"Sure." Cahya scooted over to make room for Nandini on the bench.

Once Nandini was settled, Cahya said, "So... you married my husband?"

"Oh my goodness, don't get me started!"

Cahya chuckled. "That great, huh?"

"It's like he's not even there! Don't get me wrong—we cared about each other—but it felt like constant work, and it never felt like we really got close, you know?"

"Oh, I know." Cahya had been married to Nethos in dozens of cycles, so she completely understood what Nandini was describing. Nethos was always charming and attractive, with a quality that drew people to him. But he always seemed distant, like he had a secret no one ever uncovered. It was a bizarre feeling, but Cahya had grown accustomed to it.

"You seem to be in better spirits than you were this morning," Nandini observed.

Nandini was right. Cahya hadn't thought about her secret room or that strange feeling since she woke from the cycle. She'd been so tired that all she could think about was sleep.

"Yeah, I guess I was just really tired. I think the nap helped a lot."

"I'm glad," Nandini said, smiling as she placed a hand on Cahya's and squeezed gently.

Cahya felt a rush of emotion wash over her. She didn't know what it was, but it was positive. Relief, maybe? She took a breath and smiled back at Nandini. "Me too," she said. "Shall we head in?"

Nandini nodded.

The game was fun; watching a panigêm match always put Cahya in a good mood. Still, she knew she had another cycle in the morning, so she went straight home and to bed afterward. She was determined to be on time tomorrow.

When Cahya arrived at the hub in the morning, she beamed when she realized she was the first to arrive. Only Kole and Hathina were in the training room.

"Morning, Cahya," he greeted warmly as she entered. "I've given Nandini and Nethos the day off. I've been working on a solo cycle for you, and I didn't think it would be ready for a few weeks, but it's ready now. Since they had a long day yesterday, I figured we could spare them a rest day."

Cahya felt a pang of disappointment. Solo cycles weren't uncommon, but they were a little lonely. It seemed silly because, once she entered a cycle, she wouldn't remember Nirvana, Nandini, or Nethos. Still, when she did cycles with her companions, there was something genuine about the connections with them—something that made her feel less alone.

In solo cycles, you could make friends and form relationships, but they always felt somewhat insincere. No matter how many people surrounded you, it always felt like you were on your own.

Still, Cahya knew that, as Dohan, she stood to gain a lot from solo cycles. They were almost meditative—a deep dive into the self.

Kole seemed to sense her disappointment. He gave a knowing shrug and said, "It's not so bad. You'll be a big-city private investigator named Johnny—quick-witted and wicked smart."

Cahya perked up at this information. An investigator! She thought about the evidence wall in her secret room at the Transfer Station. Maybe this cycle would give her insights to further her real-life investigation.

"Sounds interesting," Cahya said, trying not to let her excitement show. She didn't want Kole to grow suspicious.

"Alright, let's get to it," Kole announced. Cahya made her way to the active pod, which was glowing with blue light. She settled in, took a deep breath, and closed her eyes as Hathina tapped some buttons on the screen.

The dome lowered and Cahya's mind became very quiet as the pod whirred to life. She lay back, waiting for the darkness to overtake her. It seemed to be taking a while. Suddenly, there was a bright light and searing pain. Cahya had never experienced anything like this. She tried to open her eyes, tried to signal to Kole that something was wrong, but it was too late. The pain subsided, and everything went black.

✳ ✳ ✳

Johnny stomped into the coffee shop, the jingle of the bell above the door announcing his arrival. The barista behind the counter looked up from her work and braced herself, recognizing the scowl on his face.

"Black coffee," Johnny growled, slapping a five-dollar bill on the counter. He'd had a terrible day and didn't want to be here, but his assistant had gone home for the night, and he needed caffeine. It was the only way he was going to get through the pile of evidence back at his office.

The barista got straight to work, hoping to get this man served and out of the shop as quickly as possible. She nervously reached for the nearest cup and poured black coffee into it.

She placed a lid on the cup and passed it to Johnny, who immediately lifted the drink to his lips. As he did, a wave of dread washed over her—not because the coffee might be too hot; she knew he liked it hot—but because she suddenly realized that the cup she'd grabbed had sugar in it. She had started to prepare a coffee for herself just before Johnny walked in but had forgotten all about it when he stormed through the door.

Johnny took a sip, and his face twisted in rage. "What the hell is this?" he bellowed, his voice echoing through the shop. "I ordered black coffee, not this sugary crap!"

The barista's face flushed red with embarrassment as Johnny continued to rant, his words laced with profanity and insults. Customers glanced up from their laptops and books, their expressions ranging from annoyance to fear.

The barista quickly handed him a fresh cup of black coffee, even as his tirade continued. She slid his five-dollar bill back across the counter. "It's on the house," she said timidly. "Please accept my apologies for the mistake."

Johnny scoffed, grabbed the new drink and his money, and stormed out of the café, his face still red with anger.

As he walked up the street toward his office, Johnny felt a twinge of regret. Maybe he'd overreacted. He knew his temper was a problem. It made him terrible with people, but he believed it also made him a better investigator. People didn't like him, so they left him alone, which gave him more time to focus on his work.

Johnny arrived at his office and slammed the door behind him. He took a deep breath, trying to calm himself. He needed to focus on the murder case. He'd been working on it for months and felt like he was on the verge of a breakthrough. He had to concentrate if he was going to crack it.

The most critical evidence was neatly arranged on a large whiteboard mounted on the wall—crime scene photos, witness statements, newspaper clippings—all of it marked with notes in red. This was the heart of the case, the crucial details he couldn't afford to miss. Surrounding the board, a chaotic flurry of paperwork cluttered the walls—secondary information that might still prove useful. Johnny hadn't uncovered new evidence in weeks, but he was certain the answer was already there, staring back at him from that whiteboard. He just needed to piece it together.

The victim was a 40-year-old woman named Jennifer. She had died in a restaurant from an apparent heart attack. The autopsy confirmed it: heart attack. But her husband, Owen, didn't believe it.

"Jen was healthy," Owen had told Johnny. "She didn't drink or smoke. She went to the gym three times a week. She never even caught a cold. And then, just like that, she drops dead of a heart attack at 40? It doesn't make sense."

Johnny had been hesitant to take the case. Owen was grieving, and his suspicions might have been driven by denial. Johnny wasn't the type to take money for a case unless he believed there was something to solve. But then Owen had said something that caught his attention.

"She worked for Titan, the media company. She was an accountant. She'd only been there a few months, but she told me something was wrong with their books. She was digging around, trying to figure it out."

"You think that had something to do with her death?" Johnny had asked.

"Yes. One night she came home and said she'd found something big. She believed the company had an undisclosed source of income. If it was true, they could owe millions in taxes. Worst case, someone could go to jail. I told her to leave it alone, but she couldn't. A week later, she was gone."

So, Johnny had taken the case. He'd spent months on it, and everything came down to this whiteboard. Owen had provided some of Jennifer's findings—enough to prove motive. Someone was going to jail for financial crimes, but Johnny needed evidence that the company had killed her.

He scanned the board, pausing at a grainy photo of the restaurant where Jennifer had died. A still image, taken from some footage captured by a camera across the street, showed a man leaving the restaurant moments after her death. The man looked familiar, but Johnny couldn't place him. He stared at the large, sunken eye sockets in the pixelated image. Something clicked.

"Wait," Johnny muttered.

He ran to a filing cabinet and pulled out a thick folder labeled *Project Santorini*. A piece of green tape on the front read *SOLVED*. His assistant had marked it solved because the client got what they needed, but one mystery remained: the identity of a hitman. Johnny hadn't needed that information to close the case, but knowing a contract killer was still out there had always bothered him.

Johnny flipped through the folder until he found a photo of a man sitting in a blue car outside an apartment building. He held the photo next to the image on the whiteboard. His eyes widened—it was the same man.

Knock! Knock! Knock! Loud bangs on the office door pulled Johnny from his thoughts.

He gritted his teeth, annoyed by the interruption. He ignored the knocking, but it came again, louder this time.

"We're closed!" Johnny shouted, still staring at the photos.

KNOCK! KNOCK! KNOCK! The door rattled.

Johnny slammed the photo on his desk and stormed across the room. His temper boiled over. Whoever was on the other side of that door was about to face his wrath. He yanked the door open and shouted, "I said, we're—"

His words died as he stared at the pistol pointed directly at his face. Behind the gun was the man from the photo, his large, sunken eyes filled with malice.

"It's you," Johnny whispered.

The hitman smirked. "Nice to finally meet you, Johnny. I hear you're a fan of my work. You should've kept your nose out of it."

Johnny opened his mouth to speak, but a gunshot rang out before he could make a sound.

Everything went black.

Moments later, Johnny found himself moving rapidly through a tunnel filled with bright light. Scenes from his life flashed on the walls—blurry, distorted, and accompanied by static. He felt a deep, overwhelming confusion as he accelerated through the tunnel.

He sensed something important ahead and slowed. The images faded, leaving only a growing spot of light at the tunnel's end. He focused on it, waiting to reach clarity.

But just as he neared the light, searing pain exploded in his mind. The bright light turned red, then black, and everything disappeared into nothingness.

CHAPTER 4
WHERE AM I?

Johnny slipped into consciousness. He couldn't open his eyes, but sounds began to emerge. A soft murmuring came from somewhere to his right. Just above the sound of murmuring, there was a gentle hum with a distinct mechanical likeness, but it was so soft that it was almost comforting—he felt that he was being lulled to sleep by a gently whirring fan. He slipped back into the darkness.

Consciousness took hold again, his mind trying to piece things together. What happened? Where was he? He must be in a hospital room, Johnny thought. He was weak; he couldn't open his eyes or move any part of his body. The sounds he'd heard before came back—the murmuring sounded like whispers now—quiet, concerned whispers. He fell back to sleep.

He woke again and had the sense that time had passed. New sounds emerged this time, a gentle symphony slowly building around him. Footsteps drummed lightly along the floor nearby, and every so often a swooshing noise would join the mix. Then a soft rhythmic drumming, like fingertips gently tapping on a table. Everything was soft and relaxing. No sound seemed too harsh or invasive. His mind was aware enough to remember that he'd been at his office. He'd been working late. Then what? A knock. Someone at the door. A gun—the hitman—a bang. Had he been shot?

The murmuring noises began to come into focus, and Johnny was able to pick up words within the jumble.

Mumbling, "… she's very weak…," mumbling.

Mumbling, "… stable…," mumbling.

"Unlikely…," mumbling, "… more time…," mumbling.

Johnny slowly fluttered his eyelids and attempted to force them open; they were very heavy, and the soothing sounds of the room coaxed him closer to sleep. No! He had to wake up. He tried again, and his eyes were assaulted with blinding white light. He whimpered from the shock and pain of it and quickly tightened his lids.

"She's awake," someone whispered.

More feet shuffled.

Johnny felt a hand on his shoulder, and a male voice spoke gently, "Cahya?" the voice said. "Cahya, can you hear me?"

"The light…" Johnny managed to whisper.

"Myat, please dim the lights by fifty percent," the male voice requested, and though his eyes were closed, Johnny could tell that the room was less bright.

He attempted to part his lids once again, but it was an agonizing feat. He suddenly became very aware of the pain radiating from the top of his head. He pushed through the pain and forced his eyes open.

"Cahya! It's wonderful to have you back." The outline of the man whose voice was speaking began to come into focus. He sat close, hunching over slightly as he spoke to Johnny. He wore a bright blue tunic that reflected the light in the room. A warm smile stretched across his tanned face. His kind eyes matched the blue of his tunic. His chestnut hair was neatly cut to match his cleanly trimmed beard.

"You suffered a minor injury at the end of your last cycle, so your head may be a little sore."

Johnny saw the care and concern in the man's face—something familiar, even—but he had no idea who the man was. Yet, deep down, he sensed that he should. He stared, waiting for a spark of recognition. Had they worked together before? Had he been a client? Johnny's eyes lingered, his mind straining to connect the man to a memory, a time, a place. But nothing came.

"Cahya, can you hear me?" the man asked, a slightly puzzled gaze beginning to form in his deep blue eyes.

'Ah, confusion!' Johnny thought. Now this sort of look was something he could get on board with. Maybe he didn't know him after all. He definitely had the wrong name. Obviously, this man had mistaken Johnny for someone else. This made him feel a little better and a little less guilty about not being able to place him. Still, there was something strangely familiar about him; maybe the man reminded him of someone.

Johnny mirrored the puzzled gaze and asked, "Who's Cahya?" His voice sounded strange, but Johnny was still too tired to pay much notice.

"What's going on?" came another voice. Johnny tilted his head to find another attendant in the room. He wore the same tunic as the first man, but his hair was blue. How odd, Johnny thought.

"I'm not sure," answered the first man, still watching Johnny. He stared as though he were searching for something. His gaze felt intrusive and Johnny blinked, attempting to break the connection.

Whatever it was the man was searching for, he stopped abruptly, and his expression changed from puzzled to concerned. Maybe he finally realized that he'd mistaken Johnny for someone else. His gaze moved from Johnny to a hanging piece of glass located at the foot of the bed.

The glass display showed intricate images of a human body's inner workings, as though it were some advanced holographic X-ray. With the slightest motions of the man's fingertips, the images zoomed, turned, and pivoted. Finally, it zoomed in on a glimmering, multicolored depiction of a brain. Tiny blue lights orbited around it, darting in and out like sparks of energy.

"Is that my brain?" Johnny asked in a soft, raspy voice, suddenly distracted from the pain in his head. He was still weak and exhausted, but his fascination gave him a small burst of energy. If this was, in fact, an image of his brain, it was the most detailed and beautiful depiction he'd ever seen. The shape was familiar, but beyond that, it was almost unrecognizable. It was filled with more colors than he could count and surrounded by tiny blue balls of light that flickered and zipped around at random. They moved in and out of the neural mass, forming a sphere of energy that spread about a foot outward, tracing chaotic paths.

"Yes," the man replied absentmindedly. "That is your brain." He studied the image intently, his eyes squinting as he zoomed in and out of certain areas. He shot a concerned look at the blue-haired attendant. "You can see that too, right?"

"Yes, swelling," the attendant agreed.

The image dissolved, and the screen became clear once more. Johnny waited for the first man to speak. After a moment, he raised his eyes and met Johnny's gaze. When he spoke again, his voice had softened further. "Cahya is—" he paused again, considering his next words, "Cahya is... *you*, my friend. You have returned to your home," he gestured around the room, "Nirvana."

Johnny stared at the man skeptically, trying to process the words that had just come out of his mouth. 'He still thinks I'm someone else. He hasn't figured it out yet.' How was Johnny going to break the news to this man without embarrassing him? He decided to tear off the bandage; there was no sense in dragging this out. The longer it went on, the more embarrassed the man was bound to feel.

"I'm sorry, Mr.?"

"Ashatha. Kole Ashatha," he said, "and this is Kacha," he gestured to the blue-haired man. "I'm—"

"Look, Mr. Ashatha." Johnny stopped mid-sentence as though he were hearing his voice for the first time. His voice sounded different. He looked down at the bed, where his hands rested next to his thighs. The soft, dark brown hands of a woman.

"AhhhHA, holy shit! What's going on here?" Johnny shouted, leaping from the bed, wrestling the covers off him as he did. He held onto the bed for balance as he looked down at his body. Johnny wore a white linen gown, and while this body moved at his will, it was not his body. He let go of the bed and stumbled about for a moment, trying to steady himself. Suddenly, his head was throbbing again.

He looked at Kole and then back at his body—Cahya's body. He placed his hands on his chest. "I have BOCBS!" he exclaimed, a woozy feeling washed over him, the room seemed to tilt, and then everything went black.

* * *

"This is a highly unusual situation," Kole recounted. He stood next to a large, round, yellow table, which was surrounded by twelve men and women. Four of the attendees wore deep blue tunics like Kole; four wore vibrant magenta; and four wore brilliant emerald green. The tunics worn by the council were slightly more ornate than the one Kole wore. They were trimmed in elegant gold thread, making the colors appear slightly more vibrant.

Kole continued, "A trauma resulting in some memory loss is not completely unheard of—rare as it might be—but Cahya is suffering from something very different. She's displaying symptoms of a severe form of retrograde amnesia. She cannot recall faces, and she doesn't seem to know who or where she is. I'm most concerned about the extent of amnesia. Normally, an injury causing amnesia will only remove recent memories, but Cahya seems to have lost everything. She doesn't recall anything from her life here on Nirvana. She believes she's still the person she was during her last cycle."

One of the men wearing a blue tunic spoke up. "We're all very concerned for Cahya's well-being, of course, but I think that everyone would agree that the most concerning factor here is that Cahya is our Dohan. There's much at stake. We have to understand the full extent of her injuries and whether or not she'll regain her memories and be able to return to her duties. I'm afraid that we simply do not have clear protocols for this."

One of the women clad in magenta raised her hand, signaling that she had something to contribute. This woman had pale brown skin and soft pink hair that fell just above her chin. Her bangs were neatly trimmed with a fringe that sat just above a set of thick, red-rimmed glasses. The woman, whose name was Balti, began to speak. "Are you absolutely certain about the extent of the damage? Is it at all possible that she's suffering a temporary loss? That, perhaps, her memory might return?"

A man in blue leaned forward; this was Matildi, head of Human Health Studies for Nirvana. He had shoulder-length graying hair which was tied back in a couple of neat braids behind his head. His face was kind due largely to his big brown eyes and soft gray beard. He cleared his throat before addressing Balti: "I think it wise not to rule anything out at this point, Balti, but I would also hesitate to give this council false hope. We're in completely uncharted territory here. Personally, I've never seen a case of amnesia this dramatic in my ninety years of practice, and yet I have seen less invasive forms of memory loss which have left the patient permanently damaged. There's no telling if Cahya will be able to recover any of her memories, let alone all of them." Matildi let out a long sigh. "Still, I believe that we have a duty to allow Kole some time to see Cahya through this situation."

"It seems that we may have a difficult decision to make," proclaimed one of the men wearing an emerald tunic. This man had jet black hair, which was tied back into a bun behind his head. His bright green eyes glanced around the room at each of the other eleven attendees. "The Dohan is a position requiring fifty years of training on the path to becoming the Doyen. We cannot invest that kind of time and resources into a person who may or may not be able to fulfill their duties when the time comes. If she does not remember who she is, how can she be expected to lead our people one day?"

A few concerned nods circulated amongst the attendees as they pondered Kyun's concerns.

He continued, "Even if there was a chance that her memories might return, it could take years. Cahya was only at the beginning of her training—eight years in. If we make the decision now, we can select a new Dohan and work with them to make up for lost time. Nethos has participated in nearly all of Cahya's cycles to date. He seems like a natural choice. He'll be able to catch up very quickly."

"Kyun," Kole said, "your concerns are extremely valid, and I agree that this council should not hesitate for too long in making a decision on this matter; it is far too important." He paused. "However, I ask that the council consider allowing us some time to evaluate Cahya further. She's barely been awake for five minutes since the incident, and I fear that hastening a decision with so little information would be unwise."

"I disagree, Kole. I believe that the council has all of the information it requires to make a sound decision right now," Kyun interjected. "It would be irresponsible for us to leave unresolved a decision as important as this."

Just then, a door slid open, and a tall figure emerged from the opening. His long, lean body was draped in a white, shimmering tunic which flowed nearly to the floor. His silvery-white hair was tied back in a high bun, revealing his strong cheekbones. His beard, though thick, was neatly manicured around his jaw. Gentle creases formed at the corners of his kind, focused eyes as he smiled at the people seated around the table. Those lines made him unique among this group, as nearly everyone else had youthful, creaseless skin. The two exceptions were Balti and Matildi who were nearly the same age as the Doyen.

The committee members stood as the Doyen entered the room. Kole spoke, "Good afternoon, Doyen Hashen."

47

"Good afternoon," the Doyen replied, bowing his head deeply to the council members sitting around the table. "I've come to discuss the Dohan, of course. Kole, please bring me up to speed." His gaze passed to Kole as he took a seat along the wall, next to the council table.

Kole spoke, "The Dohan sustained injuries during her last cycle. We're still investigating the cause, Doyen. Her scans show swelling in her brain, which appears to have caused a devastating memory loss."

"How much does she remember?" the Doyen prompted.

"As far as we can tell at this point, Cahya can recall nothing of her life here." Kole's look was apologetic. He sighed and pressed on. "It's hardly guaranteed, Doyen, but I do believe there's a chance her memory could return." His words were hopeful, but his face and his tone were anything but.

"I agree with Kole," Balti offered with a gentle nod in Kole's direction. "Cahya is thirty-eight years old, young enough to bounce back from an injury like this. She's also eight years into her training, and I believe that's a long enough investment to justify giving Kole and his team a few days to monitor and evaluate her condition. This would also allow the council some time to discuss and explore our options."

The Doyen nodded gratefully to Balti before turning back to Kole. "Kole, I have always trusted and appreciated your counsel. You have a strong intuition, and if you believe there's a chance we might rehabilitate our young Dohan, I believe that we have a duty to try." The Doyen nodded at the council members, signaling his support for Kole's recommendation.

Kole nodded in appreciation.

"Very well, Doyen. You know that this council trusts your intuition on matters such as these. However, I vote that we apply a deadline to this endeavor so as not to waste more time than necessary," Kyun insisted.

"Yes," Balti agreed. "I think that thirty days is a reasonable amount of time to measure improvement."

Kyun interjected, "A full month? If there is any chance of regaining her memories, Cahya should show promising improvements within six or seven days. If she's made no progress by then, the council should move swiftly to replace her. I vote that we give Kole a week to work with her—no more."

Kole chimed in, "Six days? With all due respect, Kyun, I don't think a week is enough. I've discussed the matter with Cahya's medical team and they've confirmed that these sorts of injuries could take months, even years to reverse. Since we don't know the cause, it's challenging to know how long it might take."

"Unfortunately, Kole, I would have to agree with Kyun," Matildi said with a frown. As the Head of Human Health Studies, he oversaw the entire field of human health on Nirvana. More than that, he specialized in neurology, so his opinion carried considerable weight. "In instances where memory is restored, there's usually some noteable sign of improvement within the first week. If Cahya doesn't show any promising results after seven days, the research suggests that she is unlikely to regain much, if any, of her memories later."

"Very well," the Doyen said now. "Shall we vote? Green is in favor of giving Kole one week and one day, seven days total, to work with Cahya and report back to us. Red to remove Cahya from her role as Dohan immediately and proceed with selecting a new candidate."

At each place around the table, two dots appeared—one red and one green. The council members leaned forward, each of them placing a finger on the small green dot. As they did, the table slowly turned from yellow to green in small pie-shaped sections around the table. Kyun was not as enthusiastic but reluctantly reached forward and touched the green circle in front of him. The entire table was now green—a unanimous vote.

"If there are no other issues for discussion," Balti said, looking around the table. The members shook their heads to indicate that they had nothing more to add. "In that case, this meeting is adjourned. Thank you all for attending on such short notice."

With that, the members of the council began to stand and take their leave.

Kole made his way to the door, but the Doyen motioned for him to wait. As the last council member left the room, the Doyen closed the door and gestured for Kole to take a seat at the now-green table.

"Kole, does anything about this situation feel... unusual to you?" the Doyen asked, his eyes warm but speckled with the slightest hint of concern.

Kole's eyes widened in quiet understanding. He chose his next words carefully, "I really cannot say at this point, Doyen. We've experienced small memory issues from time to time, but they've become exceedingly rare in the past twenty years, as you well know. I've run checks on the system and everything appears to be functioning normally."

"I trust your instincts, Kole," the Doyen reassured him, "but do keep an open mind, will you?"

"Of course, sir. I'll run more tests and I'll let you know if anything looks... off."

"Thank you," the Doyen said, offering Kole a grateful smile. He paused, exhaling a long, slow breath. The smile faded slightly, replaced by a shadow of deeper concern. "And Kole... please, take care of our Dohan."

CHAPTER 5

ABOUT NIRVANA

Johnny opened his eyes feeling strangely clear-headed—almost refreshed. Any other day, waking up in some sterile white room, with a new name, in a new body, would have set off alarm bells. Yet he found himself... composed. Maybe too composed. As if something—or someone—was sedating his raw panic. *They must be doping me up,* he told himself, scoffing at the thought.

Johnny had been around enough hospitals and, well, shady clinics to know the good stuff when it hit him. But as he sat up, the events of the previous day flooded back: a place called Nirvana, some worried-looking guy in a blue tunic, his brain floating in mid-air... the name 'Cahya'. He peeked under his shirt just to confirm—yep... boobs.

Johnny let out a long sigh as a jolt of disorientation cracked through him. His mind flashed with the last things he could remember before he'd woken up here. His office, the investigation. A loud knocking at the door.

His chest tightened as he recalled what happened next. The hitman, the gun, the blast... a shock rose through him and his heart pounded. Was he dead? Was this... *heaven?* The panicked feeling that grew in him assured him that he wasn't on any sort of sedatives—or at least they weren't as good as he'd thought.

He took another breath, allowing the strangeness of the situation to settle in as he swung his legs off the bed. Even though he was wearing pants, he could see that the legs were not his. He flexed slender fingers, noticing how far removed they were from his old calloused hands. "Hell," he muttered in that same unfamiliar voice. *Am I even me anymore?*

Johnny Grisdale, private investigator, a man. A man who used to bark at baristas over sugar in his coffee, used to solve rich people's nasty problems. For a split second, memories battered him: *You're dead, pal—or maybe you're not. The next best scenario: you're locked in some twisted dream. Or you're dealing with some weird Freaky Friday, shit. Maybe your body is out there somewhere with someone named Cahya trapped inside.* He dragged a hand through unfamiliar purple hair, half-laughing in disbelief.

"Cahya," he tested the name. He raised his hands to his chest, cupping and lifting the unfamiliar weight of his bosom. This body was nice. If he *had* switched bodies with someone, he felt a pang of guilt for the woman who was now trapped in his body, surely her experience would be more... unsettling. Johnny hadn't showered in a couple of days. *When was the last time he'd changed his underwear?*

Everything here, on the other hand, was very clean. The room was painfully bland: white walls, white floors, a single bed, and a rolling stool. No sign of a normal door—just a smooth, slightly bowed wall across from the bed.

There must be a door, he thought, as he stepped off the bed, still holding his chest. He froze when the hanging glass screen at the foot of the bed blinked to life

"Good morning, Cahya," came an unembodied voice. "I trust you slept well. Please place both feet firmly on the floor, and I will complete a full scan."

He jumped, scanning the corners. "Who's there?" he demanded, ignoring the voice's request.

"Hello, Cahya," replied the calm voice. "I am Myat, short for My Attendant. I'm a sophisticated piece of software designed to help with daily life on Nirvana."

Nirvana. That's the word the man in blue had used. Johnny deliberately *did not* plant his feet together, instead he continued walking about, inspecting the room for any signs of a door.

"What's Nirvana?" Johnny asked the disembodied voice.

"Nirvana is a planet in the Gardia solar system, inhabited by humans in the year 8579 P.E." came Myat's response.

Johnny froze. Planet? Gardia system? What the hell was going on?

A soft blue light suddenly illuminated the floor beneath Johnny, snapping him out of his thoughts and making him jump in surprise.

Myat repeated the request, "Cahya, please place both feet on the floor for your scan."

"Johnny," he corrected bitterly—scanning the room once more.

"Would you prefer that I call you Johnny, Cahya?" the voice asked politely.

Johnny hesitated. He didn't know *what* he wanted. He just wanted answers.

"I would *prefer* that you tell me what the hell is going on here," he exclaimed.

The voice obliged, "It seems that you experienced some swelling following your last training cycle and are suffering from amnesia. You recall being Johnny, your incarnation from that cycle. I'm afraid that I'm not permitted to discuss the matter beyond that until you've spoken with Kole. However, I can refer to you as Johnny, if that makes you more comfortable," the voice offered again.

"Fine, sure." He conceded, processing this information. So no Freaky-Friday shit after all. No chance of finding and reinhabiting his original body.

"Alright, Johnny, please place both feet firmly on the floor, and I will complete a full scan."

Johnny groaned, *oh my god, this thing will not let up!* But something about being called Johnny set him slightly more at ease. He decided to do as he was asked. Setting his feet together he braced for some weird futuristic nonsense. A soft blue circle glowed under his heels.

A swirl of light climbed over his body while the glass panel lit up at the foot of the bed, displaying a rotating hologram of a tall, curvy woman with purple hair. Johnny folded his arms, refusing to show how uneasy it felt watching this happen. Words appeared on the display, Johnny leaned forward to read them:

CAHYA LIGHTHOLD - 38 YEARS OLD

Part of him—the cynical P.I.—wanted to sneer at the whole show. Another part marveled at the technology. He could feel a tug of wonder. He'd never seen anything so advanced, so polished.

He forced out a gruff sigh, fighting the wave of panic that threatened to creep up. Then Myat spoke, snapping him back into the room and out of his head, "You're slightly dehydrated, here's some water." A hidden shelf extended from the wall with a single glass of water.

"Seriously?" he mumbled, snatching the glass. "No nurse to bring me water in person?" But the dryness in his throat reminded him he was parched, so he drank it in one go before placing the glass back on the shelf.

The small shelf retracted, sealing seamlessly. Johnny stared, suspicious. "So you can pop out shelving whenever you like, but you can't open the *actual* door to let me leave?"

"It appears you would like the door opened, Johnny," Myat said. "However, the room is set to 'Limited Patient Operations' mode. You are not authorized to—"

"Right," he cut in. "Gotta wait on the doc or whoever. Great."

"Would you like me to reduce window opacity instead?" Myat offered.

"What windows?"

In answer, the curved wall faded from opaque white to translucent glass. Blinding sunlight poured in, revealing a sidewalk bustling with pedestrians, thriving flowerbeds, and a crisp blue sky. Johnny shielded his eyes, a jolt of wonder stirring in his chest. The city outside looked so... *clean.* Peaceful. He took a step forward, unsettled that it *enchanted* him. Johnny wouldn't be enthralled by a well-manicured city block, right?

He tried to cling to that cynicism. *Focus on who you are, or were.* The last thing he recalled as Johnny was the muzzle of a gun, a swirl of red, collapsing. He shivered, letting the memory wash over him.

His introspection broke when a new, real voice spoke behind him. "Thank you, Myat."

Startled, Johnny whirled around, fists up. A man in a tidy blue tunic stood near the newly opened door, hands raised in a placating gesture. "Easy," he said gently. "It's me—Kole." He offered a polite half-bow. "I see Myat's been driving you a bit crazy."

"A bit," Johnny allowed, letting his fists drop. "I, uh..." He hesitated, not wanting to reveal that swirl of fear and awe inside him. Instead, he shrugged, going for a casual, unimpressed air. "Could use a real conversation."

Kole smiled, crossing the room. "I know this must be overwhelming."

Johnny eyed him warily, noticing how calm, almost *compassionate* he seemed. That unsettled him as much as anything else. "Overwhelming. Understatement of the century, doc."

Kole tilted his head. "I'm no doctor, but I do care about your well-being, Cahya."

There's that name again. He clenched his jaw. "Look, people keep calling me Cahya, but that's not the name I go by. At least not up here." He tapped his temple, ignoring the dull ache from behind his eyes.

Kole nodded, understanding. "You remember being Johnny Grisdale. I get it. And we'll talk about it in detail. For now, can I ask you to sit? I want to show you something—something we show our children so they understand Nirvana, but it might help you, too."

"A cartoon, huh?" he said curtly. "Why not, my self-esteem's in great shape today."

Kole pulled over a white stool, gesturing for Johnny to sit on the edge of the bed. He took a seat on the stool next to the bed. "Myat, please play 'Nirvana: Beginnings'"

At Kole's instructions, the room dimmed and the curved wall across turned into a giant display. Stars winked into existence, spinning across an unseen horizon.

Johnny scanned the room for projectors but couldn't find any.

"Here we go," Kole said. "I can pause the presentation if you have questions."

"Be prepared," Johnny muttered, arms crossed defensively. "I confuse easily these days."

The screen flickered to life, revealing a stunning image of Earth, its swirling blue oceans and verdant continents suspended in the vastness of space. Johnny's heart clenched at the sight of something so achingly familiar. He'd seen photos of earth many times, but they'd never caused him to feel this way; like seeing an old photograph of a life long forgotten—comforting, yet deeply unsettling. Before he could fully grasp the moment, the scene shifted.

The Earth began to darken, its oceans turning murky and landmasses veined with the scars of deforestation and pollution. A lyrical, voice—Myat's documentary tone, Johnny realized—began a soft narration:

"Centuries ago, humankind spread across the stars, seeking new homes whenever they exhausted their old ones. World after world, each brimming with promise, fell victim to the same cycle: war, ecological collapse, or resource depletion, until the planet was irreparably damaged. In time, more than two dozen human-colonized worlds were lost."

As Myat spoke, clusters of planets floated forward, each spinning in silent majesty. The presentation zoomed in on each one—greens and blues signifying habitability—before showing them blackened under cataclysms or vanish in fiery explosions.

Johnny's stomach churned. *This is... too big.* He fought the urge to scoff. *There's no way humans destroyed that many planets.* But another part of him felt sorrow. The scope of destruction triggered a stab of empathy he couldn't wholly deny. These illusions felt *real.* He swallowed down an unexpected lump in his throat.

"Despite technological leaps, humans repeated old mistakes. Nations quarreled, greed overtook reason, and each planet's downfall arrived faster than the last."

One planet—the biggest projection yet—turned gray and crumbled in swirling dust. Johnny clenched his fists. "You're telling me humans did all that?" he whispered bitterly. "That we keep messing up, world after world?"

Kole raised a hand and the images froze. "It's a bleak history, but yes. Humans have an astounding capacity for progress—and an equally astounding capacity for self-destruction."

Johnny caught his reflection in the hanging glass: a face with purple hair, wide brown eyes. *Not the face of a world-weary detective.* "I guess I always suspected we were good at messing things up, but not *this* good."

Kole nodded and waved his hand. The imagery whirred back to life. A single planet—blue-green, reminiscent of Earth. Myat's narration continued:

"Eventually, Carta was the final human planet. Barely stable, it teetered on the brink of nuclear war. Many believed it was doomed. So, a group of five thousand fled in a desperate exodus, boarding a starship that slipped away mere days before Carta destroyed itself."

A flash of blinding light signified Carta's end. Johnny felt the same hollowness he'd felt on bleak cases—like that pang when a cold-case victim's family never found closure. He realized a wave of memory was surfacing: *he'd been shot... murdered. That's what humans do, right? We destroy.*

He inhaled sharply, forcing the thoughts aside for now.

The starship in the presentation soared across a field of stars until it reached another solar system. The planet they approached glowed gently with swirling oceans and lush landmasses.

> *"Their ship arrived in the Gardia system, discovering Nirvana."*

The view zoomed in on Nirvana's surface, revealing circular cities, each with farmland belts and elaborate waterways. "So we found a perfect place," Johnny said softly. "And we... didn't ruin it this time?"

Kole let out a gentle breath. "Not yet."

With a flicker, the scene changed: rows of sleek white pods lined up in a laboratory, each with a glass dome overhead.

> *"To guide humans away from their destructive instincts, the Earth Life Cycle Program—ELC—was developed and made mandatory for all Nirvanians. Each person experiences hundreds of lifetimes in carefully curated simulations, returning with greater empathy, wisdom, and discipline."*

Figures were shown climbing into those pods. Scenes of historically war-torn cities from Earth appeared, then scenes of families weathering heartbreak, revolution, or quiet heroics. Some scenes were peaceful, others harrowing.

Johnny's pulse quickened. *My entire existence... Johnny's entire existence... is in those pods.* How? It was all so... *real.*

> *"Citizens complete two hundred fifty cycles between age twenty-five and thirty-five,"* Myat's narration continued, *"emerging as stable, well-rounded members of society. Some require more guidance, some require specialized cycles. But in all cases, the program ensures no one must learn harsh lessons at Nirvana's expense.*

We learn them in simulations, and we preserve peace in reality."

The window brightened slightly, showing children in a classroom sporting VR headsets, some older students in ELC pods, and then the shining face of an older man wearing a white tunic.

At that moment, Myat's voice softened:

"With ELC, we have eliminated war, famine, and poverty. By living entire lifetimes of suffering in simulations, we avoid repeating catastrophic mistakes on Nirvana. However, each cycle leaves an impression—real heartbreak, real love. A sacrifice we embrace for a peaceful present."

The screen faded to black, and the lighting in the room returned. Johnny stared at the blank window, grappling with the information. War after war, planet after planet, ELC, a near-utopia here on Nirvana.

Finally, Johnny broke the silence, "So I've done some of these cycles then?"

"Quite a large number, in fact," Kole confirmed.

"But I only remember... *Johnny*," his name caught in his throat. In his mind he was still that person and to speak of him as something, well, other—it felt wrong. "And it wasn't even real?"

"You might find it's not so black-and-white," Kole said softly. "The lifetimes feel real because we experience them fully and our feelings are very real. Once a cycle is complete, the experiences become a part of you, the lessons you learned remain. People come out changed—"

"How many?" Johnny demanded.

"Pardon?" Kole replied, a quizzical look on his face.

"How many fake lives have I lived and forgotten?"

"Ah," Kole muttered, nodding, "quite a few, actually. You see, you joined the program early, at eighteen."

"Early? Why?" Johnny inquired.

Kole was brief in his explanation, "Extenuating circumstances."

"Extenuating circumstances?" Johnny repeated.

"Yes, well, early on, it was clear that there was something special about you."

Johnny scoffed, he hated that word. *Special.*

Kole continued anyway, "You had a natural intuition; we call it *'Sapoto'* which can be loosely defined as 'intrinsic wisdom'; it's an innate ability to see and understand the world beyond what is tangible, beyond what can be summarized with data or defined using words. If the council senses that a person possesses an extraordinary level of sapoto, he or she is sent to meet with the Doyen. He permitted you to start your training early. This means you've been going through cycles for two decades now."

Johnny let out a high-pitched whistle. "Twenty years of training. So if your typical human is doing 250 cycles in ten years, then this Cahya person," he said, pointing at himself, "has done like, what, 500 cycles?"

Kole smiled and responded gently, "In the past twenty years, you've lived through about sixteen hundred cycles."

Johnny let out a shaky laugh, bitterness creeping into his tone. "Sixteen hundred. "

Something new was washing over him, sadness perhaps. The information was slowly sinking in. This woman, Cahya, who's body he was trapped in, had a whole life here on Nirvana and she'd lived *sixteen hundred* other lifetimes. He couldn't even fathom all that she'd seen and done over the course of all of those experiences. And now, it was all gone—erased—and she was left with... *Johnny.* Johnny who had barely lived, he'd hardly left his office during his adult years. He hadn't had a real friend in years—no romantic relationships to speak of. What a sad, lonely life to be left with after sixteen hundred lifetimes.

Sixteen hundred. Special program. 'Nirvanian citizens complete two hundred and fifty cycles...' Johnny's detective brain was putting puzzle pieces together even as he sat in his guilt.

"So, what's this special program?" Johnny asked, "Why have I done six times more cycles than other people?"

"It may be hard to understand," Kole warned.

"I'm pretty smart," Johnny retorted.

"Nirvana has a sort of spiritual leader called the Doyen," Kole began. "While it's not a political role, the Doyen's influence is far-reaching—a very important position in our world. You see, the Doyen has lived well over ten thousand lifetimes through the ELC program. As you can imagine, that level of experience comes with great sacrifice. Two hundred and fifty cycles make for a very well-rounded Nirvanian citizen—ten thousand cycles—well, one accumulates a level of emotional breadth, insight, and intuitive perception far beyond that of ordinary citizens."

When Kole paused, Johnny jumped in, clearly impatient. "Okay, and what does that have to do with me?"

"Well, one of the Doyen's responsibilities is to select their successor—a person known as the 'Dohan.' The Dohan spends decades in training, preparing for the role they'll one day inherit," Kole continued after a brief pause. "*You* are Nirvana's Dohan."

Johnny let out an exasperated chuckle. "*What?!*"

He shook his head, processing the new information. "So, let me get this straight—you've got *one* big, important leader, and *one* leader-in-training," he said, pointing a finger at himself, "and you're telling me that you've just wiped out decades of training after a routine cycle?"

Kole nodded somberly. "It's not good."

"So, what now?" Johnny asked.

"As you can see, there's a lot at stake, so we're going to do everything we can to help you recover your memories. I've got a number of things we can try. With any luck, you'll be back to your old self in no time."

"And if that doesn't work?" Johnny pressed.

"We'll cross that bridge when we come to it. I hope it won't come to that. We have lots of things we can try and I'd prefer to focus our energy there for now."

Johnny searched his mind, searched for anything that might exist there which wasn't from his life as Johnny, anything that might offer a glimmer of hope that there was still something left of Cahya inside of him. But he couldn't find anything.

Kole rose, watching for a reaction. "I know it's a lot," he said gently. "If you need time to absorb—"

"Time?" He chuckled harshly. "I've apparently lived for centuries inside these VR coffins. What even is *time*?" Kole was right, this *was* a lot.

"Well, if you're up for it, I'll send a friend over to take you to dinner later. Getting out into the city could help to jog your memories."

Johnny looked out the windows, where people continued about their day. As beautiful as it was, something about joining that world without knowing anything about it felt unsettling. He chuckled in spite of himself. *You grew up in New York City, man. You've worked in some of the roughest neighborhoods in the world. I think you can handle this.*

"A man's gotta eat," Johnny said finally.

Kole raised an eyebrow but didn't argue.

Johnny looked down at Cahya's female form, "You know what I mean," he said.

Kole nodded, "Feel free to ask Myat to play more lessons for you while you wait. Could be helpful," and with that, he slipped through the door of the room and Johnny was alone once again.

Johnny stood in the center of the room, feeling suddenly exhausted.

"Uh, Myat," he said.

"Yes, Johnny, how can I help you?" Came the reply.

Johnny looked down at his new curvy body once more and, pulling his collar open, he stared down at the bosom under his shirt.

He took a deep breath and let out a long, defeated sigh. Whatever else might be going on here, whatever sort of strange fever dream this might be, one thing seemed fairly clear: he was no longer Johnny, and whoever this Cahya person might be, though he didn't really understand it, *he* was now *her.*

"It's ok, Myat, you can call me... Cahya."

"Okay, Cahya, how can I be of assistance?" Myat inquired.

"Could you, uh, darken the windows again? I think I need a nap."

Instantly, the windows fogged until they were completely opaque and the room felt suddenly smaller.

"Thanks," she muttered.

"You're welcome, Cahya. Would you like me to play some soothing background noises for your nap?"

"Sure."

Cahya lowered herself onto the bed as rhythmic whirring sounds gently filled the space. She held her hands in front of her face, inspecting them once more, her mind still swirling with the rush of information Kole had shared with her. Johnny had been used to processing a lot of information at once, but this was different.

She tucked her hands under the covers and closed her eyes. *Doyen, Dohan, ELC program, cycles, Nirvana.* These new terms floated through her mind, as Myat's soothing soundscape lulled her to sleep.

CHAPTER 6
THE NAPILI

A dinging noise woke Cahya from her nap. She opened her eyes but strained to see anything in the darkened room.

'Ding ding,' the noise rang again.

"What the hell is that dinging?" Cahya growled into the empty room.

"That's the door, Cahya," Myat replied, causing Cahya to jump, startled by the response. She'd forgotten about Myat.

"Are you always listening?" Cahya asked, throwing the blankets off her legs.

"Of course," Myat replied. "That is how I am best able to be of service to you."

'Ding ding.'

"You have a visitor, Cahya," Myat announced.

Cahya really wanted to dig into this idea of Myat listening to everything. But she made a mental note to bring it up later.

Cahya got out of bed and made her way to the door where Kole had exited from earlier in the day. When she got there, she realized that she had no idea how to open it. There was no handle. "Hello?" she called out to the person on the other side of the door.

"Hello, Cahya, what can I do for you?" Myat asked.

For a super-intelligent program, Myat was acting pretty dense. "Well, Myat, let's see if we can work this out together, hmm? The room went 'ding ding,' and you told me I had a visitor. Now I'm standing in front of what I'm pretty sure is the door—though you guys seem to like to hide things around here—and I'm waiting. What do you suppose you can do for me?"

"It seems that you may want to learn how to open the door. Is that correct?" Myat responded.

Cahya rolled her eyes. "That *would* be helpful, Myat."

"Very well!" Myat exclaimed. "The door is along the far wall. When you approach a door, a glowing circle will appear. If you wave your left hand over it, the door will open."

Cahya moved toward the wall, and sure enough, a glowing circle appeared which was about the size of a doorknob. She waved her left hand over it, as Myat had instructed.

The glowing circle turned from white to green and emitted a soft, chiming sound. The door immediately slid upwards, and Cahya found herself standing face-to-face with a man poised with one arm up as though ready to knock.

"Hi. I thought the bell might be broken," the man explained simply. His expression was flat; his thin lips stretched into a tight line across his face, and his green eyes stared blankly at Cahya. He lowered his knocking hand and lifted the other. In it, he held a sleek gold hanger draped with a black tunic. "I brought your clothes."

"Thank you," Cahya said to the strange man, reaching to take the clothes from him.

"Kole asked me to take you to dinner if you're feeling up to it." He shrugged his narrow shoulders under his own black tunic.

"Right, Kole mentioned that he'd be sending someone." The pair stared at one another in silence for a moment before Cahya said, "I'm sorry, who are you?"

"Oh! Right. I'm Nethos," the man replied. "Nethos Portos. We're—well, we used to be friends, I guess. But you don't remember me at all, do you?"

"No, I don't, but don't take it too personally; I don't remember anyone," she told him matter-of-factly.

"If you'd prefer to stay here," Nethos said, "I can have food delivered to your room."

Cahya looked around and realized she was dying to get out of this room. "Uh, no, that's okay. Lead the way."

"I'll give you a moment to dress first," Nethos said, gesturing toward the black tunic in Cahya's hand. "I'll wait out here."

Cahya took the tunic and slipped back into the room. The door slid shut. Cahya placed the garments on the bed and stared at them for a moment. The black tunic was nice enough—not too feminine, which she was grateful for. The evening sunlight cast itself across the room, dancing over the tunic's surface so that it sparkled. The hanger held a pair of plain black pants and a small pouch containing a pair of sleek black shoes.

Cahya removed all of the garments from the hanger and laid them out across the bed. The first garment she took was a light, almost silky pair of pants. She slid them onto one leg and then the other. They fit her perfectly. They were light and hung in a straight line to the floor. The fit was impeccable, almost as though they'd been perfectly tailored for her body.

She picked up the next garment. It was a simple, sleeveless shirt—all black—and was made of the same material as the pants. There were no seams; it was one solid piece. 'How was that even possible?' she wondered. Cahya slid the shirt over her head and pulled it down over her torso. Another perfectly fitted garment. Incredible.

Next, she slipped her feet into the shoes and then reached for the tunic. It looked quite heavy and substantial, but it was surprisingly lightweight. The material was soft, almost velvety, but it was far more structured. She pushed one arm through the sleeve and then the other. She adjusted her shoulders and the collar and then made her way to the small bathroom, where she knew there was a mirror. She found herself staring at the strange woman in the reflection. Her long purple hair fell over the shoulders of the black tunic. She looked into her soft violet eyes and then quickly looked away. She couldn't stare at this stranger for long; it didn't feel natural. It didn't really feel like her. She looked again, avoiding her own eyes. Myat had said that Cahya was thirty-eight. *Thirty-eight?* She wondered. How could she be thirty-eight? The girl in the mirror looked no older than eighteen.

'Ding ding!' came the door again. Oh right! Nethos.

Cahya made her way to the door and lifted her left hand to the glowing circle. The door slid upwards, and Cahya made her way out to meet the man waiting outside. He stood waiting a few feet from the entrance, his hands folded behind his back.

Nethos looked at Cahya, head to toe, nodded his approval, and said, "Alright then, let's get on with it. I reserved a table for us at Menza."

Nethos turned to walk, and Cahya followed. This Nethos guy didn't seem particularly keen to be babysitting the amnesia patient, Cahya thought, a little annoyed.

The tunic was long and fell nearly to the floor, hovering just an inch or so above the surface. Cahya worried about tripping over the garment, but for the moment, it was fine. They made their way down a white hallway to a set of glass doors, which retracted quietly as they approached. As soon as the doors opened, a wave of chatter and laughter burst through the silence. The large common area was full of people, and though they were still indoors, it felt as though they'd just walked into a beautifully designed park. A large glass dome overhead filled the space with sunlight.

Cahya looked back at the building they'd just emerged from. It was a large, round building covered in mirrored glass and surrounded by a wide garden bed which was lush with flowering plants and shrubs.

Everywhere Cahya looked, there were chairs, benches, swings, and strange furniture she didn't recognize. Maybe they weren't furniture at all.

A small pond with a fountain splashed and danced in the center of the space. A path made of white material—'Is it marble?' Cahya wondered. It sure looks like it.

The path encircled the pond and radiated out weaving around the large domed hub. The rest of the space was covered in pristinely manicured grass and stunning gardens. They made their way along the pathway, walking past a group of children sitting in the grass. They were playing some sort of digital board game that hovered in the air on its own, so there was no need for a table.

As they continued down the path, a woman seated on a bench smiled at Cahya, gently bowed her head, and said, "Good evening, Dohan."

Cahya raised her eyebrow at the woman and stared at her as they walked by. More people greeted her in this way as they made their way through the park. Nethos looked back and caught sight of Cahya's face.

"Stop that!" Nethos demanded.

"Stop what?"

"Stop looking at people like they're aliens. You're the Dohan." Nethos managed to keep his face calm, but his tone was clearly irritated.

Two can play that game, Cahya thought. "I'm not sure if anyone filled you in, but I lost my memories, so as far as I'm concerned, these people *are* aliens. Besides, I'm not used to people being so nice." She cringed. "It's weird."

"Just refrain from looking disgusted. Could you manage that much?"

Cahya caught sight of her face in the mirrored reflection of a window as they walked by. Okay, Nethos was right; she did look pretty disgusted. She tried to lower the corner of her lip and soften her eyes.

"It's no good," she told him. "It's stuck like this."

Nethos inhaled deeply and closed his eyes, clearly trying to ignore Cahya's comment.

'Ha! I'm getting under this guy's skin,' she thought. 'Maybe everyone here is just playing nice, but they're really all a bunch of jerks deep down. Humans, she thought, 'send them to the outer edges of the galaxy, give them fancy technology and some fandangled educational system, but they're still just a bunch of turds playing at being civilized.'

A woman with soft pink hair passed and Cahya poked Nethos, "Hey, speaking of aliens. What's with all the strange hair colours? Your hair looks normal, but mine's purple and that guy over there, his hair's blue."

Nethos placed a hand over Cahya's to stop her from pointing at the man with blue hair. "Hasn't anyone ever told you it's not polite to point?" He let out a sign before he continued, "Nirvana's star emits a spectrum of radiation that interacts with melanin biosynthesis pathways, resulting in structural modifications in select individuals."

"English, please." Cahya prodded.

"The sun causes some people's hair to turn shades of pink, purple, or blue." Nethos replied curtly.

"So it's not some weird trend, then." Cahya confirmed, watching as another woman passed with two purple-haired children.

"No, it's not a trend. Those are their natural hair colors." Nethos confirmed.

At the center of the domed building was a tower that stretched a hundred feet in the air, all the way to the glass ceiling. The white building was filled with glass windows split between ten floors. Around the outside of the building was a large, lush garden highlighted by several trees, some of which stretched nearly to the top of the dome as well.

"What's that?" Cahya asked Nethos, pointing at the tower.

"You ask a lot of questions." Nethos pointed out before answering Cahya's question, "That's the central tower; it's filled with office spaces for various governing bodies, ELC labs, stuff like that.

The top floor is the council chamber, where the Nirvanian Council meets to discuss the various issues of the day."

"It's beautiful," Cahya remarked in spite of herself, staring at the top of the tower.

"CAHYA!" came a voice from behind. Cahya turned to see a ball of curly brown hair bobbing toward her, arms outstretched. "How are you?" said the hair, wrapping its arms around Cahya and squeezing tightly.

Cahya shot a look at Nethos; she was certain that the disgusted look had returned, and she wasn't sure she could control it. Nethos widened his eyes in an expression that clearly said, 'Keep it together!'

But... kids! Ugh, if there's one thing Johnny hadn't been able to tolerate, it was kids. They were so loud and messy. They made everything miserable. Cahya tried to adjust her face, but it was a struggle. It took everything in her not to peel the child off of her and shove it into the nearest bush.

"Ash," a man jogged up to meet the group, an apologetic look on his face. "I'm sorry, Cahya; I haven't had a chance to tell her about your accident."

Cahya stared at the man, his soft curly hair fell in front of his face as he gently coaxed the girl's arms from around Cahya's waist. Cahya breathed a small sigh of relief and softened her face as much as she could manage. The girl looked up, her big brown eyes meeting Cahya's.

"What accident?" the girl asked, eyes fixed on Cahya.

The man didn't answer but turned to Cahya instead. "Sorry, I'm Carsen," he told her, hand outstretched.

Cahya nodded and shook the man's hand. "Cahya—or so I've been told," she replied, exhaling sharply, relaxing a little. Okay, adults she could do.

"What is going on?" Ash demanded. "Cahya knows your name, Papa!" She looked from Cahya to her father, a puzzled expression on her face.

"Ash, honey," the man said, kneeling down to meet the girl's gaze. "Cahya had an accident yesterday, and some of her memories were lost. It may take a bit of time for her to feel like herself again."

The girl's eyes were skeptical; she looked from her father up to Cahya and said, "She wouldn't forget me, Papa. I'm her best friend in the whole world." She stared at Cahya, her gaze determined. "You wouldn't forget me, Cahya, would you?"

Panic suddenly rose in Cahya's chest. Those eyes! Dammit! She didn't know this kid. But Cahya knew her—the real Cahya. Full-memories Cahya... *that* Cahya knew this kid.

Was she about to break this kid's heart? She didn't like kids, and tossing them into a bush was one thing... but telling a little girl that her best friend was gone, somehow, was something she couldn't do.

Could she fool this little girl into thinking she still remembered her? Cahya shot a glance at Nethos, who stood with one eyebrow raised as if to say, 'Well, what are you going to do about this?'

'Great, thanks for the help, Nethos,' Cahya thought.

She took a breath and looked back at the girl. "No, of course not, Ash. I'd never forget you." Cahya managed the most convincing smile she could muster. "How are you today?" she asked, unsure if the child would be convinced.

"I'm great!" the child exclaimed. Cahya breathed a soft sigh of relief. She didn't know why, but somehow she knew that she'd done the right thing. The girl continued, "Do you remember the boat I told you about last week? Well, Papa and I are going to go spend the whole day at the beach, and we'll get to take a ride on that very same boat! Isn't that exciting?!"

"Yes, it is," Cahya agreed. "I am very excited for you. I hope you have a great time." She looked up at the girl's father, who gave her a grateful smile, tears welling up in his eyes.

"I will! See you soon, Cahya!" and with that, the girl bounced away. Her father gave a gentle bow to Nethos and then to Cahya. "Dohan," he said, putting his hand on his chest in a gesture that said, 'thank you.' Then he turned and followed along behind his daughter.

Cahya watched them until they were out of earshot. "Are there any other clingy children around here I need to know about?"

Nethos shot Cahya a look but didn't respond; instead, he turned and resumed his walk toward the restaurant.

"Alright, fine, at least tell me who she was," Cahya said, jogging to catch up.

"Ash-Lynn Potiva," he told her, without turning around. "Her mother died in an accident two years ago. Ash stopped talking for about six months afterward. Eventually, she took a liking to you, and somehow, you got her to come out of her shell again. You've spent several hours with her every week since."

Cahya looked back over her shoulder; she could still see the young girl chatting away with her father as they walked. "I don't remember her," Cahya admitted, a pang of guilt cutting through her.

"Like you said, you don't remember anyone," Nethos shrugged. "I wouldn't feel bad."

"I'm sure you wouldn't," Cahya agreed. She didn't know much about this guy, but she got the feeling that he wasn't overly emotional.

They continued walking until the restaurant came into view; it was an open-air building with a short wooden fence running along the outside of it.

Large, sleek silver boxes on wheels rolled out of the building, each headed in a different direction. One rolled right past Nethos and Cahya.

"What's this?" Cahya asked as the cart wheeled away past the center of the dome.

"Food carts," Nethos replied. "They deliver fresh meals all over Deshka—to the office buildings, the schools, people's homes—anywhere hungry people might be. Here we are."

A gate on the fence swung open as they approached; next to the entrance there was a small sign which spelled out 'Menza' in bright green letters.

As they entered the space, a holographic person appeared above a white, glowing circle on the floor. It was the shape of a tall, handsome man. As they approached, the figure smiled broadly and spoke, "Welcome, Dohan; welcome, Nethos. Table 3 is ready for you. Please follow the lights on the floor, and they will guide you to your seat."

Nethos nodded to the hologram and then followed a series of frosted dots which lit up on the floor ahead of him. Cahya followed along until the path of lights ended with a single glowing dot which pulsed next to an empty table. Nethos sat in one of the empty chairs and motioned for Cahya to take the seat across from him.

As they settled in, Cahya had an opportunity to take a closer look at Nethos. He had olive skin, and his eyes were a deep, bright green. His head was shaved on either side, with a pile of caramel-colored curls sprouting out on top of it. He wore a curious band around his arm, over the sleeve of his tunic. It was metallic black, and as Cahya looked closer, she realized that it was actually two parallel bands held together by a sort of black medallion.

"That's an interesting, uh, armband," Cahya pointed out. She hesitated because she realized that she wasn't sure what to call it. She wasn't accustomed to seeing people wear what looked to be jewelry around their arms.

"Thank you," Nethos said. "It's from my mother."

He didn't seem keen to talk about it, so Cahya didn't press him, but she found the band fascinating, and she studied it discreetly. The medallion was embossed with three spirals that looked like waves, cresting over one another. The black metal caught the light of the evening sun on its glossy surface, shimmering slightly when Nethos moved.

"The symbol looks familiar," Cahya noted, ignoring the fact that Nehthos didn't seem to want to discuss the trinket.

"It's a kind of triskelion, I guess," he observed, "Not an uncommon symbol."

They sat awkwardly for a few minutes until Nethos broke the silence, his voice warmer than before. "So, can you remember anything at all?"

"Nope, not a thing," Cahya replied indifferently, shifting her focus to the room around her.

"It must be challenging," Nethos suggested.

"I imagine it's harder for those who know me," Cahya pointed out. This line of questioning was making her uncomfortable, and she was eager to change the subject. She wasn't sure how 'old Cahya' felt about discussing feelings, but this Cahya wasn't particularly into it. Besides, if she was being honest, she still didn't really know how she felt about all of this. It was a lot to take in, and it took all of her energy just to keep her cool.

A small robotic trolley rolled up with two covered trays. Nethos took the first tray and placed it on the table in front of Cahya before taking the second tray for himself. The lid of her tray had a small screen that was lit up with the words 'Cahya. Table 3.' Nethos lifted the cover from his tray, then took Cahya's and placed them both back onto the trolley. He pressed a finger on the machine, and it rolled off in the same direction it had come from.

The tray was piled with roasted vegetables and nuts on a bed of rice. It smelled amazing, and Cahya was suddenly very aware of how hungry she felt. She leaned in to grab her fork and then stopped. "Wait, who's paying for this? I have no idea how money works here."

"Food is a basic need, Cahya," Nethos explained. "All basic needs are covered on Nirvana."

Cahya raised an eyebrow. "So, All-You-Can-Eat?"

"I think you'll find that you can't actually eat as much as you might think," Nethos suggested.

Cahya picked up her fork, stabbed it through a pile of veggies, and lifted the food to her mouth. "Challenge accepted," she told him, as she ate her first bite.

"Nethos," came a deep voice.

Nethos spun about quickly. "Hello, father," he said in a surprisingly chipper voice. Cahya raised an eyebrow suspiciously at Nethos as she continued to chew, her cheeks puffed out with food.

Nethos stood and bowed courteously to the man as he approached. Cahya took another forkful of food and observed the interaction quietly.

"Ah, please sit. I didn't mean to interrupt your meal. I only wanted to say hello to Cahya," the man explained. A look of disappointment briefly shot across Nethos' face as he sat back down.

The man, Nethos' father, looked at Cahya, who was chewing far more food than her mouth ought to have been holding. The man stifled a repulsed look, but Cahya saw it. She saw most things.

"Cahya," he continued, "Sam and I heard about your accident. We're terribly sorry. How are you feeling?" He forced a smile that made Cahya's stomach churn.

'Huh, that was strange,' she thought.

Cahya finished chewing and swallowed hard before she replied, "As well as can be expected." She forced a smile, but something about this guy felt off.

"Father, I'm afraid that Cahya doesn't remember anyone," Nethos explained. "Cahya, this is my father, Kyun. My mother is Sam. They've both asked about you several times since your accident."

"I see," Cahya replied. "How very kind of you." She bowed her head slightly but kept her eyes trained on Kyun as she shoveled another forkful of food into her mouth.

"Yes, well, hopefully, this all gets sorted out quickly so that the lot of you can get on with your lives. Maybe this is a blessing in disguise." Kyun said, looking at Cahya and then Nethos. "Well, I've got a council meeting in a moment, so I'll be going now. Enjoy your dinner," Kyun said this last part slowly as he watched Cahya shovel another spoonful of food into her mouth.

Nethos stood as his father turned to leave. "Will you be staying in Deshka for the evening, father? Maybe we can meet up for the game later," Nethos suggested.

"No, I'll be heading home after the meeting, I'm afraid. Maybe next time, Nethos," Kyun replied, and with that, he turned and walked away.

Cahya, still chewing, leaned out of her seat to watch Kyun as he left. Her eyes followed him as he made his way through the gate at the front of the restaurant. She swallowed and turned back to Nethos, who was sitting again, looking bitter.

"What did your father mean by 'the lot of you'?" Cahya asked, ignoring Nethos' gloomy disposition.

"He meant the three of us," Nethos replied, pushing a carrot around his plate with his fork. "You, me, and Nandini."

Cahya waited, but Nethos was clearly going to need more prompting. "Uh-huh, what about us?"

Nethos looked up and seemed to snap out of his drudgery. He was back to his cool, unphased tone. "Every Dohan has a pair of companions who join them regularly through the cycles. It's a method of building bonds and trust, providing the Dohan with a team they can call on for guidance once they become Doyen."

"I see. So then you and this, Nadidi?"

"Nan-di-ni. Yes, she and I are your companions; we've done most of your cycles with you."

"Companions are also 'back-up Dohans.' They're meant to replace the existing Dohan should anything happen to them." He didn't look up when he said this. "But nothing ever happens, so Dohans are never actually replaced." He put his fork down and looked around the room, avoiding eye contact with Cahya.

'Interesting,' Cahya thought.

Neither said anything for a little while. Cahya pondered this new bit of information: why hadn't this occurred to her before? She'd been an investigator; it was her job to be suspicious of everything. And yet, somehow, it hadn't occurred to her that her 'accident'

77

might have actually been part of a bigger plot—a plan to displace Cahya as Dohan. To put Nethos or Nandini in her place instead. Maybe there was way more going on here than she'd originally imagined.

Nethos may know more than he was letting on, but she couldn't let him think that she was suspicious of him. If she was going to get him to spill the beans, she'd have to establish some level of trust with this guy.

As she pondered this, Cahya took some time to look around the room. The restaurant was large and very open. It was divided in half by a large wall that spanned the entire length of the room. She hadn't noticed the wall when she first arrived, but seeing it now, she had no idea how she'd missed it. The entire wall was a floor-to-ceiling vertical garden. Lush plants covered the wall, and all of them were filled with fresh fruits, vegetables, and herbs. Bright red tomatoes shone in the light that poured in from the glass dome above. There were also peppers in every color, vines filled with green and yellow beans, and tons of herbs. A little further down the wall were patches of strawberries and bunches of leafy greens that Cahya couldn't identify. She wondered if she'd known them before but had forgotten them along with everything else.

"Does Menza grow all of its own food?" Cahya asked, grateful to have thought of something new to discuss.

Nethos looked across the room at the garden wall and shook his head. "No, not all of it. But they do grow a lot. Most of the food comes from the agricultural belt of the city. There's more room there for trees and big hydroponic systems."

As he spoke, a strange-looking robot appeared by the garden wall; a rolling basket with arms. Cahya was transfixed as she watched the bot pick a large, ripe tomato from the vine and place it into the basket before making its way to the herbs. One of its hands opened to reveal scissors and it snipped a few leaves from the next plant before disappearing through a small door in the garden wall.

Nethos, seeing Cahya's reaction to the robot, spoke up. "The garden bots pick the food and bring it into the kitchen to be prepared. Would you like to see it; the kitchen?"

"Are we allowed?" Cahya asked, feeling strangely intrigued. This was it. This was why she was off her game. Everything here was so new and novel. It kept her bouncing between wonder and wariness. She had to keep her guard up; she had to be vigilant, especially now that she suspected there was more to find out.

"Absolutely," Nethos enthused. "School children take field trips to the kitchen at a very young age. You and I went when we were eight. I remember..."

He stopped and gave a shy smile.

"What? Tell me," Cahya insisted. If she and Nethos had a friendly history, it couldn't hurt to make him recall it. Maybe that fondness would cause him to drop his guard long enough for Cahya to figure out what really happened to her.

"Another time," he told her. Nethos straightened up, and his face was serious again. "We should probably finish up; I think Kole needs you back for some tests tonight."

"But I was going to order a second plate," Cahya protested. She wasn't ready to go back yet; she could sense that Nethos was going to give her something if she could just keep him talking a little longer. Besides, she *was* going to order a second plate.

Nethos opened his mouth to protest, and Cahya knew she had to cut him off quickly. She noticed a couple sitting at a table not too far from them. "Do you have a, uh, girlfriend?" she blurted out. "Or boyfriend—I don't want to assume anything. Or is dating not a thing on Nirvana?" It seemed like a trivial topic, and it might totally backfire, but it was the best she could come up with on the fly.

"No, dating isn't really a thing here," Nethos replied.

"Really?" Cahya was genuinely intrigued now. Dammit! 'Vigilance, Cahya!' she reminded herself. "So how do people, you know, couple up?"

"Coupling-up, as you call it, is arranged."

"Arranged marriage, huh? Seems a bit archaic for such an advanced civilization."

"Whatever notion you might have of arranged marriage, it's nothing like what is practiced here on Nirvana," Nethos assured her.

"Well," Cahya prompted, "enlighten me."

Nethos took a breath. He didn't seem particularly eager to get into this topic, but he pressed on anyway. "Nirvana takes a purely scientific approach to coupling. At a young age, boys and girls are tested and evaluated. We look at many factors: genetic compatibility, biochemistry, psychological profiles—"

"The psychological profiles of children?" Cahya interrupted, raising an eyebrow.

"Our methods are sound," Nethos insisted, adding, "Using a few simple forms of examination, you can learn quite a lot about the type of adult a child will become."

He paused and took a sip of water before continuing. "Children are assigned a partner at the age of twelve. Their 'Napili,' as we call it.

"Once the pair is identified, they are partnered for life—soulmates. When they reach maturity, they participate in the cycles together. Their bond is strengthened through each cycle. After hundreds of lifetimes together and countless monumental experiences, they're basically inseparable. These relationships are crucial to Nirvanian society. It's a big part of what keeps us grounded and connected." Nethos paused, seemingly lost in thought.

"Wow, so this, uh, nap—?"

"Na-pee-lee," Nethos enunciated.

"Right, Napili," Cahya continued. "This is a pretty big deal, then. Does everyone get one, or are some people destined to be alone?" It was a genuine question. Cahya didn't have much experience with relationships, let alone multi-lifetime, monumental, soulmate-type relationships.

"Everyone gets one," Nethos replied, shaking his head. "You make it sound like we're going around handing out apples or something."

"No, no, I get it. Very scientific and life-altering. So tell me," Cahya pressed on, glad that Nethos was speaking more openly than he had all night, "what's your Napili like?"

Nethos looked away. He waited several moments, seemingly trying to decide what to say next. "I think we should head back," he said finally.

'Crap!' Cahya wasn't expecting that. "Sorry, too personal?" Cahya asked, hoping to lure him back in.

"No, not too personal. I'm just not sure how to answer."

"Alright, fine, don't tell me what she's like. How about you tell me her name," Cahya offered. She knew that one way to get people to talk was to ask them a more simple question. Sometimes open-ended questions trip people up; they worry that they'll say too much or incriminate themselves or someone close to them. But facts—simple facts—are easy: yes-or-no questions, names, places. Those were details people typically felt more comfortable sharing; it felt less threatening. She searched Nethos' face, looking for a sign that he might take the bait. 'Answer the simple question, buddy; you can do it.'

"Her name?" Nethos started. "Her name is Cahya Lighthold." Nethos looked Cahya straight in the eyes, pausing to allow her a moment to process what he'd just said.

'Well then,' Cahya thought, keeping her face as still and unemotional as she could. She was not expecting that. Cahya glanced at her plate; she'd loaded the last bit of food onto her fork moments ago, but she suddenly felt very full. Huh, maybe Nethos was right... maybe she couldn't eat as much as she thought she could. Or maybe this news took away her appetite.

"Did you say it was time to head back?" Cahya said finally, nodding toward the entrance. "Kole's probably waiting for me, huh?"

"Yes," Nethos replied, seemingly grateful and relieved to have finally come to the end of this conversation. "Let's get you back."

They stood and made their way out of the restaurant. Cahya remained silent, processing what Nethos had just told her. The idea of being paired with someone for hundreds of lifetimes felt overwhelming, surreal even. She'd always preferred to keep her distance from people. Relationships, at least in Johnny's world, had only ever brought complications and distractions. Now, she was apparently at the center of some deeply interconnected web of relationships that stretched across lifetimes.

As they walked through the garden area outside the restaurant, Cahya found herself unable to shake the question she hadn't asked: what did Nethos think of this arrangement? Did he want this? Did he resent her for not remembering him?

Nethos walked slightly ahead of her, his posture rigid. His silence told her everything she needed to know: this wasn't easy for him either.

The sun was lower in the sky now, casting long shadows across the dome's interior. People moved leisurely along the pathways, some stopping to chat, others simply enjoying the evening air. Cahya noticed a few people glance in her direction and bow their heads slightly, murmuring, "Dohan."

She didn't know how to respond, so she offered awkward nods in return. The reverence made her skin crawl. How was she supposed to live up to these expectations when she didn't even remember who she was?

"Does this kind of thing happen a lot?" she asked Nethos, breaking the silence.

"What do you mean?" he asked without looking back.

"The bowing, the 'Dohan' thing. Do people treat me like this all the time?"

"You're a public figure," Nethos replied. "People respect you. It's part of the role."

"Great," Cahya muttered under her breath. "Just what I needed."

Nethos smirked slightly. "You'll get used to it."

They continued walking, eventually reaching the building where Cahya's room was located. The glass doors slid open silently as they approached. Cahya stepped inside and looked around the sterile, high-tech cage.

"I'll let Kole know you're back," Nethos said. "He'll probably be here soon to check on you."

"Thanks," Cahya replied, her voice flat. She hesitated for a moment before adding, "And, uh, thanks for dinner. I mean, for coming with me."

Nethos nodded once, then turned and walked away, leaving Cahya standing just inside the entrance. The door slid shut and she was alone once more.

CHAPTER 7
PANIGÊM

After her dinner with Nethos, Cahya spent several hours at the lab with Kole. He asked her a series of questions and ran a number of tests, hopeful that a few hours with a close friend might have triggered some memories, but nothing seemed to have changed. Still, Kole didn't seem discouraged.

Despite the late night, Cahya woke early the next morning, ready to take on the day. Kole had a full 'memory rescue' day planned for her. She'd spend the day with him and both of her companions, Nethos and Nandini. Kole's plan was to continue exposing Cahya to familiar people and places in Deshka, hoping that eventually, something would jog her memory.

Cahya was less preoccupied with regaining her memories than she'd ever admit to Kole. Her mind was more focused on solving the mystery she might have stumbled upon during dinner last night. She hadn't managed to get too much out of Nethos, but she'd learned enough to become a little suspicious that there was more to her memory loss than a mere accident.

She had to wonder if this was just the P.I. in her. Maybe she was just looking for a way to make herself useful in this strange place. Either way, she was anxious to meet her second companion,

Nandini. If there was any foul play involved in her accident, she was sure that either one or both of her companions were involved; they had the most to gain. Nethos had been pretty tight-lipped, but maybe Nandini would be more willing to share.

She had no idea what to expect for the day, but Kole had brought her some casual clothes to wear: a long-sleeved white shirt, white pants, and a long, dark blue vest that popped against her lavender hair.

"So, where are we headed?" Cahya asked when she'd finished getting dressed.

Kole waved his hand by the door, and it slid open. "We are going to the recreational district, to the Panigêm Arena."

Cahya was intrigued, but she reminded herself... vigilance.

The train ride to the arena was beautiful. Even in her hyper-vigilant state, Cahya couldn't ignore how stunning everything was. Every bit of Deshka was beautifully designed and lovingly maintained. There was no trash, no graffiti, no beggars or sketchy people walking the streets. It was a far cry from New York City.

As the train came to a gentle stop, the arena emerged into view. From the outside, it resembled a giant white egg crowned by an enormous, metallic-blue structure that looked like an upside-down basket made of thick, woven mesh. Yet this was no ordinary basket—the outer mesh rose from the ground and split neatly into eight sections, each forming a grand arched opening that led into the arena's main lobby. Crowds poured into the building through these imposing entryways, and as they drew near, Cahya noticed that parts of the metallic weave were interlaced with a mirrored material that brilliantly reflected the trees and gardens surrounding the structure.

"See those mirrored bits?" Kole asked, noticing Cahya's gaze. She nodded. "They're solar bands," he continued. "They absorb enough energy from the sun to power the entire arena."

"Wow!" Cahya exclaimed, genuinely impressed.

The building sparkled in the sunlight. It was by far the most spectacular building Cahya had ever seen.

Kole raised his hand, waving toward the building. Cahya looked ahead and caught sight of Nethos standing with a woman just outside one of the arches.

The woman, who Cahya assumed must be Nandini, studied Cahya as she approached. She didn't smile or wave; she just watched.

Cahya couldn't help but notice how beautiful the woman was. She wore a long blue tunic with a white crest over the left side of her chest. Her lush brown hair cascaded softly over her shoulders. Her sharp jawline and high cheekbones were softened by the warmth of her large brown eyes and her full red lips which stood out against her porcelain skin. Cahya had never seen anything so beautiful; the grand building suddenly paled in comparison.

Vigilance, Cahya, dammit! She was sure this was Johnny's taste coming through. He wouldn't have been particularly attracted to Nethos—she still couldn't believe he was her soulmate—but Nandini... she was definitely Johnny's type.

This was going to be harder than she thought. She had to focus. Nandini could be the reason she'd lost all her memories. She couldn't be distracted by a pretty face, even if it was the most gorgeous face she'd ever seen in her entire life.

Focus!

"Cahya, this is Nandini Corteza," Kole gestured toward the woman as they approached.

"Hi," Cahya said, staring a little too intently.

Nandini blushed. "Hi, Cahya." She searched Cahya's face for a moment. "You really don't remember me, do you?"

Cahya frowned. "I don't. I'm sorry."

Nandini stifled a sob and, without warning, lunged forward and threw her arms around Cahya. "I'm so sorry," she whispered. "I should have been there."

Cahya froze, not knowing what to do, and before she could react, Nandini was already pulling away. "I'm sorry," Nandini said, wiping a tear from her face as she stepped back a few feet, seemingly trying to compose herself.

Cahya studied her. She was good at reading people—well, *Johnny* had been good at reading people. Still, she could feel that she'd retained that skill even in this strange world. Nandini's pain appeared sincere. She seemed to feel genuinely guilty. The question was, did she feel guilty because she could have prevented this, or did she feel guilty because she knew she had caused this? Cahya wasn't about to let her off the hook, even if she was pretty. Really, really pretty.

Focus! You should say something, Cahya thought.

"It's okay," she said, forcing a slight smile. "Kole's working really hard to help me get my memories back." She gave Kole a hopeful look. "I'm sure he'll figure it out."

Kole nodded. "We will do everything we can. And to that end," he continued, gesturing to Nethos and Nandini, "we've got two of Cahya's closest friends together to watch Cahya's favorite sport in Cahya's favorite arena on all of Nirvana." Kole smiled. "Let's go see if we can't spark some memories."

Kole led the group through one of the large archways and into a vast lobby space that surrounded the grand egg-shaped arena. As they approached the shell, several doors slid open at once, and guests began to move into the arena itself. The inner portion of the egg was breathtaking. Thousands of seats lined the walls of the building in neatly tiered rows, but the most prominent feature by far was an enormous cylindrical tank in the center of the arena. It was forty feet wide and rose eighty feet into the air.

Cahya tried her best to take it all in as they made their way to their seats. A number of people in the crowd wore red, but a greater number were wearing blue. Cahya deduced that these must be the team colors. Several of the blue outfits bore the same crest she'd noticed on Nandini's tunic—a white shield. Some people were not wearing red or blue, but Cahya noticed that a number of them had red or blue crests on their clothing—shields that looked similar, though the shapes were slightly different. The blue shields were straight across the top and curved down into a single point at the bottom, matching the white shield on Nandini's tunic. The red shields had three points along the top and a longer, sharper point at the bottom. Cahya took her seat, sandwiched between Nandini and Nethos.

Ugh, Nethos, she thought—grateful that Nethos wasn't trying to be intimate in any way. She wasn't sure what to expect now that she knew they'd been partnered. Cahya didn't want to think about it. Besides, she decided she could ignore Nethos for most of the game since she'd already spent dinner with him. It wouldn't come across as rude if she focused on getting to know Nandini now.

She needed to build some rapport with Nandini. If she could get her to let her guard down, she might learn what Nandini knew about the accident. Cahya leaned over so that her mouth was just inches from Nandini's ear. "Okay, please fill me in here. What is this place?" she asked.

Nandini turned and smiled at the question. Cahya couldn't help the warmth that shot through her at the sight of Nandini's gorgeous smile.

Nandini sat up and leaned toward Cahya, speaking loudly enough to be heard over the hum of the crowd. "Well, this is a panigêm match. You love panigêm; we go at least twice a week." She paused for a moment, looking at the ground before she continued. "Sorry, you *used* to love panigêm, I guess? I'm not sure how to navigate all of this."

Cahya smiled and said, "It's okay. This is strange for all of us. Keep going."

Nandini nodded. "You're right. It's very strange. Okay, so Deshka is playing against Almatar today."

Just then, several splashes echoed through the arena as people in blue bodysuits dove into the giant cylindrical aquarium and began zipping around in the water at high speed. The crowd cheered loudly, waving shimmering blue flags above their heads. Nine swimmers maneuvered through the water in a V-formation, arms tucked tightly to their sides, tails flicking gently behind them.

"Wait, do they have tails?" Cahya asked, leaning forward in her chair, straining to decipher what she was seeing. Were these humans or mermaids?

Nandini let out a huge, beautiful belly laugh. "Not really, no. Well, I guess they do sort of look like tails, don't they? The swimmers are wearing HydroGliders, a sort of propulsion suit. The suits allow the players to breathe underwater for extended periods, and they have a sophisticated system that helps them move through the water at high speeds without creating bubbles or visual distortions. It has something to do with pressure changes or water disturbance—I'm not entirely sure." Nandini smiled. "Anyway, the suits let them zip around the pool really fast without churning up a bunch of bubbles, so the spectators can still see everything that's happening."

"Got it," Cahya replied. "And what do you call this giant human aquarium?"

Nandini laughed again. "That's the AquaHenger, but everyone just calls it the henger."

Another sequence of splashes rang through the arena, and the building erupted with cheers once again. Nine swimmers in red suits got into a V-formation and began to zip around the outside edge of the henger, moving in unison up and down through the water, showing off their brilliant synchronization skills. Watching the two teams move around was like watching an intricate dance. The crowd loved it, and they cheered and hollered as the swimmers continued with their sequence.

"This is the best part!" Nandini bellowed over the sound of the crowd.

The eighteen swimmers made their way to the bottom of the henger and hovered there for a moment, their tails floating just above the floor of the cylindrical aquarium. All at once, they burst upwards with tremendous energy toward the top of the tank. They broke through the surface and crisscrossed one another mid-air. Some did flips, some spun through the air, but somehow each of the swimmers dove swiftly and gracefully into the pool, breaking through the surface at the exact same time. Their splashes echoed through the arena.

Cahya gasped and clapped, cheering loudly with the rest of the spectators.

"Wow!" she said, leaning toward Nandini.

"Right?!" Nandini exclaimed. "They're amazing."

A woman's voice boomed out over the crowd: "Ladies and gentlemen, welcome to today's panigêm match featuring Deshka versus Almatar." More cheers erupted. "Athletes, please take your places."

The swimmers split up around the tank, with eight swimmers closer to the center of the aquarium and eight swimmers along the outer edge, dispersed across the height of the eighty-foot tank. Two swimmers, one from each team, circled the bottom of the pool like a couple of sharks waiting to attack their prey. A beam of light shot up through the center of the henger, creating a glowing tube about ten feet across.

The beam of light began to pulse, and numbers appeared on four sides of the glass of the tank, counting down in time with the pulsing light: 10, 9, 8, 7. The crowd counted along in time with the numbers, "Five! Four! Three! Two! One! Panigêm!"

Where the countdown had been, the numbers "0 - 0" appeared, one zero in blue and the other in red. Suddenly, a series of large blue and red balls splashed into the water, one at a time, from somewhere above the tank. Each ball fell into the beam of light and began to sink toward the bottom—red ball, blue ball, red ball, blue ball.

The players sprang into action as a timer below the scoreboard displayed a countdown from 30 minutes. One of the blue players raised his hand, and a pulse erupted from it, shooting straight across the pool and knocking one of the red balls out of the beam of light. A red player on the other side of the pool shot a pulse toward the center, but a blue player raised his arms to form an X, and a large blue shield appeared in front of him, absorbing the pulse from the beam.

Nandini leaned back over toward Cahya and said, "Each team gains points when one of their balls makes it through the hole at the bottom of the henger." She pointed to a large black ring at the base of the tank, which surrounded the beam of light. Just then, a blue ball sank into the ring, and the crowd erupted in cheers. The scoreboard updated to 1 - 0 for the blue team, and the game continued without pause.

Nandini pointed to the players on the outside edge of the tank. "Those guys, the ones hanging out around the edge, they're called Punchers. Their suits throw off an energy pulse from their hands. They use that to knock the balls out of the light stream, which stops them from going into the ring. The players in the center are the Shields. They can create a light shield with their suits, which blocks the pulse from knocking a ball out of play."

Just then, a player from the blue team swam upward and tried to block a pulse from the red team, but she didn't get her arms up in time. The pulse hit her in the shoulder, sending her flying across the tank and into the glass wall on the other side. The crowd responded with a mix of cringing moans and muffled celebration. The flung player bounced off the glass wall, swam back to her position in the center, and, without missing a beat, blocked a pulse with her crossed arms as she arrived.

"Ouch!" Cahya shouted. "That looked like it hurt!"

"Not really," Nethos chimed in. "The suits are designed to absorb the impact of the pulse. It sends the players for a ride, but it doesn't hurt them."

Cahya had almost forgotten that Nethos was there. "I see. What about those guys?" she asked, pointing to the two players swimming along the bottom of the pool.

"Those are the Feeders," Nandini replied. "They collect balls that get knocked out of the stream. Once a ball hits the floor, the

Feeders can pick it up, swim to the surface of the pool, dive out of the water, and drop the ball back into the light stream. They have to be careful not to drop the ball before they're completely out of the water, or their team gets a penalty and loses one of their four Shields for two minutes."

Pulses continued to blast across the tank, knocking blue and red balls out of the stream and sending them to the bottom of the tank. A Shield from the red team crossed her arms into an X, and Cahya realized that the shield she created was the same shape as the crest—three points at the top with an elongated point at the bottom. When the next blue shield appeared, it also matched the crest on all of the blue team's attire.

A red ball made it through the hoop at the bottom of the henger, then a blue ball, then another blue ball. The crowd cheered as the scoreboard updated with each point. Currently, Deshka led 3 - 1.

One of the red Shields caught a pulse on her fin, which knocked her backward through the beam of light and into the wall on the other side of the tank. A red timer appeared on the glass, counting down two minutes. Kole and Nethos stood up from their seats and cheered loudly as the red player swam to the surface of the pool and waited.

"What happened?" Cahya asked.

"The Almatar player got knocked into the light stream. Players aren't allowed in the stream, so if a player swims into it or gets knocked into it by another player, there's an automatic penalty. Shields have to be really careful," Nandini explained.

The match continued like this for two more thirty-minute periods. Almatar pulled ahead by the end of the first period and led through to the end of the second period. Deshka pulled together in the final period, and the game ended with a score of 28 - 22 for Deshka. The Deshka fans sang and cheered as they left the arena, waving their shimmering blue flags in the air.

Kole nudged Cahya on their way out. "So! What did you think?"

"It was very exciting," Cahya told him. "I really think I got a handle on the rules by the end of it."

"Kole!" came a voice from somewhere in the crowd. "Nandini, Nethos, Cahya! How are you all? It's good to see you." A man wearing a bright red shirt with the Almatar crest approached them, waving and smiling heartily. "What a game, am I right?!"

"Hi Walter, yes, it was a close one. Up until that last period, I thought you guys might have had us," Kole replied.

"You and me both!" the man exclaimed. "Oh well, we'll get you next month; just you wait!" He smiled broadly, his trim white beard following the upward curve of his lips, making his smile seem even larger and more jolly.

"Oh, I'm sorry, Cahya, this is Walter Kenzinnia; he's one of Nirvana's leading horticulturalists. He's been working with a team to improve the agricultural belt in Almatar. His research could revolutionize the way we grow food."

Cahya nodded in greeting and said, "It's very nice to meet you, Mr. Kenzinnia."

"Oh yes, well, we've met before, Cahya. I did hear about your accident, though. I'm very sorry for you. I hope you're able to recover quickly. Nirvana needs you, after all," he replied.

Nethos jumped into the conversation and began discussing the work his father was doing with water energy and how it related to Walter's horticultural work. Kole became very engaged too, remarking how the new systems had great potential for medical applications.

While the three were engrossed in conversation, Cahya glanced around and caught sight of a sign for the washrooms. She leaned over to Nandini and whispered, "I'm going to pop into the washroom quickly. I'll be right back."

Nandini nodded. "I'll be here when you're done."

The washrooms were nice and very clean. As Cahya waved her hands beneath the sanitizing laser, she heard a commotion rising up outside the washroom. When she stepped out into the lobby of the arena, she saw a group of young men in red arguing with a group of young men wearing blue.

"You guys rigged the system!" one of the men in red shouted. "There's no way Kashov missed that beam in the last period. Everyone saw his arm hit it."

"You can't rig a panigêm system," one of the men in blue shouted back. "Stop being such a sore loser."

"I'll show you what sore looks like!" another man in red exclaimed, and he lunged forward, knocking one of the men in blue to the ground. He kicked him three times in the ribs before some of the spectators pulled him away.

"What's wrong with you, man?" one of the Deshka fans called out, pulling his injured friend to his feet.

"He's a damn Dakaï; that's what's wrong with him," proclaimed the injured man as he regained his balance, clutching his side.

People in the crowd gasped, their mouths gaping open, clearly shocked by what they were seeing and hearing.

Cahya watched from her place just outside the washroom entrance. *Dakaï*, she thought, the word swirling about in her mind. It sounded familiar. It made her feel uneasy. She felt the urge to jump into the conversation and interject herself in their altercation. But what would she say? She had nothing to contribute; she had no clue what they were arguing about, let alone how to make them stop. Even still, she couldn't shake the feeling that she needed to be a part of this exchange.

She looked around for Kole, anxious to leave now before she did something stupid, but she couldn't see him through the large crowd that had gathered around the feuding men.

Everyone was engrossed in the altercation, whispering to one another as they looked on.

Just then, a person in a red hooded cloak slipped up close to Cahya and paused for a moment. She spoke in a whisper without revealing her face, "Do not give up, Dohan. Play this when you are alone. Don't let anyone else see it. You don't know who you can

95

trust." With that, the woman placed a small, smooth object in Cahya's hand and then disappeared into the crowd. Cahya tried to follow the woman with her eyes, but several Almatar fans were wearing the same red cloaks.

The feuding men had become loud by now, and the crowd around them grew larger by the second. Some people were trying to get the men to stop, and others were joining in the banter. Suddenly, one man lunged at another and knocked him to the ground. Gasps filled the arena's halls as the two men began rolling around, engaged in their scuffle.

A woman flew into the mix out of nowhere. She yanked the burly man off the other man in one swift movement. He tried to fight back, but she took him down and restrained him in seconds.

A group of two men and three women in dark purple jumpsuits intercepted the group. "What's going on here?" one of the women asked.

Cahya strained to hear what the feuding men were saying to her, but more people had crowded around. One voice rose above the rest, silencing the group with its authority. It was the woman who'd restrained the larger man: "Whatever it was, it was inappropriate, and you should all be ashamed of yourselves." It was Nandini! *Nandini?* How on earth did she do that? She was half the size of some of these men and she'd flung them around like rag dolls. Cahya was in shock.

"Here," Nandini said to one of the people in purple jumpsuits as she handed the man over, "you can have this one."

Cahya made a mental note that she probably shouldn't mess with Nandini.

The jumpsuit people corralled a handful of instigators and carried them away through the crowd.

"Cahya!" Nandini said when she caught sight of the Dohan. She moved through the dispersing crowd and made her way over. "Hey! You ok? You look like you've seen a ghost."

96

Cahya didn't respond right away; there was so much she was processing. Nandini, the sweet, blushing, beautiful woman, was some sort of ninja. Some cloaked woman had given her an object and a very obscure message. She suddenly felt very disoriented; she didn't know who she could trust.

Discreetly, she slipped the device into the pocket of her vest and smiled at Nandini. "Yeah, I'm fine. I was looking for Kole, and then these guys started fighting," she said, nodding in the direction of the men being led away.

"Yeah, I don't know what all of that was about. That sort of thing doesn't really happen here." Nandini frowned. "Kids," she shrugged. "They haven't done their ELC training yet."

"Who are those guys?" Cahya asked, pointing to the team in the purple jumpsuits.

"Oh, they're E.R.F.—Emergency Response Force."

"Where are they taking them?" Cahya asked.

"To the hub. They'll have to do some sort of rehabilitation. They're too young for the ELC program, but they'll have to take some courses and do some counseling. Maybe even some community service."

"For a little scuffle like that?"

Nandini raised an eyebrow. "Little scuffles can grow into big problems if we don't deal with them early on. Those kinds of outbursts are usually the result of poor communication skills, a lack of empathy, an inability to process negative emotions, and, you know, that kind of stuff. They just need a little refresher."

"Sure," Cahya replied, nodding slowly, "negative emotional processing refresher. Casual."

Nandini laughed. "Exactly. Come on. Kole has a few more things planned for today."

CHAPTER 8

FIRST CYCLE

Cahya had spent the entire day touring Deshka with Nandini, Nethos, and Kole. She learned a lot about the city, but she hadn't gained any new memories.

Kole seemed undeterred, though; he was confident that getting Cahya into a round of Life Cycles could help jog some memories.

"Don't be nervous, Cay," Nandini said, clearly sensing Cahya's discomfort from across the table.

Cahya, Nandini, and Nethos sat at a dining table at Menza. Nandini continued, "Look, I know that you don't remember going through this life cycle stuff before, but you've done this sixteen hundred times, and it's always been fine."

"Right. Except for that one time," Cahya pointed out, raising a single eyebrow.

Nandini frowned at her. "Nethos and I are going to be with you the entire time, and Kole is going to oversee everything while we're in there. It's perfectly safe. We're all going to be just fine, right, Nethos?" Nandini turned to Nethos for some backup.

Cahya could tell that Nandini was trying to calm her own nerves as much as Cahya's.

Nethos seemed to have been pulled from deep thought and answered only half-heartedly, "Huh? Oh, right, yeah, of course. There's nothing to worry about, Cahya. Today's going to be an easy day anyway."

This was true, at least. They'd gone over the details of their cycles after the game yesterday. They'd be doing a series of insect cycles just to get Cahya reacclimated to the system. They were to pay attention to the instinctual drive of the tiny beings they would inhabit today.

Cahya wasn't actually as concerned about the cycle as Nandini had assumed, but she didn't feel the need to correct her. She was distracted by the cloaked woman at the panigêm match yesterday. She heard the woman's voice repeating her words over and over in her head:

'Don't give up, Dohan. Play this when you are alone. Don't let anyone else see it. You don't know who you can trust.'

This mystery just kept getting more mysterious. Who was that woman? A friend? Or perhaps a foe pretending to be a friend?

She also had this device now, something she was supposed to listen to. She'd tucked it away in her room at the medical center. She hadn't listened to it. She had to wait until she was alone, and with Myat listening to everything all the time, she was never really alone.

There was one thing she knew for sure, though: someone was out to get her. This meant that her accident was no accident at all. She'd been suspicious before, but now she was sure. Someone wanted Cahya's memories wiped—either because she knew something or because someone wanted her out of the Dohan role. Maybe both.

She still didn't know who she could trust.

The three of them finished their meals and made their way to the ELC building, where Kole was waiting for them.

"Good morning, everyone."

There were already several others in the room when they arrived. A man and a woman stood next to Kole wearing blue tunics;

the woman had freckled skin and long golden-red hair tied in a French braid. The man had pale skin and short blue hair. He looked vaguely familiar to Cahya. An excitement rose inside her; maybe this was a sign that her memories were returning.

"My name is Kole, and here with me today is Hathina," he gestured to the woman with the red hair, who smiled, "and Kacha." He gestured to the man with the blue hair. "We three will be administering and monitoring your Life Cycles today."

Kacha—from the medical center when she'd first woken up from the accident. Her heart sank a little. She wasn't remembering anything new after all.

The first-year students in the room wore pale yellow tunics. Cahya wore her black tunic along with Nandini and Nethos. Cahya felt silly wearing black—the distinguished color of the Dohan and her companions—when here she was about to embark on a basic ELC program designed for first-year ELC students.

As if reading her mind, Kole instructed, "You can all remove your tunics and, once I've called your name, you can hang them on the hook by your pod." Kole motioned toward a row of ten pods that lined the wall next to him. Each pod was fitted with a large glass dome. They didn't seem like much to look at, Cahya thought, and yet, a knot tightened deep in her stomach.

Nandini took Cahya's sleeve. "I almost forgot about this," she said, pointing at a small hole on the cuff. "We need to get this fixed. Don't forget, ok?"

Cahya chuckled. *Don't forget. Rich.*

And then, horror fell over Nandini's face. "Oh my goodness, that was terrible! I am SO sorry. Great job, Nandini. Tell the person who's lost their memories not to forget something. Wow."

Nethos snickered at this.

Kole cleared his throat to get everyone's attention.

"These are the Life Cycle Pods," Kole announced to the group. "Each of you has your own personal journey to take through the Life Cycle program, a path that you must walk in order to reach your full potential as a member of Nirvanian society. However, every person must begin at the beginning. And so, today, you will not be entering into a human life cycle. You will begin by living through several very short insect cycles. This will ease you into the system, and it will allow us to test your responses to the program.

"Today, you will each live ten Life Cycles. Your first cycle will last 1 second in our time. You'll live through the twenty-four-hour life cycle of the common mayfly. Every second of our time is one full day in ELC time. Each cycle thereafter will become progressively longer. Your final cycle of the day will last 10 seconds in our time, though it will feel like several days for you on Earth.

"Between each cycle, you will be asked to pause and reflect on your experience. There are private spaces where you can record your thoughts at your discretion. We encourage each of you to take this time to reflect.

"Each pod has been calibrated according to the student's brain waves. When I call your name, please lay down in the pod we've assigned to you. Theo," Kole motioned to the first pod. From the back of the group emerged a young man that Cahya hadn't noticed at first. She had been entirely lost in her own thoughts. Seeing him now, she wondered how it was possible to have missed him.

The young man, who Kole called Theo, was clearly not human. He had long, curly white hair, half of which was tied back. He had several intricate braids, which were adorned with silver jewelry. His long, narrow ears poked through his hair so that the small, pointed tips were visible. His skin was shimmering white with the slightest pink undertone and had a soft, dewy, almost translucent quality about it. He had large green-gray eyes and a small, distinguished nose. He wore a warm smile across his wide mouth, which softened his strong jawline.

The young man stepped cautiously forward and laid in the first pod. No one else in the room seemed surprised by Theo's presence, so Cahya tried hard to act perfectly normal. Kole sensed Cahya's confusion, though, and put her out of her misery. "Most of you know Theo, of course, our exchange student from Octavia. He'll be participating in these cycles with you as part of his Human Cultural Studies program."

Cahya's eyes met Theo's, and she quickly looked away. She didn't want to give him the impression that she was feeling uncomfortable or anything. *Act normal,* she told herself as she shifted her gaze back to her instructor.

Kole continued calling names, gesturing to the next available pod as he went, "Yara, Galem, Roxalli, Wendu, Nandini, Cahya, Nethos, Jarex, Jennah, Kwindi." One by one, each pod found itself occupied until they were all full, and the only people left standing were Kole, Hathina, and Kacha.

"Ladies and gentlemen, remember that when you come to, it's important that you remain still until we've cleared you. Now, please relax and close your eyes," Kole instructed. Everyone did as they were asked. Kole tapped the floor in front of him with the tip of his foot, and a screen appeared in the air in front of his face. On the screen, there were ten sections, each showing the outline of a body. Lights swerved and flitted around each figure. Above each body on the screen was a series of numbers and buttons.

The two attendants stood next to Kole and each tapped the floor, activating their own monitors, which showed them the same information. All three studied their screens carefully. Kole announced, "Looks like we're all set."

"All clear," Hathina agreed.

"Ready to go," Kacha announced.

Kole nodded and drew his finger across the bottom of his screen. As he did, each glass dome came to life, glowing with blue light. One pod after the other glowed blue, following the direction of Kole's finger. When all of the pods had been lit, a timer reading '00:00:01' appeared at the bottom of Kole's screen with a glowing blue button flashing next to it.

Cahya felt a surge of anticipation race through her. Kole had convinced her that the cycles might shake something up in her brain and free up her memories from wherever they had been locked away. He'd also warned her not to get her hopes too high—it was just a theory, after all—but Cahya couldn't help but consider the consequences. There was a part of her that wanted her memories back, but there was a bigger part that wasn't sure. She didn't know who she had been before this. Would regaining her memories mean losing who she was now? That thought terrified her.

"Ladies and gentlemen," Kole announced, "we'll see you in 1 second." He pressed the glowing blue button.

✳ ✳ ✳

A feeling came over her—a need to move and expand. She felt a weight pressing against her, and her instincts told her to push back. As she did, the weight shifted. It became lighter, and movements became easier. And then, everything became very wet. She pushed herself from the muddy bottom of the shallow river water. Light pierced the water, and her eyes began observing a blur of dancing reflections. She kept moving, compelled to rise further from the river's depths.

Within minutes, she broke through the surface, her wings flapping and cooling as they hit the morning air. The current tugged at her, dragging her across the water's surface as she struggled to stay above it. A tree branch lay ahead, caught in the flow. She reached it and clung to a leaf with her tiny legs, pulling herself out of the water. Exhausted, she rested for a while on the branch.

Hours passed before she felt the urge to move again. Something within her stirred—a need to fly. She flapped her large wings and found herself releasing her grip on the branch. She took to the sky, the fresh air invigorating her as the sun's warmth seeped through her wings.

Suddenly, she was surrounded by thousands of others like her, their wings shimmering as they danced in the air. Instinctively, she sought a mate. She joined him mid-flight, their tails connecting.

Together, they flapped and drifted in a chaotic, exhilarating flight until the bond broke, and her partner fell away.

She descended to the water's surface and danced above it, feeling her eggs release into the depths below. Others mirrored her actions all around her, completing the same ritual. A fish leapt from the water, snapping up one of her kin. She kept dancing, unfazed. Soon, exhaustion overtook her. Her wings no longer obeyed her commands. She floated on the surface, her body rocked by the river's gentle flow.

Darkness crept in, erasing the light from her world. The journey was over.

But then, a new light emerged in the distance. She hurtled down a tunnel of brightness, flashes of her brief existence streaking past until she was consumed by the final burst of light.

✳ ✳ ✳

Kole's timer counted down from *00:00:01* to *00:00:00*. As quickly as he pressed the button, it was all over—done in the blink of an eye. For a brief moment, the domes above the pods glowed with darting, white lights. The lights gradually slowed and faded, leaving the domes softly illuminated in blue once more.

One by one, the students opened their eyes and gasped for breath. Their expressions were filled with shock, as though they'd just survived a violent storm. From an observer's point of view, it appeared as if nothing had happened at all, yet each participant looked like they'd been through a harrowing experience.

"Please remain still while we observe your vitals and brain activity," Kole instructed as Kacha and Hathina scrutinized their screens.

"I was eaten by a fish!" Nandini announced, her voice giddy with amusement. She peered through the sides of her dome and noticed no one else shared her enthusiasm. She quickly tried to rein in her excitement.

"A frog got me," Theo muttered from the first pod, his wide eyes fixed on the ceiling. His voice was quiet and maybe slightly shaken.

"Oh, that's awful!" Nandini replied. "A frog got me my first time too. It takes longer than the fish for sure. A friend of mine said the worst is being eaten by a small bird. Their tiny beaks aren't big enough to swallow you whole, so they mess around with you before figuring out how to eat you. Anyone get a bird?" She glanced around at the group. Everyone shook their heads, still too dazed to speak. "Looks like we've got a lucky group here!"

Cahya remained silent, her eyes shut tightly. A wave of nausea and a pounding headache threatened to overwhelm her. She took slow, deep breaths, searching her mind for any sign of new memories. There was nothing—no spark of familiarity, no breakthrough. A pang of disappointment pierced her chest. A single tear escaped down her cheek, but she wiped it away swiftly, hoping no one had noticed.

"All clear," Hathina announced.

"Everyone is good," Kacha confirmed.

Kole nodded. "The domes will now retract. You may feel a bit tired, which is normal. If needed, there are private rooms with beds where you can rest. We'll begin the second cycle in 15 minutes. In the meantime, take a moment to reflect on your experience."

The glass domes lifted, freeing the students from their pods. Cahya swung her legs over the side of the chair and faced Nandini and Nethos.

"How'd you guys do? Feeling ok?" Nandini asked cheerfully.

"Uh, yeah, I think so," Cahya replied, sitting up cautiously. "A little tired, but I'm alright."

She turned toward Nethos. "What about you?"

"Me? Oh, I'm fine. No birds, frogs, or fish for me," he answered, standing up and adjusting the armband on his sleeve. "I think I'll take my fifteen minutes to reflect. See you in a bit."

Nethos walked across the room, raised his hand to a sensor on the wall, and disappeared through a door that slid open before him.

"I think I'll do the same," Cahya told Nandini.

Nandini nodded with a smile. "Take your time."

Grateful for the privacy, Cahya stood and followed Nethos' lead, entering a reflection room of her own. The quiet space helped her steady her thoughts and ease the nausea.

Fifteen minutes passed quickly, and soon, Kole called everyone to return to their pods. The timer on his screen now read *00:00:02*. He slid the glowing blue control, and once again, Cahya felt herself plunging into the darkness of another life cycle.

The cycles continued in a similar pattern. Each time, Cahya inhabited a different life form with its own instincts and experiences.

She was a mosquito, then a spider in a rainforest. Later, she became a housefly, spending much of her existence trapped inside a light fixture. Halfway through the day, Kole put them through a plant cycle for fun. It was a completely different experience from all of the other cycles, she couldn't quite describe it. She'd been a dandelion, where the sensations of sunlight and rain dominated her existence. Cahya loved that one.

Next, she became a dragonfly, then a cockroach, an earthworm, an ant, and finally a bumblebee.

Each life began in darkness, followed by a rush of experiences and instincts, before fading back into darkness once more. Cahya would then emerge in her pod, gasping for breath like the others.

Despite the wonder of the experiences, the physical toll on her body increased with each cycle. The only round that didn't make her queasy was the dandelion cycle, perhaps the absence of movement helped.

* * *

By the end of the day, the students were exhausted. Kole encouraged them to rest and spend time with loved ones in the coming days.

As the students began to disperse, Nethos stretched and grinned. "I'm heading out to play a round of spot. Anyone want to join?"

"Spot?" Cahya echoed, puzzled.

"It's like golf but with energy balls instead of golf balls," Nandini explained.

Cahya gawked at Nethos. "Sports? After all that? I can't even think about moving. How are you not tired?"

"No idea," Nethos shrugged. "These things never wear me out. Must be genetic. My dad's the same way. Lucky, I guess."

Cahya shook her head in disbelief. "Seriously? Is he always like this?"

"Yup," Nandini replied with a smirk. "It's very annoying."

Kole approached Cahya. "How are you feeling?"

"Tired," she admitted, standing up cautiously. "But good, I think."

"Any new memories?"

"Not yet," she said quietly.

Kole's face betrayed a hint of disappointment, though he tried to hide it. He gave her a reassuring smile. "I have an idea—something that might help."

"Oh?" Cahya asked, unsure of what he had in mind.

"You've been staying at the medical center so we could monitor you, but you're perfectly healthy. You're also familiar with Deshka now. Cahya, it's time to go home."

CHAPTER 9
CAHYA'S HOME

Cahya didn't have any sort of concept of 'home.' Home was meant to be familiar—a place to escape the world. She couldn't remember ever feeling that way about any place.

Johnny had an apartment, but he hadn't spent much time there, and it never really felt like home. He basically lived at his office when working a case, with a small cot to sleep on when he needed to. Still, his office didn't feel like home either. As a child, his family moved frequently, so he learned not to get attached. Nowhere had ever truly felt like home to him.

Whatever her feelings, Kole believed this was the next logical step for Cahya. The swelling in her brain had long since subsided, and aside from her memory loss, she was in perfect health. There was no medical reason for her to stay at the center.

Maybe if she started getting back into her regular routines, something would shift. "You never know what might do the trick," Kole had said.

Nandini insisted on coming along.

After packing up Cahya's belongings at the medical center, they made their way to the residential belt. Now, the three of them walked along a marble sidewalk in the residential district.

Over the past ten minutes, they passed several beautiful homes. Every building was brilliantly white with large planting spaces integrated into their designs. It created the illusion that plants and trees were growing out of the walls, making each home appear vibrant and alive.

Their journey was a quiet one. Even Nandini was silent—a rarity, as Cahya had come to learn. Both women were exhausted from the cycles, with Cahya still feeling queasy. Kole, on the other hand, seemed lost in thought. Cahya welcomed the silence.

White bicycles zipped past on a parallel pathway designated for cyclists.

Birds chirped loudly from the treetops, flitting between branches and playing with their companions. The ground around the path was entirely green, except for areas with ponds or other water features.

Finally, Kole stopped in front of a white, glimmering house and gestured toward it. "Home, sweet home," he announced.

Cahya's gaze followed his arm until it landed on the building. The house had a rounded, mushroom-cap shape, with a door at the center and a window on either side. Each window had a planter box overflowing with greenery and herbs.

A white marble path led from the sidewalk to the front door.

"This is my place?" Cahya asked, her voice tinged with disbelief.

Kole nodded. "Look familiar?"

Cahya examined the house, hoping something would trigger a memory. It truly was beautiful—sleek and modern, yet warm and inviting, thanks to the plants. The door had soft, rounded edges with a glowing spot at its center.

"No," Cahya finally replied. "Not really. Not yet, anyway." She smiled apologetically.

"Well, what are you waiting for?" Nandini teased, giving Cahya a gentle nudge. "Go check it out!"

Cahya chuckled and made her way up the path. As she neared the door, a glowing white circle appeared which brightened and turned green at her touch.

"Welcome home, Cahya," said a familiar voice. It was Myat—the same AI that had spoken to her in the medical center.

"Well, hiya, Myat," Cahya replied, amused. The door slid upward, revealing the interior of the house.

"We'll give you a minute," Kole said. He and Nandini stayed outside to give Cahya space to explore.

The interior was bright and spacious, with large windows that made it feel connected to the lush backyard beyond. White furniture, wooden tables, and an abundance of plants filled the room, creating a serene atmosphere.

Cahya wandered through the living area and approached the glass wall. A pane of glass slid upward into the ceiling, revealing an exit to the backyard. She stepped onto a round wooden deck that stretched across the back of the house.

The yard was lush and private, thanks to dense hedges and towering trees along the perimeter. One tree stood out: a massive, fifty-foot-tall giant with thick, deeply creased bark. Its branches twisted high above, forming a vast green canopy.

The gardens surrounding the yard were perfectly maintained, with a marble walkway encircling the space. In the center lay a large patch of soft, manicured grass. Cahya couldn't resist stepping down from the deck to lay on it.

The scent of fresh grass soothed her stomach for the first time since the cycles ended. She closed her eyes and relaxed, letting the exhaustion wash over her.

She heard Kole and Nandini shuffle onto the porch but didn't move.

"Well?" Nandini prompted.

"It's a bit of a dump, if I'm being honest," Cahya quipped.

Nandini rolled her eyes and settled onto the grass next to Cahya. A gentle, low hum vibrated through the ground beneath them. Cahya sat up, pressing her palm to feel the subtle tremor.

"You didn't tell me Nirvana's grass had a massage setting," she joked, glancing at Kole, who pointed toward the massive tree across the yard.

"It's a bumble tree," Nandini explained. "They vibrate to scare off predatory insects. Usually, it's so faint you barely notice."

Just then, a tuft of grass at the tree's base shot several feet into the air, sending bits of dirt scattering before gravity reclaimed it with a soft thud.

Nandini laughed. "Oh wow—a root blast! Something must have set it off."

"A root blast?" Cahya echoed.

Nandini nodded, brushing soil off her pants as she rose to inspect the uprooted clump. "It's the same mechanism that makes the tree hum, just stronger. When they're extra agitated, the roots can fire a short burst of energy that pops up anything sitting above them." She stooped to pick up the tuft. "Poor little plant. We'll have to replant you."

The ground's humming eased, fading to stillness. Cahya huffed a breath of surprise. "Well, that was unexpected."

The three of them sat quietly for a moment before Kole spoke again. His tone was serious. "Cahya, we only have a few days left before I have to meet with the council."

Cahya nodded. She was already aware of the deadline. Kole had explained that they had seven days to show progress in restoring her memories. Without improvement, the council might vote to remove her, and the Doyen would have to choose a new Dohan.

"I'm aware," Cahya replied calmly.

"I have a lot of ideas to help you, but we don't have time to try them all," Kole said.

"Then let's stop wasting time," Cahya urged. "This house is great, but it's not helping. What else have you got?"

"This next idea might be tough," Kole warned.

"Lay it on me, Doc."

"Still not a doctor," Kole smiled, "I want to talk about Johnny.".

Cahya blinked, surprised. "Johnny? Really? How would that help me remember Nirvana? Johnny was a simulation. He wasn't real." As she spoke the words, a pang of sadness hit her. Johnny's life was all she could remember, and it felt more real than anything else in Nirvana.

"Your experience with Johnny was real," Kole countered. "Since those are the only memories we have to work with, it's worth exploring, don't you think?"

Nandini placed a comforting hand on Cahya's shoulder, sending a tingling sensation through her skin. Cahya instinctively glanced at the tree, wondering if it was vibrating again. It wasn't.

"Cahya, we need to try everything we can Nirvana needs you," Nandini said softly, her eyes filled with sadness.

Cahya sighed and nodded. "Alright. What do you want to know?"

"Tell me about Johnny," Kole prompted.

Cahya hesitated for a moment before answering. "He was a private investigator in New York City. He solved cases for wealthy clients when the legal system failed them. He was... angry. Really angry. All the time."

"Good," Kole said encouragingly. "Now, walk me through the day Johnny died."

"It was a normal day," Cahya began, her voice steady but distant. "I'd slept at the office because I was working on a tough case. I felt like I was close to a breakthrough..."

"I didn't see anyone that day, except for my assistant when he brought me lunch. I was too focused to eat. Late that night, I started to lose steam, but I couldn't stop. I was close. I went to grab coffee since my assistant had already gone home by then. The barista messed up my order, and I was pissed."

Cahya paused, catching herself. People in Nirvana didn't swear. "Sorry," she muttered.

Nandini gently prodded, "Then what?"

"I went back to my office. I was studying the evidence and... I'd figured something out. But then someone started pounding on the door. Hard." Cahya's brow furrowed as she tried to recall the details. "When I answered, there was a man with a gun. He shot me."

Kole shook his head, confusion contorting his face. "No," he said. "That's not how Johnny was supposed to die."

"What do you mean?" Cahya asked, puzzled.

"I wrote that program myself," Kole explained. "Johnny was supposed to die much later. Older. He was meant to have a spiritual journey through Tibet—"

Cahya snorted, unable to help herself. She imagined Johnny surrounded by monks, meditating in a temple.

Kole frowned but continued, "It was supposed to be very rewarding, alright? Anyway, Johnny wasn't supposed to die like that. Who shot him?"

"It was a hitman-for-hire. Someone I'd been investigating," Cahya explained, remembering the man's sunken eye sockets. The memory caused her to wince.

"Did he say anything?" Nandini asked.

"Yeah. Something like, 'You should've kept your nose out of it.' I can't remember exactly."

Cahya's mind latched onto the phrase. Was it a warning for her now? Should she keep her nose out of this mystery surrounding her accident?

Kole muttered under his breath, "It doesn't make sense." He stared off into the distance, deep in thought.

"Perhaps Johnny made some decisions that caused the cycle to deviate?" Nandini offered.

Kole shook his head. "No, Nandini, this was a predetermined event. You know that certain events in a life cycle are locked in—it's part of the training. They happen regardless of what the student does. The journey to Tibet was non-negotiable as was Johnny's death at 73. Someone must have tampered with the program. How did I miss this?"

Kole suddenly snapped to attention. "Myat, privacy mode."

A faint sound echoed through the yard, like a computer powering down.

"What was that?" Cahya asked, looking around.

"Just ensuring that Myat isn't listening," Kole explained. "Otherwise, someone could access this conversation later."

"Wait... you can do that?" Cahya asked, bewildered.

Kole nodded and continued, "The Doyen asked me to watch for anything suspicious, and this is definitely suspicious. If your life cycle was altered, someone might have wanted you to lose your memories."

Nandini gasped, but Cahya remained calm. She had already suspected foul play. This confirmation didn't surprise her. What still nagged at her was whether Kole or Nandini might be involved. This entire conversation could be a carefully orchestrated ruse to throw her off. She wanted to trust them, but she couldn't afford to let her guard down.

"Why would someone want to erase my memories?" Cahya asked, leaning into her investigator instincts.

"Could be several reasons," Kole replied. "Maybe someone thought you knew something dangerous. Or maybe someone didn't want you to become the next Doyen."

"And if I'm not chosen, who would take my place as Dohan?" Cahya pressed.

"Ultimately, it's up to Doyen Hashen," Kole answered. "But it would likely be either Nandini or Nethos, since they've completed the most cycles with you."

"I see," Cahya said, turning to eye Nandini suspiciously.

"What?" Nandini looked horrified. "You don't think I had anything to do with this... do you?"

"I don't know you, Nandini," Cahya replied. "I have no idea what you're capable of."

Nandini's eyes filled with tears. "I guess I don't know you either," she whispered.

Without another word, she stood and stormed into the house.

Kole sighed and shook his head. "If your plan is to alienate the only allies you have, you're going to have a tough time solving this mystery."

"I don't know who my allies are," Cahya retorted. "I have every reason to distrust everyone."

"You could start by trusting the people who are trying to help you," Kole suggested pointedly.

"That's too simple," Cahya countered.

"Why?" Kole asked.

"Because anyone can pretend to help for seven days if it means getting what they want. And what if I don't even want my memories back? Maybe it's safer to stay here and start over. I don't have to be the Dohan. I don't have to be the future Doyen. If someone else wants it, let them have it!"

The words tumbled out before Cahya could stop them. Saying it out loud felt both terrifying and liberating. Maybe she didn't have to fight this battle. Maybe it was time to live a peaceful life. Johnny hadn't known much peace; maybe Cahya could find peace for him here.

Kole sat silently for a moment, then spoke softly. "The Doyen mentioned you might say something like this. That you might give up."

Cahya raised an eyebrow. "Oh, did he now? What else did he say?"

"He said that if you ever voiced this, you should see him directly." Kole stood and dusted off his pants. "So that's what's next. The Doyen will see you tomorrow. What you do from there is your choice."

He turned to leave but paused. "I understand how you feel. I'll leave you to settle in for the night. Myat can order food for you if you get hungry."

"Myat, user mode," Kole instructed. The familiar beep sounded, signaling Myat's reactivation.

Before leaving, Kole glanced back at Cahya. "For what it's worth... I hope you find what you're looking for."

Then he was gone.

Cahya stood in the quiet yard for a while, Kole's words echoing in her mind. She couldn't shake the feeling that maybe he was right. Maybe she had been pushing away the very people trying to help her. But could she really afford to trust anyone yet? She sighed deeply and made her way back inside the empty house.

She wasn't hungry—her stomach still felt queasy from the cycles—but she was bone-tired. All she wanted was to go to bed and sleep off the stress of the day. As she reached down to pick up the bag she'd brought from the medical center, a small object tumbled out, rattling across the floor.

Cahya froze for a moment, then crouched to pick it up. It was the device from the stranger at the arena. She'd been so busy that she had nearly forgotten about it. Now, with the house quiet and empty, she finally had a chance to inspect it properly.

It was a simple-looking object—like a smooth, black stone with a slit running through the center, as if it were designed to hold up a business card. On one side of the slit, there was a small indentation perfectly sized for her fingertip.

She hesitated, then pressed her finger into the groove. The device lit up instantly, a narrow beam of light projecting from the slit. Cahya yelped softly and quickly covered the beam with her hand, her heart racing. She glanced around nervously, though she knew she was alone.

"Myat, can you darken the windows, please?" she asked quietly.

"Of course, Cahya," Myat's calm voice responded. The windows dimmed until the room felt sealed off from the outside world, cocooned.

Cahya exhaled slowly pulling her hand away from the stone. The light had dissipated so the stone appeared unassuming once again. "Uh... Myat, privacy mode," she said, recalling Kole's earlier instructions. The familiar shutting-down sound echoed through the room.

The house was now eerily silent. Cahya pressed her finger into the groove once more and the light beam rose followed by the sound of a soft voice—feminine and unfamiliar.

"Conducting a facial recognition scan for authentication."

A soft, blue light washed over Cahya's face.

"Authentication successful," the voice announced. "Please select a file from the list."

A small holographic screen appeared above the device. Only one file was listed: *The Link*.

Cahya hesitated for a moment, then reached out and touched the file name. A man's voice—deep and commanding—began to play from the device.

"I won't waste your time. We have much to discuss. It's time to put an end to the Doyen and our treaty with the ònakai.

"We've waited a very long time for this—too long. For generations, our ancestors worked quietly in the shadows, waiting for the right moment to act.

"Rumors of 'The Link' are spreading. Link or no link, we can't stand idle. We've placed people in positions to influence the council. As soon as we finalize our device, everything else will fall into place. Each of you has your assignments. But before we begin, we must address something critical–"

The recording abruptly cut off, leaving only a whirring static sound.

Cahya's mind raced as she played the recording back several times. The man's voice was familiar, but she couldn't quite place it. She had met so many people in the past few days that it was hard to keep them all straight.

What was clear, though, was that this conspiracy was deeper than she'd imagined. Whoever these people were, they wanted to sever ties with the ònakai, and they'd been planning it for generations. Now they were worried about something called *The Link*, which had forced them to accelerate their plans.

Cahya didn't sleep well that night. The recording looped in her mind, word for word, as if burned into her memory. She couldn't stop analyzing every sentence, every inflection in the man's voice, hoping for a clue she might have missed.

But there wasn't enough to go on—not yet.

Eventually, exhaustion overtook her, and she drifted into a restless sleep filled with fragmented dreams of shadowy figures, crumbling treaties, and the ominous hum of the bumble tree.

CHAPTER 10
THE DOYEN

When she opened her eyes again, she had no idea how long she'd been asleep.

"Myat," she called out to the empty room.

No answer.

"Myat," she called again.

Nothing. What on—oh. She hadn't reset the privacy mode last night, so Myat wasn't listening.

"Myat, user mode," she instructed, which was followed by a beep that indicated Myat was back online.

"Good morning, Cahya," came the familiar voice.

"Good morning, Myat. Uh, can you tell me what time it is?"

"Of course, Cahya," Myat replied.

Cahya waited. Myat did not continue.

"What time is it, Myat?" Cahya demanded.

"It is 6:35 in the morning, Cahya. Did you appreciate my attempt at humor? I didn't tell you the time because that wasn't the correct answer to your initial question, 'Can you tell me what time it is.' You see, I understood that you were asking for the time even though you did not ask for it, but I opted to engage in some tomfoolery instead. Did you find it amusing?"

"Yes, Myat, I found it very amusing," Cahya replied absent-mindedly as she rose from bed and made her way to the washroom.

"I thought you might. Would you like to take a shower, Cahya?"

"Uh, yes," Cahya replied, stopping in her path. She heard the water from the shower begin to run in the bathroom.

"The temperature is set as you like it, Dohan."

"Thank you, Myat," Cahya responded as she made her way into the bathroom. At the far end of the room, a shower flowed steadily, its cascading water generating a plume of steam that filled the glass panel designed to contain the water within that area.

Cahya began removing her clothes and then stopped.

"Uh, Myat."

"Yes, Cahya?"

"Can you... see me?" she asked, suddenly feeling a pang of intrusion.

"No, Cahya, not in the sense that you are likely referring to. There are no visual monitors in your space, so while I can observe biological markers and changes, I cannot, as you say, see you."

"Okay," she replied, not quite sure if that answer gave her any comfort.

Cahya stripped off her robe and began making her way to the shower. As she did, she caught a glimpse of herself in the glass. She suddenly realized that this was the first time she'd seen her full reflection since she awoke here in Nirvana.

Her figure was slim, but the definition of muscles was evident in her arms, legs, and abdomen. She turned to examine her butt and smiled in appreciation for the pronounced lump of muscle and fat that was her posterior.

"Not too bad," she smiled at herself.

"Quite right, ma'am!" Myat chimed in.

"Myat! You said that you couldn't see me!"

"I cannot, Cahya. But I can interpret your movements to suggest that you are, as they say, 'checking yourself out.'"

Cahya rolled her eyes and jumped into the shower. She didn't have time to argue with a computer. She had to get going.

* * *

Cahya stood outside a small domed building that looked like a large golf ball made of glass. A patch of grass snaked up the side of the building, curved upwards, disappeared over the top, and then reappeared along the opposite side, trailing back down along the front of the dome. This made it so that about a quarter of the dome-shaped building was covered in grass with tiny white flowers.

"This is where the Doyen lives?" Cahya asked skeptically.

"It is," Kole replied. "You don't like it?"

"Oh, it's very nice. It's just not very grand. I expected some sort of palace for the leader of the entire planet," Cahya explained.

Kole had picked her up so that she wouldn't have to find her way to the Doyen's home on her own. It was kind of him, considering how dismissive Cahya had been the night before. Still, he was quiet.

"We don't have palaces on Nirvana. Or mansions, for that matter. Our largest buildings are those that are meant to serve many people at once. There's no waste here. People have everything they need, but we don't indulge in excess for individuals. There's no reason any one person would need a palace—not even the Doyen."

"But he's special, isn't he? What does he get for all his hard work?" Cahya asked, still trying to figure this out.

"I know it's hard to understand, your memories being what they are right now, but our perception of success is very different from that of the cycles. On Earth, people sought out success in the form of power and money, and they showed off their success with big houses and fancy cars—things that most people couldn't afford.

"On Nirvana, we don't recognize individual success. We accomplish everything in teams. Even if one person makes a discovery, they recognize that their findings are dependent on the research of those who came before them.

"The Doyen, for all of his success and sacrifice, realizes that his wisdom is a gift granted by the Ọnakai, due to their willingness to share their technology with us; it's also due to the people who maintain the program and all of the real-life stories of people who lived on Earth thousands of years ago. Without their sacrifices and their hard-earned life lessons, we would have nothing to base the ELC program on."

Cahya nodded. "I see," she said, still skeptical. "But what does he get, though?"

"He gets to help build a world that is safe and sustainable for what's left of humankind. A place where people can live a happy, safe, and productive life."

"I still don't get it," Cahya shrugged, looking at the small house again.

Kole motioned for Cahya to follow a stone path that led around to the back of the building.

Cahya led the way, with Kole following close behind. The path led to a door framed by two large mounds of grass-covered earth, which tapered down into gardens on the ground.

"Wait here," Kole instructed. "The Doyen will be out momentarily."

"Wait, what? Are you leaving?!" Cahya almost shouted.

Kole laughed. "You are perfectly safe, I promise. The Doyen doesn't bite. I'll see you at the lab later."

With that, Kole turned and made his way back down the path.

Cahya stood by the entrance to the Doyen's home, waiting.

After a few moments, she began to take notice of her surroundings. Next to the path was a small pond surrounded by mossy rocks and filled with koi fish. The yard was smaller than the space behind Cahya's home, but it was overflowing with beautiful shrubbery and gardens.

In the center of the yard was a small mound of grass, which stood about two feet tall and was nearly as wide. It was flat on top, and Cahya found herself staring at the curious feature when she heard a noise from behind.

"Hello, Cahya," came a warm, raspy voice.

Cahya turned to see a tall figure standing in the doorway. He was a slender man dressed in white trousers and a brilliant white tunic that caught the sunlight as he moved. His silver-white hair and matching beard were neatly styled; half of his hair was pulled back into a bun at the back of his head, while the rest fell in loose silvery curls around his shoulders.

He offered Cahya a kind smile. "My name is Doyen Hashen. Please, come in."

He raised his right hand to his heart, closed his eyes, and bowed his head slightly, gesturing with his left arm for Cahya to enter his home. Cahya didn't sense even an ounce of ego coming from him, which one might expect to feel in the presence of the most influential human on the planet. The Doyen had a quiet, humble strength about him.

Inside, large parts of the domed glass were covered with white wave-shaped panels that stretched up from the ground and across the ceiling in the same pattern as the grass on the outside.

Between the two waves, which were stunning art installations in their own right, the sun shone through, casting the most interesting patterns. The play of light and shadow added to the artistic flow of the space.

The room was round, which Cahya assumed meant that the Doyen's sleeping quarters were below ground—a common feature for these homes, she'd learned. At the center of the room was a set of four large white armchairs and a round coffee table with a plant covered in delicate white blossoms which cascaded over the side of an intricately carved wooden container.

The Doyen tilted his head toward the plant, "Jasmine," he explained. "My favorite—especially when it's in full bloom like this. Please, have a seat, Cahya. I'll get us some water."

Cahya obliged, sinking into one of the large chairs.

Across the room, a curved wooden counter followed the curve of the white wall. The Doyen made his way there now and, with a touch, created an opening in the wall from which two glasses of water appeared. The Doyen took the glasses and made his way over to Cahya. He placed a glass on the table in front of her and took the seat to her right.

"How are you feeling, Cahya?" he asked with such tremendous warmth and empathy that Cahya felt a rush of emotion overcome her.

'Dear Lord, pull yourself together, Cahya!' she told herself. Parts of 'old Cahya' must have been coming through, she thought; Johnny would never have been so emotional.

She smiled softly, doing her very best to maintain her composure. "I'm feeling very well, Doyen; thank you for asking."

She let out a soft sigh; surely the Doyen would have noticed.

"Uh, nice place you've got here," Cahya said, looking to shift the conversation as quickly as possible.

"Hmm, yes, it's quite lovely. I grew up here, actually. It's a very comforting place for me," the Doyen told her, looking around the space, his eyes full of gratitude as though he were remembering a special moment in time.

"Kole told me you wanted to speak with me," Cahya prompted, hoping this would move the conversation along.

"Ah, yes, well, we have a very unusual situation on our hands, don't we?" He inhaled, exhaled, and took a sip of water. He was in no hurry; that much was clear.

"If you'll allow me the luxury of distilling the situation, it helps me to bring clarity to my thinking," the Doyen offered.

"Certainly," Cahya agreed.

"Well, we have a young Dohan, eight years into her training, who suddenly loses her memory following a standard learning cycle. Though you've retained your memories from that cycle, is that correct?"

"Yes, that's correct," Cahya conceded.

"That must be even more strange for you. Waking up with no memories whatsoever is challenging enough, but waking up with memories of another time and place must be incredibly disorienting."

It was disorienting, but Cahya felt she was adjusting well. Besides, she never liked to let on when she was struggling. "I'm surviving," she offered.

"I can see that," the Doyen agreed. "Now, you've been through several first-year cycles, and they seem to have agreed with you."

Cahya nodded, though she wasn't sure she agreed.

"I see," the Doyen said. "The cycles haven't really agreed with you, have they?"

Cahya was stunned. Could he read her mind? Maybe her poker face wasn't as good as she thought.

"Well, I felt a bit nauseous afterward, if I'm being honest."

"Well, that's not a good sign, Cahya. The cycles can leave people feeling tired, certainly, but one shouldn't feel ill."

"I thought that might be the case," Cahya admitted. "I didn't say anything because I didn't want anyone to worry for nothing. I can handle a bit of nausea."

"Well, that's admirable, Cahya. Still, as I understand it, even with the cycles and the many familiarization activities Kole has coordinated, you've not regained any memories to date. Is that correct?"

"Correct," Cahya agreed.

"Last evening, Kole informed me of a new development in this very unique situation. He shared that the manner in which your cycle ended provided him with strong evidence that the cycle had been tampered with in some way."

"Yes, that's all correct," Cahya agreed.

"Is there any important detail I've left out? Anything that might further add to this unique puzzle we have in front of us now?"

Cahya thought about the stranger at the arena and the strange recording she'd received. 'You don't know who you can trust,' the

127

woman had said. She felt like she could trust Doyen Hashen, but what did she really know about him? She'd spoken to him for all of ten minutes. It was too soon.

"No, I think you've just about summed it up, Doyen." Cahya wondered if the Doyen could tell she was lying. If he could, he didn't let on and he didn't press her on the matter.

"Well then," he said, "the only question that remains for the two of us at this moment is, what now?"

"Well, I assume that I will continue working with Kole, for a little while at least. The council gave him seven days, didn't they?"

"They did, yes. Today is day four, I believe. Kole has three more days before he'll have to share his findings with the council," the Doyen confirmed.

"And you don't think Kole can do it?" Cahya challenged.

"I have every faith that Kole will do whatever he can to help you regain your memories. But tell me this, Cahya: do you *want* to regain your memories?"

Obviously, Kole had shared their conversation with the Doyen; but the wording of the question caught Cahya off guard. Was he suggesting that Cahya wasn't trying hard enough? That it was somehow her fault she wasn't making progress? Or could he sense her hesitation? Could he tell that she was worried she could be in danger?

"What are you suggesting, Doyen?" Cahya asked with a slight edge to her tone.

"I apologize, Cahya; I did not mean to offend. I simply wondered, genuinely, if there was any part of you—perhaps even just a very small part—that might not want to regain your memories."

Cahya decided that it was pointless to play dumb with this man.

"I have to at least consider the possibility that someone wanted me to lose my memories, Doyen. I don't know why, but if that's true—if someone caused this—then they definitely don't want me to get those memories back. And if they do return... who knows what that person might do to stop it. So yes, I suppose a part of me is afraid. A part of me doesn't want my memories to come back. It might be safer for me to stay in the dark. Maybe I could live with that."

Even as she said the words, they felt false. The logical part of her knew that everything she said was true, but the curiosity in her knew, deep down, that she'd never be able to go on without knowing the truth. She'd never be able to leave the puzzle unsolved. She'd have to try to mitigate the danger to herself—that was the best she could manage. It wasn't in her nature to leave things be. Still, she wasn't about to share this with the Doyen. If he was on the side of whoever did this, he could easily do away with her right here and now. Eliminate any threat she might pose.

"Well, that's a reasonable deduction, Cahya," the Doyen told her. "May I share something with you?"

"Sure."

Doyen Hashen leaned forward in his chair and smiled. "Before your accident, you weren't known for being particularly reasonable," he told her, chuckling softly at the thought.

"You have never been a reckless person, Cahya; let me make that clear. However, you've never been a person to shy away from taking a chance on a long shot."

He continued, "Let's take your last cycle, the one before Johnny, as an example. You were a nurse named Sandy. You sacrificed yourself to save a young girl who was dying of radiation poisoning."

"That's very heroic," Cahya suggested.

"Yes, it was. It may have also been very stupid."

Cahya's eyes became wide. 'Stupid' wasn't a word she expected to hear from the Doyen's mouth. She laughed in spite of herself.

"Stupid? Saving a child?" she asked, still laughing.

"Yes, well, there would have been a very small chance of the child surviving even after you revived her. So in all likelihood, you died for nothing."

"Wow, that does sound stupid—but wait, I thought that the way people died in the cycles was predetermined," Cahya said, remembering what Kole had said about Johnny's death. "Doesn't that mean that I was supposed to die trying to save that girl?"

"Sometimes the end is decided, yes," the Doyen confirmed, "but not always. Certain parts of a cycle are determined in advance. There are milestones the student will hit no matter what. Sometimes those milestones are tied to how the cycle ends, and sometimes they are not. It simply depends on the learning objectives of that particular cycle."

"I see," said Cahya. "So I suppose that dying to save a girl who was likely going to die anyway does sound kind of stupid, doesn't it?"

"It does," the Doyen agreed. "But when Kole ran the simulation through, he found that the girl went on to live a very long, very fruitful life," he smiled.

"You see, Cahya, you have an intuitive sense about you. You sometimes make decisions that seem statistically unwise, and yet, as fate would have it, you're nearly always right."

"Sapoto," Cahya mumbled, remembering the word Kole had said to her shortly after her accident.

"Yes, exactly," the Doyen confirmed.

Cahya didn't know how to respond to this. She thought back to her life as Johnny; he'd always followed his intuition—it's how he'd solved most of his cases. Was that just Cahya's true nature guiding him all along?

"There are some things that computers simply cannot do, Cahya. All of the best, most sophisticated programming in the world will never bring them anywhere close to having the intuition that lives within you. That is why you are so important to Nirvana. That is why I chose you as Dohan."

He sighed deeply. "I suspect that you're correct and that someone is trying to displace you as the future leader of Nirvana. If that is true, then we are both in danger.

"I've never had the level of natural intuition that you have, Cahya, but I feel very certain of one thing: whatever happens next, Nirvana needs you on its side."

'Well, shit...' How was she supposed to respond to that? How was she going to pretend she could be content living a quiet life while staying out of whatever was happening?

"I'm not sure how I might help if my memories don't return, Doyen."

"You would be surprised," the Doyen assured her.

He continued, "In one of my past Life Cycles, I lived in a poverty-stricken neighborhood where the roads were always in disrepair, the garbage cans were always overflowing, and our neighbors cared very little about how our properties looked, inside or out. This was such a familiar sight that it became normal in my town. If someone tried to clean their yard or paint their fence, the neighbors would taunt them for trying to act like they were better than everyone else. In this way, we held one another back.

"One day, the city came to repair the roads. It was the first time this had been done since anyone in town could remember."

He took another sip of water and then continued, "When the workers had gone and the roads had dried, we noticed that they had left a gap between the road and the sidewalk. It wasn't an awfully large gap, but certainly an elderly person's cane could get stuck in it.

"At first, a few concerned citizens made calls to the city, asking them to return and repair the mistake. They promised they would, but no one ever came.

"As we waited, children began to make a game of jumping over the gap, pretending that all manner of creatures lived in the small, dark space. People stopped calling the city to make the repair, and the gap became a normal part of life, like the messy porches and the overgrown lawns.

"Over time, the elements picked away at the gap, and it became gradually larger and larger. It wasn't until a relative came to visit me that I was reminded of the gap. As she approached my porch, where

I sat, she announced, 'I damn near killed myself stepping over that damn hole on the road! Someone ought to call to have that repaired!'

"Unfortunately, no one called to have it repaired, and a week later, a young girl who had been playing in the street got her foot caught in that gap. When she tried to pull her foot out, she couldn't move it. She cried and screamed for help. Then, as a car raced toward her, she screamed louder, tears streaming down her face as she tugged furiously at her trapped foot. She was pulled out of the way at the last second by a young man, and she only suffered a broken ankle from the ordeal. It could have been much worse, of course, but it didn't have to be as bad as it was."

He continued, "You see, Cahya, humans—even ones as advanced as we have become—have a tendency to ignore small problems because there is always something bigger or more important to worry about. Over time, these small problems become invisible. We wouldn't recognize them even if we were looking for them. They become imperceptible to those who have lived with them for so long. And small problems can become very large problems if we lack the perspective to see and fix them.

"You have a unique mind, Cahya, and with your memories gone, you have a unique opportunity as well. You, and perhaps you alone, will be able to perceive gaps where others do not.

"If you regain your memories, Nirvana will be very lucky indeed. If you do not, you will be of great service to our people in a different way. Either way, you have an important place here, Cahya."

Cahya nodded. This guy was good; she'd give him that much.

∗ ∗ ∗

Cahya was deep in thought on her way home from the Doyen's. Maybe this memory loss was a gift, as the Doyen had suggested. Maybe it would allow her to see things that 'full-memory Cahya' might have missed.

On the other hand, Cahya suspected the Doyen knew more than he was letting on. Could she trust him? He had *chosen* her for this role, after all. Surely, he wouldn't be trying to undermine her now. Besides, if he did want her out, couldn't he have just made that decision himself? He was the Doyen, after all. Or... maybe admitting she wasn't the right choice would be admitting that he'd made a mistake. Did Doyens even make mistakes? Maybe this was his way of quietly pushing her aside—an elaborate move to protect his own reputation. Or was he testing her, trying to gauge how much she knew? Was he simply trying to gain her trust so she'd open up to him? And what about all those comments about her intuition? Were they genuine praise or just manipulative flattery to lower her guard? She couldn't be sure. Not yet.

She hadn't given him anything. She'd nodded, listened, and agreed to look for gaps, as he'd requested. But beyond that, she was careful not to give him too much.

"Are you going home, Cahya?" came a small voice.

Cahya looked up to see Ash standing on one leg mid-hop. Below her, a hopscotch course was etched in blue tile on the marble sidewalk.

'Oh no,' Cahya thought. 'I can't "kid" right now.'

"Hey, Ash. No, I'm on my way to the hub." She hoped this would be enough to shoo the kid away.

"You were at the Doyen's, weren't you?" Ash finished her last two hops, her curls bouncing in sync. "What did you guys talk about? Are your memories back yet? Are you still Dohan?" she asked in a flurry of questions as she ran to Cahya's side, but she didn't wait for an answer to any of them.

"You probably can't answer any of those questions, huh? That's okay. Oh! You're going to the train station, aren't you? I'll walk with you." Ash took Cahya's hand and started walking in the same direction Cahya had been going.

"Uh... where's your dad, Ash?" Cahya looked around for Ash's father, who she spotted walking down the pathway from his house to the sidewalk.

"Ash, I'm sure Cahya's very busy. We should probably let her get on with her day."

"I walk with Cahya to the train station all the time, Papa!" Ash pointed out, but she didn't wait for her father to respond. "Do you remember that my dad made this?" she asked, pointing to Cahya's tunic.

"Uh, no. No, I had no idea," Cahya told her, sincerely surprised by the revelation. She looked down at the garment; it was very impressive and by far the most comfortable and elegant thing she could ever remember wearing.

"Yeah, my dad's an awesome designer! He designed all of the new panigêm hydroglider suits," Ash told her, smiling a little too proudly.

Cahya could sense what the girl was up to; she was buttering her father up a little so he'd be a bit more willing to let her walk with Cahya. Smart kid. Cahya was impressed.

She decided to go along with it to see how it would play out. "Wow, that's very impressive," she replied, looking at Carsen.

"It's not that big a deal," Carsen contended shyly.

"Are you kidding, Papa?" Ash asked. She turned to Cahya. "Before my dad redesigned the suits, players were getting hurt all the time. Dad invented a new fabric that protects Shield players from the impact of a pulse when they don't get their arms up in time. All the players use it now; it's regulation."

"That was a long time ago, Ash," Carsen reminded her.

"Yeah, but now you're working on new uniforms for the Council of Nirvana," Ash exclaimed. "It's a big deal. That's why we moved to Deshka," she said, turning to Cahya.

Cahya nodded and widened her eyes, doing her best to look impressed. Ash was probably right; designing uniforms for the council was likely a big deal, but it didn't exactly get Cahya excited.

"It's true," Carsen admitted. "Though I've been at it for two years, and I don't feel any closer to having the uniform completed than I did when I first started. Everything I send to the council gets rejected for a myriad of reasons. I really can't figure out what they want."

"Oh! You should show Cahya the latest design you've been working on. It's so beautiful!" Ash pressed.

"I'm sure Cahya has better things to do," Carsen objected.

She did, in fact, have better things to do. She needed to get to the hub; she had cycles scheduled with Kole. But something told her she ought to check out these new uniforms. She was supposed to have great intuition, after all.

"I don't, actually," Cahya lied. "I have cycles later, but I have some time to kill right now."

"Oh, okay then. I'd be happy to show you what I've been working on." Carsen led them up the path and into the house. A small room off the entrance was filled with piles of fabrics. Sketches lined the walls of the room, and there was a machine that Cahya didn't recognize, but she assumed it must be some sort of sewing device. Then she remembered that none of her garments had seams, *hmm*. She was pulled from her musings when Carsen spoke again.

"I like old-school pencil and paper for my initial sketches," Carsen explained, noticing Cahya's gaze scanning the images around the room.

Cahya got that; Johnny had also preferred paper to screens. There was something about it that made his notes feel more substantial.

"Please ignore the mess. I wasn't expecting to have anyone in here today."

"I actually find it to be refreshing," Cahya admitted. "In my last cycle, I was a P.I." Carsen's face twisted in confusion at this term.

"Private Investigator," Cahya clarified. Carsen nodded in understanding. "This room reminds me of my office from that cycle. It was covered in evidence and papers all over the walls. This is the first time I've seen anything in Nirvana that felt the least bit chaotic. And it's strangely comforting."

Cahya was taken aback by her own bewilderment. She cleared her throat, bringing herself back into focus. "These sketches are great," she remarked.

Carsen smiled and walked across the room, where he waved his hand at the wall. A door slid upward, revealing a small closet with several garments hanging inside.

He pulled out a piece—a tunic similar to Cahya's—but the fabric appeared heavier. The garment was made of a shiny silver-gray material. The tunic was long, as she had become accustomed to, though it was markedly shorter than the current standard. The garment was accented with intricate silver embroidery around the cuffs, the collar, and along the bottom edge. Patterns of leaves interlaced with geometric shapes. A pair of matching gray pants hung behind the top—a complete outfit.

"It's magnificent," Cahya told him, still holding the sleeve of the garment. She was being completely honest, too. It was a gorgeous piece. She ran her hand down the sleeve, admiring the soft texture, which felt both heavy and silky beneath her fingertips.

"Well, I hope the council thinks so. I'm supposed to present it in a couple of weeks. I have a few tweaks to make, but it's nearly ready. This is just a sample, of course, once approved, I'll have to create each version in the correct colors."

"What's that?" Cahya asked, pointing to a black outfit hanging in the closet.

"Oh, a personal project for one of the council members. Super top secret," Carsen winked, and then he laughed in spite of himself. It was nice to see him relaxed, Cahya thought.

Cahya's gaze lingered on the sleek black garment a moment longer. Something about the mention of a hush-hush council project reminded her of an older rumor she'd heard. She swallowed and turned to Carsen, lowering her voice so that Ash wouldn't hear.

"Can I ask you something a bit... sensitive?" she said gently. "It's about—Ash's mother. People keep telling me how rare it is for someone that healthy to pass so suddenly. Wasn't there... an investigation?"

Carsen's smile faded. He shot a glance toward Ash by the doorway, then took a step closer to Cahya, speaking in a hushed tone.

"We did investigate Tashina's death at first. A lot of us demanded a full review of her scans—myself included. For a few days, the chatter was everywhere: How could this happen in a place like Nirvana?" He sighed, eyes downcast. "But after about a week, talk just stopped. Some big voices in the city council said that the 'official logs' showed nothing unusual. We were... encouraged not to pry. It was never right, but I had Ash to worry about. I couldn't change anything."

He cleared his throat, as if to shake the memory loose. "I got the sense that Tash was working on something big, she wasn't allowed to talk to me about it, but whatever it was, it wasn't good. It ate at her, I could see it. I'm telling you this in confidence, Dohan. That's all I know."

Cahya pressed a hand to Carsen's arm. "Thanks for trusting me," she said, her mind already churning with fresh questions. She glanced at Ash, who was now standing patiently just outside the room. That poor girl. No wonder she clings so tightly.

Ash stood in the doorway, waiting for the exchange to reach a natural conclusion before she interjected. "They're gonna love the new uniforms, Papa! Can I go with Cahya now?"

"Ash-Lynn," her father started, "I don't think—"

"It's okay," Cahya offered. "I wouldn't mind the company."

This was also sincere. What the heck was going on? Was she really looking forward to having a private chat with this kid?

"Okay, Dohan," Carsen agreed. "Ash, you'll be on your very best behavior for Cahya, won't you? And straight back home afterward, okay?"

"Of course, Papa." Ash hugged her father. "Okay, bye!" she said. She immediately grabbed Cahya's hand and tugged her toward the door, leading her out of the house and toward the train station.

Ash continued holding Cahya's hand as they made their way up the marble pathway, past several homes.

"So, what *did* you talk to the Doyen about today?" the young girl asked finally, her eyes full of excitement.

"A few different things," Cahya replied, studying the child curiously. "I'm sure you'd find it all very boring."

"I never find it boring! I love hearing about the council and the big decisions the Doyen has to help them make. Is your memory back yet?"

"Nothing new yet, I'm afraid. But Kole has some ideas on how we might get them back. That's where I'm headed now—to see Kole."

"What will you do? Shock therapy? Hypnosis? Sensory deprivation?" The kid sounded a little too excited.

Cahya looked at Ash, eyebrows raised.

Ash laughed and explained, "I've been talking to Myat about all the different ways that people try to heal their memory loss after an accident."

Cahya laughed. "I see! Well, we're not trying anything quite so dramatic just yet. Kole seems to think that a few sessions of ELC training might help spark something. But I'll be sure to share your ideas with him... just maybe not the part about shock therapy."

"Well, whatever he has planned, I hope it works," Ash confessed.

"You do?" Uh oh, maybe this kid was onto her after all. Did she know Cahya was lying about remembering her?

"Yeah," Ash's face became somber. "You seem more lonely since your accident. It makes my heart sad for you."

Cahya looked down at the curious child. She was just seven years old, but she had empathy and compassion far beyond her years. It made no sense; Ash had lost her mother in a tragic accident just two years earlier. This kid had every right to be angry at the world.

Instead, here she was, worried about the well-being of her 38-year-old friend.

"You're a very special young lady, Ash. Do you know that?" Cahya didn't try to hold back her awe this time. She was genuinely amazed by Ash, and she didn't care who knew it.

"Oh, I know," Ash confirmed. "You tell me all the time."

Cahya chuckled softly. Somehow, for the first time in days, she didn't feel quite so lost. Maybe she wasn't alone in this after all.

CHAPTER 11

ELC TRAINING

Cahya got off the train and made her way to Menza for lunch. Nandini, Nethos, and Theo were waiting for her by the entrance. Kole had planned an afternoon full of ELC training for the four of them.

Cahya wasn't sure why Theo was joining them, but she had to assume that Nandini had something to do with it. Cahya hadn't spoken with Nandini since last night, after she'd left Cahya's place in tears.

Nandini and Theo had become fast friends, and maybe Nandini needed someone other than Cahya to talk to between cycles. Nethos would be of no use in that department, that's for sure.

"I'm glad we'll get to do some of the more challenging cycles today," Nandini said, popping a bright red cherry tomato into her mouth. "I mean, being a bug is fun for a day, but after that, you really want to get into the tough stuff, you know?"

"Well, I'm grateful that you convinced Kole to let me join you guys," Theo said, plucking a piece of lint from his pale yellow tunic. "I appreciate that they start exchange students out at the first level, but since I've done over 5,000 cycles on Octavia, I'm anxious to join in on some of the more advanced human cycles."

"Five thousand!" Cahya exclaimed. "I didn't even know that you had cycles on Octavia."

"Well, of course we do, Cahya. Where do you think humans got the technology? We set you guys up about 500 years after you arrived here."

"I see, so you were here first, then?" Cahya inquired, realizing that she didn't know very much about the ònakai. There hadn't been any mention of them during the intro video she'd watched with Kole. *This is a gap,* Cahya thought to herself—a pretty glaring one. She made a mental note.

"Oh yes," Theo confirmed, "Octavia is our original planet, our only planet, in fact. We've explored space in the past, but we've never colonized anywhere else."

"And where is Octavia, exactly?" Cahya asked, suddenly aware of how little she knew about Nirvana's neighbors.

Theo's eyes lit up, as though this was a topic he loved to discuss. "Oh, now this is really fascinating! Have you ever wondered why the sun rises and sets at the same time on both Nirvana and Octavia? Or why we're able to follow the same calendar system? 12 months, 5 weeks per month, 6 days per week?"

"Honestly? I didn't even realize that it did." Cahya admitted. "I'm new here, remember?"

Theo's grin expanded as he grabbed one large plate from Nethos and two smaller plates from Cahya and Nandini, arranging them in a triangle.

"Imagine this larger plate is the sun, and these two smaller plates are our planets," Theo continued with a grin. "Octavia and Nirvana share the same orbit around the sun. They're what's called 'Trojan planets,' caught in a gravitational balance. Think of it like this—Octavia leads, Nirvana follows," as he said this, Theo pushed the two smaller plates around the larger one. "They're always separated by sixty degrees in orbit. It's a cosmic dance and neither planet can catch up or fall behind."

"So... we're stuck together?" Cahya asked, wiping her mouth with a napkin.

"Exactly. Gravitationally locked, perfectly synchronized. That's why the ònakai refer to Nirvana as their 'Sister Planet.' We've always been tied together."

"Huh." Cahya leaned back in her seat, processing the idea. "So if Octavia suddenly vanished, what would happen to us?"

"Not good," Theo said with a chuckle, though his tone carried a hint of seriousness. "Without that balance, Nirvana would drift off its orbit—or worse, get pulled straight into the sun."

Nandini chimed in, not making eye contact with Cahya, "Let's just say we're very lucky to have a stable partner out there."

Theo nodded in agreement.

"So the ònakai created the Life Cycle program." Cahya

"Yes. We'd been using it ourselves for quite a long time before humans arrived, over 18,000 years or so. We shared the technology with you after the Dakaï uprising in 506..." Theo's voice trailed off. *Dakaï!* That word reverberated in her mind. *Dakaï.* Something about that word sent her heart racing.

"What's Dakaï?" Cahya asked, cutting Theo off mid-sentence. The alarm in Cahya's voice caused everyone to stop eating and look at her, even Nandini, who, up until that point, had avoided even glancing in Cahya's direction. *Keep cool, Cahya,* she told herself, and she managed to relax her expression.

Nethos stepped in to explain. "The Dakaï were a group of vigilante warriors. Their mission was to end the Gardia Treaty and sever ties with Octavia."

"Their fear and hatred of the ònakai almost started a war between Nirvana and Octavia," Nandini chimed in. "It was a terrible time in Nirvana's history."

"Maybe they had some valid points," Nethos told them, shoveling another forkful of food into his mouth.

Nandini shot him a look of honest shock. "What on Nirvana do you mean by that?"

"I mean, maybe the Dakaï were on to something. Oh, come on, don't look at me like that. At every point in human history, countries and planets have sought independence from their sovereigns, right? Eventually, we want to get out from under Mom and Dad's rules and chart our own course. It's only natural."

"Sure. Except that we made a deal with the ònakai. In exchange for our safety and protection, we agreed to abide by their rules, and they've been nothing but wonderful to us. We've had the luxury of peace and prosperity for nearly two thousand years on Nirvana."

Nethos raised an eyebrow and Nandini conceded, "Ok, aside from that nasty Dakaï business 1500 years ago. But that's the point, we've lived in peace since the ELC program and we wouldn't have that program without the ònakai. No other human civilization can say they've lived in peace for fifteen hundred years. We've also improved quality of life to the point where people get to live to be 200 years old, and some are living even longer than that!

"Humans have consistently proven themselves incapable of charting their own course without destroying everything along the way. Besides, chart our own course for what? What more could we hope to accomplish for humanity that we can't accomplish right here on Nirvana while living under the protection of the ònakai?" Nandini finished her rant by taking a deep, exasperated breath.

"Well, space exploration for one," Nethos shot back.

"Can someone else talk some sense into this guy? I can't." Nandini sat back in her seat, defeated.

Theo chimed in. "Both of our species have had extensive opportunities to explore the galaxy; you know that there's nothing out there but destruction and grief. If you don't believe me, check out some of the cycles from later in Earth's history, when galactic exploration was at its peak of popularity. Maybe you could even come to Octavia and check out some of our exploration cycles during the Peace Accord era. It's very interesting, but it makes you grateful to have a home planet with everything you could ever need."

Nethos shrugged. "It's not about what's out there. It's about being allowed to go out there if we want to. It's about freedom."

Cahya tried to hide her look of disappointment. She couldn't believe how childish Nethos sounded. *My rapili is you,* she heard Nethos say. How on earth was this guy her soulmate? Did they share anything at all in common?

"So wait, what's the Gardia Treaty?" Cahya asked, remembering the recording: *'It's time to put an end to the Treaty with the ònakai.'*

Nandini replied, "The Gardia Treaty basically says that humans can't be irresponsible or shortsighted and that they have to take care of the planet they were so generously gifted by the ònakai."

"It's a bit more restrictive than that," Nethos corrected. "Take care of the planet, yes, but we're not allowed to make weapons, we're not permitted to build ships or to explore space, and we have to follow the ònakai's systems of governance."

"Those rules have allowed us to flourish," Nandini insisted.

"Well, not everyone agrees with that, Nandini," Nethos told her, but he shrugged and returned to his meal, suggesting that he had nothing more to say on the matter.

Nandini stared at him in disbelief, but she didn't press the issue further. It was clear they had reached an impasse.

Cahya was putting pieces together in her mind. The Dakaï wanted to end the treaty; the men were fighting outside the panigêm arena... one had called the other Dakaï. The recording also said that they'd been at work for generations. There were too many coincidences; the meeting she'd heard on the device must have been a secret meeting of the Dakaï. But who were they? How would she be able to tell if someone was Dakaï? Was Nethos Dakaï? He seemed to agree with a lot of the issues that caused the first Dakaï war.

She couldn't focus on that right now; she had training.

After lunch, they made their way to one of the ELC classrooms. Cahya let Nethos and Theo get ahead a bit. The two were engrossed in a conversation about space exploration and Octavian Life Cycles.

"Nandini," she whispered, taking Nandini's arm. "Can I talk to you for a second?"

She knew that she couldn't leave things the way they'd ended last night. Whatever was coming next, she got the sense that she needed Nandini on her side.

Nandini slowed her pace to match Cahya's, creating a bit more space between Theo and Nethos.

"Look, I'm sorry about last night," Cahya confessed. "I didn't mean to upset you. This has all just been... a lot."

Nandini forced a smile. Even a fake smile looked beautiful on her face. Cahya knew it was fake, though, because her big eyes remained sad.

"I know," Nandini said. "I get it. It's not your fault. I just really miss my friend."

She stopped walking and took Cahya's hand, forcing Cahya to stop too. She turned and searched Cahya's eyes, looking for her friend behind those big purple irises. "Wherever she is, I hope she comes back to me soon."

When they arrived at the classroom, Kole waved them in and began the lesson immediately: "Good morning, everyone."

Cahya, Nethos, Nandini, and Theo sat in chairs around the perimeter of the small room along one wall. Opposite them was a set of windows that reminded Cahya of the hospital room she'd been in just days earlier. They were shaped in the same way, bowed outwards, creating a crescent space.

Kole made his way to the windows and said, "Myat, please display today's Life Cycle summaries."

The windows darkened, and the faces of infants popped up on the screen in front of them.

As they watched, the images changed. Each face evolved, aging slowly from infant to toddler, toddler to young child, young child to teen, teen to young adult, young adult to older adult, older adult to elderly adult, and then back to infant again.

Cahya realized that not all of the faces became elderly; two of the faces returned to the infant phase immediately after the young adult phase, suggesting that these cycles would be ending early.

"These are your incarnations," Kole told them, gesturing to the faces on the screen as they continued to evolve. "Your cycles will take place approximately 4,000 years before Earth's destruction, known in Earth's history as the third century BC. Your incarns are all living in Rome, crossing paths with one another at various points throughout the cycles.

"Cahya, you will be Vitus."

One of the four floating images moved to the forefront, becoming larger than the rest. Cahya studied the face of the person in front of her—an infant with black wispy hair, a toddler with white-blond hair and playful brown eyes, a young boy with pudgy cheeks and darker blond hair, a handsome teen with sharpened features and thinner cheeks, and a young man with tanned skin and light brown hair.

Kole continued, "Vitus is born in Capula and travels to Rome as a teenager in search of a better life for himself.

"Nethos, you will be Antonia, a woman born in Rome to a poor family. Antonia and Vitus will become lovers before his death."

As Kole spoke, the image of the woman moved forward, and the group watched as it cycled through the phases of this woman's life. She grew from a young, brown-haired spark of a girl to an old woman with wrinkles framing her sunken eyes.

"Next, we have Cornelius." Another young man's image came forward as Antonia fell into the background. "Nandini, this is your incarnation. You'll live in a small village outside of Rome, and you'll find yourself in the big city, sold into slavery at a young age and then freed to join the Roman army as a teenager. You and Vitus will become friends during your time there."

Nandini nodded as she stared at the face of the young man in front of her. He, like Vitus, didn't age or wrinkle; he was a red-headed, red-faced boy, covered in freckles that darkened and multiplied as he grew older.

"Finally, we have Sirius, your incarnation, Theo," Kole said as the final image came to the forefront. This man did grow old and wrinkled, his hair receding over time until there was nothing left on the top of his head, and what little hair did remain was silvery white. "Sirius is Antonia's father. Theo, this means that your cycle will begin a little earlier than the rest. Sirius will become very fond of Vitus since his son will have died at the age of ten."

Kole stepped forward as the image of Sirius returned to the background with the other images, and the four faces continued to float and age behind him.

"These cycles will present some unique challenges," Kole told them. "All of you will suffer through poverty, disease, and war, but the challenges you face together will help to strengthen you as individuals and as a team.

"Fun fact," Kole continued with a small smile, "this cycle includes one of my very early incarns, Mathis; so I will see you in there, so to speak. Please don't judge, I was very young."

"What do you mean, early incarns?" Cahya asked.

"Oh, well, once you've incarnated as someone in a cycle, they're yours forever. Anyone who joins the cycle later must do so as a different incarnation, thereby building on the existing experiences. Because of this, many of the people you interact with in any given lifetime are the past incarns of someone you know here on Nirvana. That's why certain people feel familiar as soon as you meet them."

Cahya nodded slowly, "Interesting."

"Any other questions?" Kole asked as the screen faded to black and then dissipated until the windows were revealed once again. No one had questions. "Alright, kids," Kole said. "Let's get started."

They stood and made their way to the ELC Training Lab. Cahya was ready.

∗ ∗ ∗

Vitus stood tall on the front lines of the battlefield, his Roman companions lined neatly at his sides, holding their enormous red shields out as they advanced.

In his 19 years of life, he'd never seen such a sight. Eight legions of Roman men stood shoulder to shoulder, facing the Carthaginian army, which moved toward them from the south. He looked to his right at his dear friend Cornelius. He could see the determination in his friend's eyes.

They were told it would be a quick and easy battle. There was little the smaller Carthaginian army could do—the Romans outnumbered them by nearly double; or so the commanders had told them. Vitus trusted his generals. Still, he was anxious to be done with this battle; they'd been marching for days, and they were exhausted.

He didn't really care much for this war; if he was being honest, he was here because he'd been promised a pension and vast farmlands for his service to the Roman army. It was an offer he couldn't refuse. Land of his own, a place he could settle down with Antonia, have some children, grow his own food, and raise his own meat. The promise of that life was more glorious than he could bear. It was all he could think about, even now as he marched closer to the enemy. All he had to do was slice through a few Carthaginian pigs, and he could go home and start his quiet, peaceful farming life. Perhaps he and Cornelius would get property next to one another.

He recalled the first time he'd met Cornelius, when he arrived at Campus Martius for training. They'd become fast friends, something about him made Vitus feel that he'd known this man his entire life. He looked forward to the end of this war when the two could raise their families together in peace.

The armies closed in and the order came to begin their attack on the enemy's center lines. Vitus cried out and ran forward with his comrades. With shields out and swords raised, they pushed through the Carthaginian army easily. The enemy retreated further and further back. The sound of blades clashing rang all around him. A sword swung by Vitus' head, narrowly missing his shoulder.

As he twisted away from another flying blade he caught sight of his friend, Cornelius, and was transfixed. Cornelius moved through the fray like a force of nature. Amid the chaos of clashing swords and the roar of battle, Cornelius exhibited an almost supernatural grace—each swing of his sword was executed with the precision of a master. His red shield flashed brilliantly in the sunlight as it intercepted enemy blows, while his footwork allowed him to weave seamlessly between adversaries. Vitus's heart pounded in awe as he watched Cornelius dispatch his foes with fluid, dance-like movements, his every strike a testament to years of relentless training and unwavering focus.

"Vitus!" came the voice of a soldier. Vitus turned to see an enemy charging at him and he got his sword up just in time to cut him down. The Carthaginians were closing in and Vitus found Cornellius at his back. He was grateful for this.

Suddenly, screams began to come from beside him and then from behind him. The men of Carthage pressed their way into the Roman center, forcing Vitus and his companions backward. He continued fighting, finding himself forced further and further back, but his comrades held the line, and he couldn't move back any further.

Screams continued all around him. "They've surrounded us!" one Roman soldier yelled. "There's no way out!" screamed another.

The Carthaginians had trapped the Romans, who now found themselves being attacked from all sides. The center of the army, where the strongest soldiers had been positioned, was so densely packed that the men could not even raise their swords.

The sound of metal clashing against metal rang loudly in the morning air, and the screaming continued as the sun rose higher in the sky.

"Vitus! Vitus!" came a panicked voice. It was Mathis, one of Vitus' fellow soldiers, he screamed, grabbing Vitus' arm and shouting above the growing din. "Vitus, there's nothing for this. There's nothing for any of it. Please, my friend, I beg of you, force your dagger through my heart quickly so that I may be done with this."

Vitus couldn't comprehend what his comrade was asking of him—Mathis was a year his junior and they'd become close friends through their training.

"Please!" Mathis begged once more. But his plea was cut short as a blade pierced through his chest, the tip slashing toward Vitus. Mathis' eyes widened in shock before his body crumpled lifelessly to the ground. Cornelius roared in fury, thrusting his sword into Mathis' killer without hesitation. Vitus gave him a quick nod of grim gratitude before turning back to the fight.

The battle surged around them. Soldiers pressed in so tightly that neither Vitus nor Cornelius could fully lift their weapons. The crush of bodies became suffocating—arms, shields, and armor tangled in a desperate struggle for space and air. Cornelius caught Vitus' gaze, giving him a knowing, resigned look. This was the end. There would be no promised land, no victory celebration waiting for them after this fight.

Vitus gritted his teeth and made one final effort to raise his sword, but he caught sight of the tip of a blade exploding through the front of his armor as agony ripped through his chest like fire. His strength faltered, and the world blurred. The clash of weapons and the anguished cries around him faded, swallowed by a deafening silence and darkness.

The channel of light appeared to Vitus, and as he traveled through it, images began to appear—Antonia waving him off as he left for his final battle, Antonia's father, Sirius, hugging him after a deep conversation they'd had, the day he met Cornelius, and more. Finally, the light, growing ever larger and brighter, exploded.

Vitus found himself standing next to another figure in the tunnel. As it moved toward him, the figure came into focus. It was a dark-skinned woman with long purple hair and piercing purple eyes.

"Hey," the figure said, smiling and reaching a hand toward Vitus.

Vitus raised his arm, reaching for the woman, but before their fingers could touch she dissolved and Vitus was pulled violently through the tunnel.

* * *

Cahya awoke, gasping for air. She erupted in a puddle of tears as she tried furiously to catch her breath. She felt like she might be sick, and a searing pain cut through her head. She tried to keep it together; she knew she couldn't move until her vitals had been checked.

'What was that?' she thought. She couldn't focus; her head was spinning.

"It's okay, Cahya," came Kole's voice. "It's okay, you're safe."

Nandini reached her hand out from under her dome, and Cahya took it, staring up at her own glowing blue dome. Nethos and Theo lay in the pods next to them, asleep, their domes glittered with white light still bursting with activity.

"You're both clear," Hathina told them.

"Let's go rest in the other room for a bit," Nandini said, still holding Cahya's hand. "They'll be a few more hours."

"No," Kole interrupted. "You two are headed to ELC Room 3. You'll have another cycle while you wait for Nethos and Theo."

"What? That's too soon; Cahya needs a break," Nandini protested.

"Something spiked at the end of the cycle," Kole explained. "Cahya, did you see anything? Do you remember anything new?"

"I think I might have seen... myself," Cahya admitted. "It was very brief, and it happened so quickly that it could be nothing."

"I knew it," Kole said, turning to Nandini. "The Dohan needs her memories back, or the council is going to strip her of her title." Kole reminded her, "We may finally be getting somewhere; we have no time to waste. This is our final push. You've got 15 minutes to catch your breath."

"It's okay," Cahya said. "I want to go again." She didn't want to get anyone's hopes up, but she knew she had to get back in there.

When Cahya rose from the pod, she felt dizzy and very nauseous. She steadied herself by placing a hand on Nandini's shoulder.

"You okay?" Nandini asked.

"Yeah, fine." She took a deep breath. "Let's get to Room 3."

This cycle was a quick one. Cahya and Nandini were friends who died as teens in a car accident after a party they'd been at together. The cycle only lasted a little under two hours.

Cahya didn't see the figure when leaving the tunnel this time; a pang of disappointment hit her when she awoke.

Nethos and Theo hadn't yet finished their first cycle. Cahya tried to hide it as best she could, but she felt awful. She couldn't think clearly; she was weak, and that dizzy feeling still swarmed around in her head.

"Again," Cahya said.

"Nethos and Theo will be done in an hour," Kole told her.

"Great, we have time for a quick one," Cahya insisted.

Nandini shot Cahya a worried glance, but Cahya forced a smile. "I'm fine," she lied.

Nandini was not convinced, but she didn't push.

This cycle was even faster—thirty minutes or so—and Cahya and Nandini were hardly five years old before their lives were taken from them—famine.

Cahya passed through the bright tunnel, and this time a figure appeared in the light, but it didn't reveal itself before Cahya woke up.

When she came to, Theo and Nethos were waiting.

"Cahya, you look awful," Nethos remarked. His words were stated as an observation, not out of concern.

"I'm fine," Cahya insisted, but she was not fine. She had a hard time catching her breath. The room was blurry too, so when she responded to Nethos, she didn't try to make eye contact since she wasn't sure which blurry figure was him.

"I think it's time for dinner," Nandini announced, shooting Kole a worried look.

"Yes," Kole agreed. "Take an hour. We'll resume afterward."

"Kole, you can't be serious," Nandini replied, her voice stern.

"Dead serious," Kole confirmed.

"You have to see that this isn't going well. Cahya can barely stand on her own." Nandini gestured toward Cahya, who was pulling herself out of her pod without much success.

"Pushing Cahya through these cycles may be exactly what she needs to break through whatever's blocking her memories," Kole insisted. "This reaction could just mean that we're close."

"I want to keep going, Nandini," Cahya told her, shooting Kole a look. "You don't have to worry about me; I'm fine. In fact, let's order our dinner to the classroom; that way, we can get a jump on the next cycle as quickly as possible."

Nandini was clearly not convinced. "Cahya, this could really be hurting you."

Nandini shot Cahya a pleading look, but Cahya's determination was unwavering.

"Dinner is on the way!" Nethos announced. He had been ordering for the group while Nandini, Kole, and Cahya sat debating. "Can't wait," he continued. "I'm starving."

"Nethos, you're an idiot!" Nandini shouted, and she stormed out of the room.

They wasted no time after dinner. Cahya had barely eaten for fear that she might be sick, but she did her best to act normal. Nandini seemed to have calmed down over dinner, and Cahya didn't want to set her off by acting the way she felt.

Their next cycle was just over seven hours long and would last until the wee hours of the morning. It was a tough one, emotionally, with lots of abuse and loss.

When Cahya woke from the cycle, she rolled over and started to vomit.

"Whoa, whoa, whoa!" Kole shouted as he rushed to Cahya's side. He lifted the dome and pulled Cahya's hair back from her face.

"I haven't cleared her yet," Hathina told him.

"Obviously," Kole said.

It was late. Cahya was exhausted, and she knew she wouldn't be able to get out of the pod. She looked to her right and saw that Nandini was already gone, and she immediately felt relieved. She knew Nandini would lose it if she saw Cahya vomiting.

To her left, Theo was still asleep, his dome still glowing white with activity. Nethos' pod sat empty.

"We're done for tonight," Kole told her. "I'd like you to stay at the medical center for the next few hours, for monitoring."

"I'm not sure I can get there on my own," Cahya admitted, her voice weak.

"I know; I'll get you transport." Kole nodded to Hathina, who nodded back and pressed a few buttons on the screen in front of her.

Cahya fell asleep the moment she lay in bed at the medical center. Kole wanted to run scans but assured her they could all be done while she was sleeping, so she wasted no time.

Still, it felt like she'd barely closed her eyes before Kole was gently coaxing her awake again.

"Morning," Kole said when her eyes had opened. "We need to talk."

Cahya sat up; she still wasn't feeling great, and she was tired, but she felt much better than last night.

"I pushed you too hard yesterday, and I'm sorry. It was wrong; I was just so sure that we were close."

"It's okay, Kole," Cahya assured him. She'd pushed as much as he had, maybe more.

"Tell me, have any of your memories returned?" Kole asked her, though his tone was doubtful.

Cahya tried to think. Was there anything she could remember about Nirvana from before her cycle as Johnny? Could she remember Ash, Nandini, or Nethos? Any places she hadn't recently been to? Anything?

She thought hard, but there was nothing. Nothing new. She shook her head.

Kole exhaled a long, slow breath. "I thought so," he admitted. "We ran scans all night. I've looked at this from every angle, Cahya, and no matter how much I hate to admit it, your body is not reacting well to the cycles.

"You've done hundreds of these; you should be able to pull off several rounds of cycles without breaking a sweat. But that's not what's happening. It's like your body is rejecting the program.

"If we keep going, well, I'm not sure what will happen, but it's not good. That much I'm sure about."

Cahya threw her legs over the side of the bed and got up slowly. "I'm fine," she insisted.

"You're tough," he corrected, "and stubborn. But that's not the same as fine. Your scans tell a different story."

"What changed?" Cahya asked. She didn't understand how she could have been through so many sessions in the past but struggled with even the simplest insect cycles now.

"From what I can tell, you've lost all of your conditioning. Your body is starting from scratch. Whatever caused you to lose your memories also caused you to lose your capacity to handle this training."

"So let's do some insect cycles, then. They were tough but I can manage. Let's build up my tolerance," Cahya offered.

"People spend years conditioning their minds and bodies for human cycles, Cahya. It takes a lot of time—time that we don't have. I have to report to the council in two days. They're expecting good news—any sign of progress. But this really isn't looking good. I can't see the council standing behind a Dohan who has to start conditioning from scratch."

"I saw... myself, Kole. That has to mean something. We're close; I can feel it. We can't stop now."

Kole studied her, "I know. But did you see yourself again? After the first time?"

Cahya shook her head.

"We touched on something during that first cycle, but I don't know why. There may have been a trigger, or it could have been a fluke; who knows? At any rate, we can't keep putting you in there while we try to figure it out. The risk is too high. If we push too hard, it could kill you."

Cahya thought for a moment; she didn't have an answer. She hated this. Finally, she had no choice but to concede. "Okay, so no cycles then. There's got to be other ways we can keep working before your report. I've heard shock therapy can be effective." She forced a smile, thinking of Ash.

Kole sighed at this; his face was troubled. "I'm not giving up, Cahya, but I need some space to think. I think it would be good for you to rest today—try another familiarization activity, something low-key.

"Nandini had some ideas. I'm going to let her tag in for today. We'll talk tonight."

"Okay," Cahya agreed. She was too tired to argue. She didn't know enough about this stuff to make much of a compelling argument anyway.

CHAPTER 12

BEACH DAY

"We're taking you to the beach!" Nandini seemed genuinely excited about the excursion she had planned. "Then I have a special surprise for you," she teased.

Cahya smiled. She had told Kole that she would go along with this, but it felt like a waste of time.

Theo was joining Cahya and Nandini on this adventure, and his silvery-white curly hair was tied back into a high bun on his head.

"Yeah," he agreed. "We all need a break from thinking about the Cycles today. Besides, I've heard Triton Beach is amazing. I've always wanted to see it."

The three made their way down the white path toward the transportation hub. As they approached, a train pulled out of the station, bound for the center of the city.

"Where's the beach?" Cahya asked. "I didn't see one in any of the footage of the city."

"Nope! It's about an hour outside of Deshka. We'll have to take a car," Theo told her.

"Oooh! Can I drive?" Cahya asked.

"Whoa... Right, you've only done really old cycles, huh?" Nandini laughed. "Cars drive themselves here."

She smiled at Cahya as they approached the transportation center. Cahya followed Nandini toward a section of the building where several white cars with domed glass roofs lined the wall. The vehicles had no obvious front or back—they looked the same from both directions.

Nandini walked up to the first car in the line and pressed her hand to the door. A blue circle lit up, and the door popped open.

Theo placed his hand on the door behind Nandini's, activating a glowing blue circle before it unlatched with a soft pop. The panels swung outward like French double doors, forming a wide entrance that allowed them both to climb in together.

Cahya circled around to the opposite side of the car and did the same. Her door released with a quiet click, and she slipped into the seat beside Nandini

Inside the car were two rows of seats that turned inward to face one another. Cahya and Nandini sat side by side, facing Theo, who sat across from them.

The seats were made of a soft, strong silver material. They were very comfortable.

"Good morning, Nandini," came Myat's voice from inside the car. "Please confirm your destination."

A translucent screen appeared in front of Nandini, showing a map with a route drawn from the transportation center to the beach. A blue light pulsed next to the map, with the word *ACCEPT* flashing above it.

"Woah!" Theo shouted. Nandini and Cahya inclined their heads to look at him and see what was the matter. Theo broke his gaze away from the floating screen and met Nandini's eyes.

"Sorry," he exclaimed a little breathlessly. "I've seen these a few times since I've been here but not up close! We've pretty much done away with touch screens on Octavia," he explained, looking back at the floating screen. "The elders hate it," he chuckled at the thought.

"We really only use telepathic commands or voice prompts. This is old tech, but I get the appeal; it's so... tactile." He stretched his hand out toward the screen and then looked at Nandini again. "May I?"

"Be my guest," Nandini chuckled.

Theo pressed his finger to the glowing *ACCEPT* button, and the map disappeared.

"Thank you," Myat's voice said once again. "Please secure yourselves, and we will begin our trip to Triton Beach."

"Cool," Theo said, a huge, goofy smile stretching across his face.

Nandini smiled back and shook her head. She tilted her head toward Cahya, her smile widening. "To the beach!"

The next moment, they were off. Cahya felt uneasy since, to her, the car appeared to be driving backward.

Cahya craned her neck, looking out the window behind her so that she could see what was happening. The car pulled ahead and a large, vehicle-sized door opened in the wall. They pulled through the door and out into the open air.

A path paved with gleaming gray tiles stretched ahead of them. To their left, a second, identical route ran parallel, separated by a narrow strip of grass.

As they followed the curve, another white vehicle passed on the parallel lane, heading in the opposite direction. It glided toward the transportation center, where an opening appeared to allow it inside.

After a few minutes, Cahya was able to let go of the anxious feeling that she was moving backward and settled into the drive.

The car drove very smoothly, and Cahya found her attention drawn to the stunning scenery that suddenly surrounded them.

"Are those bumble trees?" Cahya asked, pointing to the forest of tall trees. They stretched a hundred feet into the air and formed a canopy that scattered shimmering, speckled light across the grassy forest floor.

"Yes, they are!" Nandini replied. "The one in your backyard might be that tall one day."

The road followed a brilliant blue river, beyond which rolling green hills filled the view from every vantage point. Further on were enormous, snow-capped mountains that stood tall and clear in the bright blue sky.

Their journey carried them away from the mountains and into a vast forest. Towering trees stretched hundreds of feet into the sky, their trunks wide enough to dwarf entire homes. They stood like sentinels, silently watching over the landscape—perhaps the entire planet.

After passing through the towering forest, a mountain loomed ahead, its slopes thick with needle-leaved evergreens that crowded the winding road as it snaked upwards. Eventually, the dense woodland gave way to a sprawling clearing at the top of the mountain.

The vehicle pulled into a small drop-off area and came to a stop. Myat's voice once again rang through the car, "We have arrived, Nandini. Have a wonderful day."

"We're here!" Nandini squealed. All the doors opened at once, and the three made their way out of the car.

"Please stand clear of the doors," came Myat's voice from inside the vehicle before the doors closed. The car began driving backward, making its way toward the city.

Cahya watched the car pull away and drive into the thickset trees, out of view. She turned around to take in the scene in front of her. She couldn't believe what she was seeing. This wasn't like any beach she had ever been to.

A pathway led from where they had been dropped off and wound down through sandy white banks, which led to several large pools of water tucked into the side of a mountain. Some of the pools steamed with heat, while others sat still, glimmering in the sunlight. Waterfalls fell from rocky cliffs into sparkling pools below. Other pools were connected to one another through gently winding streams.

The mountain was alive with the sounds of splashing, bubbling, and rumbling as the water moved about. It was strangely relaxing.

"What kind of beach is this?" Cahya asked as they made their way down the winding path toward the closest pool of water.

"This is a mountain beach. It's a combination of natural pools and hot springs mixed with some man-made elements. Isn't it great!?" Nandini squealed as she ran down the path.

An older couple sat in one of the steaming hot spring pools as they walked by.

"Let's head to one of the waterfall pools first!" Nandini insisted.

"Lead the way," Cahya smiled.

The three of them settled into one of the steaming pools midway down the mountain. The pool had a small waterfall that flowed gently along one edge. The view was spectacular! From where they sat, they could see the shimmering ocean stretching out beyond the sand and trees at the base of the mountain. Cahya settled in, closing her eyes, feeling surprisingly grateful that her friends had insisted on this little trip.

"I'm worried about you, Cahya," Nandini said, breaking the silence.

Cahya opened her eyes and saw the concern on Nandini's face.

"I'm okay, Nandini," she assured her.

"Yeah! Cahya's tough. She's got this. They don't just make anyone a Dohan, you know. She was chosen because she can handle this sort of pressure."

"*This* isn't the sort of pressure they had in mind," Nandini snapped.

"Sorry, Nandini, I only meant—"

"It's okay, Theo. You're right," Cahya reassured him. "And honestly, Nandini, I appreciate the concern. But I really am okay."

She looked up at Nandini, their eyes meeting and holding for a long moment. There was something more in Nandini's gaze—warmth and longing.

Cahya felt it too, her own eyes reflecting the same intensity. Nandini's hand found her arm, giving it a gentle squeeze. Slowly, they leaned toward each other, caught in a quiet, unspoken connection.

"Okay, well, I'm going to run to grab a glass of water. Do you guys want anything?" Theo asked.

Cahya pulled back; she had completely forgotten that Theo was there. So much for vigilance.

Cahya shook her head, avoiding eye contact with Nandini.

"We're okay, thanks, Theo," Nandini told him. Theo pulled himself out of the pool and the sunlight sparkled across his pale skin. He made his way back up the main path toward the canteen.

It suddenly dawned on Cahya that Nandini had never mentioned having a partner. Nethos had said that everyone got a napili... wouldn't that mean that Nandini had one too? Or had she sacrificed that sort of partnership when she decided to become Cahya's companion?

"Can I ask you something," Cahya said, finally. She had to know.

"Of course," Nandini replied.

"Do you have a napili?"

"I do," Nandini smiled, "His name's Alori."

"Really? How come I haven't met him?"

"Well you have, you know, before—"

"Right. Before the accident," Cahya confirmed, half-smiling. "I know you've done nearly as many cycles as I have. Didn't your napili want to join you for some of them?"

"He did. For a while. We did several years of cycles after I turned 25, but then I was selected as Companion to the Dohan. It's been almost two years since we've done a cycle together. We're still close, just... on different paths. He's an agricultural researcher in Almatar now."

"Doesn't that make things... complicated? Relationship-wise."

"Not really. Napili pairings are determined by genetic compatibility, ensuring healthy, stable offspring. The partnerships are very important for Nirvana, of course, but they're not always... romantic. While most pairings blossom into deeply intimate relationships, some napili simply maintain profound friendships. Each pair finds their own path. When it's time for children, Alori and I will figure it out. For now, he's free to explore what life brings him, and I—"

"You're busy. With me." Cahya allowed this knowledge to sit with her for a moment. Nandini had made so many sacrifices to work with Cahya, to be her companion. Maybe it was time to let her in; time to share what she had uncovered so far. She could tell her about the device she had been given at the panigêm match, about her suspicions around the Dakaï, and about her accident. Maybe Nandini knew something that could help her.

"Cahya, this is serious," Nandini said finally, breaking the silence, her eyes wide with fear. "I think someone might be out to get you," Nandini whispered, leaning in close and looking around to make sure no one had heard.

"I know," Cahya confessed. It felt good to have someone she felt she could trust. "But I think that there are also people who are out to help me. I just don't know who's who."

"I know," Nandini admitted. "We should just run away, Cahya. We should go live in a house in the woods. We could make a life out there, away from all of this. You could be safe." Nandini's voice had a pleading tone.

Cahya considered it. There was something about that idea that was so tempting. Nethos had told her about people who lived far from the cities, high in the mountains—the Montori, some called them. They chose a simple life, beyond the reach of the city's tech and scanners, rarely venturing into Deshka or anywhere the advanced technology held sway. Entire enclaves existed out there, quietly self-sufficient, untouched by the demands of modern Nirvana. Johnny would have loved that, Cahya knew.

The thought caught her off guard, and she thought about Johnny as though he were a different person, as though he wasn't her. Something was shifting, she realized. She wasn't the Cahya everyone remembered, but she felt that she had grown beyond who she had been when she was just Johnny.

This shift meant that she knew she couldn't take off to the mountains to join the Montori. There was more to this mystery; she knew there was something very big at stake, even if she wasn't sure what it was. There were pieces of the puzzle she still needed to solve. She had a role to play in all of this, whatever this was, and she was surprised to realize that she wanted to figure it out.

She smiled at Nandini, grateful for her concern and for her willingness to walk away from all of this—her whole life on Nirvana—for Cahya. To protect her. "We can't leave yet," she told her. "There's more to this, and I need to figure it out."

Theo returned with a tray filled with fresh fruit and nuts.

"I have enough to share," he announced, setting the tray on the edge of the rock before jumping back into the pool.

"Thanks, Theo," Cahya smiled, giving Nandini an apologetic look. This would have to be the end of their conversation for now; she wasn't sure how much she should say in front of Theo.

The drive back to Deshka was beautiful. The sun had begun to set, and the tops of the trees were highlighted with a pink glow. The three rode in silence, each of them watching the scenery as it passed by outside the window. Cahya's mind wandered to her moment with Nandini. She had nearly leaned in to kiss her. It felt so natural.

The towering bumble trees just outside the city came into view, while the grass outside zipped by in a hypnotic wave. As the car slowed near the city's edge, the waving grass moved past more gently. Something felt off. Ahead, the grass shifted from upright and swaying to bent and flattened. Cahya sat up, her eyes narrowing as they neared the trampled section, catching a glimpse of a small opening in the forest's edge as they passed.

Watch for the gaps, came the Doyen's voice in Cahya's head. Cahya chuckled quietly to herself.

"What's so funny?" Nandini asked with a playful, inquisitive look on her face.

"Hmm? Oh, nothing," Cahya told her, and though she did think it was silly to think twice about some bent grass, she couldn't help but feel drawn to it. Something in her said that she needed to take a closer look. She vowed to do so... someday.

"All right, one more surprise," Nandini announced as they arrived at the transportation hub and hopped out of the car.

"Aren't you tired?" Theo asked.

"A little," Nandini admitted, "but this is important."

"All right, well, I'll leave you two to whatever this important business is," Theo said, bowing gently. "I'm going to grab some dinner and head home. Thanks for the great day." He smiled and was off.

"All right, what's the surprise?" Cahya asked, genuinely intrigued.

"Come with me."

The two left the transportation hub and turned, heading away from the center of town. Nandini had a fast pace, and Cahya had to work to keep up. They didn't speak; Nandini was on a mission. She slowed only after they turned a bend and a large building came into view.

The building looked older than some of the buildings in Deshka, though it was still well-maintained. It was a long, rectangular structure with rounded edges and large windows across the front.

The gardens lining the pathway to the building were beautiful and contained some flowers Cahya hadn't seen around Deshka. Nandini must have noticed Cahya's curious gaze, because she clarified, "Most of these flowers are from Octavia. We use them to line the path to the Transfer Station as a sign of friendship when the ònakai come to visit."

The Transfer Station. Okay... Cahya wasn't sure what Nandini was getting at, but she followed her up the pathway to the main door.

When they arrived, Nandini took Cahya's hand, blushing as she did, and pressed it to the door; it slid up and opened in response.

"Ha! Still works!" Nandini exclaimed. "Seems that they haven't changed your clearance."

"My clearance?" Cahya asked.

"Yeah, you spent a lot of time here as a kid. Both of your parents worked here a lot, so you had access to go in and out as you needed. I wasn't sure if they'd updated your file after your parents died, but I guess not."

Nandini's eyes widened. "Oh wow, that's the first time I've mentioned your parents. Has anyone else talked to you about them?"

"Nope," Cahya told her nonchalantly. "But I hear they died."

Nandini looked mortified. "I'm so sorry; I don't know how I could be so insensitive. Sometimes I think I should just talk less."

"It's not insensitive, Nandini; just add it to the list of things that people assume I should know about. Besides, I can't be too upset about dead parents I didn't know, right?"

"I guess," Nandini admitted.

Cahya was intrigued by this new information and she wondered why it hadn't come up before. Normal people had parents who were involved in their lives but Cahya had never stopped to ask about hers. Though, she supposed it wasn't all that odd. Johnny was estranged from his parents so there was no intrinsic instinct to 'go to mom and dad'. Besides, the last few days had been a whirlwind. She'd hardly had time to think about anything—let alone relatives.

Upon entering the building, they found themselves in a small lobby stretching the length of the front windows. Beyond it, a wide doorway opened into the main hall. Just inside, a console stood near the entrance, while a large platform dominated the center of the room. Overhead, a massive circular skylight bathed the space in natural light.

"What is this place?" Cahya asked.

"The Transfer Station is the link between Nirvana and Octavia. Dignitaries and students come through here. Theo would have—"

"Wait! Say that again," Cahya demanded.

"Dignitaries and—"

"No! Before that."

"The Transfer Station is the link between Nirvana and Octavia?" Nandini asked.

"Yes! The link." Cahya suddenly remembered the recording—the speaker was saying something about a link... What had they said? Was this it? Was the Transfer Station the link they were talking about?

Cahya studied the space; there wasn't too much to see. It was fairly industrial. There were exposed beams and panels that presumably held all the techy stuff that Cahya wouldn't understand.

"Is this it?" Cahya asked. "Is this the whole building?"

"Well, no. There are a few levels below us."

"Show me," Cahya demanded.

Nandini cocked her head, unsure of what Cahya was looking for, but she obliged, taking Cahya back out to the lobby space and directing her to the end of a long hallway.

Cahya walked over and found a small glowing spot on the wall. She held her hand to it, and a door slid open. Inside, it was dark, but a black metal stairway led down to a space below the main level.

"I'll just be a second," she told Nandini.

Cahya followed the stairs down to a big empty room. There wasn't much to look at here either; more beams, pipes, and electrical systems, and it was darker down here.

Cahya scanned the room and noticed that one of the wall panels was slightly ajar, creating a strange opening along one side. A gap! She moved toward it. She didn't know why, but something inside of her was guiding her toward this space.

She approached the panel and studied it a moment before reaching down and pulling it free from the wall.

There was a cavity just beyond the opening, larger than Cahya would have expected, but it was dark, so she couldn't quite see just how big it was.

She checked behind her. Nandini had waited upstairs; she was alone. Carefully, she stepped in through the opening and squinted, waiting for her eyes to adjust. She took another step, and her foot made a crunching sound. No, not her foot—something under her foot. She reached down to pick up the object; it was small and round, but she couldn't tell what it was.

She held it close to the panel entrance where light filtered in from upstairs. It was a small metal button—a cufflink—which just so happened to match the missing cufflink from her tunic sleeve.

There was something else in here: a table and a chair.

She took a few paces, and she was standing in front of the table. The small amount of light coming through the opening in the panel revealed to her that there were papers scattered across the surface. Someone had worked in this space. There must be a light somewhere.

She searched the desk and felt around on the walls; she couldn't find anything.

"Myat," she whispered.

Myat whispered back, "Yes, Cahya?"

"Lights, please," she directed softly.

Immediately, a soft glow began to grow from a light over the panel entrance. Cahya turned to see where the light was coming from, she squinted allowing her eyes to adjust. When she turned back to look at the table, she saw it.

CHAPTER 13
PLANT CYCLES

The wall above the desk was covered in paper. There were notes, tons of photos, printed articles, drawings, and schematics.

What was this place?

Then the realization hit her like a ton of bricks: Cahya had been investigating something before she lost her memories. The investigator in her, Johnny, became very excited. She did love a good mystery.

She stepped closer to the wall, studying each piece of paper in turn. A photo of a man and a woman in silver robes standing by the console of the Transfer Station. That photo was taken here, right above where she was standing.

The same couple appeared in another photo outside a large mountain full of windows. A young girl stood with them; she looked to be ten or eleven.

That's me, Cahya realized. The young girl looked just like her. So those people—they must be my parents. She looked more closely at the photo of the couple now; their eyes were kind, and they looked genuinely happy.

"I bet you were great parents," Cahya whispered to the photo. She stepped back, catching herself. Vigilance.

The floor plans of the Transfer Station were also stuck to the wall. The building had three levels; there was another below her. There didn't appear to be anything out of the ordinary with those.

She moved on to an article, printed from a digital source. Cahya realized that there were no electronics in this space; no technology at all. She suspected that was intentional.

She leaned closer to the article and read the heading: *Deshka Couple Perishes in Transfer Station Accident.* The article went on to say that Laurel and Trebolt Lighthold were working late, updating critical systems, when a power surge caused an explosion.

A photo of the damaged Transfer Station was included in the article.

Another photo showed a large mirrored glass column with trees around it. Judging by the height of the trees, Cahya guessed the tower had to be eighty to a hundred feet tall. The caption below the image read: *T'Dava Tower; Octavian Mobile Citadel.*

"Huh," Cahya mumbled.

On the floor, next to the desk, was a box. Cahya reached down and lifted the box, placing it on the surface of the desk. Inside, she found more photos of her parents, and she recognized a few of the locations, like a few buildings around Deshka and Triton Beach.

Most of the photos Cahya didn't recognize, but she hadn't been to very many places on Nirvana, so that was understandable. But one image caught her attention. An image of Laurel and Trebolt standing next to a large glass tower. Cahya looked back at the wall—the T'Dava—it was the same tower. But that isn't what drew Cahya into the photo.

In the sky, three moons were clearly visible, but just behind the tower, peeking out ever so slightly, was a fourth moon. *Nirvana doesn't have four moons,* Cahya thought. *Nirvana only has three moons. Octavia has four moons.*

As far as Cahya knew, humans didn't often go to Octavia. Ònakai visited Nirvana from time to time, but humans rarely left their planet. She didn't know why, but it hadn't struck her as odd until this moment. It was even more odd now that there was a photo of Cahya's parents on Octavia.

Cahya found a small container of magnets on the desk; she took one and stuck the photo to the wall, next to the photo of the T'Dava.

"Cahya?"

Nandini's voice startled her, and she spun around, knocking the box off the desk. Papers, books, and photos plastered the floor of the small room.

Nandini stepped into the space, her eyes fixed on the wall above the desk. "You were taking a really long time, so I... What is this place?"

"I think Cahya—me—I mean, I..." Cahya took a breath so that she could start over. "I think I was investigating something before the accident. Something to do with my parents."

Nandini twisted her face. "But why?" she asked, her eyes continuing to scan the room. "You'd accepted that your parents' death was an accident," her eyes stopped on the article right above the desk, "hadn't you?"

"You didn't know about this place, then?" Cahya asked, studying Nandini's face. Nandini looked up from the paper and scanned the room again.

"No," she said, her expression sad. "I guess you didn't trust me enough to tell me."

"Why would I be looking into my parents' death?" Cahya asked.

"You always suspected that there was something going on beyond the official story. For years, you were obsessed with figuring out what it was. But eventually, you accepted the evidence. You moved on," Nandini replied.

She picked up a photo from the floor, and a smile crossed her face. "I remember this," she laughed. "I took this photo. This was just outside of Almatar, the Balaski Caves."

She handed Cahya the photo. Cahya and her mother stood with arms stretched out, smiling, next to a huge cave opening. Cahya looked older in this photo, maybe fourteen or fifteen.

"This was the summer that your parents..." Nandini started but caught herself, seemingly unwilling to discuss something so sad.

"The summer they died," Cahya confirmed. Nandini nodded.

"Explosion caused by an electrical surge," Cahya continued.

"That's the official story, yes," Nandini told her, scanning the wall and running a finger along the sheet of paper containing the article announcing the accident.

"You never accepted it. Eventually, people got tired of listening—they'd all moved on, and they wanted you to move on too."

"I guess I'm guilty of that too," Nandini admitted. "I hated seeing you sad. I wanted you to move on so that you could live a happy life, you know? I thought that dwelling on it was just holding you back.

"I guess that's why you didn't tell me. You must have known that I'd try to convince you to let it go."

Nandini turned and picked up a book from the floor. It was bound with a flexible metallic cover. The pages inside were thick—not quite paper, not quite plastic—something in between. Nandini flipped through the pages and handed the book to Cahya.

On the cover were the words: *Octavian Governance.* Inside, Cahya found a short inscription etched into the cover; it read:

"Dearest Laurel, may the wisdom herein serve to guide Nirvana through her next great evolution. Yours, Chellesëgust."

"Who is Chellesëgust?" Cahya asked.

"I have no idea, but it's definitely ònakai," Nandini confirmed.

"Were my parents working with the ònakai?" Cahya asked.

"They worked at the Transfer Station—that's all I knew about their work. I suppose they may have been; they had fairly direct access," Nandini said, gesturing upward, suggesting the transfer room above.

"Do you think I knew? Before the accident, I mean?"

"You never said anything, but I suppose that doesn't mean you didn't know," Nandini admitted, gesturing to the wall above the

174

desk. "I didn't realize I was being such a terrible friend. I can't believe you didn't trust me." Nandini stifled a sob.

Cahya took her by the shoulders and said, "I can't tell you why I kept this from you, but I suspect that you were not a terrible friend." Nandini's eyes met Cahya's, tears welling up. "Maybe I was trying to protect you."

Nandini's gaze intensified. The two stared at each other for a long moment, an energy growing between them. Nandini leaned in and pressed her lips against Cahya's.

Cahya stood frozen for a moment, then relaxed and wrapped her arms around Nandini. They held each other like this, kissing and pulling each other closer.

Nandini suddenly pulled back. "I'm so sorry," she exclaimed, touching her fingers to her lips.

Cahya's lips were pulsing, and her face was flushed.

"Sorry?" Cahya asked, confused. "Why?"

"Because you're not you—not really, not wholly. You wouldn't have wanted me to do that if you had all your memories. We're friends," Nandini explained. "Just friends." She turned and lifted herself through the opening and out of the secret room. Cahya heard her footsteps as she ran up the metal staircase.

Cahya didn't chase after her; she sat in the chair by the desk and tried to catch her breath.

Vigilance, she reminded herself. Nandini was right. Cahya didn't know everything; she didn't have the history, the memories; she didn't know if this was something she would have wanted.

What she did know was that she had been committed to solving something very big.

In that moment, she also realized that she didn't have the memories she needed to finish putting the pieces of this puzzle together. She stared at the wall ahead of her for a long moment. There was more to this—way more—and she would need all of her memories if she was going to figure it out.

She needed to see Kole.

"Plants!" Cahya announced, barging into the ELC lab where Kole sat, focused on the screen in front of him. He jumped when Cahya entered.

"Excuse me?" he asked, turning to look at her.

"Plants," she repeated. "You said the plant cycles would barely impact me; I can do plant cycles. Over and over and over until my memory comes back."

"Cahya," Kole interrupted, shaking his head gravely, "the plant cycles barely affect you because they operate on an entirely different level than human cycles. Our consciousness doesn't resonate with plant consciousness—if you can even call it that. The ELC program was designed to replicate human experiences so that we can see, feel, and live lives that feel as tangible and real as this one. We know plants have a form of awareness and can communicate in their own way, and we've developed a program that we believe closely mirrors a plant's perception of the world. But the truth is, we can't be entirely sure."

He paused, his gaze drifting to the ceiling as he searched for the right words. "Plants are... different. I don't think we could have even constructed these cycles without the guidance of the ònakai. And if I'm being completely honest with you, Cahya, I don't fully understand them myself. I really don't see how it could be of much help."

"But, Kole, it's *something!*" Cahya pleaded, snapping him back into the present conversation.

Kole shook himself from his thoughts and trained his eyes on Cahya. "It won't make a difference," he said. His tone was sad now, defeated. "I have to report to the council tomorrow. They're going to remove you as Dohan."

"I don't care about being Dohan!" Cahya exclaimed. She lowered her tone, seeing the shock on Kole's face. "This is bigger than that."

"Bigger than training the next leader of the entire planet?" Kole asked, raising his brow suspiciously.

"Believe it or not, yes," Cahya insisted. "There's something going on here. I knew what it was before the accident, or maybe I was getting close to figuring it out; I'm not sure. But whatever this is, I've forgotten about it right along with everything else."

"There's still no guarantee," Kole warned.

"I know. The chances aren't great. It's already been a week—I may have missed my window. But I saw myself last night, Kole. My memories were trying to push through; I know it. The closest I've come to any sort of shift was at the end of a cycle. I have to try if there's any chance that something might click," she told him.

Kole nodded. "Okay, what do you need?"

"Put me on a loop, 24/7 plant cycles—as much as you can set me up for back-to-back," Cahya told him.

"Slow down. I can't do 24/7," Kole told her. "but I can do 12/12. Twelve-hour cycles followed by twelve hours of recovery."

"Great! Can we start now?" Cahya asked eagerly.

Kole looked at the time. "It's late, Cahya, I should have gone home hours ago."

"You don't have to stay. Just get me set up and come back to check on me in the morning."

"I can't leave you here alone. I think Kacha was planning on being here overnight, maybe he wouldn't mind keeping an eye on you.

"Great! Put me in, coach!"

Kole nodded, a look of awe on his face.

"Alright, Cahya Lighthold, strap in," Kole gestured to the pod nearest them. Cahya sat and laid back while Kole made his way to the panel and began to swipe and poke with his fingers.

"Plants are different from other living creatures in that most of them don't 'die' in the traditional sense. Plant life is very interconnected and incredibly resilient. If you cut down a tree and leave its roots in place, it will grow again, and most plants go through these sorts of cycles of contracting and expanding but never really dying.

"Seeds are just an extension of an existing plant consciousness," he explained as he continued to tap at various spots on his screen. "Its consciousness fades slightly when it falls from its parent, but as it grows, its roots connect back into the overall consciousness at full strength.

"As such, there's no natural ending to the cycle—or a natural beginning, for that matter. I'll set you up for a certain amount of time, and you'll connect to the existing plant consciousness, and when the cycle is over, you'll disconnect."

As Cahya settled into the pod, she realized just how exhausted she felt. If given the chance, she could probably sleep for a week straight, but she couldn't tell Kole that. She needed to press on. She didn't know exactly what she was facing, but whatever it was, it was bigger than her—and she might be the only one who would see it coming.

She watched as Kole made a few more motions on the screen. The countdown clock read *12:00:00*.

"Ready?" he asked her.

"Tree me." She smiled.

Kole pushed the blue button, and everything went black.

✳ ✳ ✳

The darkness deepened, vast and empty, but it was not void. A sense of awareness stirred and began to take form. Slowly, a shape emerged—soft, glowing neon green against the expanse. A leaf, flitting gently in an unseen breeze.

The light of the leaf expanded, illuminating the branch that held it. From that branch, more light erupted—leaves and limbs grew into awareness. The outline of a trunk solidified, glowing brighter as it stretched downward, pulling into roots that branched deep and wide, mirroring the tree's upper canopy. Energy pulsed gently through the full outline of the tree, from its furthest root tip to the highest leaf, vibrant and alive.

The awareness extended further. More trees began to appear, their outlines glowing softly in green. A wide field of grasses formed at the base of the first tree, their faint pulses connected beneath the surface. Flowers dotted the field, their outlines flickering as though lying in quiet anticipation. Everything radiated a subtle yet unified rhythm.

A sudden disturbance broke through the stillness. The image refocused near the base of the large tree, where a new shape glowed into view—amber and blue, contrasting sharply with the plant's green hue. A small animal, its outline softly shimmering, came into focus. It was a squirrel, frozen mid-movement, paws working around its mouth as it ate. Energetic blue flecks danced around and within its form, zipping chaotically, a sign of heightened awareness.

The scene shifted outward again. The network of interconnected life expanded into view—everything a tapestry of light and energy. Ants scurried along a glowing anthill, their amber outlines flickering in rapid bursts. Mice darted through the tall grass, tiny pulses of light moving quickly across the ground. Along a distant hill, a fox's outline ducked into a burrow. The glowing world was alive, vibrant with motion and awareness.

The focus narrowed once more on a tiny caterpillar inching along the edge of a flower. It chewed methodically at a leaf—chomp, chomp, chomp. The flower's energy flared, sending out a pulse.

Danger, the pulse declared—not as a word, but as a distinct shift in energy, a resonating message recognized instinctively. The warning spread outward, rippling across the network of nearby flowers. *Danger.* The plants reacted, releasing a slow mist of chemicals into the air, coating their leaves in protection.

The caterpillar took another bite—*chomp, chomp*—and then froze. Its outline glowed brighter for a moment before it recoiled. The taste had changed. Displeased, its amber form pulsed irritably as

179

it climbed down the stem and retreated, leaving the green energy of the flower calm once more.

$$* * *$$

Cahya awoke to a quiet room with the soft shuffling of feet moving about. The morning sunlight filtered in through the curved windows nearby.

"Hi, Cahya. How are you feeling?" Kole was standing next to her chair instead of being by the hanging screen like he normally was.

Cahya let out a yawn and stretched her arms and legs a little. "I feel good," she said, very relaxed. "Did you end the session early?"

"No. In fact, the session ended an hour ago, but you continued to sleep, and you looked so peaceful that I decided not to wake you. Any sense that you might have recovered any memories?" Kole asked hesitantly.

"I don't think so. I feel the same as before, and nothing is striking me as a new memory at the moment." And even though this was true, she wasn't upset. This was the first time she'd come out of a cycle feeling refreshed. She actually felt really good.

"Well, I think this course may have some benefits, and I think we should stick to it for a little bit. It's accessing a part of your brain that isn't normally activated, and this could have a domino effect by activating other portions of your brain," Kole said. It was the most optimistic he'd sounded in a while.

"Well, I feel as though I've just been treated to a spa day, so if you're telling me you think this could help, I'm all for it. Can I get up?" she asked.

"Yes, you're clear to go."

"Thanks, Kole. Same time tonight?"

"You've got it. See you then! Now go get some rest."

"Okay," she replied... but she knew that was a lie. She wasn't the least bit tired; she wouldn't be able to sleep.

Now, she had work to do.

CHAPTER 14
THE COUNCIL OF NIRVANA

"Cahya! Tell me where we're going, please," Ash pleaded, looking up at her friend as they walked side by side down a quiet sidewalk on their way to the center of the city.

"It's a surprise, Ash! You'll see."

It was a beautiful morning. Cahya went straight to breakfast after waking from the plant cycle, and now she had tons of energy and lots of questions that needed answering. If she was going to go on a learning journey today, Ash would be her best partner.

They made their way into the city's hub and turned left, following along the building's curved glass wall. After a few minutes, they approached the Learning Commons, a large white-domed building that had no windows and was partially covered in grass, small bushes, and flowers. It was a beautiful sight to behold. People walked, unhurried, around the parks and communal areas which surrounded the Commons.

As they walked up the pathway which led to the arched entrance of the dome, Ash turned to her friend and asked excitedly, "Are we going to the theater, Cahya?!"

"Yes, we are! You said that you loved hearing about the council and all the things that most kids find super boring. I have a bit of learning to do too, and I thought you might want to join me."

"Yay! I'm so excited, Cahya! I love the theater, but Dad says that it's always booked for students and stuff, and we don't get to go very often."

"Well, it turns out there are some perks to being Dohan. We have the theater for two full hours!"

Cahya held her hand to a stand outside the building; the white glowing light turned blue, and the doors slid open. As they walked into the room, the lights turned on, and they found themselves standing in a huge, empty dome that stretched nearly thirty feet into the air. Around the outside of the dome were eighty large, comfortable-looking white chairs. Ash ran across the center of the dome and plopped herself into one of the soft chairs, sinking in. She looked so tiny, Cahya thought.

Cahya took a seat in one of the chairs next to Ash. "Hello, Myat," Cahya said into the emptiness above her head.

"Good morning, Cahya. What would you like to watch today?" came Myat's voice, booming through the large room.

"Myat, do you have any lessons about the Council of Nirvana?" Cahya asked, winking at Ash, whose smile beamed larger than Cahya had ever seen.

"I do indeed. Would you like to watch *An Introduction to the Council of Nirvana*?" Myat asked.

Ash nodded at Cahya and said, "Yeah! Let's watch it!"

"You crack me up, Ash," Cahya told her. "Somehow I doubt that there's another 7-year-old on all of Nirvana who would be so excited to watch a video about the Council of Nirvana."

Ash laughed. "Nope! I'm the only one. Let's watch it!"

"Okay, Myat, please play *An Introduction to the Council of Nirvana*," Cahya instructed as she laid back and waited for the show to start.

The lights in the presentation arena dimmed, and Myat's voice began to speak.

"Welcome! Today, children, you will learn about the branches of government that help shape our lives."

Ash squealed with glee and Myat continued.

"Our special guest, Doyen Hashen, will tell you a little more about it. Doyen Hashen, the floor is yours."

As Myat said this, an image of the Doyen slowly came into view, floating in the middle of the room above them.

"Thank you, Myat." The Doyen smiled as he spoke in no particular direction. "Hello, children. I'm very excited to speak to you today about the committee that serves to keep us and our planet healthy and strong."

Cahya looked over at Ash, who stared at the Doyen, listening intently. The holographic Doyen continued, "Nirvana is governed by three major branches, representing three very important markers of health in our society. They are Human Health, Planetary Health, and Technological Health. Our home needs good systems and programs in all three categories to ensure that we all live the best lives we can here on Nirvana."

The Doyen's image dissolved, and an image of a man with graying hair, appeared in his place. He wore a shiny blue tunic and smiled as he spoke. "My name is Matildi. I am a council representative for the first branch of governance, which is the Human Health branch."

As he spoke, the images behind him flashed through a series of moving clips. First, young people sat in what appeared to be an outdoor classroom—the children sat in twelve large white chairs that encircled a man who stood at the center and spoke while making large gestures with his arms. The children smiled at him, seemingly very engaged. As this image faded, young adults were shown in a similar scene, though they sat in large white chairs in a round room with a holographic Nirvana in the center.

Next, the scene changed to a group of friends gathered around a dining table talking, eating, and laughing, then to a person sitting and meditating on a grass mound. *A mound identical to the one in the Doyen's backyard,* Cahya thought to herself.

Next, an elderly woman stood in a white room surrounded by a blue swirling light, while a woman in a blue tunic pointed to a hanging glass panel where her shape appeared and lights moved through and around it. After this, we saw a man in a blue tunic sitting across from a young man who was talking to him. The man in the tunic nodded empathetically.

"This branch focuses on everything relating to the health and well-being of individual persons. We look at social health, physical health, mental health, and education. Our main goal is to ensure that people stay well so that they can learn and grow and be the best version of themselves that they can be."

Matildi's image dissolved from the screen, and another person formed in his place. This time, it was a woman wearing a bright magenta tunic. She had soft pink hair falling to just above her jaw, straight-cut bangs, and red-rimmed floating eyeglasses.

"My name is Balti. I am one of the council members representing the Planetary Health branch of governance."

As she spoke, images of Nirvanian forests flickered onto the screen. Some of the forest appeared earth-like and then there were bits which were distinctly Nirvanian—vast groves of bioluminescent flora and translucent shimmering ferns. Ethereal herds of multi-hued grazers moved slowly through a grassy field, and jewel-tone fish splashed about in mountain-side ponds.

Balti continued, "Our goal is to monitor and protect the natural balance of our planet, ensuring that our activities work in harmony with the natural rhythms of Nirvana and that we are always protecting and preserving the animals and plants with whom we share this beautiful home of ours."

Balti's figure began to fade, and a new figure took her place. This time, a man wearing an emerald green tunic, which gleamed and sparkled, appeared. His hair was jet black and tied into a bun at the back of his head. His green eyes looked out at the audience.

Behind him, fields of crops, hydroponic buildings, and restaurants with various forms of garden walls flashed into the background. Then came scenes of water—oceans, ponds, lakes—energy buildings that seemed to be powered by water, buildings that captured sunlight and turned it into energy, and people moving onto and off of trains.

Technology used in the medical centers flashed across the screen next, followed by technology used in the schools, and in the ELC labs.

"My name is Kyun, and I am a council representative from the Technological Health branch of governance. We are always looking for new technologies to help make our lives better. We also have to study the impacts of the technology that we are currently using to make sure that it is safe for the people who use it and for our planet."

"The Technology branch of governance also works with the Health branch and the Planetary branch to account for all of the resources needed in order for people to eat and drink, to move from one place to another, and to have the energy required to power our homes and cities."

As Kyun spoke, Cahya felt a wave of panic wash over her. Her heart raced, and her throat felt dry. She tried to swallow, but she couldn't get her cheeks, her tongue, or her throat to do what she was telling them to do. She inhaled deeply and looked over at Ash, who was still wearing her goofy grin.

Kyun's image dissolved, and the Doyen reappeared in his place.

"These branches of governance work together to ensure that there is harmony and balance in our world. Every human gets what they need in order to live a healthy and productive life, and our planet and its resources are protected and sustained in order to ensure that we can continue living here in peace and harmony for generations to come.

"My job, as Doyen, is to listen and to help guide the head of each branch and the council when I'm needed."

Twelve figures appeared next to the Doyen: four wore blue tunics, four wore magenta red, and four wore emerald green. Myat's voice took over now:

"The council of 12 members—four from each branch of governance—and the Doyen work with many community leaders," behind the council of twelve, a large group of citizens appeared wearing all manner and colors of tunics, waving at the audience in every direction, "to help shape the world we live in. Perhaps one day, you too could join this council and help take care of our world. It's a big responsibility, but everyone has the capacity to help make a difference."

The video ended in a swell of music, and the screen faded to black. Slowly, the lights brightened the space, revealing the white dome and Ash, sitting next to her, who looked like she'd just been on a roller coaster ride.

"Woah!" Ash exclaimed. "That was amazing! Can we watch it again, Cahya? Can we?"

"We have this place for two hours, and that's a ten-minute video. We could watch it a dozen times if you wanted to," Cahya laughed. "But we can also watch something else if you'd like."

"Maybe after," Ash exclaimed, settling back in. "I want to watch that one again first."

Ash stared at the ceiling, waiting patiently for Cahya to give Myat the instruction.

"Hey, Myat, could you please play *An Introduction to the Council of Nirvana*?"

The lights dimmed, and Myat's voice came through: *"Hello, children, I'm very excited to speak to you today..."*

As the video played through once more, it confirmed for Cahya one very important thing: something about Kyun made her very uneasy.

Kole was waiting for her at 6 p.m. sharp when she arrived for her next round of plant cycles.

"How was your day?" he asked. "Did you rest?"

"A little," she lied. In reality, she had spent a few hours with Ash in the morning, learning everything she could about Nirvana and the council. Then she went to the Transfer Station to start putting some of her ideas on paper. She wrote notes and attached them to the walls, working hard to piece together this strange puzzle that was taking shape before her eyes.

"How was your day?" she asked.

"Not bad. I still haven't figured out what might have triggered you in the Vitus cycle. I've been poring over it and going through Johnny's cycle, and I can't figure it out."

"If there's something to find, I'm sure you'll find it," Cahya reassured him.

"Thanks," he smiled. "All set?" he asked, gesturing toward the waiting pod.

Truth be told, she was very tired now, and she was looking forward to settling into a plant cycle.

"I am," she told him.

When Cahya woke from the cycle at 6 a.m., Kole was asleep at the console desk. She didn't want to wake him, but she knew she needed to be cleared before leaving her pod.

"Pssssst... Kole," she whispered. He didn't move.

"Oh, Kole," she said in a sing-song voice. Still no movement. Panic came over her. *Oh no! Was he dead?!*

"Kole!" she shouted firmly this time.

Kole jumped from his seat, confused and trying to get his bearings. He saw Cahya and seemed to remember where he was.

"Right! Sorry, Cahya," he said, tapping some buttons on the console. "All clear," he instructed.

"Late night?" Cahya asked, springing from her pod with tremendous energy.

"Yes. I think I've found something, but I can't quite say what it is yet. I must have fallen asleep while I was trying to figure it out."

"Something promising?" Cahya asked, hopeful.

"Too soon to say," he admitted.

"Look, Cahya, we've had our seven days—we're out of time. I'm so sorry. I really did think that we could figure this out." Kole looked defeated.

"Kole, I think you need to go get some rest. You have a council meeting tonight."

"And what do I tell them?" he asked.

"You tell them the truth. We've got nothing. Nada, Zilch. We did our best, but we couldn't make it work with the timeline they gave us—a fair timeline, don't get me wrong—but we're out of time now."

"They'll strip you of your title," Kole reminded her.

Cahya nodded. "I know. Maybe it's for the best."

Kole shook his head. "I don't think that's true. But you're right. I do need to get some rest. You should too," he told her.

"I will," she smiled.

Cahya didn't rest, though; she split her day between the learning commons and the Transfer Station. Things were finally starting to come together.

CHAPTER 15
CATITHIA

"Then it is decided," Balti announced, a grim expression on her face, looking over the red rim of her glasses at the green table in front of her. "Cahya will step down as Dohan. We'll notify the Doyen immediately so that he can begin planning for his new successor."

Kole nodded at the group. "Thank you for your consideration," he said, "and for giving me some time to work with Cahya before you made the decision."

Kyun replied, "Yes, well, it all proved to be less than fruitful, didn't it? At least now we can move on and start making plans for the new Dohan."

"Cahya would like to continue working through some plant cycles, if the council has no objection," Kole told them.

The council members looked around at one another. Balti spoke up, "That would be fine, Kole. We can give Cahya some time before she has to choose a new vocation. It sounds as though she will not be able to act as a companion to the new Dohan, based on her poor reactions to the human cycles."

"I'm afraid that's true," Kole confirmed.

"Very well," Balti said.

***

Cahya spent the next couple of weeks in plant cycles every night. It had become a sort of escape for her—an escape from the guilt she felt. She wondered what would happen if she did get her memories back? What was 'old Cahya' coming back to? She'd lost the title of Dohan; she'd lost all of her friends; and all her body could manage was a series of plant cycles that could hardly be called cycles at all. Whatever life Cahya had had before the accident, it was all gone now.

By the beginning of the third week, Cahya's guilt was getting the best of her. Maybe she hadn't tried hard enough in that first week. She could have done more; she could have seen more—if she'd been more committed, maybe she'd have her memories back already.

At that point, Cahya had convinced Kole to let her try an animal cycle, even though Kole insisted that her biomarkers indicated that nothing had changed. That turned out to be a disaster—Cahya had to be pulled out of the cycle, and after throwing up all over the pod, she spent three days recovering at the medical center.

She'd also begun to really miss her friends.

Nethos was the only one who didn't seem to be upset with her; he'd mentioned (more than once) that his parents wanted the two of them to return to visit them in Catithia, which Cahya continued to put off, citing that she was far too busy with her cycles to leave Deshka at the moment. Truthfully, there was nothing she wanted to do less than spend the day with Nethos and his parents, even if Nethos was her only 'friend' right now.

After the kiss at the Transfer Station, Nandini was avoiding Cahya completely. She'd see Nandini and Theo at Menza together every now and then, but Nandini never spoke to her. Instead, she'd shoot Cahya lingering glances that felt layered with guilt. She seemed sad, but Cahya could sense that she wanted space. So Cahya spent a lot of her free time hanging out with Ash. She'd grown sincerely fond of the kid; she could see why 'old Cahya' had connected with her.

Cahya felt like she could have been helping more with the investigation that 'old Cahya' had started—but she'd hit a wall. She had spent hours staring at the evidence, but nothing new had struck her. She knew that Cahya's parents had spent some time on Octavia, something no one here seemed to know about, so it was either a big secret or, maybe, Cahya was mistaken—either way, there was nowhere left to dig.

The lack of progress was becoming increasingly distressing. To calm her nerves, Cahya had started meditating for several hours a day. While it helped ease the stress, it did very little to alleviate the guilt. She sensed that losing her memory had robbed her of the ability to help her people. Each passing day without any breakthrough felt like a clock ticking steadily down to... something ominous. She didn't know exactly what, but she knew it wasn't good. Time was slipping away, and despite her efforts, she couldn't figure out what else she should be doing. The uncertainty fed her anxiety.

This morning she sat in her backyard, cross-legged under the large bumble tree, eyes closed, deeply entranced in the moment. She felt the grass beneath her, heard the water gently sputtering about in the pond next to her, and felt the gentle breeze of the wind kiss her face. She was so relaxed that she thought she might fall asleep. And then she did—her awareness drifting into a dreamlike state where the surrounding grass and trees glowed softly against a dark, endless backdrop. The plants pulsed with gentle green light, vibrant and alive, like a vivid scene projected within her mind. A warm, calming energy spread through her, easing the tension in her chest and soothing her soul.

The vision expanded outward, revealing the entire city as a web of glowing energy. Buildings shimmered in clean, white outlines while amber and blue flecks of life darted between them—vehicles and people moving along paths lined with vibrant green. Slowly, her awareness refocused on a spot just beyond the edge of the city, where the glow dimmed.

A patch of grass appeared within the treeline beside the road leading out of Deshka. The grass was bent and trampled, its light dim and weary. Cahya sensed a subtle call from the muted blades of grass, beckoning her forward. She followed the pathway deeper into the forest, noting that the energy of each trampled plant along the trail was faint, nearly extinguished.

The view expanded again, allowing her to connect with the towering trees nearby. They radiated immense, steady waves of green energy, their presence grounding and ancient. As her awareness drifted ahead, she found a circle of massive trees, their trunks forming a perfect ring twenty feet in diameter and stretching a hundred feet into the air.

The energy here shifted—dense and impenetrable. Cahya could feel the presence of the trees surrounding the circle, but she could not push beyond the boundary. The vibrant energy of the forest paused at the edge of the ring, as though holding something secret within.

Cahya woke with a jolt from her dreamlike meditation. The bumble tree vibrated softly so that the grass beneath her hummed for a moment, and then everything went silent.

"What the hell was that?" she mumbled to herself.

She stood carefully, feeling a little dizzy, and made her way back into the house for some water. Maybe the fact that she wasn't sleeping was starting to get to her. She pushed the thought out of her mind.

Kole must have noticed a change in Cahya's demeanor because, a week later, he insisted that Cahya take some time off and that it would be good for her to spend some time with her friends.

Cahya assumed that this was not a coincidence and that her friends had pushed Kole to make this decision.

Nethos was the first to reach out; she couldn't put off going to see his parents now.

"I know you don't really remember them," he had said, "but they'd really like to see you. My mother, especially. I told them I'd talk you into going down for dinner."

Cahya had agreed, since she really had no excuse to get herself out of it, and so she found herself on a train, sitting next to Nethos on their way to Catithia.

The ride to Catithia was smooth and quick. It took less than an hour for them to arrive at the city's transportation station. The train hovered along the monorail tracks with no sound or friction. A soft, whooshing hum was the only perceptible sound resulting from their journey across the green and mountainous lands. Even as it zipped by, Cahya could appreciate the immaculate beauty of this world. The skies here were bright and clear. The summits in the distance rose up for miles, and yet the tops could be seen as well as if they were only a short distance away. Large white birds soared through the air in a waving and whirling dance of beautiful acrobatics. Brightly colored yellow birds called séquins floated on sparkling blue ponds. A herd of constanian burrows galloped through vast plains; they were deer-like with blue-green fur, their long tails and manes of silver-white hair floated behind them as they ran.

"That's Almatar," Nethos said, pointing to the mountains in the distance.

"In the mountains?" Cahya asked.

"Yes, there's actually a valley and a natural lake up there. If you look closely, you can see some of the houses."

Sure enough, she could see small white buildings speckled around the mountainside. It looked like a beautiful city, and she vowed to visit it one day.

As they approached Catithia, the enormous city hub came into view. Rising two thousand feet into the air and covered largely in bright mossy greens, the mountain had been hollowed out, reinforced, and transformed into one of the most stunning central hubs on Nirvana. Enormous sections had been carved out and replaced with the ònakai's unbreakable glass, creating the largest

193

windows on the planet. From a distance, they looked like huge chunks of shiny black onyx. Intricate carvings adorned the parts of the mountain which were not covered in glass or moss.

Having been built just 84 years ago, Catithia was one of the more modern cities on Nirvana, and though its center hub might have appeared intimidating to a newcomer at first glance, the city itself was anything but. The buildings in Catithia were not all white like the ones in Deshka and many of the original cities. In Catithia, the trend was for most homes and buildings to be designed in bright colors like red, green, pink, blue, and yellow.

Many of the buildings were still largely composed of windows, a feature that tended to dominate most building designs on Nirvana. There were also large, colorful gardens everywhere. Every single home in Catithia had a brightly colored garden in its front yard, all with complementary flowers, so that the garden seemed painted to match the home perfectly.

Another feature of the modern city was that its pathways had been enhanced to be interactive, mostly for children. Kids could push a hand to the sidewalk and cause a hopscotch course to appear on the path, or a small character, like a fish, would appear to walk or swim with the child on their stroll.

Catithia didn't have a separate transportation center outside the city hub, like Deshka. The train made its way through stretches of vineyards and rows upon rows of hydroponic greenhouses, slowing only slightly as the shadow of the mountain overtook them. They passed through a grand arched opening and into the heart of the mountain.

It took Cahya a moment for her eyes to adjust to the change in light, but when she opened them, she was astounded by what she saw. Inside, the enormous windows allowed the sunlight to fill the space with a glittering glow. Large black metal trusses reinforced the mountain from within.

Like Deshka, the hub was filled with restaurants, office buildings, parks, gardens and trees—but the scale was very different, you could fit the entire city of Deshka inside Catithia's mountain hub.

"Well, here we are," Nethos announced once the train had come to a stop. "We'll have to take a car out to my parents' place," Nethos told Cahya.

Cahya did her best to take it all in, wondering if anything in this city might spark her memories. After all, she'd learned that she'd grown up here with Nandini and Nethos. This mountain city was once her home.

They made their way through a vast open garden pathway, doubling back in the direction from which the train had just arrived. On their way, they passed a garden café where tables sat full of guests chatting, laughing, and enjoying their day. Next, they passed a restaurant—the structure of which was formed and framed with enormous trees, which must have been transplanted and carefully placed, for they sat perfectly, equally spaced. Between the trunks were heavily tinted windows, which Cahya imagined provided a darkened romantic atmosphere. She could see the flicker of candlelight floating throughout the dining room but could see no tables, chairs, or people through the darkened glass.

Eventually, they reached the long row of white cars, which waited patiently for passengers to come and acquire them. The cars were identical to those in Deshka. Nethos made his way to the front of the line and held his palm to the door of the first car, which popped open so that both he and Cahya could climb in.

"Hello, Nethos," came Myat's voice as the map screen appeared in front of Nethos. "Where are we going today?"

"To my parents' house, Myat," Nethos responded. An address appeared on the screen, and Nethos tapped 'Accept.'

The car followed a narrow road, winding through the last section of the mountain hub before passing through a wide arched opening that led out of the heart of the city. It moved steadily onward, distancing itself from the mountain until reaching a dense barrier of bushes and trees, which separated the central hub and the residential area.

Once they'd entered the residential area, the car turned left and followed the tree-lined street for several blocks before turning right.

"Catithia wasn't designed like Deshka," Nethos explained. "The areas around the central hub are divided into pie-shaped sections instead of belts. With the mountain terrain, it made more sense to structure the city that way. The recreational area is up in the more rugged, mountainous region, with lots of hiking trails. The agricultural section is over in the flatlands to the east, and the residential area sits between the two, where there are plenty of natural water features like ponds and waterfalls."

Cahya observed one home which floated serenely in the middle of a broad pond. It was a red saucer-shaped structure with a long floating path leading from the sidewalk to an expansive patio that wrapped around the structure. The patio was adorned with lush flowering plants that cascaded over the rails, some brushing the water's surface. The blooms displayed a stunning palette of deep burgundy, crimson, raspberry, and pink—a true work of art.

All of the homes followed this pattern, each uniquely beautiful and captivating. A child hopped along the sidewalk, stepping onto glowing green circles that materialized before her. Everything about this place exuded beauty and warmth. Cahya wondered if she had been wrong to expect anything ominous lurking here.

The car turned left once more and came to a stop in front of a striking blue home. The structure was a long, low rectangle with softly curved corners, and its front façade was a wall of windows. To the right, as Cahya faced the house, stood a narrow, taller rectangular tower of the same blue metal, featuring three evenly spaced round windows. The front yard overflowed with vibrant blue and purple blooms, while a white path meandered from the sidewalk around the left side of the house, opposite the tower, leading to a door.

Nethos led the way up the path, with Cahya following a few steps behind. Her heart pounded in her chest, the thought of spending dinner with Kyun made her uneasy. She tried to distract herself by admiring the vibrant flowers lining the walkway. Cahya reached over and ran her fingers across the leaf of a nearby shrub. A jolt shot through her and she closed her eyes. In the darkness of her mind she saw a slight flicker of light, bright green, in the shape of a leaf. Cahya pulled her hand away from the shrub, and stood frozen.

"You coming?" Nethos asked, he was now standing at the door, looking back at Cahya.

"Yes, coming," Cahya replied, still in shock. What *was* that?

As she reached the door, it opened to reveal a woman with dark brown hair and striking green eyes. She wore an emerald-green dress that wrapped elegantly around her body, crossing over her left shoulder before flowing nearly to the floor behind her. Cahya noted how it resembled the saris worn by women in the Earth cycles, though this garment was meticulously tailored, fitted, and secured in place, unlike the draped style of a sari. The dress had no jewels or elaborate embellishments, only a delicate yellow embroidery that trimmed the neckline, arm openings, and shoulders. The same golden trim bordered the hem of the skirt, which hovered just above the floor.

"Nethos!" The woman beamed, pulling her son into a warm embrace. Still holding him, she glanced over at Cahya, her eyes lighting up. Letting go of Nethos, she stepped toward Cahya, gently taking her hands. "Cahya, sweetheart, how are you?"

"I'm well, thank you, Mrs. Portos," Cahya offered with a kind smile. By now, she was used to people approaching her with this sort of familiarity and warmth.

"Please call me Sam, Cahya," Mrs. Portos replied. "Come in, come in. Are you hungry? Can I get you anything to drink?"

Cahya glanced back at the shrub, eyeing it suspiciously, as Sam ushered them through the door and into the open living space.

Both the front and back of the house were made of windowed walls. The wall with the door, where they'd just entered, stood about ten feet above their heads, stretched across the room, and curved down toward the floor. The wall opposite them also had a door, which Cahya assumed led into the tower-portion of the home. On the right, toward the front windows of the house, was a seating area with four soft green chairs, several small wooden tables, and lots of plants on the tables and the floor. On the other side of the room was a long wooden island, which served as the kitchen space. There were more plants on the counter and four stools sat along one side.

"Water would be great, Mrs.—Sam, if it's not too much trouble," Cahya replied.

"Of course, of course. Come." Sam made her way to the kitchen counter, and on her way, she said, "Myat, please open the back wall."

As she arrived at the counter, the entire glass wall next to the counter began to rise like a garage door, concealing itself in the roof as it went. The door opened onto a beautiful backyard where a wood table sat with seating for six. A large pond filled the yard, and as they made their way out, Sam handed a glass of water to Cahya. A yellow séquin swam around in the pond, and Cahya watched it with great fascination as she took a seat at the table.

"I'm sad that we haven't seen you since your accident, Cahya, but I know you've been very busy. How are you feeling these days?"

"Well, my memories aren't back, and I'm no longer Dohan," Cahya reported matter-of-factly, taking a big sip of water from the glass in front of her. She caught sight of the worried look on Sam's face. "But I'm sure that's for the best, of course. I'm feeling fine, though, which is what you were actually asking."

"Yes, well, I'm sure you're dealing with a lot," Sam added. "Nethos seems to think that your memories may not return at all. Is that true?"

"Yes, well, there's certainly a possibility that they won't return, I'm afraid. But, on the positive side, I've been given a rare opportunity to discover Nirvana all over again. Like this place, for example. What a marvelous city!" Cahya was anxious to change the subject.

"Yes, it's quite a beautiful city. What a wonderful opportunity you have to see the world with fresh eyes, Cahya." Sam smiled warmly and placed her hand on top of Cahya's. "That's something I've always loved about you, dear; you always manage to find the bright side of every situation. It's truly inspiring."

"Thank you, Sam; that's incredibly kind of you."

"Nethos also tells me that you've been spending time with Ash recently. How is she holding up? I can't imagine what that poor girl is going through. First, she loses her mother, and then," she paused and raised a hand to her chest, patting gently as though to soothe the sorrow she seemed to be holding back, "well, it must be hard for her," she said finally.

"She seems okay. I wasn't completely honest with her when I saw her," Cahya admitted. "I told her that I still remembered her."

Sam smiled and said, "Ah, well, that may have been for the best. I'm not sure her poor heart could take any more loss. I know children are resilient, and she may be more resilient than most. Still..."

"So you know Ash, then?" Cahya asked.

"I've met her a few times, yes, but it's her mother I knew most—Tashina. You won't remember, of course, but Tashina grew up right here in Catithia with you and Nethos. I remember how Nethos used to follow her around like a duckling glued to a mama duck. I'd say you were five when the two of you met, which would have made her thirteen or so. Isn't that right, Nethos?"

Nethos nodded, and his mother continued, "Oh, the trouble they'd get into, the pair of them." Sam smiled as she recalled her memories. "Nethos was heartbroken when Tashina went off to Deshka to start her ELC training. I swear she was the reason you ramped up your studies and ended up in Deshka at twenty, Nethos"

Nethos blushed. "Please, Mother."

"What happened to her? To Tashina?" Cahya asked.

"No one really knows for sure. She and Carsen were visiting Penchewaga. She'd gone for a swim in the morning, and then she disappeared. Her body was found quickly, but it was too late. An autopsy ruled that she'd suffered an aneurysm of some sort, and that's what went into the official report, but some people didn't like that explanation."

"How come?" Cahya asked.

"Myat scans citizens regularly—weekly for most." Sam explained.

Nethos chuckled, "I haven't been scanned in three months." He popped an olive in his mouth, intentionally avoiding his mother's criticizing gaze, "What? It takes too long, I have places to be, mother, I'm a very busy man, you know." He gave her a wink.

Sam rolled her eyes, "Well, for those of us who care about our health, regular scans are important. And you shouldn't skip them, Nethos. I'm sure that Tashina was more conscientious. The system would have picked up on any abnormalities that might have led to an aneurysm. People don't die at forty-three on Nirvana. We've eradicated illness and disease, and we've made it so that our planet is extremely safe. Accidents are exceedingly rare—almost unheard of. People die when their bodies tire and wear out after a couple of centuries. Tashina's death was tragic."

Cahya wondered if Tashina's death and her parents' deaths were somehow related. They'd happened over two decades apart. But then she remembered the recording: the group that was working to take down Nirvana's systems, the Dakaï, had been working on it for generations. Who knew what they might be capable of in that amount of time?

"But this is a very sad topic," Sam said, frowning. "Maybe we could move on to something else? Cahya, do you know if the Doyen will select a new Dohan soon? It's been a month now, has it not?"

Cahya opened her mouth to speak, but it wasn't her voice that filled the room.

"No, the Doyen seems to be taking his time." Cahya turned in her chair to see Kyun approaching the table.

"Oh! Cahya, you probably don't remember Nethos' father, Kyun." Sam gestured toward the door behind them.

Cahya nodded. "We met briefly the day after my accident. Hello, Mr. Portos." Cahya and Nethos stood as he approached.

"Hello, Cahya. Please call me Kyun." Kyun offered his hand and Cahya shook it, not wanting her discomfort to show.

"It's nice to see you again, Kyun. Thank you for inviting me to dinner."

"It's our pleasure, Cahya, of course."

"Son." Kyun turned to Nethos and shook his hand. The greeting wasn't as warm as his mother's had been.

"Hello, Father, it's good to see you." Nethos said, "Any updates on your project on geothermal research in Almatar?"

Kyun took his seat at the table. "Well, son, if you'd been paying attention, you'd know that our research has taken us out of Almatar and over to Penchewaga."

"Oh yes, now that you mention it, I had heard that you'd moved your operations to the beachside resort. Focusing on quantum tidal currents, I believe," Nethos said.

"Yes," Kyun answered tersely. "Cahya, tell me—why do you think the Doyen is taking so long to name a new Dohan?"

"I'm sure I couldn't pretend to grasp the Doyen's mind, Kyun," Cahya replied evenly.

"Maybe the Council could put a bit of pressure on him," Sam ventured. "It does feel like it's dragging on."

"The Council does not 'pressure' the Doyen, Sam—you know that." Kyun's tone sharpened.

"Grandmother would have," Nethos chimed in, smiling. "She always had something to say about council matters."

Kyun perked up at that. "Yes, well, my mother was quite a force on the Council in her day."

Cahya caught the flicker of pride in Nethos' eyes—he'd at last garnered some approval from his father.

"Where is she?" Cahya asked, curious. "Your grandmother?"

Sam gave a wistful sigh. "She retired ages ago and moved to the mountains with the Montori. It's a quieter life—simpler in many ways. She hasn't visited in years. We all miss her, but Kyun speaks to her now and then. He assures me she's perfectly happy."

The rest of dinner was only slightly less awkward than the start. Sam deftly shifted the subject to underwater travel destinations, noting that Octavia boasted nearly fifty such resorts, whereas Nirvana still struggled to expand beyond its two. "It's high time," she declared, "we have to keep up with modern progress."

"Oh, Kyun, you should show Cahya that old device you found. The one for breathing underwater," Sam said.

"I'm sure Cahya and Nethos want to get back to Deshka," Kyun told her.

"Oh, nonsense," Sam argued. "Nethos hasn't been home in two months; there's no need for them to rush out just because dinner's over."

"I'd love to see it," Cahya smiled, sensing that Sam was craving some alone time with her son. But as soon as the words left her lips she wished she could take them back. She was anxious to get back home, and she didn't want to spend any quality time with Kyun. *What had she done?*

Sam smiled at her gratefully. Okay fine, Cahya thought, maybe it won't be that bad.

"Very well," Kyun said as he stood from the table. "Follow me."

"You two go ahead," Sam told them. "Nethos and I will tidy up, and my son is going to catch me up on all the latest news from Deshka." She smiled at her son playfully.

Cahya followed Kyun across the house to the door opposite the entrance. Beyond the door was a staircase that led up, presumably to the bedroom, but Kyun didn't go to the staircase. Instead, he walked over to the wall opposite the staircase and waved his hand. A small crack appeared on the floor at first, and then it grew to reveal a hidden staircase that led somewhere under the house.

Kyun gestured to the floor. "After you," he said.

Cahya swallowed hard and told herself that she was perfectly safe, trying to calm her sudden urge to run. *You're being silly!* she told herself.

Cahya made her way down the stairs and found herself in a large room that was mostly empty. A metal table sat along the wall with two chairs; a large frame hung above it displaying an image of an elderly woman with white hair tied into a tight bun. She stared at Cahya with dark, unhappy eyes.

"My great-great-great-grandmother," Kyun told her, pointing at the photo. He picked up a small device which sat on a table under the photo. "Here we are," he announced, handing the object to Cahya.

It appeared to be a shallow bowl made of a soft metallic material. "The breathing device?" Cahya asked.

"Indeed," Kyun confirmed, but he didn't offer any further explanation. "If you want to see some truly interesting devices, you really have to look at some of the ancient Octavian tech." He walked over to the photograph of his grandmother, lifting it off the wall revealing a small door.

"What is this place?" Cahya asked finally, trying to hide the slight tremor in her voice.

If Kyun noticed that she was nervous, he didn't let on.

"This is a bunker room," Kyun told her casually, pressing a hand to the door, which popped open at his touch. "A few homes in each city are built with them. It's generally council members who have them, sometimes senior members of the E.R.F., people like that. They're shielded from all tech and scanners, so you don't want to lose something in one," he said, raising the corner of his lip slightly, "because Myat can't help you find it."

A chill ran down Cahya's spine. She wanted to run back upstairs. *Keep it together, Cahya!* she told herself. Lots of homes had bunker rooms—the homes of council members and senior E.R.F. Cahya strained to remember what E.R.F. stood for; she knew she'd heard it before. Right! She remembered—*Emergency Response Force.* That's what Nandini called the team in the purple jumpsuits at the *panigêm* match.

Behind the small door in the wall was an opening, a type of safe, Cahya deduced. Inside the safe were a series of small devices arranged neatly across three rows of shelves. Cahya caught sight of a gold metallic object on the top shelf, but Kyun pulled out a different piece and handed it to Cahya. She took it and turned it over in her hands, inspecting it. It was long and thin, like a sleek white pen, that looked to be made from the same metal as many of the buildings in Deshka.

"What is it?" Cahya asked him.

"Well, I haven't given it a name, but I can tell you what it does. This device emits a high-frequency laser, which can cut clean through the toughest metal without making a sound."

"Wow!" Cahya exclaimed, wondering how such a tiny instrument could hold so much power.

"If you think that's impressive, have a look at this." Kyun took a small container of red balls out of the safe. "These little guys can create a huge energy burst and cause quite a bit of damage." He took the pen-like object from her and dropped one of the red balls into her hand.

Cahya flinched as the ball landed in her hand, afraid that it might blow up.

Kyun laughed. "You can't activate it, Cahya. It's Octavian," he told her. "Nearly everything in this safe is Octavian—devices and weapons used by the ònakai military. Fascinating pieces, all of them."

He pulled another object from the safe, turning it over in his hands. This one looked like a cog from a clock, but he didn't bother describing what it did. He continued, holding the cog up between his thumb and forefinger, "The ònakai design their weapons with a biomechanical safeguard; they only work for people with ònakai biometrics."

"That's interesting," Cahya said. She wasn't sure if it *was* interesting, but she didn't feel she had anything else to contribute to the conversation at the moment. Her mind was too busy trying to process why Kyun would have a stash of ònakai military devices in a safe in his private bunker.

"It's very interesting," he assured her. "It ensures that their enemies can't pick up their weapons and use them against the ònakai people. A very clever feature. See, *you* can't do anything with that little red ball in your hand, but an ònakai need only roll it around in their palms for a few moments to activate it.

"Tashina was a brilliant biomechanical engineer, though, and she managed to crack the code on these devices, making it so that they would work with *her* biosignature. She developed an adaptation which tricked the device into recognizing a protein in her DNA as ònakai. It's a shame that her research was cut short."

He spoke fondly of Ash's mother, almost as though he had been very close to her. It was a warmth Cahya hadn't thought Kyun was capable of.

He returned the cog to the safe and pulled out the gold object from the top shelf. It was a beautiful piece of equipment, whatever it was. It curled around into itself, forming a spiral shape. Kyun turned the object over in his hand and Cahya noticed a hole at one end and a trigger where the spiral seemed to curve into a handle. A gun, she realized.

"Why do you have these?" Cahya asked and regretted it immediately. It was too blunt—almost accusatory. She didn't think that Kyun was the kind of person to take accusations lightly.

He eyed her for a moment, seemingly trying to decide whether or not to answer her question. "I'm the head of Technological Health for all of Nirvana, Cahya. Technology is my passion. Some of these items were gifted to me over the years. Some items I found."

"Found?" she asked.

"Yes, on an expedition in the mountains of Talem. I went cave diving and found a bag tucked away in a hidden cavern. Some of these items, that included," he said, pointing to the red ball in Cahya's hand, "were in that bag."

"How did they get there?" Cahya wondered out loud, peeking at the other objects inside.

"How indeed?" Kyun agreed. "And perhaps the more pressing question is *why*. Why would the ònakai have a bag of military weapons and devices tucked away in a cave on Nirvana? All their weapons were supposedly destroyed. And perhaps more disturbing than that is this question: Was this the only bag?"

Cahya contemplated the question. What was he trying to imply? That the ònakai had stashed a bunch of weapons on Nirvana? Why would they do that? '*Why indeed?*' She imagined Kyun saying to her.

Cahya offered the red ball back to Kyun.

"Keep it," he told her.

Cahya pulled her hand back, a puzzled look on her face. "Why?" she asked.

"Consider it a reminder to remain vigilant," he told her. "There may come a day when you need to choose a side, Cahya. It's important that you remember which side you're meant to be on. This ball," he said, lifting the ball out of Cahya's hand and examining it, "is a symbol—a reminder that, when we become complacent, we create weaknesses that others can exploit." Kyun placed the ball back in Cahya's hand and said, "We must remain awake and aware so that we can see clearly."

Cahya didn't really understand what Kyun was trying to tell her; he was speaking in riddles. Still, she tucked the red ball into her pocket and watched as Kyun placed the gold object back in the safe. He closed the door of the safe and placed the photo of the old woman back over the opening.

"It is best that we keep this between us, Cahya. The council doesn't want the general public to know that these objects exist. It might cause a bit of panic."

"Why would it cause panic?" Cahya asked him.

"People might suspect that the ònakai are building and hiding weapons on Nirvana for some malicious purpose. People tend to jump to the worst possible conclusions, don't they?"

Cahya hadn't jumped to that conclusion, but it was certainly rolling around her head now. Could the ònakai be planting weapons on Nirvana? And if they were, what would be the purpose?

The two rejoined Sam and Nethos upstairs. Cahya had never been so grateful to see Nethos as she was right now. He'd already gathered their jackets and seemed ready to leave.

"Ready to head out?" he asked. "We have a busy day tomorrow."

"Yes, you're right. We should probably get home and turn in early," Cahya told him, relieved to be leaving. She'd felt very uncomfortable with Kyun and was eager to get back to Deshka. Cahya thanked Sam and Kyun for their kindness and generosity, and they were on their way.

Cahya was tired on the ride home. All of that anxious energy must have worn her out. The sun had tucked itself away for the evening, and the stars shone brightly in the night sky. Only one moon was visible tonight and rose high over the mountains in the distance.

"I'm sorry about my father," Nethos said to Cahya as they passed through a field of tall grass that shone purple in the light of the moon. "He means well, I'm sure, but he's always been a little abrasive."

Cahya wondered if Nethos knew about the stash of devices in his father's safe. He must, she concluded, but she still decided it was best not to discuss it on a train full of people.

"It's okay, Nethos," Cahya told him. "You don't have to apologize to me for your father."

"He just has such a strong sense of what's right, you know? He really understands the world, and he's just... I don't know, he's just very passionate."

"I can see that," Cahya told him, smiling at Nethos' desire to defend his father. "You really look up to him, don't you?"

Nethos smiled shyly and looked out the window. "I do; he's my father."

Cahya watched him for a moment. He looked so young to her just now, with the moonlight shining on his face and smoothing his features. His eyes were soft as he stared up at the moon above. She still didn't fully understand him, but she was seeing a piece of him right now that she hadn't seen before—an innocent, unconditional love for his father. A man who barely seemed to pay attention to him or care much for what he thought. Cahya felt a little pang of sadness tugging at her chest. Poor Nethos, to love someone so completely—like a puppy—without receiving the same love in return. Maybe that's why he kept a guard up with everyone else.

The two rode the train the rest of the way to Deshka in silence, looking out the windows and up at the starry night through the glass-covered roof of the train.

When they finally reached the station, Cahya yawned and stretched before stepping off the train with Nethos. They walked together for a short while before reaching the street where they would part ways.

"Thanks for coming with me today," Nethos said, stopping at the corner. Cahya noticed his caramel curls, highlighted by the moonlight. He really was very handsome.

"Of course. Thanks for inviting me," Cahya replied, "sorry it took so long."

"See you tomorrow?" he asked.

"Yeah, I'll see you," Cahya confirmed with a smile.

Nethos gave her a small wave before turning to walk in the opposite direction. Cahya watched him for a moment, then turned toward her own home. The night air was cool but pleasant. She wrapped her arms around herself and let her thoughts wander as she made her way back.

She couldn't stop thinking about the safe and the objects inside it. Why had Kyun shown those things to her? Was he trying to send her a message? She didn't trust him, but something about the way he'd spoken about vigilance and choosing a side had struck a chord.

When she reached her front door, she paused, noticing the small shrub in the garden next to the entrance. She suddenly remembered the strange jolt she'd felt just before entering the Portos' home. It had been so jarring, but she'd been fully immersed in her visit and she'd forgotten about it until now. Had she imagined it?

Slowly, Cahya reached down, hesitating a moment before placing a finger on one of the shrub's leaves. She waited. Nothing.

Letting out a huge sigh of relief, she laughed in spite of herself. She must have imagined it. Cahya turned and looked up at the sky. There was just a single moon casting a soft glow over the quiet street. It felt almost earth-like. She let out a deep breath and stepped inside.

CHAPTER 16
THE T'DAVA

Cahya slept in her own bed for the first time in weeks, and it felt great. With her evenings taken up with plant cycles, she'd almost forgotten what real sleep felt like. She woke up feeling refreshed.

She'd agreed to meet up with Nandini for breakfast. The two had stealthily avoided one another since the kiss, but Cahya missed her friend, and she was anxious to do away with the awkwardness they were feeling.

Nandini arrived at breakfast looking beautiful. Her hair was tied up in a high bun on top of her head and she wore a red jumper which matched her bright red lips.

"Hi," Cahya said as she approached the table.

"Hey," Nandini smiled, taking her seat. "Look, I'm sorry I've been avoiding you. I've been feeling really guilty about... well, you know."

"You don't have to apologize; I get it," Cahya told her. "Besides, it gave me some time to focus on some personal stuff."

"Oh," Nandini laughed, "I didn't realize that my friendship had been taking up so much of your time."

Cahya smiled. "So, what's the plan for today?" Nandini had insisted on planning a morning activity for them but refused to share any details.

"You'll see," Nandini winked.

After breakfast, they made their way to the recreation belt. Cahya hadn't spent much time here; she'd been so busy that taking any time out for recreational activities felt like a waste of time.

The area was huge. There were bike paths, running paths, several large fields, a spot course, and several indoor arenas. There was even a small panigêm arena for amateur players. There were people everywhere; apparently the recreation belt was a hot spot in Deshka. Who knew?

"Am I finally going to learn how to play spot?" Cahya asked, gesturing to the course where players were hitting a small energy ball toward the side of a grassy concave hill with several holes in it.

"Nope, not today. I think you need a bit more of a challenge. When's the last time you had a good workout?" Nandini asked with a devious look in her eyes.

Oh no, Cahya hadn't done any sort of workout since the accident. Unless she counted all of the walking she'd done to get around Deshka. Somehow, she got the feeling that the walking wouldn't count.

They approached a field where a group of people stood chatting. "We're going to do a bit of Ai Chi Fu," Nandini smiled.

Ai Chi what?

"Hello, all," Nandini said as they approached. "Welcome. If you would please take your places, we'll get started with a warm-up."

The group moved around to form two lines, facing Nandini. Cahya took up a spot next to Theo and looked around to see if she recognized anyone else. She did, as it turned out. The man she'd met outside the panigêm arena—what was his name again? Wallace? Walter. That was it, Walter. He had something to do with horticulture, if she remembered correctly.

Nandini led the group through several warm-up exercises before she paired them up for drills. Cahya was paired with a short blond man named Seth.

Nandini and Theo demonstrated the movements that the teams were meant to replicate. When they showed the movements at full speed, it made Cahya dizzy.

Try as she might, Cahya was anything but a natural. She was slow and awkward with every move.

"It seems you lost all of your martial arts skills along with your memories," Seth joked after Cahya's fifth failed attempt at a simple movement.

"Huh," Cahya mumbled, breathless.

"You used to be really good at this stuff Almost as good as Nandini."

Cahya looked at Nandini, who was sparring with Theo. The two were rolling, jumping, and lunging so quickly that it was hard to keep up. Everyone had stopped to watch them at this point; it was mesmerizing. They were both tremendously skilled and nearly equally matched, but eventually, Theo pinned Nandini, and she tapped out.

"Don't feel too bad." Theo smiled, helping her up from the ground. "I've done about 3,500 more cycles than you. You'll catch up one day, I'm sure." He winked and laughed.

Nandini shook her head, a big goofy smile on her face. She was having a blast.

"Alright, everyone, final move of the day," she told the group. She demonstrated a high kick, which the opponent would have to block. It seemed like a simple enough move, and Cahya was sure she could manage.

She and Seth practiced slowly a few times: Seth kicked, and Cahya blocked. Seth kicked, and Cahya blocked. Seth kicked, Cahya blocked.

"I think we've got it," Seth said. "Shall we speed it up a bit?"

Cahya agreed and braced herself for the kick, ready to block, but just before Seth kicked, Cahya felt a rumble rising up from the grass. She turned her head to look for a bumble tree and looked back just in time to see Seth's foot as it connected with her face.

Everything faded into darkness. In that void, a flicker of light appeared—a trembling leaf outlined in a soft, neon green glow. Gradually, the branch holding the leaf came into focus, followed by the sturdy, glowing outline of a towering bumble tree—it trembled with a warning energy. *Danger.*

Other patches of light soon emerged: clusters of grass blades swaying gently, small flowers sparkling faintly in their stillness. Soon the whole field came into awareness. Glowing figures outlined in amber light moved about the field—players engaged in a game of spot and a small group now huddled around a body, which lay motionless in the grass.

The awareness began to drift, gently at first, then rapidly accelerating. It floated above the field, where clusters of plants glowed in vibrant green. The black void behind it all deepened, making the energy and light stand out starkly. Shapes formed—buildings outlined in a clean, steady white light, their structures rigid and motionless. The shifting amber energy of people and vehicles moved swiftly through the paths between these white silhouettes. Sweeping past glowing trees, their energy pulsing in rhythmic harmony, the branches and roots forming a vast network of green light. Faster and faster, rushing along the glowing road until, abruptly, the movement halted.

Ahead, the forest loomed, a solid presence in the darkness. The tall trees glowed faintly with green outlines, their roots threading deep into the earth. At the forest's edge, a gap broke the continuous wall of energy—a patch of grass flattened and dimmed, creating an opening in the line of trees.

Go! She heard a voice say in her mind.

Cahya opened her eyes; she was gasping for air, and the entire field was vibrating loudly. A group had formed around her, and

Nandini was bent over, calling her name. Walter was there too, pressing his hand into the grass and staring at Cahya.

Cahya finally caught her breath and felt the relief of cool air rushing in. As her breathing calmed, the vibrating slowed and eventually stopped.

"Cahya, are you okay?" Nandini asked, checking Cahya's face for breaks or blood.

"Yeah, I'm okay, I think," Cahya said.

"I'm so sorry, Cahya," Seth told her, stepping forward from the crowd. "I really thought you were ready."

"It's fine; totally my fault; I got distracted."

Walter helped Cahya to her feet. "What happened just now, Cahya, while you were out?"

What a strange question! Why did he suspect something had happened?

"I'm not sure what you mean," Cahya said. "I was out."

"Yes, but did you see anything? Feel anything unusual?" He searched Cahya's face, and seeing that she was unwilling to share, he continued, "It's just that I've heard that you've been working through many hours of plant cycles lately. And sometimes, though it's exceedingly rare, well, I've heard rumours about people who have reported being able to sort of... communicate, if you will, with the environment."

Walter continued, "Ka'ana, it's called, if I'm not mistaken: the ability to connect with plants. I'm not suggesting that you have it; I only found it odd that the bumble trees began buzzing just as you were about to be kicked very hard and then only got louder and more aggressive until you came to." He looked up at the bumble tree which now sat perfectly still, "It could be a coincidence, of course, but given my field of work, I find this topic tremendously fascinating." He smiled broadly.

"Some people have even reported being able to travel without moving an inch, just by communicating with the plant life around them. Truly fascinating stuff," he said again.

215

"Sorry to disappoint you, Mr.—Kenzinnia, was it? I'm sure it was just a coincidence." Of course, Cahya knew that this was not true. Everything Walter described had happened to her, and now she knew she hadn't imagined it.

"Ah, yes, well, an old horticulturalist can dream, can't he?" He stood and turned to Nandini, "Thanks for a wonderful class, Ms Corteza."

* * *

Nandini walked Cahya home so that she could rest. But she couldn't settle, not now. Not since learning that her visions were likely real, that she'd somehow tapped into the ability to... what—talk to plants?

And so, instead of resting, she found herself standing on the side of the road, staring at the opening in the treeline. She couldn't help herself. The urge to jump in a car and make her way to this spot was far too compelling to ignore. Was there anything worth exploring beyond the flatten grass?

She watched the small, egg-shaped car roll away until it vanished into the distance toward the city. Turning back to the gap, she pushed aside the tall grass and stepped through the treeline, venturing beneath the gnarled canopy of the hundred-foot trees. Her breath caught when she realized the gap continued—a narrow pathway stretching deeper into the forest.

She paused only briefly before moving on, treading carefully. Ten minutes in, she had seen nothing unusual, but the trail continued, so she pressed forward. After twenty minutes, there were still no towering trees. The entrance to the treeline was now so distant she couldn't make it out, and ahead—nothing but forest.

She nearly turned back, dismissing the whole thing as a foolish pursuit. "What were you expecting, Cahya?" she scolded herself. The grass was likely trampled by larger animals, this whole thing had been a huge waste of time.

Wait, what was that. Something broke the silence—a noise—someone talking. They seemed far off, maybe they weren't voices at all. But then it came again, clearer this time—closer. Cahya ducked, afraid that she might be seen.

Under the cover of the tall grass, Cahya could hear a man and a woman speaking. Their voices carried clearly enough that she caught the tension between them, although they were still too far away for her to discern every word. Slowly, she crept closer, moving quietly through the swaying grass until she was near enough to listen.

"If you ask me, he should be worried," the man said curtly. "Any sign of recovered memories, no matter how slight, is bad news. He ought to handle her before it's too late."

"She hasn't remembered anything," the woman replied, her voice tinged with what sounded like forced calm. "All she did was see herself in the recovery channel at the end of a cycle."

There was a slight tremor in her tone, and Cahya thought she detected an undercurrent of fear.

The man snorted. "Close enough to be a problem. If she starts remembering things, they'll reinstate her."

"I... I won't let it happen," the woman insisted, her words tumbling out too quickly.

"You're letting her do the cycles," the man blurted impatiently.

"The Council approved these cycles—what can I do? Besides, they're plant cycles. She's basically sleeping."

"It's still risky," he warned, voice tight. "And you know what happens if you fail."

The woman sucked in a sharp breath, and Cahya caught the tremor in her voice. She's terrified, Cahya realized, pressing herself lower into the grass.

"I'll do what I can," the woman murmured, though she sounded anything but confident.

Cahya felt a jolt of recognition. That voice—it was Hathina's, she was sure of it. Carefully shifting her weight, she tried to get a better

217

look. Her foot landed on a dry branch, and the sharp crack echoed through the still air. Cahya's pulse thundered in her ears.

"Did you hear that?" Hathina asked, stepping toward Cahya's hiding spot. Her tone grew tight—whether from the source of the noise or from the man beside her, Cahya couldn't tell. Heart hammering, Cahya tucked down under the grass and pressed herself tight against the tree, trying to vanish.

She squeezed her eyes shut and felt a jolt as a bright line of neon light flashed against the black backdrop in her mind. A towering trunk took shape revealing a towering 100-ft bumble tree, complete with a soaring canopy of glimmering leaves. Only a few feet from the tree, she could see Hathina's outline glowing in soft amber. Blue orbs flitted in and around the figure. Cahya forced her eyes open, startled, and her body heaved as she tried to take in air without making a sound.

Ka'ana! She thought. Was this really happening to her?

"Probably just an animal." The man's voice was dismissive, but had an edge to it. "Come on, get inside."

Hathina lingered, only a few feet from where Cahya crouched.

"Let's go!" the man called again, more forceful this time.

Cahya released a slow, silent breath and peered around a nearby tree to get a better view. She had to be sure this was Hathina.

Rising inch by inch from the grass, Cahya spotted them again—backs turned to her. It was definitely Hathina; that long, golden-red hair was unmistakable. Standing beside her was a short, orange-haired man. Both wore long red cloaks with large hoods bunched around their necks. Cahya had never seen him before.

Hathina stopped between two large trees, gave a quick, tense wave of her arm, and an enormous glass tower materialized from thin air. Cahya's jaw dropped. The tower rose nearly to the canopy, an awe-inspiring sight. A small door slid open, and the pair stepped inside—oblivious to Cahya's presence. The door closed behind them, and the tower dissolved into nothing. Six towering trees stood in a silent ring, as though the structure had never been there.

Cahya froze, her mind racing. *What was that tower? What was Hathina doing here?*

Cahya ducked into the grass, crawling quietly along the path until she was far enough from the cluster of trees to be out of sight. Once sure she couldn't be seen, she stood and sprinted toward the opening in the treeline. Bursting out of the forest, she darted across the road and crouched behind a towering tree hidden in the tall grass. She paused, heart pounding, and scanned the area to ensure no one had followed. Satisfied after a few tense moments, she raised her hand and called for transport. The soft hum and gentle braking of a small white car broke the silence. Slipping out from behind the tree, Cahya crept to the car, tapped her wrist to unlock the door, slid into the seat, and gave the instruction: "Deshka."

She stayed low in the car for several minutes before poking her head up to peek outside, making sure she hadn't been followed.

"Cahya," Myat's voice rang through the vehicle, causing Cahya to jump, letting out a quick scream. "Kole has sent a message requesting your presence at the ELC labs."

* * *

It was starting to get dark, and Cahya's purple hair shone brightly in the deep blue and pink tones of the evening sky.

On her way to the labs, all she could think about was what she had seen and heard in the forest.

"I've found something," Kole told her as she arrived at the lab.

"So have I!" Cahya exclaimed. "And I think I need to go first."

Cahya told Kole about the invisible tower in the forest and how she thought she might have found it using ka'ana, something she'd just learned about today from Walter Kenzinnia. She also told him that she suspected the invisible building was a Dakaï hideout, and she told him about Hathina.

Kole sat in stunned silence for several minutes before he responded, "We have to go to the Doyen."

"Are you sure we can trust him? Are you sure he isn't a part of this?" Cahya asked.

"I'm sure," Kole responded, and he shot Cahya a look that made it clear that the topic was not up for discussion.

Cahya closed her mouth, choosing not to push the matter further. Then she remembered Kole's comment from earlier and asked, "Wait, what did *you* find?"

Kole had begun gathering his things while he answered, "I think I figured out how to get your memories back."

Cahya's eyes widened, and she opened her mouth to speak, but Kole was on the move as he said, "Myat, arrange an emergency meeting with the Doyen." He paused, looking at Cahya before he continued, "And the Tosha Council, code word Dakaï."

"The Tosha Council has been notified," Myat confirmed.

Kole gave Cahya an apologetic look and said, "Let's go."

CHAPTER 17
TOSHA

Kole refused to answer any of Cahya's questions as they made their way to the transportation hub, they were in public after all.

"Everything will make sense soon enough," he insisted, which did not make Cahya feel better.

They boarded the train to Catithia. *Catithia?* Why Catithia? Were they going to see Kyun? Was he a part of this secret council? Didn't they realize he was probably Dakaï?

Her mind raced—questions piling up like the distant hum of the train. Every unanswered query tightened the knot in her stomach, yet she knew that in public, she had to appear calm—even if she was no longer Dohan.

As they moved through the train's compartments, they passed the seating area and the lounge before heading farther back. The train was nearly empty today, and by the time they reached the final coach, it was deserted. After all, the most comfortable seats were near the front.

At the rear of this last coach, wide windows offered a view of Deshka fading into the distance. A door led outside, and Kole stepped up to it, pressing his hand against a white glowing panel that turned blue.

Cahya's thoughts whirled. Were they about to jump off the train? Why would they do that?

Before she could voice her concerns, the door slid open to reveal a hidden section. Kole entered first, and Cahya followed, eyeing the windows as she went, trying to discern how her vision was being fooled.

"The last coach is cloaked," Kole explained, his tone bright with amusement. "Come."

Cahya's heart thumped. Why did they need a secret compartment? And how would they have entered it if there had been other passengers around? She glanced back at the empty coach, confirming once more that no one was there. As she stepped through, she opened her mouth to question Kole but froze when she saw who was waiting: Doyen Hashen, Balti, Matildi, and Theo, all seated around a table near the back of the hidden train car.

Woah! She thought, the Doyen and two prominent council members, and... *Theo?*

"Thank you for being here on such short notice," Kole said to the group as he took a seat at the table. He gestured for Cahya to sit too. She took the last empty seat at the table and glanced around at the concerned faces.

"We've all stayed in Deshka these past few weeks for this exact reason," Balti began in a tone that was just above a whisper. "What have you found?"

Cahya had so many questions. What did Tosha mean? How did Kole know that everyone in this car was trustworthy? Why was Theo here? He was an exchange student, wasn't he?

There was no time to ask these questions, though, because Kole went straight into his briefing.

"Cahya has discovered the Dakaï's secret base, a tower in the woods on the outskirts of Deshka. When she found it, Hathina was there with a man that Cahya didn't recognize." Kole took a breath, "Cahya suspects that Hathina is helping them against her will."

"That's huge," Matildi exclaimed.

"There's more," Kole continued, sliding a device onto the table. It was a silver cube, and when he tapped it, a small holographic screen rose in the air above it. On the screen, lines upon lines of code began to scroll across the surface of the hologram.

"What are we looking at, Kole?" Doyen Hashen asked, scanning the lines of code as they continued to scroll.

"It's a subroutine," Kole explained, "that was buried deep within the ELC Program. I can't be certain how it got there, but I believe that this," Kole pointed at the screen, "is what caused Cahya to lose her memories."

Cahya studied the lines of code as they flashed across the screen. She'd seen some kind of internet code back on earth, in her life as Johnny, she knew absolutely nothing about it. What she did know was that this looked nothing like any of the code she'd seen. The lines ran vertically across the screen and they were filled with symbols she didn't recognize.

"This subroutine was planted in the system months ago, just before Cahya's accident," Kole continued, giving Cahya an apologetic look.

A flicker of disappointment crossed the Doyen's face. "Do we have an understanding of how this subroutine evaded our sweeps?" he asked.

Kole nodded grimly. "Yes, we run routine integrity checks daily, of course, but whoever wrote this code disguised it as part of our standard ELC updates—likely borrowed from Tashina's old encryption routines. It looked like normal patch data, so the system recognized it as harmless. It has only been activated once, on the day Cahya lost her memories."

The Doyen pressed further, "And we know how to detect this sort of thing in the future then?"

"Yes," Kole confirmed, "Though I doubt they'd try the same trick twice. Still, this subroutine included a unique trigger in this code that doesn't exist in standard ELC updates. I've added a safety check which will flag these triggers going forward."

"Trigger?" Matildi asked.

Kole nodded. "The code would not run unless it was activated by signalling the trigger code. That's the part that still had me stumped this morning until I spoke with Cahya. This code would have had to have been activated manually and I couldn't figure out how that might have happened. Then Cahya said that she saw Hathina at the tower—and it hit me."

A realization washed over Cahya. Hathina had direct access to her during her cycles. She hadn't ever considered how vulnerable a person was once they'd entered a cycle. You were left entirely in the hands of the ELC instructors, you had to surrender yourself completely. The fragility of the situation was terrifyingly glaring—what happened if you could not trust those people?

Kole let out a huge sigh. "She was standing right next to me, and I didn't see it. But I know now that Hathina had to have activated the code."

"So let's go get her!" Cahya exclaimed. Even if Hathina had been coerced, she had to be held accountable.

"It's not that easy," Balti pointed out. "We can't go after a single member of the Dakaï. If they knew we were onto them, they'd just go deeper underground, and we wouldn't know what they were up to until it was too late. We're playing a long game, Cahya. We have to; they've been playing for longer. We can't be rash."

"So what do we do?" Cahya asked.

Theo jumped in this time: "We have to let them maintain their confidence; let them believe that they've got the upper hand somehow."

Cahya had forgotten that Theo was sitting at the table. How was he a part of this? The question had sparked in her when she walked into the car and now it burned fiercely so that she couldn't hold back the urge to speak.

"Okay, Theo, great idea, sure, but how are you here?" Cahya asked. "I'm sorry, everyone; I just have so many questions. I don't think I can focus until I understand what's happening."

Doyen Hashen nodded. "Of course, Cahya, we should have given you an opportunity to catch up before now." He motioned to Kole to fill Cahya in.

Kole clarified, "The Tosha Council was formed twenty years ago when whispers about a secret Dakaï plot began to circulate. We needed a team who could quietly track their activity without raising suspicions.

"As for Theo," he continued, "Theo is an emissary from Octavia. He was sent to aid our council with the situation regarding the Dakaï. Theo is a well-respected expert in the subject of the Uprising of 506."

"I've done 357 cycles from that era," Theo explained. "When the Tosha Council was formed, they thought that my input could be helpful."

"And it has been," Matildi exclaimed.

"Okay, I'll buy that... and he's helping the Tosha Council, not the Council of Nirvana."

"Correct," the Doyen confirmed, "named after Doyen Tosha, who led Nirvana to peace and helped implement the ELC Program following the last uprising."

Cahya sighed heavily. "Does Nandini know about this?" Cahya asked. "Sorry, that's my last question."

"No," Theo admitted. "The fewer people who know, the better. Before your accident, you didn't know about this council either."

"Why not?"

Kole answered this time, "Because you were too focused on your parents' deaths. You tried to hide it, but we knew. We wanted to make sure you had enough energy to focus on your Dohan training, and we weren't sure you could handle the added pressure."

"I see," Cahya said. "So what do we give them?"

"Sorry?" Kole asked.

"Theo said we have to give them something. What do we give them?"

Doyen Hashen sighed. "There's only one thing we have to give them right now." He looked Cahya in the eye and said, "The Dohan."

✳ ✳ ✳

The members of the Tosha Council remained on the train as it left Catithia to return to Deshka. They hashed out their plan, which would begin with a meeting with the Council of Nirvana.

The sun shone brightly through the glass roof of the central tower. The entire council of twelve members sat around the yellow table. Doyen Hashen, Cahya, and Kole stood.

"I've called you all here for a very important decision. As you are all well aware, Cahya has been removed from the position of Dohan. I'll admit that I have hesitated to name a replacement for her. I suppose I had hoped she might yet come back to us.

"I apologize to you, our council members, for my tardiness. You can't blame an old Doyen for holding out for hope. Cahya has decided that she would like to begin on a new path, to find her way in Nirvana, and I believe that she deserves that opportunity.

"To that end, Kole will be working with Cahya to create an integration program that will allow her to study and find a vocation that is well-suited to her skills."

Many of the council members smiled kindly at Cahya, as though giving her their blessing.

"And so, as our old Dohan charts a new path, a new Dohan must come forward to take her place. As you know, it's the Doyen's responsibility to select a new candidate to serve as Dohan. However, as the council, you have the opportunity to voice concerns and cast a formal vote on my selection.

"I have spoken with Kole and with Cahya, and I have decided to name Nethos Portos as Nirvana's new Dohan, successor to the role of Doyen of Nirvana."

"Nandini and Cahya will step down, and Kole will begin the process of seeking out companions to accompany Nethos through his training.

"I will now provide you with the opportunity to air any concerns you might have with my decision."

The committee members exchanged glances, but no one spoke.

"Very well then, would you all please cast your formal vote in the matter of naming Nethos Portos to the role of Dohan of Nirvana."

Each member reached forward and touched the green dot on the table in front of them.

"Thank you all for your time today. I'm sure you have many things to get back to, so I won't keep you any longer. We'll hold the formal swearing-in ceremony tomorrow."

As the councilors stood to leave, Cahya looked out the windows at the gardens below. The view of the central hub was stunning from this vantage point. She could see Menza, full of diners eating and chatting, and she could see the park, where children were running around in the grass and along the play structures.

"I'm sure this is for the best, Cahya."

Kyun's voice made Cahya's skin crawl. She turned to find him standing close. The rest of the council members had left.

"Yes," Cahya said to him. "I'm sure you're right."

Cahya wasn't sad to let the Dohan position go permanently, but she wondered if, once she'd regained her memories, maybe she'd feel differently. Was she letting Old Cahya down?

It really didn't matter what she wanted anymore; this was bigger than her. Once the Dakaï had this win, the Tosha Council would have the space to plan their next move.

CHAPTER 18
BYE JOHNNY

"I don't understand; how does Kole know this is going to work?" Nandini asked, following Cahya to the ELC labs.

"He doesn't," Cahya admitted. She did her best to fill Nandini in on what Kole had told her about the program·bug, but she wasn't sure she fully understood it herself.

"Kole thinks that the program activated during the cycle, causing me to be murdered and end the cycle early. He thinks that's why I saw myself in the channel after Vitus' cycle. Vitus was also murdered, and he thinks that it forged a connection to Johnny's cycle.

"So, the theory goes that if I go back into Johnny's cycle and complete it the way it was meant to be completed, without interruption from the Dakaï program, it could help me regain my memories, but there's no guarantee."

Nandini shook her head. "But you can't do human cycles anymore. Your body can't handle it."

"Right, but I've already done Johnny's cycle, and so my body is already primed for it. I won't reject it like the other cycles; it's familiar," Cahya assured her with an uncertain smile. "At least that's what Kole said."

As they entered the lab, Nandini took Cahya's hand, "What if it doesn't work? What if it's worse than that? You're finally starting to seem like yourself, even without your memories, what if you forget everything that's happened since you woke up? I can't lose you again, Cahya." Nandini's eyes were full of fear, and Cahya didn't know what to say to make her feel better.

Kole and Theo were both in the lab, and Kole gestured toward the pod, "I'm ready when you are."

Cahya gave Nandini an apologetic look. "Just be here when I wake up, ok?"

Nandini nodded at first, but then she started to shake her head. "No," she said, staring at Cahya. "No, you're not going in alone. I'm going with you."

Cahya looked at Kole, who shook his head. "Nandini, this is a solo cycle; I can't just put you in."

"Figure it out, Kole. You don't have to create a new incarn; just connect me to someone who's already in there."

"Can you do that?" Cahya asked, becoming more confused by the second.

"Technically, yes," he admitted, "but there's a chance that having another person in there will set things off course."

"I won't set anything off course," Nandini insisted. "Get me in there, and I'll bring her back."

Kole looked at Cahya, who nodded.

"Okay," he conceded, "I'll need a few minutes to get you set up."

Nandini took off her jacket and sat in the pod next to Cahya. It was strange to be doing a cycle together when neither of them was in uniform. They laid back quietly until Kole indicated that he'd finished.

"Are you two ready?" Kole asked.

They looked at each other and smiled, "We're ready."

Kole set the timer to seven hours. "See you soon," he said, smiling at Cahya as he pressed the blue button.

***

Johnny stomped into the coffee shop, the jingle of the bell above the door heralding his arrival. The barista behind the counter looked up from her work and braced herself, recognizing the scowl on his face.

"Black coffee," Johnny growled, slapping a five-dollar bill on the counter. He'd had a terrible day, and he didn't want to be here. But his assistant had gone home for the night, and he needed caffeine if he was going to get through the wall of evidence waiting for him back at the office.

The barista got straight to work, she knew how impatient he was when he wasn't served quickly. She nervously reached for the cup that sat closest to the coffee pot, pouring black coffee into it.

Johnny took a sip, and immediately his face twisted in rage. "What the hell is this?" he bellowed, his voice echoing through the shop. "I ordered black coffee, not this sugary crap!"

The barista handed him a fresh cup of black coffee even as his insults continued. She slid his five-dollar bill across the counter. "It's on the house," she announced timidly. "Please accept my apologies for the mistake."

Johnny scoffed, took the new drink and his money, and stormed out of the café, his face still red with anger.

Johnny arrived at his office, slamming the door behind him. He took a deep breath and tried to calm himself down. He really needed to focus on this murder case; he'd been working on it for months, and he felt sure that he was on the brink of a breakthrough.

The evidence was all laid out on the wall of his small office. Pictures of the crime scene, witness statements, and newspaper articles about the victim. Johnny hadn't found a new piece of evidence in weeks, but he was sure that he had everything he needed to figure out what was going on. He studied the wall, trying to find the missing piece of the puzzle—that one detail that would help him solve the case. Just as he thought he was getting close, there was a loud knock at the door.

Johnny gritted his teeth, annoyed at the disruption.

Knock! Knock! Knock!

"We're closed!" Johnny shouted at the door, his eyes still fixed on the wall of evidence.

The knocking came again. Johnny stormed across the room and opened the door, ready to give whoever was on the other side a piece of his mind. But he was not prepared for what he saw.

"Hi, Mr. Grisdale." The woman from the coffee shop wore a timid, apologetic smile. "I know you're very busy, so I apologize for the intrusion. Your assistant, Cameron, he's a friend of mine."

Johnny stared at the barista, baffled by this interaction. What on earth was she doing here? He wished she would just get on with it.

"Anyway, I told Cameron what happened just now. I felt really bad. He said that you likely hadn't eaten today." She noticed the cold, uneaten soup on the desk and pushed a bag toward Johnny. "He said I should bring you a sandwich and remind you that you rarely solve a case on an empty stomach."

Johnny studied the woman as he made a mental note to fire Cameron first thing in the morning. He'd hire him back immediately—he'd need someone to pick up his dry cleaning, after all—but first, he'd fire him.

The woman was very beautiful; he hadn't noticed before. "I yelled at you, and you're bringing me dinner?" Johnny asked, confused.

"I know how much good you've done working in this small room, all alone, day in and day out." She caught herself. "I mean, I don't know any details; of course, that's all very private, but Cameron says you're a brilliant man and you've helped a lot of people. I imagine you feel a lot of pressure to find the answers you need. I'm Courtney, by the way." She managed a shy smile.

She pushed the bag toward Johnny again. "Anyway, I know you're very busy, and I don't want to keep you from your work. I just thought I could bring you something to eat. Please don't be angry with Cameron."

Johnny took the bag, and the woman turned to leave. Johnny closed the door and brought the bag back to his desk. He opened it and found a roast beef sandwich inside, his favorite. He really was very hungry.

He approached the board, pausing at a grainy photo of the restaurant where Jennifer had died. A still image, taken from some footage captured by a camera across the street, showed a man leaving the restaurant moments after her death. The man looked familiar, but Johnny couldn't place him.

He took a few bites, staring at the papers on his wall again. His eyes widened and he leaned in closer to the photo of the man with the large, sunken eye sockets. Something clicked. The hitman, he thought, Johnny recognized him from a past case. He found the old file and compared the photos. Sure enough, same guy! He inspected the grainy photo more closely and realized that the license plate number was reflected on the mirrored surface of a nearby food cart.

"Well I'll be damned!" Johnny muttered as he circled the license plate number in the photo and then, sitting at his desk, he searched for the plate number in a database. *BINGO!*

The face of a man named Gerald Harper was displayed on the screen, his large sunken eyes stared back and Johnny. I found you, you *son-of-a-bitch.*

Johnny looked back at the half-eaten sandwich on his desk. He hated that Cameron was right. He was definitely going to fire him before he started work in the morning, and then he was going to give him a raise.

Years later, a very old and wrinkled Johnny lay in a hospital bed, with an old, wrinkled Courtney by his side, squeezing his hand.

A nurse held a stethoscope to Johnny's chest, listening intently. She raised her eyes to meet Courtney's. "It won't be long now, Mrs. Grisdale."

Courtney nodded in understanding.

"I'll give you some privacy," and with that, the nurse slipped out of the room, closing the door silently as she left.

Courtney leaned in close and whispered, "Thank you, Johnny. Thank you for the beautiful life you've given me. Thank you for loving me." She squeezed his hand once more. "It's okay to let go now," she told him, tears streaking her cheeks.

Johnny could feel himself fading, edging further and further away from the clutches of life. He was grateful for his wife, and so sad to be leaving her. *I'm sorry, my darling wife,* he thought, but he couldn't speak. He felt Courtney's head on his chest and then the darkness creeped in.

The monitor emitted a long, low *beeeeeeeeeeep.*

A bright light appeared, and Johnny found himself moving quickly through a long tunnel, major life moments playing on screens lining the walls: his trip to Tibet with Courtney, their wedding day, the birth of their daughter... On and on, the screens flew by at an ever-increasing pace until they melded and then exploded into one bright, blinding light.

As the light dissipated, a figure stood in front of Johnny: a beautiful young woman with gorgeous brown skin, soft purple hair, and matching purple eyes.

"Hello, Cahya," Johnny said.

Cahya smiled at Johnny, tears in her eyes. "You did it."

"We both got what we wanted," Johnny told her. "I got to live out the life I was meant to live, and now you get to go back to Nirvana and finish what you started."

Cahya nodded, closing her eyes. When she opened them again, tears slid down her cheeks. "I'm scared," she admitted.

"Good," Johnny told her. "I'd be worried if you weren't." He handed her a small box with a bow on top.

"What's this?" she asked.

"You'll see," he told her, pulling her in for a hug. "Good luck, Cahya."

Cahya gasped for air, and her eyes popped open. The light of the blue dome cut through her like a sharp knife, and she squeezed her eyes closed again. She kept them closed as she tried to slow her breathing.

"You're clear, Cahya," Kole said, waiting by the console.

Cahya opened her eyes slowly, but she didn't move. She looked over at Nandini, whose dome was still glowing with flitting white lights.

As the lights slowed and faded, Nandini's eyes fluttered open.

"You are clear, Nandini," Kole announced.

Nandini pushed her dome up and went directly to Cahya, kneeling down next to the pod. She pushed Cahya's dome up and searched Cahya's eyes, waiting.

"Cahya?" she asked hesitantly.

"Ask me about something," Cahya said quietly.

"I don't—" Nandini started.

"Anything," she insisted, "something from before the accident." Her head was spinning. Were her memories back? She couldn't be sure. She needed a test.

"Okay, um, do you remember the cycle we did as waitresses in Nevada? We went to Reno, and you stole a purse from a lady at the hotel."

Cahya closed her eyes again and concentrated. She searched her mind for the memory. *Reno... waitress... purse.*

"I don't remember that," she finally admitted. Nandini's face flushed with disappointment. "I'm pretty sure that *you* stole the purse in Reno," Cahya corrected her.

"Oh yeah," Nandini laughed. Then her eyes became large with realization. "Wait! You remember!" Nandini's eyes filled with tears, and she let out a sob.

Cahya sat up, throwing her legs over the side of the pod. "Yes. I remember." She looked at Nandini and said, "But I don't blame you;

that lady had it coming. She was so mean to the concierge—she deserved to look like a fool when she tried to pay for her room."

Nandini laughed, tears streaming down her face. "And when we got caught, you told the cops it was all your idea."

"And then you convinced them that I was a liar, and they sent us both home just so they didn't have to listen to us argue anymore," Cahya reminded her.

"Exactly. Yes, that's exactly right!" Nandini laughed. She wrapped her arms around Cahya. "You remember."

Cahya hugged Nandini back for a moment and then took her by the shoulders, looking her in the eyes. "I remember," she said softly. "I remember that in Rome, you were Cornelius, and you were Adam—oh, I loved Adam!" Cahya laughed and hugged Nandini again.

A flood of memories rushed into Cahya's mind from past lives she'd had with Nandini. There were so many—Nandini was always there, always by Cahya's side. Always there to protect her, to love her, and to support her.

They'd been lovers in some of these lifetimes, and those cycles stood out in her mind now, cycle after cycle of stolen kisses, secret rendezvous, passionate, intimate encounters. They'd been drawn together by fate over and over again.

Cahya released Nandini from her embrace and looked into her eyes, as though seeing her clearly for the very first time. This woman *is* her love, her soulmate. "Nandini," she whispered, "I remember." She leaned in close and kissed Nandini tenderly on the lips. Nandini froze, surprised by Cahya's affection, but then she pulled her in tighter and eagerly returned her kiss.

Kole and Theo pretended not to watch, doing their best to give the two a brief moment of privacy.

"I love you," Cahya confessed between breaths.

"I love you, Cahya," Nandini cried. "I can't believe you're back! You're really here!"

They stopped kissing and stared into each other's eyes, drinking one another in. They'd crossed a threshold together just now, and they both knew it. There was no going back from this.

"Sorry to interrupt, ladies," Kole said, pulling the two back into the present moment. "Cahya, I'm glad you're back, and I wish we had time to celebrate, but we have to get ready to swear in the new Dohan."

CHAPTER 19
NEW DOHAN

Cahya stood on the flower-lined path that led to the entrance of the Transfer Station. She wore a white outfit with a long purple vest covered in deep purple embroidery. She wanted to look nice for the ceremony.

She couldn't be late; otherwise, people might start wondering if she didn't really support Nethos in this transition. Yet something had drawn her here. She made her way through the main entrance and down to the lower level. Her breathing slowed as she approached the access panel along the far wall.

She pulled the panel, sat it on the ground next to the opening, and climbed into her secret room.

"Myat, lights," she whispered into the darkness.

The lights flickered to life, and Cahya squinted, allowing her eyes to adjust. When she opened them, she could plainly see what she had been up to these past few weeks. It had been foggy, like a dream, the time she'd spent without her memories. She'd been Cahya in some ways, but she'd felt Johnny's presence with her always. He had become the biggest part of her for some time, quieting all of the other noise that came with being the version of herself who remembered her parents and her grief. The version blinded by what was right in front of her.

There was a certain clarity that came with knowing nothing; she could see it plainly now.

The walls had been stripped of all but a handful of the photos of her parents. She saw the extras piled up in the box next to the desk. In their place on the wall, she'd written notes, placed large red circles on diagrams, and used string to make connections between pieces of the puzzle.

Cahya stepped closer to the wall to have a better look at what she'd pieced together with the clarity afforded by her memory loss and Johnny's investigative mind.

Next to a photo of her parents standing with a T'Dava, she'd circled the moon with red ink. Next to it, a note read, *'Parents worked with the ònakai? Spent time on Octavia.'*

Another note read, *'Tashina Potiva, murdered? Why?'*

Another read, *'The link? Transfer Station?'* The words *Transfer Station* had been scratched out, and below it were the words, *'Thing?/Person?'* and then below that, *'Not on Nirvana.'*

Another note read, *'Who are the Dakaï?'* Below which she'd written *'Hathina'* with a question mark. Below that, with a great big question mark, she'd written *'Kyun?'* and then *'Nethos?'*

There were two objects on the desk below the notes and photos. The first was a smooth black device with a long slit along the top. The other was a small red ball, the size of a marble. Cahya picked up the ball and rolled it around in her hand, remembering when Kyun had given it to her the night she and Nethos visited Catithia.

She set the ball back on the table and picked up the smooth black device, pressing a finger into the groove at the center.

A light emerged, washing over her face, as a voice said, "Conducting a facial recognition scan for authentication," followed by, "Authentication successful. Please select a file from the list."

Cahya clicked on *'The Link'* and listened:

"I won't waste your time. We have much to discuss. It's time to put an end to the Doyen and our treaty with the ōnarai.

"We've waited a very long time for this—"

The recording continued to play, but Cahya had a flashback, a memory. She was preparing for her swearing-in ceremony shortly after she'd been named Dohan. Sam and Kyun were there, along with Nandini and Nethos. Sam tended to Nethos, adjusting the buttons on the front of his plain black tunic. Kyun turned to Cahya, took her hand, and, shaking it, leaned in and said, "We've waited a very long time for this—"

The memory played over in Cahya's mind as she listened to Kyun's voice. *"We've waited a very long time for this—"*

"We've waited a very long time for this—"

A whirring, rustling sound cut through the transmission, and the audio clip ended.

The voice on the recording was the same as the voice in her memory. The voice on the recording was Kyun. She hadn't been able to place it before, but now it was clear as day. Cahya picked up the red marker from the table and drew a line through the question mark next to Kyun's name. He was Dakaï; this confirmed it.

Cahya stepped back and took in the wall, staring at all the pieces that were finally fitting together. She had needed that memory of her swearing-in ceremony in order to hear Kyun's words and put that very big piece into place.

Oh no—the swearing-in ceremony!

Cahya checked the time; she was going to be late. Dammit!

Cahya raced out of the room, put the panel back in place, and flew out of the Transfer Station at top speed. She slowed slightly when she reached the populated area around the hub, but then she remembered that she was no longer Dohan. She didn't have to be quite as prim and proper. Instead of slowing down, Cahya picked up the pace, smiling in spite of herself.

She saw Nandini waiting for her behind the rows of chairs that had been set up by the central tower. She slowed her pace and stopped in front of Nandini, breathing heavily.

Nandini had her arms crossed, and her face was stern. "You were supposed to be here 20 minutes ago."

"I know, I'm sorry," Cahya said with her most apologetic smile.

Nandini rolled her eyes. "This was a part of you I didn't miss," she said. "You were more punctual when you didn't have your memories."

"Shhhhhhhhh—" Cahya hushed.

"Right, sorry," Nandini said, glancing around to see if anyone might have heard, but no one was within earshot.

It was imperative to the plan that no one outside of the Tosha Council knew that Cahya had regained her memories. Nandini was the sole exception, and now Cahya was wondering if that had been a good idea.

If the community found out that Cahya was whole again, many would fight for her to retain her role as Dohan, and that couldn't happen. The Dakaï needed this perceived win. If they thought their plan was going smoothly, they might let their guard down enough to slip up.

Nandini and Cahya made their way to the hub, where the ceremony would take place. As they took their seats close to the stage, a young man approached Cahya.

"Nethos is asking if you'll meet him in his dressing room, Doha—I mean, Cahya." The young man smiled, a little embarrassed. He gestured to the large curtain at the back of the stage, which had been erected for the event. Cahya looked up at the mirrored windows above the curtain. She knew that Nethos would be waiting there because she'd waited in the same room just eight years ago when she'd been sworn in as Dohan.

"Okay," she said, smiling at the young man. She gave Nandini a nod. "I'll be right back. Save my seat?"

She arrived at the dressing room and pressed her hand to the door. Inside, Nethos stood by the windows, staring down at the stage below. He turned to face Cahya as she walked into the room, his black Dohan tunic, covered in detailed embroidery, flowed just above the ground.

Cahya studied Nethos for a moment. His father was a member of the Dakaï—was he? Everything in Cahya told her that he wasn't. Sure, he was a bit brash sometimes, and he kept to himself often. He even sympathized with a lot of things the Dakaï stood for; he'd made that clear many times. But he didn't want to start a war. Did he?

Nethos turned from the windows and saw Cahya watching him. "This doesn't feel right," he said.

"What do you mean? You look great!" Cahya smiled, walking toward him. She brushed a small piece of lint from his shoulder and stepped back to look at him. "It fits you perfectly."

"I don't mean the tunic, Cahya. I mean this whole situation. None of it feels right." Nethos frowned, looking back at the stage through the windows. A large food cart from Menza stood next to him, full of untouched food.

"Looks like you haven't eaten yet. You shouldn't go out there on an empty stomach."

"I'm not hungry," he told her absentmindedly. "Do you know what the worst part of this is? I want to ask you how you felt when you had to go through this—if you felt like me, if you had doubts, if you were nervous—but you can't tell me because you don't remember."

Cahya felt awful for lying to Nethos about having regained her memories, but she had to keep up the charade.

"I don't, Nethos. I'm sorry. But here's what I can tell you: This feels right. I'm not meant to be wearing that tunic anymore. I don't know what I'm supposed to be doing, but I finally feel like I'm free to figure it out."

"And as for you, the Doyen believed that you were the right choice for Dohan. You wouldn't dare challenge the wisdom of the Doyen, would you?"

Nethos laughed. "I wouldn't dare," he admitted.

She placed her hands on his arms and gave him a little squeeze, feeling the metal of his armband under her right hand. It blended in with the tunic so much that she'd barely noticed it before.

"You've got this," she said. "Take a deep breath and relax. This part is just a formality, a chance for the citizens of Nirvana to see your face and welcome you as the new Dohan. Just smile and wave. You'll be fine."

"Thanks, Cahya," Nethos said, leaving the room and making his way down to the stage. Cahya watched from the window of his dressing room as the Doyen announced, "Ladies and gentlemen, I am very pleased to present to you Nethos Portos, Dohan of Nirvana."

Nethos climbed onto the stage, greeted by kind cheers and applause. He smiled and waved, just like Cahya told him to. The crowd filled most of the open area around the central tower. Some people were sitting on benches in the park, and some kids were standing on play structures to get a better look. Cahya caught sight of Ash sitting on her father's shoulders, watching the proceedings with tearful eyes. Poor Ash. She loved that Cahya was Dohan; this must feel terrible for her.

Next, Cahya saw Nandini in the front row, sitting with an empty seat next to her. Oops! She really ought to make her way down so that Nandini didn't have to sit alone.

Cahya turned to leave the room, but she was knocked to the floor by a large, muscular arm.

Gasping to catch her breath, Cahya looked around to see what was going on. A burly man and a tall woman stood in front of her. They reached down, grabbed her arms, and hoisted her to her feet. They held her firmly in place. Cahya tried to speak, but nothing came out; she was still trying to catch her breath.

"Myat, privacy mode," the woman said. The familiar tone sounded, and Kyun walked through the door, smiling at Cahya with his tight, snaky smile. "Hello, Cahya. I hope we're not disturbing you."

Cahya managed to find her voice and sputtered, "What is this, Kyun?"

"Isn't it obvious, my dear? I'm taking care of you once and for all. You know, you hire people to do these things, and you can never really trust that they're going to be done properly. This all could have been avoided, you know, had you just left well enough alone after your memories disappeared. But you've never been one to leave well enough alone, have you?"

"I don't understand," Cahya choked out.

"You don't? Well, allow me to spell it out for you. I know about your close call with regaining your memories during one of your cycles. It helps to have eyes everywhere. Cahya thought of Hathina; all of her progress was being reported back to Kyun.

"You may have made peace with stepping down as Dohan, but you will always be a threat to Nethos. If your memories return, people will call for you to take up the role once again. Nethos would be little more than a blip in the history books.

"So now that Nethos is in place, it's time to make you disappear. For good this time."

"It was you, wasn't it? You caused me to lose my memories."

"Well, I can't take all of the credit, though I did write a pretty sophisticated piece of software to make it happen. So I suppose I can take most of the credit."

"Nethos?" she asked. "Was he in on this too?"

"Oh goodness, no. Nethos doesn't have the stomach for the dark side of governance. No, Nethos will remain in the dark; he'll be a very important little puppet in the war to come."

"War?" Cahya gasped, horrified.

"There is no revolution without war, Cahya. Major change requires major sacrifice."

245

"Nethos may trust you, but I can't believe that he would follow you into war, Kyun."

"Nethos will see reason; I'm confident of that."

"There's nothing reasonable about what you're doing."

"I was like you once—young and full of hope. Full of faith in our planet's leaders. Full of a false belief that we are free and autonomous beings of the universe. But I was duped. And so are you, poor Cahya."

Cahya listened intently; she wanted to make sure he kept talking because once he stopped, she wasn't sure what would happen.

"We are being controlled and manipulated by the ònakai, but I'm going to help free our people once and for all."

"How?" Cahya asked. *Keep talking.*

Kyun's eyes sparkled. "Technology, of course! You remember my collection, don't you?"

Cahya nodded.

"Well, there's one device I didn't show you, but it's perhaps the most special one of them all. The ònakai developed a coding device—not for computers but for the mind. This device rewires the neural pathways of the human brain."

"How does rewiring someone's brain help with your revolution?" Cahya was afraid to hear the answer, but she needed to keep him talking.

"You do ask really great questions, Cahya. How indeed? The ònakai developed a tool that allows us to subvert the ELC program. This device projects a signal which uploads a neurological code to the brain. Once the code has been uploaded, the program's Life Cycles are experienced as little more than a dream. The student no longer has to endure the pain and suffering we've been subjected to for hundreds of years."

"I still don't understand how that helps," Cahya told him.

"Once the human race is liberated from the ònakai's mind-control program, they'll be free to see reason, to see that we've been brainwashed. We'll never be free as long as the ònakai have us under their thumb."

"Father," Nethos said, almost in a whisper. Kyun spun around to see his son standing in the doorway, his face twisted in confusion. "Please tell me that you did not use the coding device on me."

The room remained silent for several moments. Cahya watched Nethos' face, she'd never seen him look so upset. He was frozen in place as he repeated the words, "Father?"

Kyun regained his composure and responded matter-of-factly, ignoring his son's look of distress. "I did it for your protection, Nethos."

"All of these years," Nethos said, eyes darting about the floor as he gathered his thoughts. "Everyone else spoke of the transformative power of their cycles, the bonds they'd formed with the people they'd been through cycles with. It all sounded so foreign to me. I never experienced any of that."

"It's not transformation, Nethos; it's brainwashing," Kyun told him firmly. "Now stop this."

"You told me I was special," Nethos continued, "that I was stronger than the other students. That I was better than them. I spent my whole life feeling like an outsider... because of you."

"I freed y–"

"Undo it," Nethos demanded, cutting his father off.

"What?" asked Kyun.

"Undo it! Reverse it. Change the code so that I can do the cycles. I'll go back and start over. I can't be Dohan if I can't experience the cycles. You had no right to take that from me!"

"It cannot be undone, Nethos. Once the code is uploaded to the brain, it cannot be removed; the ELC software will always find it and obey it. The only way to remove it is to reset the brain—you'd lose not just your memories but your ability to speak and walk. It's not an option."

Nethos sat, his face twisted in shock; he didn't respond.

"You'll come to see reason in time," Kyun insisted. "We cannot continue to hide from the truth."

Cahya, who had been listening quietly, spoke now as Nethos sat in stunned silence. "What truth is that?" she asked. Her captors squeezed her arms tightly and mumbled to her to keep quiet, but Kyun responded.

"The truth is that we have allowed ourselves to become inferior, docile, and defenseless against the ònakai. We must come together to terminate our treaty and prepare to protect ourselves against whatever may be coming."

"Nirvanians will not believe that the ònakai mean to harm them in any way. We've lived here nearly two millennia in peace with the ònakai," Cahya challenged.

"A blip! A tiny, minuscule blip in the timeline of the ònakai. They are patient beings, and they will wait to strike, I assure you."

"But what could they possibly want with us? Why would they want to cause us any harm?" Cahya asked.

"They don't want to harm us; they want to control us. Turn us into their slaves. And then they can do whatever they want with us."

"Why would you not bring your concerns to the Doyen? You're a member of the council, you have great influence in that space. Surely you could have brought your concerns to them and they would have listened."

"Oh yes, the council. That was my first strategy; I've had several strategies, in fact, over the years. I believed that becoming a member of the council would provide me with the platform I needed to share my discoveries and shift our fate on this planet. It took me very little time to realize, however, that the council was too far gone. They were completely brainwashed and blind in their loyalty to the ònakai and to the treaty. I would never be able to sway them. The only way to sway the council is through the Doyen." He gestured toward Nethos now.

"But a liberated future-Doyen isn't enough, we need to liberate everyone. Everyone deserves to be free of this curse that is the ELC program." Kyun narrowed his menacing eyes at Cahya.

"When did you do it?" Nethos asked, breaking his silence. A look of disbelief still covered his face as he processed everything his father was saying.

Kyun wasn't sure what Nethos was referring to. He prompted him for clarification. "Do what?" he asked.

"When did you recode my brain without my knowledge?"

"What does it matter?" Kyun pressed, clearly annoyed by the question.

"Does Mother know? Does she know what you did to me?"

"Of course not; your mother wouldn't have understood."

"When?" Nethos asked again.

"When you were twelve, Tashina helped me."

"Tashina wouldn't have done that," Nethos argued.

"No, she wouldn't have, not intentionally," Kyun agreed. "She was a child when she came to work for me, 19-years-old. She didn't have a clue. When she discovered what the device could do, I convinced her to test it on me; since I'd completed all of my ELC training, there would be very little downside if it worked."

"What she did not realize was that I'd placed you in the room right next to me, hoping that the device would also code your brain. Tashina was none the wiser for nearly 25 years. Eventually she grew suspicious after she had a conversation with you about the cycles. She realized that you weren't experiencing the cycles like others did. She's smart, she eventually put all the pieces together. There was no sense in lying to her when she confronted me about it. She was outraged, but it's only because she didn't understand either; she was brainwashed too, after all.

"She threatened to go to the Doyen and, well, we couldn't have that."

"So you killed Tashina," Cahya said, the note on her wall flashing into her mind now.

"Quiet!" The man holding her arm shouted.

Kyun ignored Cahya and said, "I couldn't be sure that the upload had worked until you started your cycles. But after a few rounds, it became clear to me that you were not having a typical experience, and I knew it had worked." The pride in Kyun's voice was something Cahya had never heard. "No one else noticed because they didn't even know to look for it."

Nethos interjected, "Why are you telling me all of this now? Why are you confessing?"

"I'm giving you a unique opportunity, son. I'll even let Cahya have a choice here too, since I'm feeling generous. Now that you know the truth, you can make up your mind to join us."

"Us?" Cahya asked. "Ouch!" The woman pinched her this time. She didn't care; she wanted to hear him say it out loud.

"The Dakaï, Cahya. The saviors of Nirvana. The ones who will free us from the ònakai once and for all."

She knew it, but there was nothing quite like a confession to make it real. "I'll never join the Dakaï, Kyun," Cahya told him.

"Oh, such a shame. Not to worry, Nethos and I will lead Nirvana into a new era of growth and prosperity, without the interference of the ònakai."

"No," Nethos mumbled, looking at his father in disbelief.

"Excuse me?" Kyun asked, his eyes narrowing on Nethos.

"No. I don't want to have any part in your plan. I'm the Dohan now, and I have a responsibility to look out for the people of Nirvana. You're trying to destroy everything we've built for the past two thousand years."

Cahya smiled at Nethos and resisted the temptation to cheer. It felt as though she was just now seeing him for the first time.

"Well, that's disappointing." Kyun frowned. "No trouble, you'll just need a little extra time to think it over. We can work on that."

"Take them both," Kyun instructed. We have to get them out while the crowds are still distracted with the celebration."

Before she could react, Cahya felt a pinch on her neck, her vision narrowed and the room went dark.

CHAPTER 20

NETHOS

Cahya's eyes fluttered open, and she found herself lying on the floor of a dimly lit room. This room seemed familiar. She blinked and gave her eyes a moment to adjust to the light. She felt weak and groggy. There was a black spiral staircase and a photo of an elderly woman hanging on the wall.

Yes! Yes, she knew where she was. The bunker in the Portos' house. To her left, Nethos lay sleeping on the ground.

"Nethos," she whispered, "Nethos, wake up." She leaned over to nudge him awake, which is when she noticed the cuffs around her wrists. She crawled a few feet across the floor to where Nethos slept and pressed on his shoulder. "Nethos, wake up."

Nethos opened his eyes and squinted up at Cahya. "Where are we?" he asked.

"We're at your place. Well, your parents' place. In the bunker."

"How'd we get here?"

"I have no idea. Your father would have had to sneak us out through a huge crowd of people. There's no—" Cahya's eyes grew large as she suddenly realized what had happened. "The food cart," she said.

"Huh?"

"The food cart. They could have wheeled us out of there using food carts without raising suspicion." Cahya inspected the room. "Is there a way to get out of here?" She pulled herself up to inspect the walls and the doorway at the top of the stairs.

"No, not from the inside."

Cahya searched around for a few more minutes but decided it was futile and eventually lowered herself back to the ground next to Nethos.

The two sat quietly for a while, processing the gravity of what was happening.

"So I guess you're not a Dakaï, huh?" Cahya teased.

Nethos rolled his eyes, "Why would I be a Dakaï?" he asked, exasperated.

"I don't know, you defend a lot of their ideologies," Cahya retorted.

"Just because I think someone has some valid points, doesn't mean I agree with everything they stand for. What the Dakaï are trying to do is dangerous and I want no part of it." He paused, quiet for a moment and Cahya studied his worried face.

Nethos ran a hand through his curls before he broke the silence, his eyes fixed on the empty wall ahead. "I always knew I was different from everyone else. How arrogant am I that I thought the reason I wasn't impacted by the cycles was because I was... tougher? I thought I was better in some way. I've worked so hard to impress my dad my whole life, and he was just using me. Who does that to their kid?"

Nethos shook his head and shifted his gaze to his lap.

After a moment he asked, "What are the cycles actually like?" a sadness in his tone.

Cahya could see the pain in his eyes. "They're like this, I suppose; they feel as real as it feels for you and me to be sitting here right now. When you're in a cycle, you're in it fully and completely. Nirvana melts away, and you become someone else for an entire lifetime. You fully become your incarn, you live their pain and grief as deeply as anyone could, and you revel in their joys and success. You fall in love, you have your heart broken, you lose people you love, you have children and love them more than life itself. It's all real." Cahya looked at Nethos and asked, "What was it like for you?"

"It was always like watching a movie for me. I was there, but as an observer, in a way. It felt like a dream. I don't know that I was ever really there at all. I was on the sidelines. Watching. Observing. Never actually participating in the game. I guess that's why it didn't make sense that others made such a big deal of it."

Nethos sat quietly for a moment, pondering. "Some of the things we've been through in the cycles... Why would anyone want it to be real? It would be so much more painful that way."

"I can't remember everything we've been through, but I remember my cycle as Johnny and the one as Vitus, and yeah, there's pain, but it's not all pain. There's also some really deep joy," she paused, "and there's love. It all goes hand in hand. Seeing the story is good; it allows you to understand life from various perspectives, and understanding breeds empathy, which is wonderful. Living the story though—that's a whole other level," she paused to consider how she might explain it, "because once you've lived every story, you become every story, you become every person, and you know every person, like this deep intimate knowing, you know? To know a person, *really* know them, is to love them, and if you can know everyone, you can love everyone." She stopped, worried that she might have said too much. "At least, that's what I've been told," she concluded, smiling shyly.

Nethos studied her. "Sounds like you've learned more about the cycles in just a few months than I've learned from them over the course of my whole life. I guess that's why you were chosen to be Dohan. Even without your memories, you're one of the wisest people I know, Cahya," Nethos admitted.

Then he continued, his eyes filled with regret. "I suppose that's why you and I never really connected in any of the cycles. I wasn't there. Not really." He glanced at Cahya apologetically.

Cahya didn't respond, but she returned his gaze, her eyes filled with regret. She suddenly realized that she'd never really known Nethos at all. They'd spent years together and had never truly bonded. She could feel that in her body and in the way he acted around her. Maybe Nethos hadn't ever formed a real bond with anyone. She couldn't let Nethos know that she'd regained her memories, but maybe that could work in her favor right now.

"Well, we're both here now. Let's see if we can't make up for some lost time." Cahya smiled at him. "We're basically starting from scratch anyway, right? I don't remember most of the cycles, and I remember nothing from our past here on Nirvana, so none of that matters right now." Cahya put out her hand. "Hi, I'm Cahya."

Nethos smiled a grateful smile and took Cahya's hand in his, shaking it warmly. "Hi Cahya, I'm Nethos; it's nice to meet you."

"So Nethos, tell me about yourself. Did you grow up here in Catithia?"

"I did. With my mom and dad and my older brother, Tennar," he recalled, "and you grew up here too, before you moved to Deshka. Our parents were friends. We visited each other a lot as children. I always admired you, Cahya."

He laughed in spite of himself. "Can I tell you something?"

"Of course, tell me everything," Cahya replied, a mischievous tone to her voice.

"My mom thinks that I rushed my studies and went to Deshka early for Tashina," he laughed again as though the thought amused him. "I wasn't in a hurry to get to Deshka for Tashina. I was trying to get back to you."

Cahya's breath caught in her chest, but didn't speak. Nethos gave her a shy look, "I was always jealous of Nandini, of how close the two of you were."

Cahya studied Nethos in disbelief. All this time, he had wanted to be with her? She had always assumed his distance came from resentment, that he hadn't wanted the role of her companion or

Napili. But he was really resentful that he wasn't closer to her—jealous of Nandini?

A pang of guilt tightened her chest as she recalled the kiss she and Nandini had shared. It had been spontaneous, but the memory lingered now with a strange weight.

Cahya opened her mouth to speak, but she was cut short when the door at the top of the stairs slid open. Kyun slipped down the staircase and into the small room. Cahya and Nethos pulled themselves up from the ground, standing to face him. Their hands hanging cuffed in front of them.

"Well! Good morning, sleepy heads! I hope you got some rest. We're on our way to Almatar today. Sam will be home soon, and we can't have her finding the two of you cuffed in here, can we?"

"So Sam isn't part of this plan of yours, I suppose?"

"Oh Cahya, some people just aren't built for the revolution. Nethos' mother is kind but very naive. She'll appreciate the new world we're about to build, but she can't be a part of the mess it will take to get us there."

"Nethos, have the two of you reconsidered your position?"

Cahya looked at Nethos, who stared silently at his father. "No, Kyun," she said finally, when Nethos didn't respond. "He doesn't want any part in your terrible schemes."

"No, indeed, but of course, we want Nethos to think for himself, don't we?" He shot Cahya with a sarcastic look.

"I'll need the two of you to come with me... voluntarily."

Cahya caught a sparkle coming from Kyun's side, and that's when she saw it. The shiny gold ònakai gun. Her pulse quickened at the sight; she knew the weapon was ònakai so humans couldn't use it, but something in her told her Kyun had found a loophole. Still, her resolve was unshakeable.

Kyun followed her gaze. "No tranq pistols today, I'm afraid; I don't have any friends here to lug you guys about."

"I know you can't use that, Kyun," Cahya challenged, "You told me that these weapons can only be activated using ònakai biomarkers, remember?"

"Who said that this gun was ònakai?" Kyun quipped, a flash of pride in his eyes.

Cahya hadn't considered that Kyun might have weapons that were not ònakai. The humans had been forced to destroy all their weapons and they were forbidden from making any more after they'd signed the treaty.

"How? The Treaty—"

Cahya's words were cut off by Kyun's sharp reply, "the Treaty will be terminated; and in the meantime, we have to prepare—we have to protect ourselves."

Cahya opened her mouth to respond but Kyun proceeded first.

"Enough of this, there's no time. Let's get moving," Kyun instructed.

"I'm not going anywhere with you, Kyun," Cahya said stubbornly.

Kyun lifted the gun from its holster, a sharp pulse noise erupting from it as it powered on. "Don't make me use this, Cahya. I've worked very hard to put our planet on the path to salvation, and I won't have it all thwarted by a know-it-all little girl hell-bent on doing the right thing."

"I will not join the Dakaï, Kyun, and you can't hold me here forever. You'll have to kill me or let me go."

"I knew that this might happen, Cahya. I knew that even though you'd lost your memory, some part of you might still be too naive to see reason, even when it's staring you right in the face." He waved the gun around, "This mission is bigger than you. If you won't join us, you'll only get in the way. You're not leaving me any choice, I'm afraid."

Kyun took aim, "NO!" Nethos shouted as he stepped in front of Cahya, "I'll join you, father."

"Nethos, you can't!" Cahya shouted at him. Nethos didn't turn to look at her. "I have one condition; Cahya cannot be harmed. I know you can't let her go yet; she's too dangerous, but you can't hurt her."

"Nethos, don't do this." Cahya pleaded.

"If she is not with us, Nethos, she's against us. She can't live." Kyun raised the gun again, pointing it at Cahya's head.

"Father, stop! I won't let you hurt her." Kyun lowered the gun and studied his son, perplexed. Nethos didn't move; he stood strong in his resolve, staring at his father.

"I'm sorry, Nethos. I didn't realize you'd grown fond of this woman." Kyun stepped away from the stairs and gestured for Nethos to walk up. "Come, let's discuss this."

Nethos moved toward his father, keeping Cahya behind him as he moved. Kyun opened his arms and embraced his son as he approached. He leaned down and whispered in his ear, "One day you'll understand."

Kyun leveled the gun at Cahya once again. Nethos's eyes went wide. He shoved his father backward, then spun around and lunged at Cahya, knocking her out of the line of fire. She stumbled over a box and hit her head hard on the corner of a shelf. A thunderous blast echoed through the room, and Nethos was flung against the wall where they'd been sitting moments before.

Everything went black for a moment, and Cahya was overtaken by a searing pain in her head. She could barely open her eyes but managed to force them open long enough to find Nethos lying motionless on the floor.

Sam burst into the room, flying down the twisted staircase. She let out a blood-curdling scream as she ran toward Nethos. Kyun dropped the gun, staring at his wife and his son, taking in the gravity of what had just occurred.

Stunned, he picked up the gun, ran up the stairs and out of the bunker room.

"Nethos! Nethos! No, please, *please no. Nethos!*" Sam screamed, holding her son's head in her lap. Cahya wanted to get up, to help, but the room felt as though it had tilted and Cahya couldn't muster the strength to pull herself up. A rush of nausea overtook her followed by searing pain and as the darkness grew in her mind, Cahya could still hear Sam crying out.

CHAPTER 21
KIDNAPPING

Cahya heard the sounds of the hospital room and knew where she was before she even opened her eyes. Her entire body hurt, but the pain in her head was the most intense.

"Cahya, can you hear me?" came a familiar voice.

"Kole?" Cahya forced her eyes open, the light in the room blinding her.

"Myat, dim lights," Kole instructed. The lights in the room dimmed, and she was able to open her eyes fully. Kole stood next to her, a grim expression on his face.

"How?" she started to ask.

"Samuella Portos, she called the E.R.F., and they brought you here; I didn't want you to go to the medical center in Catithia."

Catithia? Sam? Her memory was hazy; she knew she'd been in Catithia, but why? How did she get there? And then, all at once, the whole ordeal came back to her. Nethos!

"Where's Nethos?" She asked, her fearful eyes searching Kole's face for any sign of hope. She was terrified to hear the answer.

Kole hesitated and then shook his head. "I'm so sorry, Cahya."

Cahya felt all of the air leave her body. Her hands clenched the blankets twisting them up toward her face where tears burned hot in her eyes.

"She's awake?" Nandini whispered to Kole as she entered the room. She made her way to Cahya's side and wrapped her arms around her. "Cahya, I'm so, so sorry."

The moment Nandini's arms encircled her, Cahya's composure dissolved completely. Tears cascaded down her cheeks as she buried her face in Nandini's shoulder, her body trembling with each sob. She gasped for air and Nandini clung to her. They sat like this for what felt like an eternity.

Slowly, the sobbing turned to whimpers, the heaving turned to shudders, and Cahya's breathing changed from gasping to stuttering inhales. She breathed deeply and exhaled, releasing Nandini from her grip and staring at the ceiling. She inhaled one final stuttering breath and, releasing it, regained her composure.

"I need to see the Doyen," Cahya said.

Kole protested, "You need to rest, Cahya; you've hit your head really–"

"There's no time, Kole," she told him, a sharpness in her tone. "I need to see him now."

※ ※ ※

The sun was just beginning to set by the time the Tosha council convened at the Doyen's house. Kole helped to bring Nandini up to speed on the clandestine group while they waited for Matildi to arrive.

"We've long suspected that Kyun was involved with the Dakaï, but we had no way of being sure," the Doyen explained. "Now that he's been exposed, he'll go into hiding."

Kole, Theo, and Balti sat in the large white chairs; Cahya sat on the countertop across the room; and Nandini stood next to her.

262

A dinging noise rang out through the room, and the Doyen, who stood near the door, pressed a hand against the wall, and the door opened, allowing Matildi to join the meeting.

"Apologies for my tardiness," he said as he took a seat in the remaining chair. "I was headed to Penchewaga to spend some time with my family. I thought we might have a period of rest once the new Dohan was in place."

"The new Dohan is dead, I'm afraid," the Doyen explained.

"Oh," Matildi gasped, giving Cahya a sympathetic look. "I'm so sorry, Cahya; I know he was your Napili."

"Thank you, Matildi," Cahya said.

"We all felt that the Dakaï might rest once the new Dohan was in place," Kole explained, "We figured they'd give him some time to establish himself in the hearts and minds of the people. That's the only way he could be of value to them if he had influence."

Balti nodded. "Exactly. But now they're spooked; with Kyun being exposed and Nethos dead, they won't wait to strike. We just can't be sure what they have planned."

"I know what they have planned," Cahya told them. Everyone turned to look at her. She slid off the counter and stood next to Nandini. "But first, I have some questions."

"Yes?" The Doyen prompted.

"When I lost my memories, Doyen, you told me to look for gaps. So you'll forgive me for any perceived scrutiny."

Cahya continued, "Is there any validity to the Dakaï's concerns? Is there any risk that the ònakai are plotting against us? That they're secretly building weapons or that the Treaty is in place to keep us weak?"

She turned to Theo, "I'm sorry, Theo, I have to ask these things. I have to make sure I'm not choosing a side blindly."

Theo nodded somberly.

"You are wise to ask these questions, Cahya," the Doyen told her. "But no, I do not believe that the ònakai have any ill intentions toward us."

"Kyun found weapons and devices designed for destruction; they were hidden in the mountains of Talem. All of the devices were ònakai," Cahya continued, "why would they be here?"

The group looked to Theo now, who pondered the question. "The ònakai have dark periods in their history, like all other species in the galaxy. During our last great war, 20,000 years ago, long before the first humans arrived here, some ònakai used Nirvana as a base. It makes sense that some artifacts from that time may have been left behind, but I can assure you that the ònakai have no ill intentions toward humans."

"Fear and suspicion are a dangerous combination," the Doyen chimed in. "Humans do not trust what they don't know. In the absence of information, we're left to form our own conclusions. As it so happens, humans are terrible at drawing conclusions; we tend to default to the worst possible explanation."

Balti joined in now, "The ònakai have lived in this solar system for over a hundred thousand years. They've seen their share of wars and strife, and they relive those moments through their own Life Cycle program."

Theo nodded. "It's been so long now; we have all but bred these negative traits out of our people. We've changed our very genetics over time. Ònakai do not default to fear and hatred the way that humans sometimes do. Still, we continue the cycles so that we never forget."

Cahya nodded. "Do you think humans could achieve that? Freedom from fear, suspicion, hate, and greed?"

"With the help of the cycles, yes, absolutely," Theo confirmed. "It will take time before the changes take place at a cellular level, at the level of human DNA; but I believe that it will happen for humans too, in time."

"Then we have to stop what's coming," Cahya told them. "Kyun has this device that can reprogram our brains. It will make it so that we no longer live through the cycles; we'll experience them as a dream instead. He plans to upload it to the brains of every human on the planet."

"They were all supposed to be destroyed," Theo said.

"What was that, Theo?" Balti asked.

"The device Cahya is describing is called a dishack," Theo explained. "They were built on Octavia illegally, a few decades after the Life Cycle program had been implemented planet-wide. Some ònakai discovered that it was possible to create a disconnect between the experiences of a life cycle and the emotional suffering that comes with it."

He continued, "It was a terrible time in our history. When you're disconnected from feeling the cycles, you don't gain any of the empathy or wisdom from those hard-earned experiences. Those ònakai who had been dishacked were easily manipulated, and eventually, a group of anti-cycle activists formed an army. They rose up against the Octavian Council and the Cycle Program.

"They had never experienced war," Theo continued, his voice lowered to a somber tone. "They'd watched it, like a movie, but they didn't really understand what they were starting. I've done cycles that reenact lives from that time period; it was a terrible thing to behold."

Theo lowered his head. Cahya had never seen him look so distraught. He took a deep breath and continued, "One of our great cities was destroyed, and many lives were lost. The dishack devices were confiscated, destroyed, and banned. But much of the damage had been done. It took a long time to rebuild our world from that point—thousands of years. But we did it in time."

Matildi chimed in, "If Kyun is allowed to deploy this device, humans wouldn't be capable of experiencing the benefits of the cycles. The wisdom that comes from real experience," he narrowed his eyes, focusing on the jasmine plant that sat on the coffee table in front of him. "In just a few short generations, we'd be right back where we started when we first arrived here in the Gardia system. We'd destroy ourselves the same way we have so many times before."

"What do we do now?" Nandini asked, glancing around nervously. "We can't let that happen."

Theo was staring at the floor, deep in thought. He shook his head and explained, "The device that Kyun has, one that would be powerful enough to download the code into many brains all at once, would require a tremendous amount of gravitational power. It could only be deployed on a night when all three moons are visible in the sky. It would also have to be deployed from a high point, at least 100 feet. There aren't many buildings that tall here on Nirvana, and all of them are in highly populated areas. He'd risk being seen."

"They're not all in highly populated areas," Cahya reminded Theo.

"The T'Dava," he said, nodding.

Cahya nodded, "We'll have to go get it."

Nandini cut in, "And I suppose we're just going to walk up and ask them nicely to hand over the device? We have no weapons, and we know they have at least one gun. Who knows what else? It's a suicide mission!"

"And it's a death sentence for our entire planet if we do nothing," Kole said calmly, looking around the room.

"So he has the height and the privacy," Cahya summarized. "When does he have three moons?"

"Tonight," Theo confirmed, "but I don't understand how he plans to use it. The technology is ònakai; he'd need ònakai biomarkers to activate it."

"He's already used it," Cahya said, "on himself and on Nethos. There could be others too; I'm not sure."

"How?" Balti asked.

"Tashina Potiva," Cahya explained, "figured out a way to make the technology work with her DNA."

"But Tashina is gone," Nandini said. "How..."

Nandini continued talking, but Cahya didn't hear her because a sharp and terrifying realization swept over her.

The Doyen put a hand up to silence everyone, listening to a report that was coming through his earpiece, he wore this when Myat was in privacy mode so that he could still be reached, if needed.

He looked around the room, a sober look on his face, "They have Ash-Lynn Potiva."

CHAPTER 22

IT'S KA'ANA

Cahya felt as though her heart had been torn out of her chest. They had Ash, and it all made sense now. If Tashina had made the device work for her DNA, it would work for Ash as well.

"They'll be keeping her at the T'Dava; they don't know that we know about it. They'll think they're safe there. We need to go now," Cahya said, looking around the room.

The council exchanged looks. "We have to be smart about this, Cahya; you can't be the one to go," Kole said. "The Dohan has to be protected."

"I'm not the Dohan," Cahya reminded him. "Nethos was the Dohan, and now he's dead. Who was protecting him?" She shot the council an accusatory look.

"I'm not going to stand around and do nothing while more people get hurt."

Matildi nodded. "I'm afraid that I agree with Cahya. It has to be someone from this council. We can't involve the E.R.F.; it's challenging to know who we can trust there. If the Dakaï were able to infiltrate the Council of Nirvana, there's no telling where else they may have followers lurking."

"Nandini and I will go with her," Theo told the council.

Nandini nodded in agreement.

"Very well," the Doyen agreed, seeing no objection from Kole, Balti, or Matildi. "You'll need some supplies. The lower level of the Transfer Station has a room with night-vision glasses, tranq guns, and the like."

"I'll confirm that you'll have access," Balti said.

"I have access," Cahya told them.

"Very well," Balti nodded.

Nandini and Theo stood in the pathway of the Doyen's home, waiting for Cahya to join them. Before Cahya left, she turned to the Doyen for a private word. "Doyen Hashen," she began, looking over her shoulder at the seating area where Balti, Kole, and Matildi had resumed talking. "How did you know you could trust them? When you formed the Tosha council, how could you know that none of them were secretly with the Dakaï?"

The Doyen smiled. "When you've lived more than 10,000 Life Cycles, you become very attuned to reading people, Cahya. I trust Kole with my life; he has a good heart and a wise soul. I know that he would only ever want what's best for Nirvana.

"And as for Balti and Matildi," he said, "well, they were my companions when I was Dohan. I know them as well as I know myself."

＊＊＊

Cahya approached the transfer station with Nandini and Theo close behind. The structure's gleaming metal contrasted sharply against the lush trees surrounding it. Cahya's heart pounded with anticipation—Ash was in danger, and time was running out.

Suddenly, a faint rustle in the foliage caught Cahya's attention. She halted, turning her head just enough to see the edge of a crimson cloak peeking from behind a nearby tree. She tensed—*Dakaï!* But a hand emerged, beckoning urgently yet silently.

"Go on ahead," Cahya whispered to Nardini and Theo, who had not noticed the disturbance. "I'll be right behind you."

They shared a concerned glance but followed her instruction. Once they'd disappeared into the station, Cahya moved cautiously toward the hooded figure. As she drew closer, the figure stepped forward into a shaft of light. It was Hathina, her face drawn with worry.

"Hathina?" Cahya breathed, glancing around to be sure no one else was watching. "What are you doing here?"

"I had to speak with you," Hathina whispered. Her voice trembled with a mix of fear and resolve.

Cahya scanned the area again, then leaned in. "Talk quickly. They'll be back if I'm out here too long."

Hathina lifted her hood, revealing tired eyes. "I'm sorry for everything. I was the one who gave you the device—the recording. I hoped you would recognize Kyun's voice or at least sense there was more to your memory loss than the story you were told."

Cahya's eyes narrowed on Hathina, still not fully certain of her role in all of this, "Say more."

Hathina nodded, her voice shaky. "Kyun threatened me. He threatened..." She swallowed hard, "Ash. I loved Tashina like a sister, and when she died, I couldn't just accept it—there had to be a reason. I started digging and that led me to the Dakaï. They had a hand in Tashina's death, I'm sure of it, but I needed proof. When I finally infiltrated one of their meetings, Kyun discovered me. He told me that if I didn't do as he said, he'd hurt Ash. I—I didn't know who else to trust. Everyone could have been compromised... except you. I knew you weren't in on it because they were targeting you."

Cahya's pulse quickened. "Hathina, the Dakaï already have Ash."

Hathina's face went pale. "No..." She took a shaky breath. "Let me help."

Cahya placed a hand on Hathina's shoulder. "No. The fewer of us, the less likely we'll be detected before we reach Ash. If you go, Kyun might see you as a threat, and who knows what he'll do? We need you alive—and free—to report this directly to the Doyen once we rescue Ash. Trust me—Doyen Hashen isn't involved with the Dakaï. He can be trusted."

Hathina's voice quivered with gratitude and lingering fear. "You're sure?"

Cahya nodded. "Yes. For now, find a safe place and wait. Once this is over, I'll make sure the truth comes out."

Tears filled Hathina's eyes, but she blinked them back. "Be careful. If anything happens to Ash—"

"It won't," Cahya interrupted, her resolve unwavering.

Hathina bowed her head, pulling her hood low once more. "Thank you, Dohan." She took a step backward, fading into the shadows. "And... forgive me."

Cahya opened her mouth to respond, but Hathina was already gone. A moment later, Cahya turned and sprinted for the station. Nandini and Theo were waiting, and she had a rescue mission to lead.

In the lower levels of the Transfer Station, Cahya, Nandini, and Theo gathered up the equipment they needed, including tranq guns, night-vision goggles, and sleek black outfits that would allow them to hide in the shadows of the forest.

As they made their way up to the second level, Cahya stopped and stared at the panel on the far side of the room.

Nandini followed her gaze. "Cahya, we have to go," she said.

"There's something I need to do first," Cahya told her. "Theo, I'll need your help."

Cahya made her way to the panel; she gave it a tug, and it popped out from the wall. Theo and Nandini followed Cahya into the small room.

Cahya asked Myat to turn on the lights to reveal her secret space, the place that had been her refuge for years.

"When did you do all this?" Nandini asked, scanning all of the notes and evidence covering the walls.

"After you and I found it, while I was doing the plant cycles," Cahya said, "and it wasn't me. Not really. It was Johnny."

Theo studied the wall and said, "It looks like you pulled a lot of stuff together—information that took the Tosha council years to figure out."

Cahya nodded. "I should have figured it out sooner. The only reason I was able to do it at all was because my memories were gone, so I had stopped obsessing about my parents for the first time in more than twenty years."

She glanced at the box stacked high with photographs and said, "If I'd been more vigilant, I would have noticed the Dakaï had returned. I would have sensed that something was off about Tashina's death, I would have pushed harder for answers. Instead, I devoted all my attention to my parents. If I'd just *looked around* I might have figured out what was going on—and I would have realized that Ash needed to be protected."

"You can't blame yourself for this," Nandini told her, placing a hand on her shoulder.

"I was the Dohan, Nandini; it was my job to be there for Nirvana. Instead, I was selfish. I could only see my pain... my loss."

The realization weighed heavily on Cahya. This place, this little hole in the wall, had been her lifeline to her parents—the only place she could go to feel connected to them. Without it, without her parents, she didn't know who she was. Looking around now, she realized that she'd built herself a prison. She created it, and she was the only one who could get herself out.

"We'll give you a minute," Nandini said, gesturing for Theo to follow her out of the room.

Cahya walked up to the wall and ran a finger over the photo of her parents standing by the T'Dava, Octavia's moon circled in the corner. In that moment, she recalled Johnny handing her a gift at the end of her cycle, she smiled realizing that *this* was the gift. He'd set her free from this space. If there was anything more to learn about her parents' death, she wouldn't find it in this room. A tear rolled down her cheek. "Thanks, Johnny," she whispered.

Cahya looked down at the box of photos which sat on the floor next to the desk. The photo on top was the one of her with her parents in front of the mountain full of windows... Catithia. Cahya reached down and picked up the photo. Then she grabbed the note on the wall which referenced The Link, and the photo of her parents with the T'Dava, she slid them into the book entitled 'Octavian Governance' and tucked the book under her arm. She picked up the small red ball and met Theo and Nandini back in the main room.

Cahya squeezed the ball as Kyun's words echoed in her mind:

'This ball is a symbol, a reminder that, when we become complacent, we create weaknesses that others can exploit.'

Cahya hadn't been able to see clearly in a long time. Losing her memories had afforded her a clarity she may not have found by any other means. This space was a liability now. Her photos, the evidence she'd gathered... in the wrong hands they could be dangerous for Nirvana.

"I'll need you to activate this," Cahya said, holding the ball out to Theo.

His gaze flicked between the doorway and the orb. "Are you sure?"

Cahya nodded firmly.

Theo took the ball from Cahya's hand. "It's got a ten-foot blast radius. Once I activate it, you'll have thirty seconds to toss it and get yourself out of range."

"I understand," Cahya confirmed, holding her hand out, her eyes trained on the doorway.

Theo rolled the ball between his palms until it glowed and emitted a sharp beep. He placed it in Cahya's hand. It pulsed, counting down the seconds. Cahya stared at the orb a moment, then lobbed it into the secret room. It landed on the desk, right beneath a photo of her parents. "Goodbye," she breathed, offering one last smile.

She shoved the panel back into place and stepped away. A thunderous blast roared behind it, launching the panel halfway across the room and sending smoke billowing upward.

Nandini wrapped an arm around Cahya's shoulders, tears tracing lines down both their cheeks. Theo stood behind them, resting a steadying hand on each. "We'd better get going," he said softly. And this time, Cahya didn't look back.

*** * ***

The sun had finally set and three full moons kept watch in the night sky, making their covert journey out of the city exceedingly difficult. Still, Cahya knew that this would be the easy part.

Cloaked in black and sticking close to the shadows of the treeline, Cahya, Theo, and Nandini followed the road out of Deshka.

When they reached the place where the grass bent gently away from the road, they stopped, checked all around to ensure they hadn't been followed, and then moved quietly into the darkness of the forest.

"It's five kilometers to the tower," Cahya whispered.

As they entered the forest, the thick canopy of leaves and branches overhead cast the rest of their journey in relative darkness. The three of them took out their night-vision glasses and placed them on their faces. When they looked through the glasses, the forest around them appeared to be covered in a film of bright green. The trees, which glowed purple in the moonlight only a moment ago, now shone bright lime. The lagocici, which normally produced an amber light, sparkled in a cool green glow as they floated around above the tall grass.

The team was careful to keep their movements quiet, not wanting to raise any suspicions as they approached. The mission was a simple one: get to the bunker undetected, sneak into the bunker, find Ash, get Ash to safety, find the device, destroy the device, and sneak away unnoticed.

What could go wrong?

They kept low, watching for any guards who might be watching the perimeter of the bunker.

Three kilometers into their walk, they'd seen no one.

Suddenly, Nandini let out a muffled scream, and the three stopped moving.

"Something touched my foot," she whispered. "I'm so sorry, I didn't–"

"Shh!" Cahya hushed, raising a finger to her lips. She waited, listening for any sign that they'd been discovered—any talking or rustling about—but she heard nothing.

"It's ok, let's keep going," Cahya instructed, motioning with her hand for them to move forward. In that moment, something whipped past Cahya's head, knocking her night-vision goggles to the ground.

"Duck!" she said, just loudly enough for Theo and Nandini to hear.

The three lowered themselves to the ground and laid flat, concealing themselves in the tall grass. Cahya used her hands to feel around for her goggles, but she couldn't find them. This was bad; if she couldn't see, she wouldn't be able to help.

"Can you guys see anything?" she whispered to Nandini and Theo. She could hear them rustling around quietly, trying to get a peek at their surroundings. Something had hit Cahya, and someone knew they were there.

"Nothing," Theo replied.

"Me either," Nandini whispered in agreement.

Two more shots ignited, sending something flying past in their direction. The team kept low, trying to determine where the shots were coming from.

What were they going to do? Theo and Nandini couldn't do this alone, they needed her, and she was blind. She felt a tension rising up in her chest as the bumble tree next to her began to vibrate gently.

'*NO!*' She thought, placing a hand on the tree. She was worried that the tree's hum would alert the Dakaï to their location. At her touch, the humming subsided and the forest resumed its standard rustling.

Cahya froze. Did I do that? She pulled the tranquilizer gun from her pocket, placed her hand to the bumble tree, closed her eyes and waited.

The forest fell silent, and in the darkness of her mind, a glowing outline began to take shape—a towering tree formed in soft, vibrant green light. Cahya recognized this feeling, this consciousness, it felt... familiar.

The tree stood against the vast blackness like a beacon of life. Gradually, the forest floor emerged, each blade of grass illuminated with a gentle pulse of energy, swaying slightly in an unseen breeze. Amber outlines flickered into view—small animals scurrying between the glowing plants—each creature accompanied by tiny blue sparks of consciousness flitting around them like restless fireflies.

Cahya's focus narrowed on a tiny mouse nestled quietly in the luminous grass, nibbling on a freshly dug root. Its amber outline glowed steadily, tiny pulses of blue darting within. *Hello, little guy,* she thought.

The grass surrounding the mouse shimmered and quivered in response, causing the mouse to pause mid-chew. Its ears twitched, and it glanced around nervously before darting off, away from Cahya's position.

Could it... *hear me?* She wondered. No—that wasn't it, intuitively she knew that the mouse couldn't hear her—it was the *grass.* The grass closest to the mouse reacted to her thoughts.

She opened her eyes and pulled her hand from the tree coming back into her body. She was shrouded in darkness; she couldn't see a thing.

She closed her eyes once again, searching for the mouse in her mind. She couldn't find it. But what was that? Another animal? No—something smaller. A bug. No—many bugs. Her awareness shifted to a small anthill about ten feet from where the mouse had been. Countless tiny amber points of light scurried up and down the glowing mound, each carrying pieces of leaves which formed specks of green energy. The entire anthill pulsed with coordinated activity, a living network of light.

Cahya's perception expanded outward. Slowly, the scene zoomed out until she could see herself, Nandini, and Theo crouched low. Not as they would appear in the physical world, but as glowing outlines of amber and blue energy. Around them, each blade of grass shimmered faintly, every tree and root beneath them alive with a steady pulse. The entire forest unfolded as a living map in her mind—interconnected, teeming with vibrant life.

Then she saw him.

Thirty feet ahead, a man was concealed behind a large tree, invisible to the naked eye and the night-vision glasses. But Cahya could see him clearly—his outline pulsed faintly with amber light. She sensed his presence fully: the slow, steady rhythm of his breathing, the subtle shift of his feet as he waited for his next move.

Her awareness extended further. Another outline came into view—a woman crouched behind a tree farther down the path. Cahya stretched her senses even further, all the way to the bunker. Four more figures waited along the path, each stationed in hidden positions, their outlines distinct and watchful.

Cahya turned to Theo and Nandini, gripped the tranq gun, and whispered, "Follow me; keep your head down."

In one swift movement, Cahya leaped from her place behind the tree, eyes closed, and rushed toward the glowing T'Dava. She could see Nandini and Theo's amber outlines following close behind. The man behind the tree adjusted his position slightly, peering out from behind the tree; Cahya had a clear shot. She pointed the tranquilizer gun and, without slowing her speed, aimed: *swish—thud*. The dart hit the guard straight in the neck. She saw his amber shape pulse and the glowing grass caught him as he fell limp to the ground.

Cahya continued to lead the group further down the path, trying to keep their movements swift and quiet. The female guard was next, and Cahya felt her move into view, she aimed: *swish—thud*; another guard was down.

Then three, four, five, and six. Six guards lay motionless in the long grass, invisible to everyone but Cahya. As the sixth guard fell, Cahya found a place behind a large tree just off the path. She opened her eyes, ran to the tree, and tucked herself up close to the trunk, with Theo and Nandini following close behind her. The three paused, sitting with their backs to the tree, and tried to catch their breath.

"How did you do that?" Nandini exclaimed in a hushed voice.

Cahya shook her head, not fully understanding what had just happened.

"Ka'ana," Theo answered, a sense of wonder in his voice.

"What?" Nandini whispered.

"Ka'ana. It's a sort of plant vision—like echolocation for vegetation. Plants and trees can communicate with one another for all sorts of reasons. I didn't know humans could tap into it—some ònakai can but it's exceedingly rare. Cahya just tapped into that. Kenzinnia was right!"

"So, Cahya can talk to trees now?" Nandini whispered in hushed disbelief.

Cahya's mind flashed with a vivid memory, Nandini asking their teacher if the ònakai could speak with plants. *Ka'ana*, she thought.

"Well, I'm afraid it's more complicated than that—"

"Could we have the conversation later, please?" Cahya interrupted, whispering harshly, "We're in the middle of a mission here."

Cahya's head was swimming. She had to be able to think clearly; she couldn't let this development derail the mission.

"Right. Sorry. What now?" Nandini asked.

"Now we have to get into the bunker without being seen," Cahya instructed, "There's no one left outside the bunker, everyone else must be inside."

"You can't see them?" Theo asked.

"No. The cloaking device; it must be blocking me."

"Okay, how far are we from the bunker?" Nandini asked.

"Twenty feet," Cahya murmured, gesturing toward a cluster of trees further along the path where they had halted. She narrowed her eyes and then closed them, attempting once again to peer beyond the veil of the cloaking technology. Her awareness stretched outward, seeking any sign of the bunker's interior; but all she could see in her mind's eye was the towering form of a massive glowing tree trunk. The bunker's energy signature mirrored that of the surrounding trees so perfectly that they blended together as if one. No details, no structures—just a seamless pulse of green light that camouflaged the bunker entirely within the forest's living network.

Cahya furrowed her brow in frustration. "Ugh, nothing. I guess we're back to plan A. You two go ahead; I'll keep watch."

Nandini and Theo split up, silently fanning out around the perimeter of the cluster of bunker trees. They moved in a wide circle, keeping low to the ground and stopping every few feet to survey their surroundings. Each step was cautious but swift, their movements blending into the natural rhythm of the forest, causing minimal disturbance to the undergrowth.

Cahya remained still, eyes closed, watching Theo and Nandini in her mind as their glowing amber figures made their way around the perimeter of the T'Dava. She also watched the tower for changes or movement. Once they'd completed the circle, Theo and Nanidini slipped quietly back to the tree where Cahya sat, their footsteps barely audible against the rustling grass. When she opened her eyes, she felt dizzy and had to sit.

"We're all set," Theo announced as he approached. "You ok?" he asked.

Cahya nodded but she didn't move and her eyes remained closed. She was so tired all of a sudden. She wanted nothing more than to curl up in the soft grass and take a nap.

Theo placed a hand on her shoulder, "Ka'ana is a powerful ability, Cahya, but it takes an enormous toll on the body. You need to use it sparingly."

Cahya nodded, she needed to pull herself together. She couldn't let Ash down, "I'm ready. Do it."

Theo pulled a small device from his pocket and pressed the button at its center. Instantly, a plume of blue smoke erupted and spread outward, swirling around the hidden bunker. The smoke shimmered with tiny mirrored particles designed to disrupt the cloaking deflectors and force the hidden structure to become visible.

Cahya remained motionless, her eyes closed as she monitored the surroundings through her heightened awareness. The smoke illuminated her mind's vision, glowing with sparkling blue light as it rose a hundred feet into the air, creating a dazzling haze. Theo and Nandini crouched low on either side of the massive tree trunk, their senses sharpened as they waited for any sign of movement.

Suddenly, a shimmer rippled between the trees, revealing the concealed bunker. Its mirrored glass walls emerged from the shadows, the reflective surface bathed in hues of blue from the surrounding smoke. Cahya opened her eyes briefly, noting the tower's black glass before shutting them again to focus on the shift in energy. The singular, overwhelming tree-like energy signature had dissolved. In its place, six towering trunks stood clearly outlined in green light. Between them, a new signature flickered—glass—now transparent to her vision.

Inside the structure, she saw ten floors stretching up through the core of the building. Two grand staircases spiraled along the inner walls. Her focus sharpened further. Two men hurried down from the third floor, their energy patterns vibrating with urgency. Higher, on the eighth floor, a third man appeared, moving swiftly up the stairs with a little curly-haired girl in tow.

"Ash! I see her," Cahya said.

Just then, the two men running downstairs hit the first floor, and they ran immediately toward the entrance of the bunker.

"They're coming," Cahya told Nandini and Theo, "Two men. Now."

The bunker door slid open, and two men holding large gold guns ran out. The guns looked similar to the one Kyun had shown Cahya, but they were larger and more elaborate.

The moment they were out, Nandini and Theo pulled the triggers of their tranquilizer guns, and two soft thuds could be heard as their bodies fell to the ground.

The door of the T'Dava remained open for a moment, but then it began to slide closed.

"Hurry!" Cahya shouted as she turned to run toward the opening, eyes wide. The door continued to slide closed as she approached. Cahya dove and made it through with Theo following close behind. He made it through with just inches to spare. Cahya turned and realized that Nandini hadn't made it.

Cahya went to the door to find a button or some way to open it. She looked to Theo, who shook his head and whispered, "It's been locked down, I'll have to reactivate it from the control panel on the third floor."

Cahya nodded her understanding. They'd have to go on without Nandini, there was no time to waste; they had to get to Ash.

Cahya pointed to Theo and then to the staircase across the room. Theo nodded and quietly made his way over to the other set of stairs and began to climb. The two made their way up, silently, following the spiraled curve to the second floor. They both arrived at the same time, seeing one another from across the room. They scanned the empty space and continued their climb.

Through the windows, they could see the smoke continuing to billow upwards, blanketing the T'Dava in a blue cloud as it rose into the sky above the trees.

Cahya placed her hand on the tree and closed her eyes. The energy map grew in her mind. She could see a man and a girl waiting on the tenth floor. The man was holding the girl by the arm, keeping her close. Cahya opened her eyes; anger flashed through her. She signaled to Theo to move to the next floor.

When they emerged on the ninth floor, the scenery outside the window had changed. At this height, the tower was in the canopy of the massive trees. All around them, branches and leaves shimmered with the filtered purple glow of the night sky.

They climbed their respective staircases and stopped just a few steps before reaching the top. Cahya looked Theo in the eyes to make sure she had his full attention. She held three fingers in front of her face, and Theo nodded his understanding. Cahya began lowering her fingers one at a time in a silent countdown: 'Three, Two, One.'

The two burst up the last few steps and emerged on the tenth floor of the tower. In an instant, a burst of light shot off in Theo's direction. Theo ducked and rolled out of the way.

Kyun stood in the center of the room, holding Ash in front of him, a gun aimed at her head. Tears streamed down Ash's face and her eyes wide and pleading as she stared at Cahya.

Cahya aimed her tranq gun at Kyun.

"Drop it," Kyun shouted, breathing deeply, sweat dripping down his face. He looked as though he hadn't slept in days.

"Cahya," Ash whimpered, taking a deep breath. "I want to go home." Tears spilled down her face.

"It's ok, Ash. I'm going to get you home. I promise." She turned to Kyun, her soft look changing to a serious glare. "Let her go, Kyun. She has nothing to do with any of this."

"I won't tell you again," Kyun shouted; his usual calm was gone, and the man standing before Cahya seemed crazed. The gun aimed at Ash's head made a whirring noise, and Ash screamed, squeezing her eyes closed.

Cahya raised both hands out in front of her and slowly lowered her tranq gun to the floor. She'd seen what Kyun's gun could do, and she wasn't about to let anything happen to Ash.

"It's over, Kyun; all of your guards are asleep in the grass outside. Soon they'll be picked up and brought to the rehabilitation center in Casule."

Kyun laughed, an evil, bloodcurdling laugh. "Over? Is that what you think? We have only just begun, my dear Cahya. Soon, the device's power will be unleashed and all of Nirvana will be liberated."

"Is this what liberation looks like, Kyun?" She pointed to the gun Kyun continued to hold steady next to Ash's head. "And Nethos? Is that what liberation looks like?"

"Liberty requires sacrifice, Cahya. I'm willing to make the sacrifices that are necessary. I'm willing to do what so many of you are too weak to do!"

"The cycles are the sacrifice we make, Kyun. We suffer there so that our people don't have to suffer here. If this is what your version of Nirvana looks like, I want no part of it."

"Not everyone will make it to the other side of this, Cahya; we've accepted that." Kyun looked up at the sky above them. The highest floor of the tower was covered in a glass dome. Cahya looked around and realized that they were sitting just above the tops of the trees. From here, they had a clear view of the night sky overhead. Three moons shone brightly, surrounded by enumerable glimmering stars.

In the center of the room, where Kyun was standing, a post rose up from the ground. A round device sat atop the post. It was a black saucer with a green glowing circle at its center.

Kyun followed Cahya's gaze.

"Beautiful, isn't it? Such a simple piece of technology, and yet, it has the ability to change the course of history."

"I'm not going to let you activate that device, Kyun."

Kyun looked to the sky again and then looked back at Cahya. "I bet someone told you that you were special, didn't they? People have made you feel as though you have some unique purpose in this world."

His face twisted in disgust. "But look at you now. Weak. Helpless. You're not special at all, Cahya; you're not different; you're nobody."

His lips curled into a hideous smile. "The device has already been activated, I'm afraid. And in approximately ninety seconds, it's going to emit a burst that will save the human race."

"Kyun, you have to turn it off!" Cahya pleaded, "You have no idea what this will do to us. You're condemning us to a terrible future!"

"No, I'm releasing us," Kyun scoffed. "Besides, once it's been activated, it can't be stopped."

"He's lying!" Ash shouted, her voice trembling.

"Shut up!" Kyun shouted, squeezing the girl.

Ash let out a whimper and then continued, "I heard them... it needs the whole countdown or it won't work!"

Kyun pushed Ash toward Theo, turning the gun to Cahya. "You can have that one; she's served her purpose."

Kyun kept the gun fixed on Cahya as he backed up toward the wall. With his free hand, he searched along the wall until he found a button. When he pushed it, the dome above them opened to the night sky, and a gush of cool air whirled in around them.

"Take her down to Nandini, Theo; get her out of here!" Cahya shouted at Theo from across the room.

"Cahya, I can't leave you–"

"GO!" Cahya shouted. Theo lifted Ash into his arms and began back down the stairs. As they went she could hear Ash calling for her. She pushed the sound out of her mind and fixed her eyes on Kyun.

"Alone at last," Kyun said, moving closer to Cahya. Without Ash to shield him, Kyun's outfit suddenly caught Cahya's attention. A sleek black suit, it looked familiar, was this the uniform from Carsen's closet? The special project for a council member?

"It's such a shame to have to eliminate someone so beautiful," Kyun continued, pulling Cahya's attention from his attire, "but I'm afraid you've left me no choice. You just keep getting in the way." He kept the gun pointed at her head as he moved closer. When he was just a few inches away, he used the barrel of the weapon to move a strand of hair away from her face, studying her. A chill ran down Cahya's spine.

The device in the center of the room let out a long beep, "Ah, thirty seconds to go!" Kyun announced, his eyes still fixed on Cahya.

There was no time to think; she had to react. Cahya cut a hand across her chest, grabbing Kyun's wrist and knocking the gun out of his hand. Kyun's face twisted in confusion as Cahya grabbed his arm and shoved him hard to the ground.

Kyun flipped over, regaining his composure, and kicked hard at Cahya's leg, knocking her to the ground.

Kyun pulled himself to his feet, watching Cahya, "It's too bad you lost your memories, Cahya. You used to know how to fight."

Cahya hooked her foot around Kyun's ankle and pulled swiftly, breaking his balance, then she bounced to her feet and kicked him hard, sending him stumbling backwards. As he struggled to regain his balance, Cahya tucked her head and rolled on the ground toward him, picking up the gun as she passed.

Kyun yelled as he fell to the ground. Cahya moved forward and stood over him, gun pointing at his stunned face.

The device let out a long, sharp signal, and Cahya, startled, turned her head to look at it. While she was distracted, Kyun seized his opportunity and kicked the gun out of Cahya's hand, knocking it high into the air. As the gun rose higher the trees enclosing the T'Dava began to vibrate.

Kyun, confused by the noise, let the gun fall to the ground. When he reached for it, the vibration increased. He pulled his hand away from the weapon as the T'Dava began to shake violently.

"What's happening?" Kyun shouted. He looked to Cahya, whom he found standing at the edge of the T'Dava, holding tightly to the branch of a tree, her eyes closed.

'Danger,' Cahya thought, pushing her warning into the trees. She continued the message over and over as the vibration became louder and louder.

Cahya opened her eyes and fixed her gaze on Kyun. She watched as his face twisted in fear as the building heaved and sent cracking noises ringing through the forest. "It's ka'ana," she told him, her gaze steady.

The dishack became quiet, and a bright green beam of light began to slowly rise from it, as though being pulled upwards toward the sky. Cahya released her grip on the tree and ran toward the device. Around her, the sound of cracking glass pierced her ears. She tried to ignore the pain it caused and focused on the device just ahead.

She reached out and snatched the glowing orb from the platform and continued to run toward the edge of the T'Dava.

"NO!" Kyun shouted as the green light dissipated and disappeared from the sky.

As Cahya reached the edge of the tower, she tucked the dishack close to her body and dove off the edge of the roof just as the floor began to crumble beneath her. She crashed through the gnarled branches of the bumble trees, falling fast toward the ground.

The last thing she heard, through the shattering roar of the tower, was Ash's voice from the ground below as she screamed, "CAHYA!"

CHAPTER 23
OCTAVIA

Time slowed as Cahya fell toward the ground. The air whooshed loudly in her ears, but she could still hear the sound of the tower cracking under the vibrations of the bumble trees. Her hand brushed against the tree trunk, which sparked her connection once again; she closed her eyes, and a map of the forest lit up in her mind, allowing her to see everything around her.

Nandini, Theo, and Ash stood huddled behind a tree about thirty feet from the bunker. 'Good, Ash is safe,' she thought.

Cahya searched the map for Kyur, but she could no longer see him. She couldn't risk him getting to her friends; 'DANGER!' Cahya yelled in her mind, pushing the thought into the tree again, harder this time. A violent vibration erupted from all six trees surrounding the structure. A loud crack rang through the forest, and the glass walls of the T'Dava shattered and began crumbling toward the ground.

As Cahya neared the forest floor, panic seized her. She felt her own distress echoed back to her through the forest, and the trees around her trembled in response. The roots below her rumbled with an urgent energy. Suddenly, the trees unleashed a surge of vibration that burst upward from their deepest roots.

The shockwave slammed into her, and for a moment, everything paused, floating in midair. Cahya hovered a few feet above the forest floor, frozen, surrounded by the glittering dust of the shattered tower. She barely had time to register a dull roar in her ears before the burst dissipated as suddenly as it had appeared.

Gravity reclaimed her at once, and she landed hard, pain whipping through every inch of her body. Her vision blurred, and she thought she caught a fleeting echo of the forest's trembling hum—like a final, exhausted sigh—before the entire world went silent and dark.

In the darkness, a flicker of amber light appeared, waivered, and then disappeared. A blade of flickering grass came into view, outlined in neon green light. Then a tree began to take shape and slowly, a map of the forest grew, bright and glowing.

In the grass, a body lay still, its amber light weak and pale, nearly extinguished. The forest glowed and all of a sudden, green energy flowed from the trees and the grasses, moving toward the fading figure, filling it with a soft green radiance—filling it with life. The body pulsed several times before the green light retreated, leaving the figure imbued with vibrant amber light speckled with green flecks, and surrounded blue orbs which flitted softly. Complete. Vibrant. Alive.

Though Cahya's ears were ringing, she could vaguely make out the sounds around her. She heard Nandini scream her name, but Cahya couldn't respond. She heard Theo say, 'It's ok, Ash, it's going to be ok.'

The sounds came through as though she were underwater. She could hear their muffled words, but she couldn't respond.

All at once, she heard Ash scream, "NO! No! It's not ok! Let me go! LET ME GO!" Cahya's eyes shot open in a panic, and she began gasping for air.

"Cahya!" Ash wailed as she tore herself loose from Theo's grip and ran to Cahya's side. She threw herself over her friend, erupting into a puddle of sobs.

Cahya wrapped her arms around the young girl and squeezed. "I'm okay, Ash. We're both okay."

Nandini flung her arms around Cahya's neck, tears streaming down her face. "I thought I'd lost you again," she sobbed into Cahya's shoulder as Cahya labored to catch her breath. "Where does it hurt?"

"Everywhere," Cahya groaned, wincing as she shifted.

"Good!" Nandini exclaimed, half-laughing through her tears. "That was reckless, Cahya. You should've died from a fall like that. I have no idea how—" Her voice trailed off.

Theo just smiled and shook his head. "Ka'ana," he said softly. "The forest helped slow her descent."

Nandini's gaze darted between Cahya and the towering bumble trees, disbelief mingled with relief.

Before Cahya could muster a reply, the E.R.F. arrived, combing the shattered remains of the T'Dava and collecting the unconscious Dakaï in the grass. Despite hours of scans, they found no sign of Kyun's body.

✳ ✳ ✳

Cahya's luggage sat outside on the path; she'd packed everything she needed for her trip, and the car she'd called would be here any minute.

Her home felt empty now. It wasn't really; the furniture would stay, ready for the next person destined to take up residence here, but all of her personal belongings were gone; she'd packed everything.

The only thing that remained unpacked was her black tunic which hung on the wall by the front entrance. She moved toward it, a slight limp in her step. She winced as she raised her hand to brush her fingertips along the soft, seamless sleeve. It sparkled, picking up the sunlight that was spilling in through the windows as she moved it around. She held the sleeve's cuff in her hand, running her thumb over the cufflink which Carsen had recently repaired for her.

She'd worn this tunic almost daily for the past eight years. It had become a part of who she was. She remembered the first day she'd put it on; it was the morning of her swearing-in ceremony. She'd left her house in a hurry, having slept in. The tunic was waiting for her in her dressing room when she arrived, and she'd had just enough time to throw the tunic on and rush out to the stage.

Today she would not rush. Today, she would move into her new role with intention, with grace.

She glanced at the small news scroll on the visor in her hand. In bright letters, it read: "Reports of strange green light seen from Almatar to Casule—several citizens note mild headaches, no lasting effects." She sighed. It had only been a few days since the Dakaï's near-attack. Word was spreading fast; the entire planet now knew how close they'd come to losing their minds to the dishack broadcast. Some were anxious. Others were furious. The Doyen had already given a public address, reassuring everyone that no permanent harm was found in the few who'd felt dizzy spells. Still, a knot of guilt tightened in her stomach as she prepared to leave. Shouldn't she stay and help guide Nirvana through this aftermath? Even though the Doyen insisted this exchange trip was vital to the planet's future, it felt strange to walk away right now.

Kole had popped his head in the door as she was about to leave.

"Everything ok in here?" he asked.

"Yeah," she said, a little breathlessly, "I think I'm ready."

"Alright, let's get you sworn in."

"Kole?"

He stopped, "Hm?"

She hesitated, trying to find the words to say next, "Is this ok? Is it... right? Me becoming the Dohan again, I mean. And leaving so soon after all that's happened? It feels like I'm... abandoning them."

Kole turned to face her and took her hand in his. "Cahya Lighthold, you are an incredible individual. You have an intuition and a moral compass like no one I've ever known. I trust that you will always choose to do what is right and just for the people of Nirvana."

She bit her lip, glancing down at the visor in her palm—another incoming alert about citizen concerns.

"Kole, people saw that beam—some of them felt it. They're scared. Isn't that my responsibility now?"

"The Doyen will manage the fallout," Kole assured her gently. "He's already speaking to the council. He knows exactly what to tell the people to keep them calm and unified.

"And, thanks to your tip about the missing ònakai details in the learning modules, he's now collaborating with the educational teams to pinpoint which programs have been tampered with."

Cahya recalled how sharing that gap with Kole had led to the shocking discovery of altered videos—modules from which any mention of the ònakai and Octavia had been systematically removed. No one had noticed these crucial references slowly vanishing from the curriculum, and now restoring them was proving to be a monumental task.

"As for you," Kole continued, "your trip isn't a getaway, it's the next step we need. He believes in your plan, and so do I."

Cahya nodded, exhaling a slow, unsteady breath. "Thanks, Kole. I hope you're right."

* * *

Cahya went straight from the Swearing-In Ceremony to the Transfer Station. She stood next to the platform with her bags at her side. The glass dome overhead filled the space with glimmering sunlight.

"Cahya!" She heard a familiar voice shout from behind her. She whipped around to see Ash racing toward her, with Sam following behind at a casual pace.

"Ash! I didn't think I'd get to see you today." The two had said their goodbyes a few days earlier. Ash had been a real trooper about the whole thing too.

Cahya bent down and scooped the child up in her arms, giving her a little squeeze.

"I didn't think so either," Ash confessed, "but when Sam told Papa she was coming to see you off, I begged him to let me go too, and he said yes!"

Cahya smiled at Ash, "Of course he did!"

"Is this the outfit Papa designed?" Ash asked, looking down at Cahya's new uniform. She wore a gray tunic trimmed with silver embroidery around the sleeves and the collar. The slightly shorter tunic design revealed the matching gray pants underneath. The council had approved the design and Carsen had tailored this sample to fit Cahya perfectly. It was a gift, a small token of his appreciation for saving Ash. He'd apologized when he gave it to Cahya, feeling that no gift could convey the immense gratitude he felt for her, or the deep shame he felt for helping Kyun; *The design incorporated the pulse tech I used in the HydroGliders,* Carsen had told her, *"Kyun said it was for some sort of lab test he was working on."* Carsen was convinced that the custom suit was the reason Kyun was able to survive the 100ft fall from the T'Dava and disappear.

Cahya had told Ash's father that he couldn't blame himself, Kyun had fooled everyone.

Cahya peered down at the new tunic. The design was a genuine improvement over the old uniforms and Cahya was proud to be among the first to wear it. She'd been granted special permission to sport it for her swearing-in ceremony and her visit to Octavia. Something about the new color appealed to her. She was re-writing all of the Dohan rules, it seemed.

"It is! Do you like it?"

"I think it's beautiful!" Ash told her.

As Sam drew closer, Cahya whispered to Ash, "She's a really nice lady, isn't she? And now that she's living in Deshka, I hope the two of you will spend some time together. Maybe you'll even become friends."

Ash leaned in and whispered back conspiratorially, "Daddy said that she moved to Deshka because her son died, and I think she's really sad. Daddy said she must be. And do you know what? I'm going to take care of her just like you took care of me when my mama died."

Cahya hugged her tightly as her eyes filled with tears. "You promise?" she asked.

"I promise." Ash pulled back and looked at her friend, tears now starting to well up in her eyes. "I'm gonna miss you a lot, Cahya."

"I'm going to miss you so much, Ash. You're my very best friend in the whole world, after all. When I get back home, you'll be the first person I come to visit, ok?"

"You *promise?*" Ash pressed.

"I promise." Cahya assured her, smiling and giving her another little squeeze.

Sam joined them as Cahya lowered Ash back to the platform. "I hope you don't mind that I brought her along. She was so insistent."

"Yes, well she has a tendency to be insistent when she wants something," Cahya laughed. "I'm glad you brought her, Sam, thank you."

"I came for something else too. I wanted to see you off, of course, but I also wanted to give you this before you left." Sam reached out her hand, and Cahya instinctively reached hers out in response. Sam dropped a small item into Cahya's palm, closing Cahya's fingers around the object and giving her a little squeeze.

Cahya pulled her hand back and uncurled her fingers to find Nethos' black armband sitting on her palm. "Oh Sam, I couldn't—"

"Please, Cahya. I had it resized for you. I know that the two of you weren't given a real chance to grow your relationship. That opportunity was stolen from you, from both of you, by my husband. But the two of you really were meant to be together; I could see it in the way he looked at you, even when you were children.

"I know that he would have wanted you to have this. I hope it will continue to protect you the way he protected you in the end." Sam choked back her tears, and Ash wrapped her fingers around Sam's, looking up at her with a knowing expression on her face, wise and compassionate far beyond her years.

She would be ok, Cahya thought to herself. They both would. "Thank you, Sam. Would you help me put it on?"

Sam placed the band around the gray sleeve of Cahya's tunic, clipping it in place around her upper arm. "The triskelion is a symbol of the balance of life," Sam explained,"Life, death, and rebirth; infinity and connection."

"It's beautiful, Sam. Thank you." Cahya ran a finger over the armband before turning to hug both Sam and Ash one final time. Then she turned and stepped onto the platform.

Cahya whipped around quickly, pulling a black envelope from her tunic, "Before I forget, would you mind passing this along to the Doyen for me?" Sam took it without hesitation.

"Of course. What is it?" Sam asked.

"It's a report," Cahya told her.

"I see," Sam said, a sly smile on her face. "You know, I still don't understand how you convinced him to let you go to Octavia on an exchange program. I've never even heard of a Dohan living outside of Deshka for any extended periods."

"I can be pretty convincing, I suppose," Cahya smiled.

Sam leaned in once more and whispered to Cahya, "I am very happy for you." She leaned back, looking Cahya in the eyes. "For both of you," she clarified, and then motioned toward Nandini, who was standing on the platform, waiting for Cahya.

"That means the world to me, Sam, thank you," she leaned in and hugged Sam one last time before turning to step on the platform where Theo waited next to Nandini.

Cahya stood between them and took Nandini's hand in hers, interlacing their fingers.

"Are you two going to be super affectionate all the time now? I'm not really looking to be a third wheel here," Theo told them.

Nandini laughed, "We'll keep it strictly professional, once we get to Octavia, promise."

"Theo, I have a question." Cahya interrupted, changing the topic. "You know, I didn't realize this before; I blame the memory loss, but in all my studies about Octavia, I've come to realize that 'Theo' doesn't really sound like a standard ònakai name. Is it short for something?"

Nandini leaned forward, "Hey, that's true! Is it short for something?"

"Well yeah, of course." Theo shrugged, "I don't think you'd be able to pronounce my full name, though. Theo's fine."

"Try us!" Cahya insisted.

"Okay then, my first name is Theoshkwandula," he raised an eyebrow as if to say, 'and that's not all.' "My full name is Theoshwandula Ishquan Moëthishka."

Cahya and Nandini looked at Theo and then at each other and began to laugh, shaking their heads. "Theo it is," Cahya said.

"Exactly," Theo exclaimed.

"We're all set here," the operator at the console announced. "Are you three ready?"

Cahya looked at her two companions. She knew that what they were about to do might change everything between Nirvana and Octavia.

"We're ready," she said.

∗∗∗

Back in Deshka, Doyen Hashen pulled a crisp white paper from the black envelope Sam had dropped off moments ago.

Dear Doyen,

Thank you for believing that I had a role to play, even with my memories gone. You allowed me to see Nirvana in a new light and you afforded me the opportunity to observe and seek out gaps.

I suspect that you wanted me to find gaps similar to the one in your story: gaps which have the potential to cause harm if left unattended. Those gaps represent a breach or some sort of disparity. I did, in fact, identify some such gaps; I've outlined them on the next page of my report.

The most important thing I discovered from this project, however, is the fact that not all gaps are bad. Some gaps represent opportunities. I recognized opportunities for change and growth; opportunities to serve; opportunities to challenge the status quo. These sorts of opportunities, when they are seized by the right person at the right time, have the potential to change the world. Hopefully for the better.

I don't know what we'll find on Octavia, Doyen. But I suspect that when we find it, it will be hiding somewhere in the gaps.

Yours,

Cahya Lighthold
Dohan of Nirvana

EPILOGUE

The hour was late, and Nirvana's three moons were high in the night sky, casting long shadows across the forest floor. He could see the small house in the distance, just a hundred yards to go. He was nearly there.

The man shuffled awkwardly, dragging one leg as he pulled himself closer and closer to the building. The walls were composed of logs piled one on top of the other, an ancient building technique once used on Earth. The glowing light of the moons bounced off the metal roof, where a small chimney sent smoke swirling into the sky.

As he reached the door, he paused to catch his breath, sweat dripping down his face and long strands of black hair stuck to his cheeks. He steadied himself and pushed his hair back, making himself as presentable as possible, given his current state. Then he knocked gently.

Shuffling noises emerged from inside the house, and a moment later, the door was pulled open by a woman with long graying blond hair. She wore a long red robe, and her eyes scanned the man standing on her porch.

"You failed," she declared.

The man's shoulders hunched forward in defeat, and he nodded, lowering his gaze to the woman's feet. His black suit was torn at the shoulder, and a shard of glass punctured the side of his leg.

"Forgive me," he whispered.

The woman moved out of the doorway and gestured for the man to come inside.

The inside of the house was composed of a single room, which had a bed on one side and a large fireplace on the other. Next to the fireplace was a tall stack of wood and several long metal tools.

Aside from the bed, the room was sparsely furnished with an armchair and a small wooden table with two dining chairs. A round rug filled the center of the room.

"This way," the woman instructed, closing the front door, locking it, and then crossing to the opposite side of the room. The man limped, following slowly behind her.

As she reached the wall, the woman raised her hand, and a doorway appeared. The woman passed through the opening, followed closely by the man.

Beyond the door stretched a spacious chamber, its design akin to many Deshka interiors, though the walls shimmered in a dark gray hue. Oversized monitors lined one side where people gathered to discuss the images on the screens. In the center, a group crowded around a broad, round black table, above which hovered a projection of the planet Nirvana. To the right, three hospital beds with hanging glass screens stood in a neat row along the wall.

A woman approached from the hospital area, her eyes fixed on the piece of glass sticking out of the man's leg.

"Patch him up," the woman in the red robe instructed dryly.

The murmuring in the room stopped, and everyone turned to look at the man hunched over in the doorway.

"Go!" The woman exclaimed irritably, pointing the injured man in the direction of the beds.

"Listen, all of you," the woman called out, straightening her robe. "We may have lost the battle," she shot a piercing look at the

300

man who was now pulling himself up onto one of the beds. "But we will win the war."

Cheers rose up, filling the space.

"The Link cannot be allowed to interfere with our way of life, no matter what the cost. I've already lost a grandson to this cause," the woman declared, her gaze sweeping across those gathered. She turned to the man lying in the hospital bed. "But I'm prepared to lose much more."

A hush settled over the group.

"You all know what to do—get back to work," she instructed. "And nurse," she added, nodding at the woman beside the bed, "no need for anesthetic. I raised a durable child. He can handle it."

With that, the woman in the red robe strode out of the dim chamber, and everyone resumed their tasks. The nurse followed orders, disinfected the wound, and then, without anesthesia, extracted the glass shard from the man's leg.

Blood pooled on the sheets, and the man's body convulsed with pain. The room spun in a dizzy haze before everything went black.

Acknowledgements

As with most things in life, this book is the result of collaboration—a collection of thoughts, ideas, insights, and perspectives that came together to form a work I'm very proud of.

This book would not exist without the support of so many people. First off, my oldest daughter McKenzie—affectionately known as Kenz—was my first reader. She tackled a very rough draft of the book and pushed through to the end giving me some great feedback. When life got busy and the book took a backseat, it was Kenz who nudged me to get back into it; and when I was ready to give up on the whole project, she insisted that the story was worth telling and that I should push through. Kenz, this book wouldn't exist without you. Thank you.

My father and my husband also read early versions of the book and provided tons of helpful feedback. The final version wouldn't exist in its current form without their thoughtful insights.

My sister, Cindy, took tremendous care reviewing and assisting with much of the editing. Cindy, thank you for supporting me through this journey.

I must also thank my uncle Tim for always engaging in thoughtful conversations. In fact, ore such conversation sparked the idea for this book—without that chat, I may never have written it.

And finally, there's you; the person who is reading this right now, thank *you*. I appreciate you far more than you know.

About the Author

I never set out to be a storyteller—I'm a philosopher at heart. I studied philosophy in university, and while my life took me in a different direction, I've always been invigorated by new ideas and fresh ways of looking at the world. I love noticing the things others often miss in the hustle and bustle of daily life.

This book was born from a conversation with my uncle about reincarnation and Nirvana. What if Nirvana were a real place? What if reincarnation wasn't random, but a carefully designed curriculum? Maybe those who seem unwilling or unable to "grow up" are just early in their training, while those with wisdom beyond their years have lived through hundreds—maybe thousands—of lifetimes, gaining experience unknown to them.

The idea stuck with me in a big way; I found it so compelling that I built a story around it. Seven years later, this book is finally complete, and I couldn't be more excited to share it with the world. I'm looking forward to continuing the journey with these characters in books two and three.

When I'm not writing, I'm busy being a mom, a job I love more than any other I've ever had–genuinely. My two girls, Khori and McKenzie, keep me on my toes, but I couldn't imagine a more rewarding experience than watching them grow and become.

I also devote much of my time to running an event design business and growing flowers on our family's farm—two creative outlets that inspire me in different ways.

Fun fact: I love Disney and I've always thought it would be incredibly cool to work there. It never seemed like a realistic idea since my businesses keep me quite busy, but hey—if Disney ever wanted to turn this book into a movie I may get a chance to work with them after all. *Wink wink* Disney!

If you'd like to follow along with the progress of my second book, you can find me on Instagram at **@nirvana.novel**

Manufactured by Amazon.ca
Bolton, ON

44386420R00171